BANTAM BOOKS BY LOUIS L'AMOUR

NOVELS

Bendigo Shafter
Borden Chantry
Brionne
The Broken Gun
The Burning Hills
The Californios
Callaghen
Catlow
Chancy
The Cherokee Trail
Comstock Lode
Conagher
Crossfire Trail
Dark Canyon
Down the Long Hills
The Empty Land
Fair Blows the Wind
Fallon
The Ferguson Rifle
The First Fast Draw
Flint
Guns of the Timberlands
Hanging Woman Creek
The Haunted Mesa
Heller with a Gun
The High Graders
High Lonesome
Hondo
How the West Was Won
The Iron Marshal
The Key-Lock Man
Kid Rodelo
Kilkenny
Killoe
Kilrone

Kiowa Trail
Last of the Breed
Last Stand at Papago Wells
The Lonesome Gods
The Man Called Noon
The Man from Skibbereen
The Man from the Broken Hills
Matagorda
Milo Talon
The Mountain Valley War
North to the Rails
Over on the Dry Side
Passin' Through
The Proving Trail
The Quick and the Dead
Radigan
Reilly's Luck
The Rider of Lost Creek
Rivers West
The Shadow Riders
Shalako
Showdown at Yellow Butte
Silver Canyon
Sitka
Son of a Wanted Man
Taggart
The Tall Stranger
To Tame a Land
Tucker
Under the Sweetwater Rim
Utah Blaine
The Walking Drum
Westward the Tide
Where the Long Grass Blows

SHORT STORY COLLECTIONS

Beyond the Great Snow Mountains

Bowdrie

Bowdrie's Law

Buckskin Run

The Collected Short Stories of Louis
L'Amour (vols. 1–7)

Dutchman's Flat

End of the Drive

From the Listening Hills

The Hills of Homicide

Law of the Desert Born

Long Ride Home

Lonigan

May There Be a Road

Monument Rock

Night Over the Solomons

Off the Mangrove Coast

The Outlaws of Mesquite

The Rider of the Ruby Hills

Riding for the Brand

The Strong Shall Live

The Trail to Crazy Man

Valley of the Sun

War Party

West from Singapore

West of Dodge

With These Hands

Yondering

SACKETT TITLES

Sackett's Land

To the Far Blue Mountains

The Warrior's Path

Jubal Sackett

Ride the River

The Daybreakers

Sackett

Lando

Mojave Crossing

Mustang Man

The Lonely Men

Galloway

Treasure Mountain

Lonely on the Mountain

Ride the Dark Trail

The Sackett Brand

The Sky-Liners

THE HOPALONG CASSIDY NOVELS

The Riders of High Rock

The Rustlers of West Fork

The Trail to Seven Pines

Trouble Shooter

NONFICTION

Education of a Wandering Man

Frontier

The Sackett Companion: A Personal
Guide to the Sackett Novels

A Trail of Memories: The Quotations
of Louis L'Amour, compiled by
Angelique L'Amour

POETRY

Smoke from This Altar

LOST TREASURES

Louis L'Amour's Lost Treasures: Volume 1 (with Beau L'Amour)
No Traveller Returns (with Beau L'Amour)
Louis L'Amour's Lost Treasures: Volume 2 (with Beau L'Amour)

LOUIS L'AMOUR'S
Lost Treasures:
Volume 2

LOUIS L'AMOUR'S
Lost Treasures:
Volume 2

More Mysterious Stories, Unfinished Manuscripts, and Lost Notes

from One of the World's Most Popular Novelists

Louis L'Amour
with
Beau L'Amour

BANTAM BOOKS

New York

Published in the United States by Bantam Books, an imprint of Random House, a division of Penguin Random House LLC, New York.

BANTAM BOOKS and the HOUSE colophon are registered trademarks of Penguin Random House LLC.

ISBN 978-0-425-28492-6
Ebook ISBN 978-0-425-28493-3

Printed in the United States of America on acid-free paper

randomhousebooks.com

2 4 6 8 9 7 5 3 1

First Edition

Book design by Caroline Cunningham

WHAT IS LOUIS L'AMOUR'S LOST TREASURES?

L ouis L'Amour's Lost Treasures is a project created to release some of the author's more unconventional manuscripts from the family archives.

Currently included in the project are *Louis L'Amour's Lost Treasures: Volume 1* and *Volume 2*. These books contain both finished and unfinished short stories, unfinished novels, literary and motion picture treatments, notes, and outlines. They are a wide selection of the many works Louis was never able to publish during his lifetime.

In 2018 we released *No Traveller Returns*, L'Amour's never-before-seen first novel, which was written between 1938 and 1942. Additionally, many notes and alternate drafts to Louis's well-known and previously published novels and short stories will now be included as "bonus feature" postscripts within the books that they relate to. For example, the Lost Treasures postscript to *Last of the Breed* will contain early notes on the story, the short story that was discovered to be a missing piece of the novel, the history of the novel's inspiration and creation, and information about unproduced motion picture and comic book versions.

An even more complete description of the Lost Treasures project, along with a number of examples of what is in the books, can be found at louislamourslosttreasures.com. The website also contains a good deal of exclusive material, such as even more pieces of unknown stories that were too short or too incomplete to include in the Lost Treasures books, plus personal photos, scans of original documents, and notes.

All of the works that contain Lost Treasures project materials will display the Louis L'Amour's Lost Treasures banner and logo.

LOUIS L'AMOUR'S LOST TREASURES

CONTENTS

INTRODUCTION

By Beau L'Amour

Not long before presenting this manuscript to Random House, I attended a memorial service for a man named Oscar Dystel. Oscar had been the powerhouse president and chairman of Bantam Books from the 1950s to the 1980s. A visionary when it came to editorial content, art direction, distribution, and inventory control, he had worked at Esquire, Coronet, and Collier's magazines and had been honored for his expertise in psychological warfare during World War II. After Dad had come to Bantam full-time around 1957, and after some initial hesitation, Oscar became a great champion of my father's work and, eventually, his close friend.

The service was a strange experience for me. I recognized faces, voices, and names that I had known as a child or worked with as a young adult. There were people I had lost track of years before, some of whom, though they had seemed mature enough to have been intimidating at the time, must have been fairly young when I first met them—because here they were, older, grayer, but still alive and kicking.

There was a lot of history and a lot of brainpower in that room, men and women who steered the publishing industry through the heyday of the paperback. These were the people who made my father a legend. They were the people who had made Danielle Steel, Harold Robbins, Irving Wallace,

Clive Cussler, Sidney Sheldon, Norman Mailer, Michael Crichton, Barbara Cartland, James Michener, John Grisham, and Ian Fleming household names.

It stirred up a lot of memories, and I found myself mourning Oscar's passing, not only as a child who had looked up to this gruff but kindly man as one of the only authority figures my father ever chose to answer to, but also as a symbol of a passing era.

Louis L'Amour, just after moving to Hollywood.

My father arrived in Los Angeles in the summer of 1946. The bustle of wartime had not yet abated and the rules were such that it was next to impossible to find a hotel that would allow anyone to stay for more than five days. Short-term housing was a constant game of musical chairs. While the primary reason for the trip was the wedding of Dad's niece, the visit also served as a reconnaissance mission.

Louis was thirty-eight years old and possessed of few prospects. Like thousands of other recently returned servicemen, he needed to make a living. The war had disrupted the magazine business as much as it had everything else. Many of Dad's contacts had disappeared and, while he had written a few stories even before leaving Europe, the marketplace was changing. The world had been overwhelmed with the real-life version of the high-adventure tales he had special-

ized in before going overseas. Postwar, editors were looking for Westerns as a more comfortable and nostalgic alternative.

In the late thirties and early forties Louis succeeded in selling
about three dozen short stories. At the time, he had been living with
his parents on a small farm in Oklahoma owned by his eldest brother.
Now, however, in order to afford the independence he was looking for,
he would have to complete more stories each year than he had sold in
his entire life.

Writing forty to fifty short stories annually provided Louis with
just enough money to live comfortably as long as he kept tight control
over his budget. Maintaining his morale was also a reason for the
high productivity: "My system was to have so many stories out that
when one came back its failure was cushioned by the chances that
were left," he wrote to author and editor Ken Fowler, "and by the time
they returned I had others out."

For five years, a very nice family allowed him to sublet a ten-by-
ten room with a bath in the back of their second-floor flat. In the beginning, he'd sit on his bed and place his typewriter on a folding chair.
When he had any extra money, he would send it to his mother or
spend it on books.

Eventually Dad got a small typewriter table
and a cabinet for some of his books.

Louis was working full out, as hard as he could. He managed to sell thirty-three out of the fifty-five stories he wrote in '47, and twenty-seven out of fifty-one in '48. But around 1950 the pulp market began to weaken. Magazines that had been around for decades were failing, changing their format, or scaling back from monthly to quarterly editions. Competition for the remaining space became more and more fierce.

Some of the difficulties the fiction magazines were experiencing were due to a prewar invention: the paperback book. The Western "dime novels" and "railway novels" (so named because they were sold in train stations) of the nineteenth century were early experiments in this form. True success, however, had to wait until the 1930s, when a pair of innovations were introduced: an effective glue strip used to bind the book together and the adoption of a distribution model invented by magazine publishers.

Before World War II, there were fewer than five hundred real bookstores in the whole of the United States, and most of those were centralized in a dozen northeastern cities. The rest of the country was serviced by "book of the month" clubs and libraries. Before the advent of the paperback, at least half of all titles produced by American publishers sold fewer than 2,500 copies. The book industry was staid and predictable, organized around a group of venerable old companies. Its product came from a relatively elite group of writers and sold to a relatively elite group of readers.

On the other hand, the magazine business was a good deal more lively and inventive. While bookstores may have been in limited supply, the country had thousands of newspaper and magazine stands, cigar stores, drugstores, and railway and bus stations. Though the two businesses, books and magazines, eyed one another with a mixture of envy and contempt, it was destined that they should meet.

It was not an immediate love affair. Hardback publishers looked down on the cheap books, and believed that the American masses weren't readers. They allowed paperback publishers to reprint their titles but assumed the arrangement would be at worst an experiment on someone else's dime and at best no more than a passing fad. However, the experiment turned into a breakaway success and led to an explosion of paperback publishing houses in the mid- to late 1940s. The number of copies sold shot into the millions. Mass-market distribution changed the entire concept of success in the publishing industry.

Dad had always intended to become a novelist. That had been his plan ever since his first attempt in the late 1930s, *No Traveller Returns*. But a great many short stories could be written in the same number of months it took to write a novel, and the chance was much better that a few of them would sell.

Ten years later, with rent constantly due and his mom and dad expecting help rather than giving it, the time it took to write—and sell—a novel was an even bigger risk. Dad was living from paycheck to paycheck, and those checks came only when he was lucky enough to sell a story. Louis wanted to make the move to writing longer material, and, risky or not, the time was right. In the end, though, none of that mattered: Dad *had* to move on to the next step . . . because, with the decline of the magazine fiction business, the one on which he was standing had begun to disintegrate.

In the late 1940s, with some success selling Western short stories under his belt, Louis set out to sell a Western novel. He was still writing a few high-adventure and detective stories, but his sister had sent him a diary containing a brief account of a party of German settlers who had been swindled in a fake gold rush. That section of the diary became the inspiration for *Westward the Tide*.

Years earlier, impressed by a short story published in *New Mexico Quarterly Review*, a New York agent had contacted Louis and offered his services. The man was never particularly good at selling Dad's material, but he did represent some very respected writers and, still a relative newcomer, Dad was honored to think of himself in such august company. The agent initially expressed high hopes for *Westward the Tide*. Louis, writing to his mother, put it this way:

> "Just had a letter . . . on Westward the Tide and [the agent] believes the novel will have an excellent

chance with the <u>Post</u> or <u>Collier's,</u> which would mean
$6,000 or more for me."

When Louis mentions these two top magazines, he is referring
to the possibility of one of them serializing the novel—including a
chapter or two per issue until the entire story is printed. This method
of publishing was the best money available at the time, and the prestige gave the author an even better chance of selling the rights to a
book publisher afterward. It is worth noting that Louis had yet to
earn $6,000 in an entire year.

It breaks my heart to know that Dad was so desperate. He was
seeing his earnings decline each month as stories became harder and
harder to sell, and he wanted to show his parents that he could actually make it as a writer. As the letter goes on you can sense that des-
peration:

". . . I don't believe it will sell to them, although it might. However, I do think it's a fair
story. At that, it promises well, for if he thinks it
that good, he should know, and it means my next one
<u>will</u> be that good . . . I want to double my income
this year, but will do better than that, I think . . .
<u>Westward the Tide</u> is a fair job that I could have
improved a lot with more work. It will sell, but if
I get $1,000 for it, I shall be satisfied. And I'll
do that one way or the other . . . With luck and no
major illness, I'll be a wealthy man one of these
days."

Eighteen months later, after rejections from several publishers,
his agent finally sold the rights to *The World's Work* in the United
Kingdom for a mere $243.68 and mailed away my father's only copy
of the manuscript. Dad agreed to the deal because, by then, he was too
desperate to wait for anything better. Not only was this vastly less
than Dad might have made by cutting the story down and selling it to
the pulps, but since he'd lacked the money to have it copied, he could

not continue trying to sell the U.S. rights. He would not see a copy of *Westward the Tide* in any form for almost twenty years.

It is only now that I realize how young I was when I first heard about Dad's mysterious missing novel—the book he had never seen in published form, and to which he no longer even had a manuscript. When I was eight years old, the whole family took an extended trip to England and Ireland. The year before, Mom and Dad had made a whirlwind tour of Britain to promote the motion picture version of Shalako. Both the film's gentlemanly producer, Euan Lloyd, and Dad's publisher in the UK, Corgi, had pulled out all the stops, nearly overwhelming my parents with the best of British hospitality.

The experience was so extraordinary and Corgi was so enthusiastic about promoting Dad's books that my parents decided to return the next year to do more of the same, except this time they would bring me and my sister along and turn it into a family vacation. It would be the first we had ever taken beyond the American Southwest.

1969 was an amazing time to be in England. The country was blossoming after the grim years of postwar austerity. British music, films, cars, and fashion had taken the United States by storm, and if the acclaim Dad received on our trip was any indication, the English were indulging in American culture as well. In between seeing the various sights, Louis spent a great deal of time autographing books and doing TV and radio interviews.

Corgi did such an exceptional job that when the trip was over my mother marched into Oscar Dystel's office in New York and shoved a scrapbook of all of Dad's appearances across his desk. "This is what you should be doing for Louis in the United States!" she told him. Up until that moment, virtually all of the publicity Louis had received he had set up for himself.

After England we flew to Ireland and saw Tara Hill, the ancient seat of the Irish kings. We saw passage graves a thousand years older than the pyramids and traveled the southern coast in a horse-drawn gypsy caravan wagon. A great many of the Irish locations Louis experienced on this trip would later be used in his novels.

The L'Amour family in Ireland, 1969.

The final success of our great English adventure was that somewhere along the way Dad mentioned to Michael Legat, the editorial director of Transworld, the company that owned Corgi, that he had written a book that had never been published anywhere but England.

By the time we were home in Los Angeles a package was waiting for us. Mr. Legat had convinced World's Work *to part with its last copy, discovered in a dusty file in its office in Surrey.*

By the early '50s Dad's financial situation had become extraordinarily difficult. He was conning his way onto studio lots to sell television producers episode ideas for the shortest money imaginable and he was going to the park in the mornings so his landlady wouldn't realize he couldn't afford to buy himself breakfast. He was afraid of being asked to leave if she lost confidence in his ability to pay the rent. In 1951 he earned only a disastrous $2,200, less than half the modest amount he made in an average "good" year. His creative output remained high—he produced thirty-eight stories, some of them quite lengthy—but he was able to sell only seventeen of them. In the ledger where he noted which manuscripts had been sent to what magazines, the words *Discontinued Publication* appear again and again; the magazines had gone out of business.

Then, in September, Louis received even more bad news. It was a twist of fate that, over the next two years, would change his life in ways he could barely have imagined. He submitted a short story titled "Gift of Cochise" to *Better Publications*, a magazine outfit run by his friend and longtime benefactor Leo Margulies . . .

. . . and Leo turned it down.

Despairing—and feeling he had nothing to lose—Louis sent the story on to his agent. And at last the man came through, making a sale to *Collier's*.

Dad's fortunes immediately began to improve. In quick succession, he sold a treatment that became the movie *East of Sumatra* to Universal Studios, and another story to NBC's Fireside Theatre. Even before "Gift of Cochise" was published, Louis was able to option it to producers John Wayne and Robert Fellows. The movie, when it was made the following year, was titled *Hondo*.

Louis promptly began paying off his debts and swore that he would never allow himself to get that close to the edge again. Booking a flight to the East Coast, he set up meetings with every editor he knew and probably a few he didn't. Previously, he had relied on his agent or, more often, simply sent his work through the mail in the hopes that an editor might like it. Now, he confronted the publishing industry with the full and considerable force of his personality.

Up until this time, Louis had been a writer working in several genres who just happened to write quite a few Westerns. They were popular and he knew the West from personal experience, so the genre had been a good fit. Writing to Oklahoma author Harold Keith of his early career and the transition away from writing adventure stories, Louis said: "The thing that moved me into the western field was simple economics . . . the market was larger. However I never intended to stay with it . . ."

Using the upcoming movie production of *Hondo* as leverage, and with paperback companies always eager to take advantage of a studio's promotion efforts, Louis pitched himself to paperback and magazine publishers alike as an author who specialized in Westerns. "Success is not a trollop that gives herself to every comer," he later commented. "Success must be lured and trapped . . . Hondo was not my break through, my use of Hondo was."

Within two months he had sold the reprint rights for the magazine novels *The Rider of the Ruby Hills*, *Showdown at Yellow Butte*, and *Crossfire Trail* to Ace Books. In addition, Ace picked up *Utah Blaine*, Louis's first story written specifically for the paperback market.

After the hard times that Dad had just been through—the closest to the edge of abject poverty he had been since he was a kid—this was a major victory. Later that same summer he signed a contract with Fawcett's Gold Medal Books to expand "Gift of Cochise" into a paperback novelization, a companion piece to the release of the movie. That deal included a commitment for one new paperback original per year from Gold Medal.

Dad was ambitious, and concerned about the future. He was getting older and he had lived through tough times, not just the previous several years but the Depression and the rough (for him) decade that preceded it. He figured he could write three paperback-sized novels a year, and he was not going to let up until he could make sure that every month of every year was put to good use. He summarized his goal in response to comments made in *Inside Bookselling*:

> "Dick Carroll was then editor at Fawcett, and I approached him with the idea of three books per year. He liked the idea but the powers-that-be at Fawcett did not. I like to write and I write better when I write all the time so I went to meet Saul David."

And that meeting led to what must be one of the most profitable relationships in publishing history.

The sound of a swimming pool filter hushed in the background, sunlight reflected off greenish water and cracked cement, a white glare broken by the

Louis and Saul, late 1950s.

outline of a nearly leafless tangerine tree in a pot. The room where we sat was glass walled, the "family room" of a rambling 1950s ranch-style home in the heart of the San Fernando Valley. The place was an indication of the long, slow purgatory allotted to those no longer in favor in Hollywood. It had seen better days, and so had the small white-haired man who sat across from me dressed in tattered pajamas and a faded robe.

Saul David had once been the producer of such films as Von Ryan's Express, Our Man Flint, Fantastic Voyage, *and* Logan's Run. *He had also once been the editorial director of Bantam Books, a man who, when he left publishing to make movies, had been replaced by a staff—an entire department.*

Saul had many private demons. He could be fiercely vindictive and had never been afraid of giving anyone, from the head of a studio to the lowliest assistant, an identity-destroying dressing-down. In an industry that values deference (let's not call it "subservience") above most other traits, Saul burned many bridges, often well before he even arrived.

The only people who seemed safe from his acid tongue and flashing temper were my parents. His bond with them had been forged in the purer world of books. Neither were intimidated by him, and I think it was their unconditional acceptance that completely disarmed him. Mom and Dad were two of the very few people he actually wanted to be around.

Worried he might decide I was wasting his time, I got my tape recorder rolling and asked him how he had met my father.

Saul:

"I was in a suite at the Beverly Hills Hotel when the front desk called and said, 'There's someone here to see you.' I said who was it, and they said, 'A Mr. L'Amour.' I said, 'I don't know any Mr. L'Amour,' and they said, 'Well, he's on his way up to see you now.'

"I opened the door, and there stood Louis, who was all his life a very large guy. Maybe memory has gilded it, but as I remember . . . the sun was coming in from the doorway and Louis blocked it out.

"He was . . . enormously aggressive, in a soft-spoken sort of way. I mean he had a purpose. He was going to do something, and I was not going to interfere with it. He was going to be pleasant about it, but it was going to happen.

"He said, 'I know you've never heard of me . . .' He had a sort of set speech which I . . . I'm afraid I can't reproduce after all these years, but I do remember it came out like, 'I'm the best Western writer even though you've never heard of me. I want to join with you and I'm going to become the star of your firm . . . and you won't be sorry!'

"'How do I know this?' I said. He gave me some pages. They'd been torn out of, I guess, a magazine. And he said, 'Here's some of my stuff. You can read it.'

"So I said, 'Okay, well, uh, what's your phone number? I'll call you tomorrow or you can call me.'

"He said, 'No, read it now.'

"I considered arguing about it and I decided it was easier to read it. It was . . . Hondo ["Gift of Cochise"], and the truth of the matter was that, intimidated or not, it was terrific! It was so much better than anything we had, you know? It had a ring to

*it. It had a personal style to it. He had a very particular way of
using language. The man himself reminded me of what I thought
Jack London must be like.*

"I said, 'Okay, let's talk a deal. What do you have in mind?'

*"And, gosh he was pleased. He didn't fall down and grovel.
He sort of congratulated me, as I remember."*

In two years, Louis had gone from the edge of eviction to sign-
ing contracts with multiple publishers. It looked like his future was
set as long as he could keep churning out books that the public wanted
to buy. As a writer who was rarely at a loss for ideas and who had a
powerful will to create, one of the few obstacles he had left was jug-
gling the needs, and schedules, of his three publishers, Ace, Gold
Medal, and Bantam. More than anything, Dad wanted to streamline
the way he did business, to save as much of his energy for writing as
possible. For all his ambition, he wasn't greedy. He liked the idea that
everyone was making good money off his work and he eventually
pressured Bantam to keep his cover prices low. He wanted his audience to feel like they could always afford to buy his books.

It took Louis four years after his meeting with Saul to bring all
of his business to Bantam. The idea of publishing three books a year
by a single author was a daunting proposition in the early days of
paperbacks. Oscar Dystel, the newly arrived president of Bantam, had
come on board to solve the host of issues that had caused the market
to become oversaturated with unsold books. Faced with an excess of
material being released into an unruly marketplace, he was not initially supportive of an aggressive newcomer writing in what was considered to be a second-rate genre.

But Saul David personally went to bat for Louis. He had known
Oscar in Cairo during the war and knew how to be persuasive. It
made no sense to lose two thirds of the money Louis's books were
making to other publishers. And, *because* the market was chaotic, it
made no sense to not be in control of the release of all three books.
Louis L'Amour was successful and becoming more so; all it would
take was the guts to say yes.

Saul being Saul, he also threatened to quit.

After a successful test in El Paso and a couple of other cities, Louis and Oscar signed a deal that gave Dad the opportunity to sell three Western paperback originals a year to Bantam. For my father, it was the beginning of an era of relative prosperity and stability.

Creatively, however, the pressure to do something different had been mounting. While Louis enjoyed writing Westerns, it was far from the only genre that interested him. With the security of his new contract to protect him, he began to plan an attack on a number of other genres. But it was an effort that did not succeed for a very long time.

Before the advent of the paperback, the idea of genres, of different categories within the universe of fiction, wasn't the controlling force that it would later become. When paperbacks first appeared, they were rarely sold in bookshops, and merchants hardly cared what was in the book section of their stores. Paperbacks at magazine stands, drugstores, and supermarkets were primarily organized by publisher, the subject matter casually mixed together.

As the 1950s became the 1960s, bookstores, followed by other outlets, began a process called "integration"—organizing books by genre or category rather than by publisher. Unfortunately for many authors, this meant that publishers developed a keener interest in keeping their writers locked into the category and the specific area of bookstores where the majority of the readers expected to find their work.

In the early 1960s Louis wrote the following in his journal:

    Oscar Dystel . . . out from NY for a brief visit. Says my books are selling in great style but tries to talk me out of trying anything else, and of course, I see his point.

This conversation was probably regarding material like *The Walking Drum*, a twelfth-century adventure that Dad had just finished. Louis and Oscar had great respect for each other, and Louis understood that once Oscar found a successful author he didn't want to take any chance of disturbing that success.

As much as Dad wanted to stretch his wings creatively, there were similar issues to be considered in his own life. He was fifty-four years old, success was still new to him, and I had been born a year or so earlier. For the first time he had a family of his own to support. Louis knew the Westerns were his bread and butter and, though he had tried, he'd had no luck selling anything *but* a Western in a decade. Yet he still felt like rebelling. A few months later he wrote:

> Starting next month I shall do 5 pages of a western every day, and the rest of the time on other things. Stories I would much rather do. Yet I can't knock the westerns . . . Lando sold 103,000 copies during its first month.*

In the previous five or six years, Dad had begun work on a good number of stories in other genres, but the need to cover the costs of his growing family and to save money in case of hard times constantly pulled him away. He had even *finished* two non-Western novels, *The Walking Drum* and the so-far-unpublished *Sky Ring Water*. But *Sky Ring Water* needed a considerable amount of work, and *The Walking Drum* was rejected by a number of publishers. As soon as Dad stepped away from writing Westerns, it seemed like he was starting his career all over again. Something needed to change and, as it turned out, the social upheavals of the 1960s were already creating the opportunity he needed.

In 2012 I was working with artist Thomas Yeates on the comic book adaptation of Louis's story "Law of the Desert Born." I visited his home in Northern California several times during the two years that it took to produce the hundreds of images that went into that project. One evening, we sat

---

* Given the cover price and royalties of the day, this would have earned him around a thousand dollars. However, that money was almost certainly kept by the publisher to help pay off his advance.

in his studio as Tom played the guitar. The sky over the Pacific still glowed bright enough to see the horizon. I knew Tom had been an illustrator since the 1970s and I asked him about his familiarity with horses, Western landscapes, and cowboy gear.

He replied by telling me stories of a childhood growing up in some of the more rural areas of the Central Valley. We talked about how we found it odd that many people don't seem to recognize California as the profoundly Western state that it is. "Before I was a hippie, I was a cowboy," he said, and segued from "The Streets of Laredo" into a psychedelic riff à la Jimi Hendrix.

I knew that cultural crossover very well, though I saw it happen the other way around. I spent the 1960s and '70s traveling around the West; my sister, mother, and I went wherever Dad needed to research or promote his books. Even as a child I recognized that the hard-bitten blue-collar cowboys and miners who had once looked down on "longhairs" were suddenly beginning to get a bit shaggy themselves.

On any street in the country, you could spot a guy with shoulder-length locks and elaborate facial hair in the style of Wild Bill Hickok or Commodore Perry Owens. Women affected Indian braids and long skirts and everyone wore Levi's, vests, wide-brimmed hats, and high-heeled pull-on boots. Musical tastes were also drifting, from the British Invasion toward folk and country rock, which had clear roots in rural and Western Americana. In those days, counterculture contained an antielitist bent, regardless of political sentiment. The times they were a-changin' for everyone. The children of the baby boom, the young people of the 1960s, could see that the heroes of Western fiction had a profound antiauthoritarian streak and were seeking relief from the power of the East Coast establishment and the expectations of Victorian conformity. The hippie had met the cowboy, and they'd found they were brothers.

While Louis eschewed the outward trappings of a younger generation, like Woody Guthrie he became an elder statesman to millions of young people remaking their lives in new and rebellious ways. He knew from personal experience what it meant to be a wayfaring stranger, an outsider, a day laborer panhandling his way across a nation that didn't understand his dreams. His characters were often young and adrift, orphans and outcasts, searching for employment and community. I have read hundreds of letters he received in those years, some from girls who were hungry and lost on the streets of Haight-Ashbury, others from lonely and scared boys in the jungles of Vietnam. All discovered freedom and adventure and some sort of comfort and personal guidance in the pages of Dad's work. There are powerful reasons why Louis's greatest growth in popularity was in the 1960s and '70s.

Kathy and Louis L'Amour with original "long-haired country boy"
Charlie Daniels, celebrating the inauguration
of President Jimmy Carter.

So instead of fighting, unsuccessfully, to make a clean break from Westerns as he had in the late 1950s and early '60s, Louis's new plan was to explore the creative possibilities within the notoriously brittle boundaries of the Western genre. "I know that some of my readers do not like my going away from the straight western, but I must do it for myself," he wrote in his journal. If he succeeded, the next step would be to gently convince both his fans and his publisher to follow him into any genre he wished.

It was a cautious strategy, but Louis knew that it was the right moment. Though as skeptical as anyone who'd lived through the radicalism of the '20s and '30s, Dad also understood what he saw going on around him. From doing personal appearances and book signings, answering fan mail, and just watching the changes in our West Holly-wood neighborhood, he could tell that a younger generation was making the world ready to accept a broader definition of just about everything.

Louis laid the groundwork carefully, crafting a vision of himself as a "frontier writer" rather than a man who simply wrote Westerns. He established that he was going to write three interconnected series following the adventures of the Sackett, Chantry, and Talon families. Some of these would be traditional Westerns, but he was going to also carry their stories back to the earliest days of the North American frontier.

The plan was to convince the publisher that he had not drifted beyond their comfort zone, keep the booksellers from feeling they didn't know where to rack his books, and allow his traditional fans to find his work *while* following him into new and interesting territory. With any luck he'd be able to cross over into the arena of swashbuck-ling adventure and historical novels. Eventually, he hoped to sell lon-ger and more complex novels without rattling too many links in the complicated publisher-to-reader supply chain.

After a series of experiments throughout the 1960s, like the contem-porary Western *The Broken Gun*, the attack on audience expectations began in earnest in 1972. *The Ferguson Rifle* is a Chantry family story and takes place just after the Revolutionary War. *Sackett's Land* spends a good deal of its page count in Elizabethan England. The most sig-nificant departure was *The Californios*, which was not only set in a Mexican California slowly being invaded by Yankees, but contained elements of mysticism and science fiction too. "You've really taken a chance with [*Sackett's Land*]," Bantam's Marc Jaffe wrote in a letter to Louis, "but you were always one to take a chance. The story moves as well as any of your conventional westerns."

Chance or not, the impact on sales was positive and meshed closely with the zeitgeist of the 1970s. Carlos Castaneda's *The Teach-ings of Don Juan* and its mystical sequels had been bestsellers for some time, and the impending American bicentennial had caused historical novels set in years before the Revolution to surge in popularity. On a more negative note, the social unrest of the times, the Watergate investigations, fuel rationing, thousands of domestic bombings, and international terrorism all pushed readers to seek comfort, or a sense of American identity, in genres such as Westerns and historical novels.

The success of *Sackett's Land* and *The Californios* put Louis on course to do more of the same, and eventually allowed him to make the move away from the American frontier and to occasionally publish books like his beloved *The Walking Drum*, in 1984.

That outcome, however, as the following journal entry indicates, was initially far from certain:

> I wait warily for the returns on DRUM, out this coming wk. Some of my regulars may desert me on that one but I may recruit new readers. Yet one never knows. Many a writer as well as an actor has broken his back trying to do something different. Several people have commented on my making a change at this [late] date.

In the end, though, the book was a massive bestseller and paved the way for a similar success with *Last of the Breed* in 1986 (a cold war thriller) and *The Haunted Mesa* in 1987 (science fiction). It had been a hard road full of compromise and patience, but Dad had finally proven he was not a writer whose success was tied to just one genre.

In closing, I will return briefly to the memorial service for Oscar Dystel. For me, the most telling moment came when Patrick Janson-Smith, once an editor at Corgi, quoted Oscar saying: "The right to fail is the catalyst of creativity."

I can think of no better phrase to describe the contents of *Louis L'Amour's Lost Treasures: Volume 2*. Yet mostly I believe that what you see here was only a failure of longevity, for Dad intended to permanently abandon very few of these ideas. "Found several good story openings," he wrote in 1976, ". . . and once the opening is written the story is mine forever."

If you read the "bonus feature" postscripts that accompany the new Lost Treasures editions of many classic L'Amour novels, you will notice that Louis started and then set aside quite a few of his best-known works. Whenever possible, he would return to them a few years later and, with typical energy, blast all the way through to the end.

"So much to write and so little time!" he commented in the mid-1980s. "What will it matter if it is not written? Perhaps not at all, yet I think of Nietzsche's Zarathustra: 'I am like the bee that hath gathered too much honey; I need hands reaching out for it.'"

BEAU L'AMOUR
November 2019

LOUIS L'AMOUR'S
Lost Treasures:
Volume 2

THE BASTARD OF BRIGNOGAN

Two Beginnings to a Historical Novel

CHAPTER 1

Alone upon the darkening hillside I wait for the last lights to wink out.

There stands the castle, well-guarded and strong, yet tonight I shall enter that castle. I shall scale its walls, open its doors of oak, walk down its silent halls, a sword in my left hand.

In my _left_ hand?

I have no right hand.

My right hand is gone, struck from the wrist by the order of he who rules this castle, rules it and all the land around.

He will have forgotten me, for to him I was less than the dust beneath his feet, and the sight of my blood dripping to the floor before his eyes will have been drowned in the blood of others he has killed or maimed.

Yet tonight he will remember, and for the brief moment of his life that follows he will swallow the gall of
his hatred. He will die slowly and with time for regret.

I will go alone, yet had I an army I would disdain to
use it, for it is a part of my revenge that he realize my
contempt of him, and of the power he wields. This must be
done without help. Too long he has hidden behind his
mighty walls, behind his armored men, and I will show him
what a hand can do. Only one hand, and the hatred he fed
into me when he deprived me of that which was all and everything to me.

My right hand . . .

You ask me . . . what is a hand? A hand is a delicate, yet a mighty thing. It can weave and weigh and
strike and caress. It can grip a sword or wield a hammer,
touch with tenderness or strike a blow that will crush
bone. A hand can create a tapestry of silk, carve ivory
or jade, create a goddess from raw marble, heal the sick
or bless those who have sinned. A hand can lift a savage
brute to the heights of creative skill.

Was it not the hand that created Man? A lion walks in
the jungle and steps upon a stone, and from it receives
perhaps two impressions, a sense of hardness, of sharp-
ness? Of something rough or smooth? But a man stepping
upon that same stone experiencing the same things, can
yet lift the stone, turn it gently in his fingers, feel
its various sides, judge its weight and its balance.

The lion receives perhaps two sensations, the man receives a dozen . . . perhaps more.

So it is with each thing he touches with the hand,
and with each touch his experience grows, and with it his
knowledge. Truly, man was shaped and created by his own
hands.

Who am I? A man . . . no more, no less. Except . . .
yes, there is a difference, for I am a man with a sword.

Once I was more than that. Once I had a right hand,

that could carve, shape, test and create. My hands were born to shape the still wood or stone into things of beauty, and within me there was naught but the wish to create. I asked for nothing but materials and time. The materials were all about me, and the time stretched before me forever . . . I was younger then and there seemed no end to the years.

The will to create is still within me, but the left hand is not enough. The touch is there, as is the mind and the will, but a little something is lacking for the right hand was the master of art, the left only a servant to it.

With my left hand only, I am skilled. With a right hand I was . . . who shall ever know, now, what I was or might have become? Since childhood I had shaped and carved wood into animals and men that could all but speak, and then stone . . .

Apprenticed to an armorer, I learned to handle metal, to emboss, to inlay, to use a hammer with cunning. My skills increased . . .

Then *he* took from me my hand. He, who rules in yonder castle. Who now drinks his wine, eats his food, and prepares for rest.

His last rest.

Impregnable they say, is the castle. No army has ever taken the castle of Gingee. He sits secure behind his walls, upon his towering peak, high above all that is about him.

My boat lies by the distant shore. My men await me there. Beyond is the Bay of Bengal and a wide world of which my fellow Europeans know little.

The artist I once was is dead, but something was born from the ruins, sired by hatred, mothered by a will for revenge.

Now I am a warrior.

A warrior with but one hand? Ah, yes . . . but a war-

rior trained as no other was ever trained, a warrior
driven by such hatred as you cannot believe.

He took from me the girl I loved. He took from me my
dreams, all that I had or lived for.

Nor was ever a man trained with the skills with which
I have been trained. The teacher I had, the greatest master of his craft, a teacher without another pupil but me,
a teacher so skilled even his former master feared him
and wished him dead. Knowing his time was brief he strove
to pass on to me those skills he had acquired in a life-
time.

My fingers open and close. Soon my time will come. No
army has been able to storm those walls, or scale the
mountain upon which the castle is built. No elephant has
been able to batter down the giant gates with their
steel-spiked doors. Behind those doors he sits, spinning
out his evil like a great spider, hidden and protected.

Tonight I shall face him . . . and he will be alone.

Oh, he will have a blade! He will have one or I shall
give him one, and it is said he is a master swordsman.
Yet he will die. He will die alone with the cold steel of
my blade in his guts, die in a pool of his own blood.

Who am I? I am the Bastard of Brignogan.

My father I saw once only, and well I remember the
night he came to us. A night of storm fit to shiver the
masts of many a tall ship when he came to our door and
rapped on it with a sword-hilt to be heard above the
storm.

Ours was a poor cottage though I never thought it so,
for beyond the harsh granite of the rocks lay the steep
cliffs I loved and the long, lonely beach with the cold
Atlantic rollers coming in upon it.

Cold, did I say? Yes. But often indeed they were warm
and pleasant for our shore was touched by a current I
came to love for upon it were borne many odd things:
strange woods, bits of wreckage, fragments of things from

afar. There I splashed in the waves, tasted their salt, and there I looked upon the distance.

My father was a tall young man, but he staggered from the wind's force and swore as he slammed the door against it. He removed his cloak with a flourish that scattered drops over the room and draped it across a chair.

He swept the rain from his hat with a gesture and looked at my mother. She was brown and strong and beautiful, but with the fires of Hell in her blood.

"There's nothing for you here," she said flatly, "so why have you come?"

"Nothing for me? Once it was a different song you sang."

"Long ago. I've forgotten the tune. What is it you want?"

"I heard you'd borne a son of mine, and I wished to see what we spawned, you and me."

"He is not your son. He is mine. You've strong lads of your own. Go to them."

"I am his father, am I not?"

"You were the sire. It ended there, and you've no more to do with him."

He looked at her and laughed, from sheer pleasure.

"Ah, girl! What a woman you are!"

He looked at me. "Is this the one?"

"There is no other. That is my son."

The tall man dropped on his knee before me and put his hands on my two shoulders. His face was wet from the storm, and although I was scarcely three, I recall it well, for he was not a man to forget.

"Ah! A handsome lad, to be sure! Look at the shoulders! And the hands!"

"He has good hands, I'll grant you. Already he has taken to weaving and splicing. You'd not believe it, and him so young."

"I'd believe it of your get, lass." He stood up and

looked at her. "You know my situation. I've been off to
the wars and it was little enough I brought back but the
scars and experience. I've a great name, but with three
boys and a girl growing, there'll be little enough to di-
vide among them when all is done. I could not take him
from you, and I---"

"I would not give him up. He is mine."

"May I be seated?"

She gestured to a chair, and sat down at her loom.
"What was it you wanted?"

"I am home for a few days only. Tomorrow I must be
off again, I think. I await the word. I returned to bring
them what I could, and little enough it was." From under
his belt he took a leather purse and threw it on the
table. "I saved this for you."

From an inner pocket he drew a sheet of paper.
"Here's a name. The man's an armorer . . . makes the finest blades in France. When the boy is seven or eight,
take him there. He will take him on as an apprentice
where the boy can learn a trade and make an honest living.

"Would I could do more, but being born who I am I
have only the choice of going to the wars or bending a
knee at court, and I was never one for that. Our family
land is poor stuff, and scarcely supports the castle. My
sons have a name, lass, but I doubt they eat better than
you do."

"We have the sea."

"Ah? Of course. A fine mother but a harsh master."

He got to his feet. "They will be expecting me, and I
have far to go. Tiphaine, I wish it had been otherwise, I
wish--"

"No need to waste yourself with wishing. What was between us was my doing as much as yours . . . more, perhaps, for you were ever the gentleman. Do not worry about
the boy. I will see to him."

"What will you do, Tiphaine?"

"For the moment, nothing. The lad has a love for the sea and the shore, yet one day we shall go to Paris."

"It is a great city. Yet not an easy city."

My mother laughed. "These shores do not breed weakness, and I am strong. Paris will do nothing to me, nor will London, or wherever I go."

They stood for a moment, looking across the table and into each other's eyes, and I think, for the moment, they each remembered what it was that had been between them.

Then he took me again by the shoulders, and this time he kissed me. "Be a good lad, be a bold lad. Stand your ground."

There was a burst of wind and rain, and he was gone. My mother stared long at the closed door, and then she said, "That was your father. Remember him well. He is a better man than he knows."

Well . . . what would he think of me now? Here? Had I, over the years, stood my ground well enough for him?

One more thing he said before leaving the house, a thing I have never forgotten, for it was my mother's answer that stirred something in me.

"About a name, Tiphaine. The boy must have a name. There's my grandfather's . . . let him take that. I will go to the notary--"

Her chin lifted. "He will need no name until he can make one for himself. What is a name, after all? A thing hung upon you to seal your station in life. Let him name himself when the time comes, and when he wishes. He needs neither your name nor any other."

"It is a proud name."

"It is. And proud men have made it so. Thus it shall be with my son."

We saw no more of him, and I doubt not that after a few days he returned to the wars.

It was the next year I found the figure.

The morning was cold, the sky over-cast. A strong sea was running but I climbed eagerly down the cliffs to the shore and ran along the sand among the great rocks until I saw something white . . . something with a pale sheen.

Cautiously, I approached it. Something in the sand, half-covered. I dug around it, lifted it carefully up.

It was the figure of a woman, carved in what I now know to be ivory, her flowing garments about her, all her features perfectly shaped, her hands, her fingers . . . I had never seen anything so beautiful.

I sat down on the sand and stared, turning it carefully in my hands. Someone, somewhere, somehow, had done this. Someone had carved, taking away a little here, a little there, and so had come from the ivory . . . beauty.

Something created. Something that had not been before had become.

For days I kept my secret. For days I studied it, looked at it, longed for . . . for what?

What was it I wanted? What was that strange excitement within me? Could I . . . could I, perhaps, do such a thing? Could I, with a knife, carve such a thing as this?

I had no ivory, but there was wood. Alone, seated upon the rocks out of the wind, I began to shape a small piece of wood. Days followed. Sometimes I cut too deeply, sometimes I pared away too much. Often the thing I created was lumpy and wrong, and it irritated me, yet always I returned to my study of the figure, and again and again I tried.

One day I came up from the shore with a piece of wood in my hand. My mother saw it, and asked what it was. "It is a man," I said, "an old man with a barrow. He has sacks upon it, and he is very tired and old."

She looked at the wood, and then at me. "It is only a piece of wood," she said, "of driftwood."

"Look!" I held it up. "His head is here. The barrow with the sacks, it will be here, and--"

"I do not see it," she said gently. "I have not your eyes."

"Wait," I said, "I will show you. I will cut away some here. I will shape that curve, I will--"

"Do it," she said. "I would see what you have seen."

Days I worked. I ran no more upon the sand, I showed her nothing. At night I hid it in a crack in the rocks. I worked and worked again.

Then one day I went to her. She was doing her hair, looking in the small mirror I had found for her in some wreckage.

"See?" I said. "The old man and the barrow!"

She took it up, she turned it slowly in her fingers, then she knelt down and took me by the shoulders. "You did _that_? But who could teach you? How could you learn?"

"I had a teacher. The lady showed me how."

"A lady? _Here_?"

I took the figure from inside my shirt. "I found it in the sand. I wondered if I could do that . . . could do it as well. I have not . . . yet."

"You will. I am sure you will." She stood up then, holding the figure in her hands. "It is old," she said, "it is very, very old."

After a moment, she handed it back. "I think we will go to Paris," she said quietly. "I think it will soon be time."

Yet it was two years longer before we left.

Behind me I left carvings of ships and men, of mermaids and horses, of dolphins, whales, and strange designs I dreamed of at night or saw shaped in the sunset clouds.

We went to Paris . . .

My mother, young, beautiful. A girl from a sea-side

village who had never known a city, but a girl unafraid,
a girl very sure, and very strong, a girl with a few
carefully hoarded coins . . . not including those she had
from my father.

She took with her several of my carvings.

CHAPTER 2

The night was very still. The horses stamped restlessly, tired of their long wait.

Mahmoud looked at me and shook his head. "One man?
Against a castle? It is mad!"

"Where ten thousand could not go, one man might. I
know what I do."

"You have waited six years, so wait another year.
When the Nayak returns, the Solaga will no longer be in
Rajagiri, the citadel of Gingee. He will return to his
island in the Coleroon, and you can have him there."

"I have waited too long. I shall wait no longer. He
thinks me dead, drowned in the sack. He watched me. He
saw the sack drawn up around the girl, and I saw her
strangled before my eyes and her dead arms hung over my
shoulders, then the sack sewn shut. He watched as we were
dropped into the water from his ship. He saw us sink, my
dead beloved and I."

Mahmoud stared. "You got out of _that_? Your hands
tied? A strong sack sewn tight?"

"It was she. Somehow she had secured a knife, and in
the moment before her hands were tied, she cut mine free.
In the moment she was strangled, she slipped the knife in
my hand, and her one last word was, 'Wait!' It was whispered, softly.

"I waited, then as the sack struck bottom, I cut my-

self free, and when I surfaced it was close under the
stern where I could not be seen.

"The sun was setting, and as the ship moved away, I
dove once more and swam under water, and was careful to
come up with the sun glare in their eyes.

"I swam then, swam away from the shore where his soldiers might be. I swam out to sea."

"To sea?"

"There was a ship . . . I had seen it earlier, lurk-
ing along the shore, and when the Solaga's ship put out
from shore, it went further to sea . . . avoiding us. It
seemed to have no wish to have us draw close.

"Yet when the sack was drawn up, I saw it off there,
a mile or so away and working across the wind to get more
distance still. It was that ship I swam toward."

"It was a long chance."

"Aye, but I reached it and they took me aboard, and
truly enough, they feared the Solaga. That night again
they came in close to shore and picked up what it was
they awaited . . . some secret goods, sold without paying
the tax to the Solaga . . . and we sailed off then, far
to the east and were wrecked there."

"You survived?"

"And no other. Of them all, I lived. I was found and
cared for by an old man . . . five years I lived in his
home, and was trained by him. It is a long story."

I stood up. "It is time, Mahmoud. Do you return to
the boat on the river. If I have not come in three days,
forget me."

Black and terrible the three hills bulked against the
night. Men had called it the strongest fortress in all
India and many an army had fallen back from its great
walls. They were sixty feet high, surrounded by a ditch
eighty feet across. Beyond those walls, other walls, and
finally the dome of Rajagiri, the highest of the three

hills, a vast rounded head of stone, its sides almost
sheer, great boulders forming a part of those walls.
Within it, temporarily in command, was the Solaga, Sarbaz
Khan, a renegade Moslem, and the man I sought. It was he
who had ordered my hand cut off at the wrist.

The path to the citadel passed through a pleasant
grove, alongside a reservoir, and by a shrine, the oldest
building in the place, older than the fort itself. Yet
there are legends that tell of earlier occupation, and
not far off is the ruined city of Padaividu, some sixteen
miles in circumference, a city said to have been buried,
perhaps thousands of years ago, by a shower of dust and
stones.

The main fortress enclosed a triangular space about
three miles around, with citadels upon the three hills.
There were granaries, tanks, pavilions, barracks, pal-
aces, temples and mosques all enclosed within the walls.
There were also more than one thousand highly trained
fighting men inside that enclosure, men dedicated to the
service of Tubaki Krishnappa Nayaka.

I knew that few of these men admired Sarbaz Khan, who
had fled the Moslem forces to serve Krishnappa, for what
reason I knew not. What I did know was that he was a
cruel tyrant who hated all he could not crush.

Long had I studied design and plan, long had I worked
drawing the patterns for gold inlay upon armor, pistol
and sword-hilt until I had an eye for detail. For months
I had studied the layout of the fort, I had learned it
carefully, and now had come the time to make use of my
knowledge.

My horse walked along the dark lanes, between boulders, under trees, through thick stands of brush. In the
distant jungle I heard the coughing roar of a tiger . . .
there were many about . . . but I moved on, approaching
the castle steadily, at a pace long planned.

The Bastard of Brignogan . . . so they had called me,

and I accepted the name. Yet there was no doubt as to
whose son I was, and he was a man much known and much
loved in that corner of the coast.

Of my mother's early history, I knew nothing. Nor did
I know why she chose to live alone in our thatched cottage of stone near the shore . . . a shore notorious for
its wreckers.

There was a man who came often to our cottage. That
he was in love with my mother, I well knew, but she would
have none of him. He was a great, powerful man, and
friendly, yet I knew he was one of the wreckers. By and
large they were a bloody lot, wrecking ships and then
looting them, and no doubt killing all who survived.

I remembered once, he said, half-humorously, "What if
I took you anyway?"

She said, without any humor at all, "You might succeed, although I doubt it, and you'd look the grand fool
if you failed, but if you did succeed, I'd wait until you
slept, and then I'd kill you."

He believed her, for he did not mention it again.

That he admired her still . . . perhaps even
more . . . was obvious. He brought us gifts of food,
clothing from the wrecks, or materials looted there.
These were useful, as my mother sewed well, exceeding
well, in fact.

It was not until later that I began to wonder about
her, for no relatives came to visit. She had no ties in
the village or the country around. Whoever she was, wherever she had lived before coming to the cottage, I did
not know.

It was a time when few people traveled. Most of those
who lived along our coast had never been more than a few
miles from their homes except when fishing or going to
sea, and the women did neither.

Nor did my mother ever speak of her past, nor of anyone she had known before coming to the cottage where we

were. We were much together, walking along the shore, working in our small garden, going to Brignogan to sell vegetables or fish. After it became known that my mother sewed so very well she was often asked to sew but she usually refused . . . relenting only when the task happened to appeal to her.

She made some vestments for a priest, I remember, and a wedding dress for a young girl with whom she had talked from time to time. At night, sometimes, she sang . . . the songs were not French, yet some were Breton, or some tongue very like it.

That my mother was a woman of some mystery did not occur to me. She was my mother. It was that fact I accepted and no other, yet it did begin to appear that she was something out of the ordinary in many ways . . . her independence, her courage, her strength of purpose. I remembered the way she spoke to my father with a kind of pride, although it was not until later that I grasped all she said.

That I would make my own name was something I did consider, and once asked her about it.

"Names are important only when you make them so," she said, as we walked upon the shore. "Men are named for their trade, for the town in which they live, for the estate they possess, or sometimes for some characteristic that is uniquely theirs.

"You are Brenn. That is the name I have given you, but in your time you will choose another when it suits you, or circumstances will confer a name upon you."

How right she had been! Now I had a name, for when my hand was cut off I did what must be done. Always I had been mechanically skillful. I had designed in metal, worked in metal, wood, stone and ivory . . . so now, left without a hand, I designed one for myself, a metal hand that could be fitted over the stump of my wrist. It was not only a hand, it was a claw, as well. So they called me the Claw.

The man with the Claw. From that, the man with the Talon. And finally, Brenn Talon.

But when my mother took me to Paris, I was only Brenn.

Etienne Bressy was an old man, yet tall and strong with fierce eyes and a nose like a hawk's beak. It was an early morning when my mother brought me to his door.

He opened the door and glared at us, looking from one to the other. He wore a shirt and breeches, his sleeves rolled up to display powerful forearms. I never forgot them, and envied him his strength, wishing for such arms myself. It was years before I earned them, and it was only after much work, and much use of the hands.

She mentioned my father's name and he stepped back, gesturing for us to enter.

The room was low-ceilinged and relatively bare. There was a table, several wooden benches, and on a smaller table, several books. There was a fireplace and on the far side of the room, a bed.

He looked at her again, and then at me. "He is young," he said.

"But skillful," my mother said coolly. "You will be fortunate to have him as an apprentice. Already," she added, "he can do what you need."

He stared at her then snorted. "Such work needs skill, and skill comes from work, years of work."

She opened the bag she carried and placed before him the figure of a fisherman I had carved from bone. He looked at it. "What is that?" he asked, his voice surly.

"The work is his," she said. "It is good work."

He took it up then and turned it in his fingers. As he studied it, she took several other pieces from her bag, one a piece of inlay done with shell.

He looked at me again. "You did this? What is your age?"

COMMENTS: The first chapter of this next draft is missing but we can assume that it also begins in India, with the hero about to make his attempt on the citadel of Gingee, before flashing back to his childhood in France. In this version, Brenn is named Dorion and a character much like Etienne Bressy is named Coatlanen.

CHAPTER 2

The year was 1629, and Louis XIII was king of France.

Of the four years that followed I had only the most meager of memories, and those were confused, without focus or direction. They were memories of swimming in the sea, running over the high, lonely moors, of fishing, boating, wrestling with other boys, and of watching the change in my mother.

At first I was aware of no change. It began with the books. Gold was scarce, hard to come by, so greatly valued. My mother had the typical Breton caution with money. She improved our lot very gradually, but the books were the first thing.

My mother could read. How she learned, when so many people of all classes did not, I never knew. Now she bought cautiously, also she began to improve her appearance, so gradually as to make the change scarcely appar-

ent, yet when four years had passed my mother no longer
was the same.

She spoke quietly, rarely raising her voice. Guarding
herself from the sun, her skin was no longer brown. Her
clothes were plain but carefully chosen. My mother had
become a lady.

With her change in clothing and manner there had been
a change in the attitude toward her on the part of other
people. They accepted her for what she seemed to be.

Moreover, she had been teaching me. At first she did
the teaching herself, and then she acquired the assis-
tance of an elderly woman who had once been maid to a titled lady. She paid the woman a few coins each month to
stop by, and it was not until later that I realized that
while the woman taught me, my mother was learning also.

She learned by imitation, casual questions, and by
leading the woman to gossip of her former life.

When I was scarcely past seven years old, we moved.
My mother had prepared the ground well, but left open an
avenue of retreat.

"My uncle in Paris," she told people, "has been asking us to come to visit him. Actually," she would add
after a few weeks, "he wants us to live with him, but we
shan't do that. Maybe we will visit him."

Then one day the plans were made. She closed up the
cottage and we rode with a friend, a driver from the castle some distance off, who was going to Paris. Trust my
mother to spend no money if it could be avoided.

I was filled with excitement. I had never traveled
except to nearby villages, and to our small village,
Paris was a far off place to be imagined rather than
seen.

Yet we did see it, and after a few days of getting
settled, my mother took me to a narrow little street on
the left bank. Louis XIII was in the process of complet-

ing the changes Henry IV had begun. Richelieu had completed the Palais Royal a few years before and presented
it to the king, and the Ile de la Cite and the Ile St.
Louis had been joined by a bridge.

Not too many changes had taken place on the left
bank. The old inns that dated back to the twelfth century
when the first students began to haunt the left bank were
still in existence. And if one knew where to find them
there were even Roman ruins, for it was on that bank the
Romans had made their station.

The house where my mother took me was of ancient design and in a narrow street. The second floor projected
out above the street with heavy timber framing, and there
was a sign suspended over the walk.

COATLANEN

I was startled, for even I knew that name. It was the
Breton seaman from the Ile of Brehat who had become an
admiral in the Spanish navy, and who told Columbus in
1488 of lands that lay to the westward.

The story was an old one in Brittany, and not unlikely, for had not Breton, Basque and Norman fishermen
fished off those coasts for generations?

From the sign this Coatlanen was not a seafaring man
but an armorer. My mother lifted the latch and entered a
long, low-ceilinged room with a few chairs about, and a
wide, empty hall to our left, forty feet long and half
that wide. A room that had a board floor of amazing
smoothness. Two swords lay across a chair.

My mother opened and closed the door again, harder
this time, and then we heard footsteps along a passage,
and a man appeared who filled the width of the door, a
very short but broad and strong man with a large head set
upon massive shoulders.

"M. Coatlanen?" my mother asked.

He had looked quickly at us, but he shook his head.
"I am Jacques. If you will wait---?"

He disappeared, and a moment later reappeared with a tall, well set-up but much older man with a pointed white beard and keen blue eyes.

"I am Coatlanen," he said.

My mother said, "This is the lad of Brignogan of whom his father spoke to you. His name is Dorion."

Coatlanen looked first at my mother, then at me. He took me in at a glance, then looked again. He took one of my hands and turned it in his.

"A fine hand, a strong hand. Have you lived by the sea, lad? Have you fished? Rowed a boat?"

"I have," I said. "And I swim."

"Of course." He looked at my mother. "The lad has un-commonly fine hands, and strong wrists. He should do well as a swordsman."

"His father wishes him to become an armorer."

"Yes. I believe he said something of that." He looked at me again. "He is the son of a gentleman, a noble-man--he should handle a sword."

My mother looked at him, her eyes cool, her manner composed. "My son has no name, m'sieu. Perhaps he will make it with a sword, but I would prefer he make swords."

They were kin but stern. There was discipline in the shop. Coatlanen believed in basics. He believed in bodily strength, self-discipline, and in knowing the whys and hows of all things. It was Jacques who first took me in hand to show me how steel was tempered, how swords were hammered into shape, how the final point or edge was put on. At first he merely led me around the work-shop, show-ing me the anvils, the forges, the tools and explaining each in turn.

From the first day, I worked. I swept the floors, picked up odds and ends of metal and returned them to their respective boxes, returned the tools to their

places at the end of a working day, and worked the bel-
lows. Above all, I was expected to observe.

On my third day as I worked, an object fell from my
pocket. It was a bit of hardwood on which I had been
carving.

Jacques picked it up, was about to hand it back, then
stopped. It was a replica of a ship, not quite so large
as my fist, and carved in minute detail. He turned it in
his hands, studying it.

"Beautiful!" he said. "Beautiful! Where did you get
it?"

"I carved it. I found the wood on the shore . . .
among the rocks."

"You? You carved this? How old are you, lad?"

"Eight years . . . nearly eight."

"May I keep this for a few days? To look at?"

"You may have it, if you like. I can carve another."

He left me then and went to the room where Coatlanen
worked, and a moment later, opened the door and called me.

I was frightened. I did not know them well and feared
they would believe I had carved it when I should have
worked.

Coatlanen studied the piece in his hands, with his
eyes and his touch. Then he looked at me thoughtfully.
"Have you done much of this?"

"I have."

"Only ships?"

"Birds, animals, flowers, people . . . whatever I
see."

He leaned over his table and looked at me. "Dorion,
you are an artist. You have a gift. Continue this, and
show me what you do, but above all, study the basics,
lad, the basics. You must know the look of heated metal,
must know the sound of the hammer upon it, the sound of
it when dipped into water. No matter how beautiful a
thing is, it is nothing unless it is also strong.

"Tiny, if you will. Fragile, if you must, delicate as any rose petal, but for what it is . . . strong. Always strong. Men or metals, lad, the strong survive. And be careful of those hands . . . there may not be another pair like them in the world."

What would he think now, that good and gifted man? What would he think to see me standing here, with one hand only? Waiting for the hour when I would go up those rocks, over the wall? But he would know how I did it, for he taught me that, too.

He taught me the art of the ninja, which he had learned long ago, in Japan.

He taught me patience, and to turn each problem into profit. As a boy, cast away upon the shores of Japan, he had learned the art of the ninja, the making of swords, and the using of them, Japanese style.

Like his distinguished ancestor, he had taken early to the sea, his skill with a sword swiftly winning him an honored place, yet he had little money, and no title. He was simply a master-at-arms and a soldier, a man of peculiar skills, respected by all, feared by not a few.

His first voyage to sea at the age of ten had ended with the ship of his father wrecked on a reef in the north Pacific, and Coatlanen himself the only survivor. Washed overboard, he had struck out wildly, trying to swim in the madly churning water. On the second stroke his hand smashed hard against the side of the captain's gig, and he caught the stern and pulled himself into the boat.

Hours later he awakened with the morning sun upon his face. He lay in a small cove, his boat bobbing upon the waters, the storm clouds scattered and drifting. The cove was an indentation in a rocky and beautiful shore, ragged, wind-blown pines and what he took to be cedars

clinging to the rocks. Not far off was a small sandy
beach.

He was working toward the beach, half-hidden by an
over-hang of rocky cliff, when he heard shouts, then a
clatter of hoofs upon stone and gravel. Peering out from
his over-hang he glimpsed a party of horsemen clad in
strange armor charge along the edge of the cliff on the
other side of the cove and then into the trees. Wild and
fierce they were and, frightened, he stopped his boat and
crouched down. The men were circling to find a way to the
beach, apparently.

Clinging to the vines, Coatlanen stood up in his boat
and peered toward the beach.

On the white sand, not a hundred yards away, lay the
body of a man. Even as he looked, the man put out a hand,
trying to crawl. No doubt it was he for whom the riders
searched, and in minutes they would be upon him.

On impulse, Coatlanen urged his boat swiftly along,
reaching the sandy shore. He scrambled from the boat and
caught the wounded man under the arms. "Quick! You must
help!"

Somehow the man mustered strength, and together they
reached the boat. Toppling the wounded man into it, the
Breton sailor boy pushed off from shore. Swiftly he
skulled the boat. The nearest over-hang was only a few
yards away. He could hear the horses coming, heard angry
shouts, and then he was in the shadows and under the
vines. Once out of sight, he continued to move, using his
hands upon the rocks to move the boat silently along into
a deeper and darker part of the over-hanging cliff.

Behind him were shouts and angry yells. He could see
only a few of the horsemen in their strange armor. Most
of them carried bows, and a few had swords as well. They
rushed down upon the sand, whirling about.

Yet their very anger was a blessing, for charging

down upon the sand, even into the edge of the water, they trampled out any tracks he might have made.

They scattered out, searching.

Careful to make no sound Coatlanen worked his boat along the shore. The water was deep close up under the rocks, and even from the sea his boat would have been invisible due to the over-hang's shadow and the vines. The tide was changing and as he continued to ease the boat along it more and more often threatened to crash them against the cliff.

Suddenly the over-hang deepened and he found himself in the entrance of a cavern hollowed by ages of pounding seas. The boat was carried inward and it was only with a quick twist of the oar that he avoided a rocky barrier where a piece of the roof had fallen in. As he grew accustomed to the dim light he made out a sandy shore, but tied to the rocks was a boat, a boat with round wooden eyes on the bow . . . Japanese or Chinese, he knew that at once, and as they had been not far off the coast of Japan, he knew now where he was, where he must be. This cave was a hidden place, a secret place, but someone had been here, might still be here. Silently he tied his boat to the other.

For the first time, in the vague light reflected from the water, and filtering through a small hole in the roof, far, far above, he looked at the man he had rescued.

A small man, but compact and strongly built. The man was bleeding from several wounds, one apparently a spear-thrust, another a cut that was not deep but had bled much, and the third, an arrow through his side that still remained there.

On the voyage with his father around the Cape and into the Indian Ocean, then along the Malabar Coast and thence to Sumatra, their ship had been several times at-

tacked by pirates or others, and Coatlanen, too young for
combat, had helped the cook who was also the most skilled
hand with wounds.

He knew what to do and he pushed the arrow on through
then bathed the wounds in salt water, and tore pieces
from the wounded man's clothing to make compresses and
stop the bleeding.

On board the Japanese boat he found dried fish, rice
and some vegetables he did not recognize. There was also
tea and rice wine. He found many curious things, among
them a number of small discs, stars, and swastikas of
iron, with edges razor-sharp. There were several kinds of
weapons and a number of devices whose purpose he could
not guess.

From time to time he paused to listen, but no sound
came to this place but the lapping of the water against
the hulls and the sandy beach and the deeper sound of
surf on the breakwater of fallen rock. He was about four
boat-lengths inside the cave, which was a large, vaulted
cavern. He could see several openings that might lead to
the surface, or might only go deeper into the ground.

He prepared a small meal for himself and some hot
broth for the wounded man, careful to make no sound. Then
he heard a voice muttering.

The man's eyes were open and he was looking up, and
he said something in a strange language. Coatlanen replied, "I found you on the sand." And when the man spoke
again in the strange language, Coatlanen indicated lifting him and helping him.

The man smiled weakly, nodding his head, and then he
lay quiet and Coatlanen brought the broth he had made and
fed it to him, sip by sip from the edge of a bowl. After
a time the man signaled that he had enough, and then he
slept.

Weeks passed. The wounded man slowly recovered, but
their food supply was running low. Twice detachments of

what seemed to be soldiers had come back to search the area, and finally one night the wounded man indicated they were to load all that was left into the boat with the eyes. When that was done the man went around and carefully removed every evidence of their being here. And when they left they towed the gig after them and set it adrift at sea.

Moving only by night they crept along the shore, hiding by day in some rocky crevice in the shore cliffs or tiny cove, each time masking the boat with fish nets into which they wove vines.

From the first the wounded man had begun to teach the boy. He touched himself and said, "Sand-a-yu," and then one by one he touched the items about him, saying their names.

One day Sandayu touched the discs with the razor-edges. "Shuriken," he said, and picking one up he threw it suddenly at a beetle upon the bulkhead of the cabin. The disc cut it neatly in two.

Swiftly, his hands a blur of motion, Sandayu threw a dozen more, several of them in the air at one time. They struck the target in a rough star.

Coatlanen was amazed. Such swiftness and accuracy was unbelievable.

It was the beginning. Little by little Sandayu taught the boy his skills, working with infinite patience. He also instructed him in the language of the Japanese.

"I am ninja," he explained finally. "It is my art to be invisible, to come, to go . . . to spy and to kill. There were many of us, but there will be few now, those few scattered.

"The riders were the soldiers of Nobunaga Oda, a great lord. He sent them to kill me, and to wipe out all ninja. If he learns I live he will not cease until he kills me."

"Where do we go?"

"To Kii. It is a place where there are friends, Buddhist friends. They will hide me and protect me, and I have a farm there, a hut and some land near the sea. You will come with me, you will be my son."

"Is it far?"

"Not too far, and we can go along the coast. The Buddhists there are militant, and have no cause to love Nobunaga."

For ten years Coatlanen remained with Sandayu, and for ten years he was trained in the skills of the <u>ninja</u>. As they made their own weapons, he learned the arts of the sword-maker and armorer at the side of the master. Only when the <u>ninja</u> died did he leave Kii, and then it was by night, in the same boat in which he had come.

On the coast of China he found a Portuguese ship and returned with it to Europe.

Those were the skills he had passed on to me. The <u>ninja</u> were adept at scaling walls, using hand-cannon, poison-water guns, smoke bombs and blow-guns.

COMMENTS: Given the pieces of the drafts you have just read, I believe that the first section was actually written later and that Louis intended to take Coatlanen's adventures in Japan from this second section and hand them off to Talon, creating a narrative that would be both more exciting and more focused on its protagonist.

As many of his fans know, Louis was working on three interconnected series of books about the Sackett, Chantry, and Talon families, each following a different family through the period of European exploration and development of the North American continent. Though he did not write them in order, this novel, once finished, would have been the first, chronologically, of the Talon series.

Below are several sets of my father's notes on the early Talon stories that suggest how he might have continued on past these several chapters. I have compiled them into one continuum for easier reading:

Begin in India, flash back to Brittany. Illegitimate son. Lonely boyhood along shore. Talon . . . sees animals, fish and other objects in pieces of bone or wood . . . says "I will show you" and cuts away unneeded wood until the thing he sees is there. He has a gift for perception of form and line.

In 1569 apprenticed to an armorer in Paris, he develops his natural genius for design and sculpture, becomes skilled at trade. [He becomes an] Aid to [a] diplomat . . .

Goes to Persia by ship and caravan with Master, master dies, accused of theft by those who rob his master. He escapes into the swamps of the Tigris.

India, Talon in love: meets on the shore with a beautiful girl, is captured, replies fiercely to Solaga, who discovers how marvelous his art, then cuts off his hand, dropped in sea.

Escapes, gets aboard ship, proves useful, learns much about seafaring (use early sailing records), is wrecked in Japan . . . Stern teacher, some take him for Ainu [the Ainu were a native people in the Japanese islands]. Leaves Japan after long training, returns overland to India.

Joins pirates, takes a small boat and reaches Gingee. Using arts of ninja, enters castle and kills man who took his hand, becomes a pirate leader, raids along coast. Visits Tamil country. Stops at Krakatoa.

After capture of town or ship he examines prison-
ers for knowledge, information, etc. Those who can
teach [him something] he keeps, then releases with
presents. Finds one gathering info on his ship . . .
in order to steal it. All written down. He suggests
prisoner develop a better memory, maroons him upon an
island. Returns to find prisoner has become ruler.
Prisoner now plans to take Talon's ship again. Talon
outwits him. They become friends.

Finds Neolithic settlements, old maps, falls in
love with Rajput princess, escapes with her. Battle
at sea, raids up river, mysterious voyage up the
Indus and recovery of treasure at night. Some of his
men mutiny but he defeats them, puts them ashore on
an island and sets sail across the Pacific.

Crosses Pacific, terrible voyage, many die--1 of
4 [of his] ships disappears at sea. He sails to west
coast [of North America], fight with Spanish ship,
scurvy causes another ship to be abandoned, treasure
buried or hidden on west coast of America.

With loyal seamen he sails around horn to France.
He pensions them off, one at a time, invests some of
his fortune there. His mother has gone on to become a
famous woman, a patron of the arts. Brings the rest
of his treasure to Canada packed among bales of
clothing, etc. To Gaspe [the Gaspe Peninsula is the
southern side of the mouth of Canada's St. Lawrence
River], sees rock [from] an earlier dream and stays
there. [Perce Rock is a distinctive formation just
off shore from the Gaspe town of Perce.]

After loss of hand, he creates art in secret,
using only the left. Hides work due to shame as to

quality, actually quite good. Do not show this until close to end or at end, create mystery, show his secret pain, discards work.

Next are notes on a possible sequel, picking up after the fight with the Spanish ship and duplicating or expanding on the rest of Talon's life. The reference to "Sackett" suggests Louis was thinking of this as an opportunity to interweave this novel with the early stories in the Sackett series.

Down west coast thru [through] [the Strait of] Magellan, arrives off Gaspe, sees rock [from] an earlier dream and stays there. En route north passes another ship at sea near Carolina coast (Sackett?) then on to Gaspe with treasure. In a small bay on east coast attempted seizure of ship defeated, but some friendly seamen killed. Talon almost single-handed beats them off, his wife fighting beside him. On the Gaspe shore they hide treasure, find signs of activity on island there, signs of someone else in the area.

They sail into a small bay and begin to build a large home. (Jambe de Bois a boy on this voyage?) [de Bois is a character in a later Talon family book, Rivers West, and would, almost certainly, not have lived long enough to appear in both stories.] Attacks by Indians? Pirates? Finds remains of ancient settlement of some sort (tie in with Oak Island treasure), makes effort to recover treasure but defeated by storm and Indians. Beginning of trouble between colonies & England. Early feeling for preserving French language. Beautiful love story.

He builds a home, studies the sea through a spyglass, has children, 3 boys and a girl. One boy sails away to the West Indies. One becomes a steady man, a ship builder (a descendant of this child will become

the Character in RIVERS WEST). One travels to Ottawa
and then north. Daughter? Sometime during this period
Talon is in Quebec and meets his father.

Perhaps when he is an old man a traveler tells
him of carving found in France, the work of a great
genius, someone inspired. He alone knows he was that
carver.

Ends his days, after Indian battles, pirates,
etc., looking off to sea, his wife beside him. She is
a daughter of Rajput kings.

Louis's first journal reference to creating a series of stories covering several generations of three families was in 1962. Back then, it
was possible he was thinking that his "Three Family" stories would
all be set in the nineteenth century. However, by 1971 he was planning *Fair Blows the Wind*, a Chantry family novel that takes place a
couple hundred years before his traditional Westerns. And in 1972 his
journal produces the earliest mention of *The Bastard of Brignogan* or
its sequel when he mentions that he is looking for a certain location in
Canada:

. . . drove out and spent about ten days or more
on the Gaspe. I was looking for an old village I
could use, picked up much history, and finally decided that Perce itself was the place I needed.

In the summer of 1978 it is clear he is working on the chapters
you have just read when he writes:

Continuing my reading on pirates and piracy for
the Talon book. I read much of them years ago but
want to soak it all up now. Too little written about
any pirates but Europeans or Americans, however most
piracy was in Asia (and still is!).

The Talon book, one of those which will be done

soon requires a good knowledge of the life and action in Japan and India in the late 1500s.

And then:

Also reading for Talon. He is an armorer early in his career and I have been studying methods of work, the work itself, and the tools. I shall draw upon things seen by Manucci and other early travelers in India for his first impressions. I have several [accounts of people] who were there at the time. Also reading about Japan, same period. I am well-established in that history but one can always learn more. Have been reading books on piracy most of them of a later period, to be more familiar with that aspect. And must brush up on seamanship of the period. I shall have a bit to say about Asiatic seamen, too.

Perce, Quebec: This photo was taken from the spot where Louis imagined Talon's house would have been built.

Most of the books imply they copied it all from us,
or much of it, which is nonsense. A lot of interesting lore to be weeded from the ARABIAN NIGHTS and
OCEAN OF STORY.

Finally, there is one last slip of paper used to sketch out some of the
Three Families series. On it Louis has written:

    1. Talon--India.
    2. Chantry--Ireland, England, Newfoundland.
    3. Talon--Oak Island.
    4. Talon--Huron, Brule, Iroquois.
    5. Talon to West Coast after treasure.

Item number one is certainly *The Bastard of Brignogan*. Item two
is partly the novel *Fair Blows the Wind*, but the "Newfoundland" part
suggests a Chantry is going to end up in Talon's part of the New
World. With item three, it looks like he is considering that previously
mentioned connection between Talon and the Oak Island Treasure.
Four refers to Etienne Brule, an early explorer in Canada and a pretty
wild character. For his sins, he was tortured by the Iroquois and then
eventually dismembered and eaten by a group of Huron. Item five
suggests that Talon or a descendant decided to go after a portion of
the East Indies treasure Talon had abandoned in order to make it
home to Europe.

MAC ROSS

The Beginning of a Western Novel

CHAPTER I

He was seven or eight miles away when he saw it for
the first time, stark and lonely against the empty sky.

Upon the wide plain there was nothing else, only the
yellow-brown grass blowing in the long, low wind and the
great square house, lonely in the evening.

It was autumn, and the wind was chill without being
cold, but it was a time when a man began to wonder what
had become of his summer's wages.

He had been riding three days and had seen no living
thing but a wolf, trotting, head down, along a far off
slope. There had been tracks of buffalo and of cattle,
but even those grew fewer as he rode deeper into that
vast and vacant land. Water-holes were few, and tinged
with alkali, and it had been a week since he had seen a
tree or brush taller than his saddle.

At first he thought what he saw was an upthrust of rock, incongruous as that might be, yet as the sun dropped lower its light glinted on the far off windows . . . glass windows, in a place like this.

Uneasily his eyes strayed left and right, but there was nothing else upon the low hill but the house, a small shed that could do for a barn, and a corral. He rode with his sheep-skin coat hanging open, his gun-butt forward on his left hip. In his saddle scabbard he carried a Winchester.

He was still three hundred yards off when something moved on the grassy slope between himself and the house, yet he had ridden another fifty yards before he could make it out.

Someone slight and small, lying in a half-sitting, half-reclining position, looking back toward the house. As yet that person's attention was so strongly upon the house that he or she was not aware of the approaching rider.

There was a slight movement and he saw the figure was that of a girl in a faded brown or yellow dress. She was staring back toward the great, gaunt frame house as though frightened, but there was no movement near the house, nor any sound. From this distance he would have guessed the house to be empty, for it offered no evidence of occupation.

By now he was within a few yards of the girl, but on the prairie turf his horse's hoofs made no sound to warn her of his approach. When he was within easy speaking distance, he said, "Hello, there!"

She started as if to spring to her feet, then sagged back. The face she turned toward him was gaunt and pale.

It was also beautiful in a haunted, wistful way, with great dark eyes and black hair, a wisp of it falling over her brow and stirred by the wind.

She had reason to be startled, for he knew what she

saw. His clothes were dusty and he had a week's stubble
of beard on his lean jaws, and hard green eyes that had
small cause to be anything but cold. His hat was battered
and there was a bullet-hole through the brim. His sheep-
skin coat was worn and stained. His boots were down-at-
heel, his jeans worn thin by many washings. The horse he
rode showed none of its fine lines for his winter coat
was on, and he was long-haired and ragged, as tired and
ill-fed as his rider.

"Something wrong, ma'am?" He strove to make his tone
gentle, only partly succeeding. "If I can help--?"

"No . . . no, it is nothing."

She came suddenly and gracefully to her feet. On the
ground she had seemed wasted and thin, now she looked
lithe and lovely as a young antelope.

"It is a long ride that's behind me. When I saw the
house I thought I might find a meal and a place to
sleep."

"I . . . I don't know. You will have to ask."

She turned away and walked ahead of him toward the
house. Once he had a vague notion he saw a curtain move
on one of the ground-floor windows, but it could have
been his imagination.

He was uneasy. There was something here that disturbed him, and he liked nothing about the weather-
beaten, unpainted house. It appeared to have stood there
for quite some time yet he knew that could not be the
case for this had been Indian country until just four or
five years ago, and the only travel through here had been
a few buffalo hunters.

"Kind of a lonely place," he suggested.

"We don't have many visitors." She turned her head.
"You must not be surprised. I mean . . . he may not let
you stay. He does not like visitors."

"I'll be no trouble," he said hastily. "I need grub
and water. I can sleep out."

Anywhere but in that house, he told himself, and the thought surprised him.

"You came from the west?"

"Southwest." He hesitated, then added apologetically, "I haven't eaten in three days."

She was shocked. "I'll get something for you. No matter what he says."

Now what kind of man would turn a body away without eating? he asked himself. _That makes no sense. None at all._

At the corral he dismounted, hesitated a moment with his hands on the saddle, then stripped the rig from the dun. _The Hell with it. You're going to rest, no matter what._

He turned the line-back dun into the corral, then rousted around the barn. Surprisingly there were several sacks of corn and oats in a room at one side of the shed. He dipped up some of each and took it to his horse.

There was a trough in the corral, and the water looked good. It was only then that he saw the pump near the house, and the pipe leading to it from the trough.

He went to the pump. There was no dipper . . . at most wells a man found a tin-dipper or a gourd hanging from a wire, but not here. He worked the pump-handle and water gushed clear and cold at the fourth stroke. Cupping his hand, he tasted the water. It was cold . . . and sweet.

A sweet-water well in this country! Whoever owned this place, he was shot with luck.

The girl had gone into the house, so he worked the pump-handle a few more times to send water gushing into the corral trough to replace what his horse would drink. Wiping his mouth with the back of his hand, he started toward the house.

He went up to the door, scraped his feet, then knocked.

The knock was loud in the silence, but for a long
time there was no response, then the door opened suddenly
and an old Negro stood there, a tall, fine-looking man,
ramrod straight. "Come in, sir," he said expression-
lessly. "Whom shall I announce?"

"Mac Ross," he said, and saw the Negro stiffen ever
so slightly, then bow and turn away.

At the end of the short hall was a tall door of dark
oak panels. The Negro opened it, and said quietly, "Mr.
Mac Ross, sir."

Mac Ross stepped into the door, and stopped for a moment, yet nothing in his face revealed his astonishment.

The room was high-ceilinged and lined with books. On
the wall above the fireplace was an oil-painting of an
austere man in uniform. Before it, one heel hooked over
the edge of a brass hearth fender, stood a tall man in a
black suit. A singularly handsome man despite his long
face emphasized by the wave of hair above the brow, somewhat in the Andrew Jackson manner.

"Come in, Mr. Ross. I am General Robinson."

General is it? Well, if you're going to take a title
it might as well be a good one.

His immediate impression was that he did not like
General Robinson, and his next impression was that the
feeling was mutual. He came to the point at once.

"I was ridin' past and I'm short of grub."

"Of course. You are most welcome." There was an edge
of sarcasm to Robinson's voice and Mac Ross felt a stir
of irritation, and fought it down. He wanted no trouble.
The last thing he needed right now was more trouble.

"You came from the southwest? Is that right?" Robinson's tone was no longer sarcastic. This was something he
wished to be sure about, and Mac Ross had the feeling
that Robinson desperately wanted him to have come from
the southwest . . . hence not from some other direction.

"That's right. Been ridin' for a week."

"I was wondering. We are told there is nothing out that way, nothing at all."

"Your information is correct. It's level country for mile after mile. A few dry lakes here and yonder, probably filled up after a good rain."

"Buffalo?"

"Saw some tracks . . . buffalo, and a few cattle tracks."

"Cattle? From where?"

Again he seemed disturbed, although why Ross could not guess.

"No idea," he replied, honestly enough. "I saw nothing but tracks."

"Come! We'll have a drink, then we'll eat."

Mac Ross hesitated. "I'd like to wash up first. It's been a dusty ride."

"Certainly." He turned slightly as the black man entered. "Manisty, will you show Mr. Ross where he may wash up? And you may set an extra place--he will be dining with us."

"Of course, sir. Mr. Ross? Will you come with me?"

He led the way upstairs and to a comfortable bedroom on the second floor. "You will find warm water in the pitcher, sir. Dinner will be served in thirty minutes."

"Is there a whisk broom? I gathered some dust."

"Of course, sir. May I take your coat? I should be glad to dust it for you, and--"

"That's all right," Mac Ross said easily, "I'll take care of it."

"Of course, sir. As you wish."

When the black man had gone, Mac Ross removed his coat and took his second gun from his waistband and placed it on a stand nearby. Then he took off his shirt, and using a washcloth, washed off his face, neck and hands, then his chest. There was a livid scar . . .

a fresh scar . . . across his chest and shoulder. He was
especially careful around that only partly healed wound.

He put his shirt on once more, buttoned the collar,
and with a black string tie from his breast pocket, he
made himself appear somewhat more formal as befitted the
dining room in a gentleman's house.

He checked both guns as well as the thin knife he
wore down the back of his neck below the collar.

What was a house like this doing in a place like
this? And who was this "General Robinson"? And who was
the girl?

He had seen no one other than the black man, but assumed there was further help in the kitchen. And what of
the ranch? Or was it a ranch?

His uneasiness increased. The girl had seemed
frightened . . . of what?

He brushed his coat carefully, then adjusted it, trying to smooth out the pockets that had too often bulged
with necessaries. The haunting uneasiness refused to
leave him. Going to the window, he looked out. It was a
sheer drop, a good thirty feet to the ground, as the
house stood on a knoll that fell away sharply on his side
of the house. The other window was scarcely better.

He had turned away when something that had caught his
eye claimed his renewed attention. He went back to the
window. Some distance off, barely discernible now in the
late twilight, was something black . . . a building of
some sort, long and low, nestled in a corner of the hills
and almost hidden from sight.

He let the curtain fall into place and stood listening. All was very quiet . . . too quiet.

He stood in the middle of the room, thinking. He had
seen but three people, yet there had to be more. Did they
run cattle here? Sheep? Where were the cowhands . . . if
any?

Who built the house? Who supplied it with food? And
from where? There were some Mexicans settled on the Canadian, but how far away was that? This was new country to
him although he had hunted buffalo in other parts of the
Panhandle and High Plains country.

As a matter of fact, he did not know exactly where he
was. He had left the Pecos in a hurry, and had ridden far
and fast, changing directions several times in an effort
to elude those who pursued him. Later, he had changed direction looking for water as one water-hole after another
proved dry. He knew only that he was in the High Plains
country somewhere east of the Pecos and still upon the
cap-rock.

It was very possible there was not another habitation
of any sort within a hundred miles of where he now was.
He did not know that, of course, but from his knowledge
of the country it was a logical guess. Certainly, he knew
of none.

So then . . . what was this "General" Robinson, a
strikingly handsome, educated gentleman, whose hands
showed no indication of hard labor, doing out here in the
middle of nowhere? And with a young, and very attractive,
woman, very possibly a sister, niece or even a daughter.

Or his wife.

For some reason he found the idea distasteful. He
smiled grimly at that. Was he, Mac Ross, becoming enam-
ored of a girl he had just met? Scarcely glimpsed?

"Mac," he spoke softly, but aloud, "you've been away
from women too long."

There was a discreet tap on his door.

"Yes?"

"Dinner is served, sir. At the foot of the stairs,
sir, in the room on your right."

Careful directions . . . a courtesy? Or to keep him
from wandering about?

He glanced at himself in the mirror once more. Excellent mirror, he thought, and beautiful furniture. The house had been done by someone with taste. He opened the door and stepped out into the hallway. He glanced along it as he turned toward the steps. At least four doors opened on the hall . . . yet there could be even more rooms.

The stairs were carpeted. He walked down them carefully, spurs jingling. He did not want to catch a spur in the carpet . . . obviously Persian.

The lower hall was wider, carpeted as well. The library where he had seen the General was on the left as he came down the steps, the dining room on the right. He opened the door and stepped inside.

The table was long. There was silver and crystal, place settings as for a formal dinner. There were eight chairs.

General Robinson stood with his back to the fireplace, hands clasped behind him.

"Good evening, Mr. Ross. Jettchen will be down briefly."

"Jettchen? It is an unusual name."

"Jetta, if you wish, Mr. Ross. It is a Frisian name." Robinson glanced at him. "You have heard of the Frisians, Mr. Ross?"

"An ancient Teutonic people, weren't they? From the Netherlands area?"

"I am amazed. The Frisians are little heard of in these later days."

Mac Ross offered no comment. He was waiting, every sense alert. Something was decidedly wrong here, and it disturbed him.

Robinson took down a cigar box and opened it for him . . . Havanas. Ross shook his head. Excellent cigars, but he was no smoker. "Thank you, no."

"You are traveling far, Mr. Ross?"

He took a name out of a hat. "St. Louis, eventually.
Abilene first, as I hear the railroad's there now."

"It is? I had not expected it so soon." Robinson
clipped the end of his cigar, then lighted it. "Abilene?
I do not know the place although I have heard some rumor
of it. Kansas, is it not?"

"It is, and there's nothing there unless McCoy has
built something. A few sod houses and dug-outs, and a
sort of a saloon, I think."

"You mentioned a McCoy?"

"Joseph McCoy. He's the one who talked them into
building the railroad out there. He's convinced them
there's money in shipping beef that will be driven up
from Texas, now that the war is over."

"Ah, yes. The war. I am afraid some of us suffered
very much from the war, Mr. Ross. We . . . my family, I
mean . . . lost everything. It was no use rebuilding, no
use at all."

"You seem to be doing very well here," Ross said,
glancing around.

"A pittance, Mr. Ross, just a pittance. But we manage, we manage. Of course, as we could no longer afford
to work our estates, we were forced to sell . . . to sell
at a very bad time, Mr. Ross. It was distressing."

He paused, glanced at the end of his cigar. "Of
course, our business had not been in satisfactory shape
for some time. When the government passed the Non-
Importation Act in 1806, it was a blow. Of course, that
was before my time."

"The Non-Importation Act? You refer to the slave-
trade?"

"Of course, and an excellent business it was, too. We
had half-a-dozen ships in the trade, Mr. Ross. The family
saw the end coming, naturally, as Vermont, Massachusetts,
New Hampshire, Rhode Island, and a number of other states

had already abolished it, but we had ties with the Arab
traders . . . and the help of a few African chiefs. The
Arabs and the Portugese almost controlled the slave
trade."

"You had no doubts about all that, General?"

"Doubts? Why? There had always been slaves. The Greek
and Roman civilizations were built on slave labor, and
the same with the Egyptians and Babylonians. Race mattered little in those days."

He shrugged. "Labor has always been needed. Some men,
whether white or black, are born to be slaves."

Ross's irritation was mounting, but the man was his
host, and if such was his viewpoint, he was entitled to
it. Before he could make a reply, the door opened again
and Jettchen entered.

She was dressed in white, and she was breathtakingly
beautiful. She crossed the room to him. "How nice that
you could stay. We have so few visitors, Mr. Ross."

She went to the table, and he held her chair for her
to be seated. Momentarily as she moved up to her chair
her body pressed against him, pushing his gun against his
side. He was embarrassed by the gun, yet when the General
moved to his chair he was no longer embarrassed.

He was also wearing a gun.

COMMENTS: At this point a page is missing. The narrative picks
back up, for just a moment, after the first course of dinner:

Manisty entered and took up the soup plates. He moved
silently and smoothly, his skill that of years of prac-
tice, but there was an assurance about him that disturbed
Ross, an assurance that went beyond the fact that he knew

his business and was, perhaps, an old retainer. There was in him a sense of power, of strength that was not only physical, but something more.

———————◦LT◦———————

COMMENTS: I have always wondered if the early images in this story weren't inspired by the famous painting by Andrew Wyeth, *Christina's World*. In the early 1960s a friend of my mother's had a print of it hanging just inside the door to her apartment. I remember it, and I was just five years old, so Dad could hardly have failed to see the picture every time he visited. Then, as now, it was known that Anna Christina Olson, the inspiration for that work of art, had been paralyzed by an undiagnosed muscular disorder. That fact and the pathos that goes with it adds an interesting tension to what could be seen simply as a pastoral, if somewhat mysterious, painting. The concept of the distant house with nothing else around and of a woman trapped in some strange and unknown way is at the core of the initial moments of this oddly Gothic-seeming Western novel.

I love the creepy atmosphere Louis created, and I wish I had more information about when it was written and what my father may have intended.

———————————————

DAM AND TIMBER

Notes for an Adventure Story

LT

COMMENTS: This project was probably intended to be a short story aimed at the men's adventure magazines of the 1950s. The men's adventure genre was one of the last gasps of the once dominant pulp magazine market, and the various magazines, like *Argosy, Saga, Real Men,* and many others, were cheekily referred to as the "sweats" or "armpit slicks" (some were published on slick paper like the more up-scale magazines). They focused on "true" stories of crime, war, and often quite bizarre man-against-nature encounters. I have always suspected that they were an expression of a rather odd postwar/cold war–era psychology that I have never completely understood. In general the subject matter was fairly graphic and the art pretty kinky.

I've always considered the "sweats" to be a macho version of our supermarket tabloids, with their lurid half-fact, half-fantasy feel and their somewhat voyeuristic tales. Louis was never completely comfortable with the operatic cartoony-ness of the genre, but in the years prior to his breaking into the paperback market, he was forced to give it a try.

Regardless, Dad's notes for the following story channeled some recognizable aspects of the men's adventure genre: blue-collar manly men doing manly things in a challenging natural setting.

The location of "Dam and Timber" seems to be Arizona or Nevada, someplace very hot and remote from civilization. A dam is under construction, and the protagonist of the story is the winner of the contract to clear what is about to become the bottom of a large lake of brush, trees, and other debris. The corporation or local government must have the job done by a certain date, so there is a lot of pressure to finish quickly, and not too much concern for worker safety. From hearing Dad talk about it, I believe he was planning to incorporate a conflict in which a group wanted to stop the hero from finishing the job, or from finishing on time—but from these notes it's not completely clear why. The equipment being used to clear the brush and trees includes heavy chains stretched between bulldozers and a huge steel ball that is dragged over areas to crush the vegetation flat.

Don't be thrown as you read through—Louis experiments with a couple of different names for the female characters . . .

The first set of notes:

```
Open: Hero arrives from freight train.
He is surprised at ease of getting sub-contract.

Heavy sends thugs after him
He begins looking for help, there is none.
He begins taking bums, drunks, etc.
The fight with thugs

More grief--perhaps the dealer calls back his
equipment

So Hero goes to a really tough character and gets
equipment from him.

Make this good -

Perhaps use cloud-seeding stunt. [Cloud seeding
is a process that uses chemicals spread by aircraft
or fired into the atmosphere from the ground to cre-
ate rain.]
```

Second set of notes:

```
Opening scene: he arrives and there is tough
talk, then he bids for contract--gets it-
```

Heavy sends two thugs after him. Heroine sees it [the fight] and afterward her friends tell her he is not a man a nice girl would be interested in--she answers that even a nice girl likes a little red blood in her men. Gleason overhears this and comments--then the tramp [Louis is talking about a "trampy" woman] joins him [the Hero], and takes his arm possessively.

One of workers is knocked down in front of steel ball and Hero goes to rescue -

At climax logs fail to burn as rain, increased by cloud-seeding, stops fire. [This may refer to the debris piled up by the crew clearing what will become the lake bottom behind the dam, or it might be something completely different.]

Then Hero has pay-off fight with Heavy--terrific.

Fight between girls: Heroine knows judo--she takes off her stole and coolly beats the hell out of tramp.

Build for 8 high points and in about 30 pages.

Humor--Gleason & others [Gleason seems a bit like a comic-relief, sidekick sort of character.]

Strong character--different

Make girl unusual--simply wants her man--Gleason advises--"She's [the trampy woman] got no brand on him. Move in if you've got the guts."

So battle is joined

The job is man-killing and brutal--it goes on
through rain and sun in the roughest kind of
country -

Man falls before steel ball -

Perhaps a fight between two men with bulldozers
to deflect tumbling ball, or to push logs in its way

Sub-contract from a guy who wants him [our hero]
whipped, broken, dead. This man broke him on [the]
last job--wants to finish it. Gives him sub-contract
where he can't win--but he takes his misfit crew and
does win--two women--one a lady, the other a tramp,
but the lady beats hell out of the tramp

Strictly a fight for a man. Cathy remarks--older
man tells her she must fight with all her weapons.
She does and wins.

The third set of notes:

Part cliff, part swamp, all hell -

Use fire scene, steel ball, fight scene--make
this a honey--two really tough mugs--scene where 2
are sent out to beat up Hero--He whips them both,
takes them to boss and throws them across his desk at
him--

1. Jim Tyler.
2. Tom Bassett, of Bassett Demolition & Construction Co.
3. "Larry" Lorraine, a sexy babe with Tyler on
   her mind and Bassett on her trail.

4. <u>Ruth Sheridan</u>, visiting in vicinity of project, who falls for Jim. Wealthy but un-
   spoiled, quiet, but determined. Her father
   had been a contract mine boss and she had
   spent her early years in mining camps.

5. "<u>Doc</u>" <u>Cassidy</u>, stew-bum but old friend of
   Tyler. The first of his new crew. [This might
   be the same as the Gleason character.]

6. <u>Jack Helms</u>, Bassett's straw-boss and muscle
   man.

7. <u>Swede</u>, the ex-con; <u>Milligan</u>, ex-Seabee; <u>John</u>,
   the half-breed; <u>Lee</u>, the coward; <u>Laramie</u>, ex-
   contest rider (all bums picked up by Tyler
   for his misfit crew.)

8. <u>Louise Butler and Dave</u>: Friends of Ruth, who
   entertain Tom Bassett and later, Jim Tyler.

Some of the inspiration for this story may have come from accounts Louis heard in the 1920s from a girlfriend's father, a man who
was working on a dam project near Klamath Falls, Oregon. I also
suspect that this concept later evolved into the Western novel *Guns of
the Timberlands*, but I have only my sense of my father's career and
methodology to suggest that.

THE QUEST FOR THE BEAR

A Complete Adventure Story

Night and the cold . . . four men crouching above a tiny fire in a shallow cave, hollowed by the wind.

Black and glistening peaks towering into the silence of the night . . . a frozen surf of glaciers. Sixteen thousand feet . . .

Far off, miles away through the night, an avalanche rumbles, tearing the brow from a cliff, hurling its thundering mass of millions of tons of ice, frozen snow and rock into some vast, unknown chasm.

A lonely, prowling wind moaning along the pass, a wind seeking out every crevice, every fold, every tiniest crack among the mountains, a wind that creeps up close to the fire and flattens itself above the flames, that huddles close to the warmth of men, a shuddering wind that has known no living thing . . . a lost wind in a lost land.

These are mountains unpeopled and still, these are haunted canyons, unclimbed and unattempted peaks, these are the pillars that loom above the Roof of the World,

above the silent and somber Kuen Luns, backbone of
Asia . . . lonely as the ranges of the moon.

Three of the four men are mountain Ladakhis, skilled
guides and hunters, men of the caravans, wanderers of the
highest mountains on earth . . . but they are afraid now.

The fourth man stretches his hands toward the tongues
of flame, watching the fire as it curls lecherously about
the few chilled sticks and yak chips gathered from the
long-unused trail.

"Sir?" The Ladakhi with the scar speaks carefully. He
wears the scar as a badge of bravery, so it is he who
speaks, for the Ladakhis would not be thought afraid. "We
will go back? The season is long past. There will be another year for the bear."

"No." The tone was flat. "We will find him now. I
cannot hope to come this close again. It is a miracle
that we have found him, and he is near . . . I can feel
it."

No man among them spoke, but within them stirred
fear. The great white bears of the mountains possessed,
it was said, the souls of evil men. Some said they had
the souls of the wicked black lamas of the land of Bod,
which white men call Tibet. This man had come to them,
hunting a certain bear, just one bear in all these vast
ranges . . . and he had found it.

Frightened they were of the late season in the high
passes, knowing as they did the dangers of remaining too
long, and frightened as they were of the bear, they were
even more frightened of the man who sought the bear. They
were frightened, and yet they were filled with admiration. First among mountain men, the Ladakhis had found in
this man their equal if not their superior. He had been
able to find one trail out of the many trails, one bear
out of the hundreds of bears.

Had he not described the bear to them? Had he not
told them of the great scar across muzzle and jowl? A

scar burned by a torch in the hands of this very man? Had
he not shown that it was his destiny to find this bear?
Already the Tibetans had deserted, the food supply grew
short, and the Ladakhis knew but little time remained.
Yet the man had found his bear.

Sanju Pass was far and away to the south. The pass
upon which they camped was nameless and little known. It
was but four days before that Morgan had come upon the
trail.

They had ascended a valley, walking on crusted snow.
They had picked their way across a recent slide, and seen
other slides poised above them. They had come down upon
the new fallen snow covering a glacier, and there on the
snow were gigantic tracks.

The Ladakhis were aghast when they saw them . . .
they looked away and then looked again. How could the
tracks of any living thing be so huge? And across one of
them was the old mark, a scar like a rope across one huge
padded foot.

"He is big." The Ladakhi looked from the track to
Morgan. And Morgan had nodded grimly. "Yes," he had said,
"this bear is big. He may be the biggest bear that ever
lived. He is bigger than a Kodiak grizzly. He is bigger
than a yak. He will weigh well over two thousand pounds.
He stands more than six feet high at the shoulder. He is
The Bear."

The Ladakhis looked again at the tracks, and they
avoided each other's eyes. This was a tale they would not
dare to tell. No man would believe there was a bear of
such hugeness. This was The Bear. Now they understood why
Morgan spoke of it as he did.

They had tracked him across the glacier and down into
the forest, and they had tracked him across the rocks and
soon they became aware. The Bear knew he was being followed. He knew!

On the second day the Ladakhis pointed this out to

Morgan. "Sir, he knows we follow him. See where he
stopped to look back? See where he swung wide to go up
the hill and look down upon this trail? He has seen us.
Now he will kill."

On the third day The Bear circled back and lay down
beside his trail. This a Kodiak will also do, but when
they wait for their hunter they attack. The Bear did not
attack. He watched.

It was afternoon of the third day when they found
where The Bear had circled back to watch them. The Ladakhis shook their heads and looked all about them, super-
stitious and frightened. Yet the Ladakhi is a man of the
mountains, proud of his reputation for bravery.

And then The Bear moved away from the forest. He
climbed the long glaciers, moved over the rocky slopes,
mounting higher and ever higher into the bleak, cold
fastnesses of the mountains. The sky flattened into endless, monotonous gray, the tops of the peaks were lost in
the clouds and overnight their flanks took on the blinding white of new snow.

"We must go back now," the Ladakhis said, but Morgan
did not seem to have heard. Bowed and steady he stayed
upon the trail, and on the fourth day they came suddenly
upon The Bear.

He was standing on the slope above them and they were
almost abreast of him before he was seen. He reared up
then, a gigantic beast, so enormous as to defy calcula-
tion, his great nose thrust toward them, his little eyes
blinking as if to ask what manner of creature this was
who stayed so relentlessly upon his trail.

A full minute they stared and then The Bear turned.
Morgan jerked up his rifle but The Bear was gone!

Like that, he vanished . . . but when they reached
the spot, there were no tracks to be seen . . . of
course, it was rock where he had stood. Nevertheless . . .

It had been a forced landing, that first time. The
plane had been lost on a flight from Chungking to Iran,
and it had crashed in a remote valley high among the
peaks of the Kuen Luns. There had been four of them left
alive and they had started to walk out.

From the beginning it had appeared hopeless but they
were men and men must act. Carrying what food they could,
they started north for Sinkiang proper, hoping to strike
one of the old caravan routes and to find people. None of
them knew the country and only Morgan had a vague idea of
where to go. Their navigator had been killed and none of
them had ever been over this country before.

By the night of the fifth day they were well broken
in to the walking. Their food was holding out, and they
had supplemented it by killing an ibex that very day. At
night they camped near the foot of a black column of
rock, and it was there The Bear had come upon them.

Drawn, no doubt, by the smell of fresh blood from the
ibex, The Bear appeared. Yet at first he had not seemed
dangerous. They had seen him some fifty yards off, a gigantic creature, so enormous as to make them doubt their
senses. He had his nose to the wind and was sensing their
body odor . . . seemingly puzzled.

Ryerson had been broiling the meat over a fire. Smith
was dozing, half-asleep. Gordon and Morgan had seen The
Bear at the same moment.

"Harry . . ." Morgan's voice had been muted, low with
astonishment. "Look at that."

They stared, and then The Bear had started toward
them. Lumbering forward curiously he seemed more curious
than anything else . . . but Gordon was suddenly stricken
with panic.

No outdoors man was Gordon. He was city bred and city
stifled. To him a wild animal was an immediate danger,

and when The Bear started toward their camp, instead of
giving him a chance to satisfy his curiosity and leave,
as he might have done, Gordon grabbed up his carbine and
fired.

A .30 caliber carbine is no weapon, as either Ryerson
or Morgan could have told him, with which to tackle two
thousand pounds of bear . . . or any bear.

The bullet struck . . . they all heard it strike, and
then with a muffled roar, The Bear charged. Perhaps he
had only been curious, but these strange creatures had
lashed out at him, they had stung him, and red-eyed with
fury, he charged, thinking only to annihilate them. And
he very nearly did.

When the huge beast lunged for them, instead of holding his ground and emptying the carbine into it, Gordon
cried out, dropped the gun and fled. Ryerson sprang for
his own carbine and Morgan rolled over, grabbing up the
fallen gun. A huge paw smashed at him, caught him a
glancing blow, and he was knocked rolling.

Poor Smith never had a chance. Startled from his
sleep by the sudden crack of the gunshot, he lunged to
his feet squarely in front of The Bear. With one smashing
blow it broke his neck, and then crunched his skull between great jaws. Gordon fled and fell, and the charging
bear was upon him. Gordon's scream was to ring in Morgan's ears all during the months that followed, and the
memory of it never died.

Ryerson tried one wild shot, and then as The Bear
rushed him, he crowded himself into a narrow crack in the
rock. It snarled and muttered, reaching for him with huge
paws, biting angrily at the edges of the crack, but Ryerson was out of reach.

Morgan lay perfectly still. The beast turned to
Smith's body, and not knowing he was already dead, Morgan
could not stand to see the helpless man mauled again.

Lying within a yard of the fire, it was easy for Morgan
to reach over and grab a burning brand. The Bear saw the
movement and swung around. Morgan's flaming wood was a
heavy stick and it was filled with pitch and burning with
a bright flame. Swiftly he struck, and the blow caught
the beast across the face.

For an instant, everything seemed to stop. The flame
seared the face and Morgan smelled burning hair, and then
the monster cried out, an almost human sound, and struck,
knocking the stick from Morgan's hand, but the pitch on
his face still blazed and the eyes of the beast seemed to
stare down at Morgan with a wild sort of horror. Then The
Bear wheeled and lunged away, stopping every few yards to
rub his face in the snow.

Slowly, Morgan got to his feet, then sat back, shuddering with nervous reaction, thinking of that final,
awful moment when The Bear had looked down upon him with
that wild, helpless, tragic fear as if wondering what
sort of creature had done this to him.

Ryerson edged his way out of the crack, his body
shaking as if from fever. "Good God, man! Did you see
that creature?" His voice was shrill with shock and fear.
"I never imagined . . . !"

Gordon was dead and Smith was dead. They buried them
there with the towering black pinnacles as marker, then
left their two carbines beside the grave, and went on.
And somehow, ragged and worn, half-starved and half-
frozen, months later, they reached warmth and civilization.

Only their knowledge of the wilderness, their skill
at hunting, their physical condition could have gotten
them through. They were a good team, and they made it.
And the first night Morgan had glanced around at Harry
Ryerson. "I'm going back," he said, "and kill that
brute."

They told their story and people smiled, as inexperienced people always will. They smiled that smile that
every traveler knows, the good-natured tolerance of polite skepticism of the person who believes he is being
subjected to a wild tale, but who listens politely, any-
how. And then they stopped telling it. They stopped because nobody would believe, nobody could believe. The
people they knew had nothing by which to judge such a
story, for each judges by his own limited experience.

Ryerson was discharged a year later. Morgan remained
on a bit longer and then he too returned home. They no
longer told the story of The Bear, but to them both he
had become just that. He was no longer just a bear, just
any bear. He was The Bear, the personification of all
bears, the undying spirit of Bear.

And to Morgan he was something else. He was an obsession.

Gordon had been relatively a stranger, although a
crew member on the plane. But Smith had been Morgan's
oldest and best friend. Perhaps it was some primitive
lust for revenge, perhaps it was his own memory of that
awful instant of horror when he looked into the eyes of
The Bear. Perhaps he believed that if he returned, found
The Bear and destroyed it, the memory of those eyes would
fade.

Perhaps it was because he remembered his own awful
fear. Perhaps if he had managed to fire . . . after all
he, Morgan, was the real hunter of the lot. Time and
again he told himself that he could have done nothing,
yet a sense of guilt remained. If only . . . well, if he
had done something sooner those two might have lived.

He worked, and he did well. He married, and he was
relatively happy, but the memory wouldn't leave him. It
became an obsession. He talked of it to his wife . . . he
no longer mentioned it to others . . . and she listened

with understanding. On the subject of The Bear, Morgan
decided, he was touched. He was a little insane.

It is given to no man to judge the depths of horror
with which a certain experience may strike another. Time
often wipes away all scars, dims all memories, yet it was
not so with Morgan. The memory of The Bear rode him and
he could not shake it off.

Finally, one night as they lay in bed, he said to his
wife, "Ruth, I'm going back there. I'm going to find that
bear and kill it."

"How could you? In all those mountains? There must be
hundreds, even thousands of bears."

"Yes," he agreed, "but I'll find him. I'm sure of
it."

After that she offered no objections, but helped him
prepare for the expedition. The revolution had swept over
China and there were dangers other than mountains, land-
slides and bears. Nevertheless, he had made it.

At first, he had scouted around for their old trail.
Between them, Ryerson and himself, they had worked out
the approximate location of the crashed plane, and surprisingly, Morgan found it rather easily. He was sorry
Ryerson could not have come along, for his memory would
have been an added help, but finally Morgan found the
pinnacle where his companions had been buried. The graves
were there, undisturbed. It was evidence of the loneliness of the mountains that the carbines stood, covered
with frost, where they had been left.

The season had drawn on, their Tibetan carriers deserted them and only the Ladakhis remained. Not until
after the Tibetans had left did they find the tracks of
his bear.

Morgan added another stick to the fire in the wind-
hollowed cave. He no longer thought of home. He scarcely
thought of Ruth. He did not consider the lateness of the

season, the impending awfulness of the winter nor the difficulties of travel. Now he thought of nothing, dreamed of nothing, lived for nothing but The Bear.

Even now, as he huddled above his fire, he knew it was out there. And he was remembering something his friend had said after they had returned home. "You know, Morg," Ryerson had spoken quietly, "if you think back, I don't believe that bear intended to attack us until Gordon fired that crazy shot. I think he was just curious.

"Think of it. It's possible the creature had never seen a man before. If you remember, he didn't seem angry at first, he wasn't frightened, he was just curious. After all," Ryerson had added, "he was a king in his own land, and we were invaders. He had a right to look us over."

Maybe. But he had killed Smith and he had killed Gordon, and he had given Morgan those awful minutes of fear and horror. Minutes that could, Morgan believed, only be washed away by the blood of the monster that inspired them. Or was it simply that he used this as an excuse? He did not know.

In the morning it was colder. An icy wind whined off the glacier. Frozen snow rattled upon the rocks and the hard crust underfoot. Morgan got to his feet, the heavy rifle cradled in his arms. "Let's go," he said, and they went.

He had been right. The beast had been outside during the night. With slow care, he unwound the skein of tracks, ferreted out the mystery of The Bear's actions. And then they started to follow. All morning they worked their way through the icy mountains, descending into a deep valley, crossing a frozen stream, mounting at an angle a long, steep slope above which towered the beetling brow of a cliff.

Down a vast gorge they followed the trail, and then

up the face of a great declivity, a precipitous slope
wind-swept and bare for five miles, looking always upward
toward the brutal mass of rock that towered above them.
Yet now The Bear seemed to be going somewhere, and not
only away from them. He seemed to have a destination, a
certain goal in the unbelievable vastness of the mountains.

The icy wind gnawed at their exposed flesh, the snow
crunched under foot. They paused to rest and made hot
black tea and ate, and then they pressed on.

No vegetation now, only black rock . . . and ice. No
soft, gentle snow, but blades and anvils, frozen and jag-
ged, under their feet a crunching blanket of it, like
broken glass. And then, suddenly, The Bear stopped.

Wherever he had been going, the trail was blocked by
a vast slide of rock and snow, bigger itself than a mountain in a lesser range. But The Bear had stopped and then
The Bear turned.

The Ladakhis drew back, their faces stiff with
fright, and the great bear lifted himself to his hind
legs, towering above them, vast, yellowish white, with
open jaws. The heavy rifle in his hand, Morgan inched
forward, alert for the slightest move. Now he had him!
The Bear! The killer of Smith and of Gordon! Now . . .

Across its face was the blackened scar of the burn,
the hair scorched away from one side of the muzzle, from
the great jowl, one ear partly gone, and the flesh around
one eye snarled and wrinkled and black. And from that
scar peered an eye, a still seeing eye, but with the lid
burned away. And it was from that strangely wide-open eye
that The Bear watched him.

For a long moment they stared, fascinated, each at
the other. No Kodiak bear had ever been so huge, no gaze
from man or animal had ever been so appalling as that
strange, quizzical stare from the one, wide-open eye, the
other lidded and small.

The Bear was the first to move. It was a sudden, flicking movement of the great head, turning slightly away from Morgan, as if sniffing. And then one of the Ladakhis called out.

"Slide!"

It was a scream rather than a yell . . . and then Morgan heard it himself. The distant, faint whispering that suddenly began to rumble, and then became a roar. He took one swift, frightened glance upward and saw the whole side of the mountain was coming down upon them. He wheeled, and threw himself down the path after the Ladakhis.

The closest of them stumbled and fell. Morgan tripped and sprawled over him, then scrambled to his feet. The Bear had turned and was charging at the cliff! For one startled instant, Morgan hesitated, then he grabbed the Ladakhi. "This way!" he said, and lunged after The Bear. He had a tight grip on the Ladakhi and the man had no choice but to follow.

And then The Bear vanished. Yet they were so closely behind him as to see him rush into a cave-like crack in the cliff. It was all of sixty feet high and how deep they could not see. It was almost covered over at the top, yet they rushed in just as the slide roared above them and swept off down the mountain. For endless minutes it seemed to roar on, like a dozen express trains running abreast. Then it was over and there was a vast and awful silence.

Morgan looked at the Ladakhi. The man's face was sickly pale under the dark, drawn skin. Above them the crack was closed over. They got up and climbed over the snow that had fallen through and reached the entrance. It took them only a few minutes to push out into the day.

The trail they had followed was gone. Before them the slope was swept clean of snow, swept almost smooth of all

projections of ice or rock. There was no sign of the
other Ladakhis.

"They couldn't have made it," Morgan said.

"No." The Ladakhi looked at him. "The Bear saved us."

Morgan started to reply irritably, but could not.
After all, they had followed The Bear to safety. Not that
The Bear intended it so. The very idea that he might
phrase such a thought irritated him. Was he becoming as
bad as the natives? Thinking of a bear intending to save
a man? The Bear was his enemy.

Where was it now? The thought drew Morgan back. The
Ladakhi was looking at him. "We must go now," he said,
"we can delay no longer."

But he turned back to the crevice, and then stopped.
The Bear had emerged. It was not over twenty yards away.
Morgan lifted the rifle, steadied it against his shoul-
der, and looked over the sights at the great beast.

It stood there, head lifted slightly, staring at him.
One shot from this rifle and The Bear was his. One shot?
No, it might require several to stop him, but even if it
charged it would die. At this range Morgan could not miss.

The Bear would be dead.

The king of this lonely land slain. The thought came
strangely to him, and with it, hesitation. Suddenly . . .
no, he did not want The Bear dead. Not this way, at
least.

The Bear deserved his chance. The heavy slugs of the
rifle would smash the life from him, and he would be
slain by a machine from the outer, unrealized world. Morgan put his rifle down carefully. Then he took out his
hunting knife.

It was an eleven-inch weapon, razor sharp. With this
he could meet The Bear on his own terms. After all, as
Ryerson had said, he was king in this world . . . this
was his land . . . and maybe he _was_ only curious.

And maybe he, Morgan, was a little insane. The thought flickered through his awareness and died, lost in the greater urge. Knife in hand, he took a tentative step forward. The Bear would rear up, and he would close in. Mentally, icily cold, he calculated. The Bear would strike and in that instant he would step inside, like a good boxer, and drive his blow home to the body. He would rip open the soft belly. Slashing swiftly and wickedly. He would get clawed, but he would kill The Bear. He would fight him hand to hand, on The Bear's own terms, and then . . .

"Sir?" The Ladakhi's voice was calm. "Why should you kill him now? I do not believe he wishes to fight."

Morgan advanced another step, the knife ready. The Bear looked at him, sniffing the air toward him, still more curious than aggressive.

It was possible his memory did not recall that other day, those years ago, when he had been fired upon, that day when in a red surge of fury he had killed and killed again. It was possible The Bear did not even conceive of these humans as a threat. In its world they were something rare, something different.

Morgan gripped his knife tighter, holding it low, cutting edge up, as does the trained knife fighter. He advanced another step, and then another.

Now The Bear seemed to sense danger, for he swung a little, then reared up, sniffing toward Morgan, studying him with that curious, wide, unblinking stare.

Morgan sought out the spot for his knife. He studied with a flick of his eyes the snow over which he must cross, for to slip might be fatal.

But possibly the thought that this creature might attack him might never have entered The Bear's mind. Probably, with the exception of that one time, long ago . . . and who is to judge the length of an animal's memory . . .

this bear had never been attacked by anything save another bear. Suddenly, even as Morgan poised himself for another cat-like step, The Bear dropped to all fours and turned away.

Lumbering, slow, he walked away over the slope. Once, fifty yards farther on, The Bear swung his huge head and glanced back over his shoulder. A long minute he stood there, studying these strange invaders. Then ignoring them, he walked slowly away.

Morgan stood still, knife in hand. A chill wind moaned down the barren, icy slope, and he shivered a little. Morgan stared after the retreating bear, and suddenly he felt a desperate sense of relief . . .

Frozen snow rattled on his stiff garments, needled his raw skin.

"Sir?" The Ladakhi's voice seemed to come from far off.

"All right," Morgan said, "we'll go now."

Once, far down and away along the slope, he paused to look back. Up among the high black rocks where the icy winds prowled, he seemed to see something moving, something white, something . . .

It could have been his imagination.

COMMENTS: I've never known quite what to think of "The Quest for the Bear." I was on the verge of adding it to more than one of our past collections of short stories but always decided not to.

I have a fairly strict set of rules for myself when I'm editing or rewriting one of Dad's stories. The goal is always to help the story live up to its potential. Thus a story idea that wasn't the best to begin with might get a quick once-over to make it read quickly and easily, while a better story, one with a concept that had more potential, would get considerably more attention.

The first phase is straight editorial work—spelling, punctuation, phrasing, and the like. After that, if additional work is needed, the next thing I do is some judicious cutting. If the cuts become significant, occasionally I will add material to bridge the trimmed sections. If you know what you're after, it's pretty amazing how much can be improved with a very light touch. There was only one time when I felt the need to truly do what in the film business is called a "page one rewrite." In that case, there were so many overlapping requirements that there was no other way out. Dad wrote so much material in his life, to this date I have never felt the need to create something entirely "new" in his name, nor have I considered finishing anything of his where I did not feel I understood the direction he intended to take the story.

I considered many alternatives with "The Quest for the Bear." I felt it had so much potential and I wanted to do something special with it, yet figuring out exactly what was a real challenge.

I started to revise it to be a bit more realistic, cutting out the avalanche and Morgan's weird (and sort of hollow) impulse to try to kill The Bear with his knife . . . then I stopped myself. I started to try to build more material into The Bear's stalking of the downed airmen, trying to create a longer period of trauma for them in order to justify Morgan's near-suicidal mission into what could be considered enemy territory in order to get his revenge on this bear, which, to a great extent, was simply defending itself.

I even thought I might have The Bear lead Morgan and his Ladakhi guides somewhere more important, to a magical place of some sort that would be better at justifying this amazing bear's existence or would be more helpful in explaining Morgan's final change of heart. And I even got a few pages into a complete rewrite that reset the story in Alaska in the very early twentieth century. I tried to apply the best interpretation of the mythic and character-building aspects of this story to something that was more believable and that commented on Man's desire to hunt for sport.

In the end I did none of the above. All of that seemed to be too much of a change from Louis's original intention, even though I could tell he was struggling with many of these same issues.

I'm not entirely sure when "The Quest for the Bear" was written. The text tells us that Morgan's return takes place after the Chinese Revolution of 1949, but some evidence for the date of the story's creation lurks in an interesting connection to a couple of other L'Amour works.

Dad used the mechanism of an airplane crash to transport a modern man (or woman) into a world of adventure a number of times. The simplest of these stories was "Crash Landing," which was published in 1952, but the concept also appears in "Beyond the Great Snow Mountains," "With These Hands," and the "Ben Mallory" section of this book. I'm sure that my father, who was born just five years after the Wright Brothers' first flight, could sense the irony in using a modern aircraft as a way of transporting his heroes and heroines "back in time."

Dad's earliest notes on this story contain the following passage:

They come . . . to a high cirque [a glacial valley or hollow] and corner the Bear at last in fading afternoon and mounting wind and the man fights the Bear, hand to claw in a deadly combat. The man wins.

Later he wrote a rough description of a slightly more realistic version. That description ends like this:

The bear at last, cornered, ready to fight. Wounded by previous shot. Man closes in to end it with a knife.

The political conditions mentioned in the story seem to indicate a date between the earliest days of "Red" China and the 1959 uprising that caused the Dalai Lama to flee Tibet a decade later. That was the era of the previously mentioned "sweats." They were famous for their over-the-top man-against-nature themes but, because Louis's hero finally allows The Bear to live, this story seems to be trapped somewhere between the ethos of the sweats and something potentially greater. I'm still convinced that there is an even more interesting and meaningful story locked up in "The Quest for the Bear," but it will just have to exist, flickering and half-formed, on the edges of our imaginations.

KILLS BEAR

The First Three Chapters of a Frontier Novel

CHAPTER I

For the third time in as many days they had lost the trail and the two Delawares were casting back and forth along the hillside.

The four white men who were the Company trappers directing the chase stood together, the Bannocks gathering nearby. Kills Bear stood aloof as befitted the lone Nez Perce among them.

Kills Bear liked the Delawares well enough but was disdainful of their tracking ability, and now they wasted time. The white man they followed had tricked them again and Kills Bear was amused.

When they found the white man they would kill him, but Kills Bear respected their quarry, and it gave him real pleasure to follow the white man's trail, for undoubtedly he was a warrior fit to walk beside the greatest.

Although Kills Bear was half white, he thought of himself as Nez Perce and he had no liking for the Company trappers. They lived among the Bannocks, friends and neighbors to the Nez Perce, and Kills Bear had been visiting when the trappers came looking for trackers. He had joined for the chase, but what the trail revealed excited him in a different way.

Every action or reaction of a man is an indication of his character, his training and his experience, and this his trail will reveal. The path left by a Sioux is not that of a Blackfoot, and that of a Shoshone is different from that of a Crow. So it is that a trail left by one man is different from that of another, and to a skilled tracker not only is the path revealed but the maker of the path as well.

The four Hudson's Bay Company trappers were slovenly, untidy men, careless on the trail, and dirty about their camps. Left to themselves they could scarcely have followed a buffalo bull.

He whom they pursued was a man of another sort, for even before he knew he was being followed the man left no trail to speak of. He disguised each camp before leaving and only a shrewd tracker, after careful study, would realize that someone had indeed stopped there.

Kills Bear permitted himself an icy smile. He was nineteen, but a warrior for the past four years. And he had already been a famous hunter by the time he took his first scalp, that of a Blackfoot. Before he was sixteen he had also stolen ponies from the Crow and taken the scalp of a Sioux warrior.

"What you grinnin' at?" Higgins demanded.

"He knows he is followed."

"What do we care?" Higgins asked. Then struck by the comment he asked, "How do you know that?"

"The trail has changed. He will be dangerous now."

"So he knows we're behind him. How does that make him
dangerous?"

Kills Bear liked this white man the least of all.
"The man you follow," he said contemptuously, "is a great
warrior. To know what he knows, to move as he moves, one
must have followed many war trails, made many hunts. Soon
he will circle to see who follows him, then he will decide what to do."

"One man against twenty? I hope he decides to fight."

"The twenty must see before they can kill, and he
will choose the time and place of battle."

"Maybe," said Higgins, skeptically.

"Only he," Kills Bear replied, "knows where he goes,
and you must go where he wishes you to go, or give up the
chase."

Thinking of it from that aspect Higgins began not to
like it so much. The Company wanted no free trappers in
this country of fine fur, and spies in St. Louis warned
them of any likely party. This man had gone to the Big
Horns with a party of two dozen other free trappers but
had left them for some unaccountable reason and was pushing westward alone.

Why the Company was making such an issue of one man
Higgins could not guess, unless they feared he might
somehow break the control they held.

"When he decides to fight," Kills Bear said, "there
will no longer be twenty to face."

Higgins threw the young Indian an irritable glance.
He was too smug, Higgins decided, too know-it-all. But
there'd be time.

Kills Bear was himself curious. The Indian, in company with the wild animals among whom he lived, was curious to a fault. He knew the ways of the wild creatures

because he had studied them, often following an antelope, bear, or wild horse until all traits were made plain. And this man they pursued was westward bound. He rode a better than ordinary horse and had three pack horses with him, but he did not pause to trap although they had passed several streams where there had been beaver sign. Only now, when aware of pursuit, did he deviate from his path toward the setting sun.

The ways of the white man were confusing. Many seemed obvious fools, while others deserved great respect. Unlike many Indians, Kills Bear did not think of them as just another nomadic tribe. Their existence and their origins were a mystery and, because of that, because his father had been one of them, so were his own.

His father had first come to their village when they were in great need. Illness had been among the Nez Perce and many had died. The white man had come with meat and had shared it among the lodges as an Indian would share. Then he had gone back into the hills to hunt.

In the snow-covered Bitterroot Mountains he had killed a grizzly, and later found several elk trapped by winter snows. All this meat he had brought to the lodges of the Nez Perce. And so it was that in a time of sickness and starvation their village had survived and grown strong. Against the Blackfeet he proved a great warrior and took scalps like any Indian. Eventually, he took a Nez Perce wife and lived among them for some time.

Kills Bear could not remember his father but had grown to manhood hearing stories of him. Like his father, he had begun by killing a bear in the Bitterroots, and among his people it was taken as an omen that he was favored as his father had been.

The training of Kills Bear had been the training of any young brave. Among the tribes the words for stranger and enemy were synonymous. A stranger who came willingly into a village might remain there unmolested, would be

fed and lodged, yet that same man might be killed immediately if seen again. There was no question of right or
wrong in this. One did not kill a guest within the village, nor did one steal from his own people. To steal
from enemies was merely warfare of another kind, and a
sport as well. To steal successfully was a matter of
pride.

Kills Bear found nothing strange in the pursuit of
the white man for the purpose of killing him. Had Kills
Bear come upon the white man and found it possible he
might have killed him himself, although he had never yet
killed a white man. The four horses, rifle and goods the
man carried constituted a considerable wealth to an Indian.

From his mother Kills Bear knew the customs of the
white man were different and that white men often consulted books before deciding what should or should not be
done. Several books had been left behind by his father
and Kills Bear had examined them closely, but learned
nothing. The mystery of the talking leaves was beyond
him. They were his father's medicine, and surely his father had been a great hunter if he could decipher even
these small and complicated signs.

Kills Bear watched the Delawares. He knew where the
white man had gone but he had not been asked, nor was he
paid as were the others. He had come along simply because
he was interested in the chase, yet he was sorely tempted
to join in. To find and kill such a man, even to simply
count coup on his body would be something of which to
tell in the lodges.

Humility was not a trait to be admired among Indians.
A man was expected to tell of his victories, even to enlarge upon them, for such was the poetry of the Indian,
such were his songs, his stories, even his history. Poetry was ever the language of memory, and victory alone
was not enough; the story must be well told about a fire

in the lodges. From such stories the young boys learn to be warriors and the girls what to expect of a man.

Suddenly Kills Bear lost his patience. He turned his horse and walked him away at right angles.

"Where do you go?" a Bannock called. "Do you leave us?"

"The white man went there!" Kills Bear indicated a low saddle in the hills in front of him. They were not so far behind the white man as they believed, and this hill was exposed to view for a great distance. He believed the white man deliberately led them over this ridge so he might see them clearly, count their numbers and see who it was who followed him. And the low saddle at which Kills Bear pointed was the one place where he could cross the opposite ridge without being sky-lined for all to see.

After much debate the others followed. When he had found the vague tracks Kills Bear sat waiting for the others to come up and see for themselves.

Higgins threw him an ugly glance. "I'll kill that one," he muttered to Johnson, who rode beside him. "He's too high an' mighty."

"He's the best of them," Johnson said. "If you want to collect that money the Company has offered, save your killing until this is over."

"We got trackers of our own," Higgins replied brusquely.

Johnson thought Higgins a fool, but did not say so. Higgins was the best shot with a rifle that Johnson had ever known.

"All Indians are not good trackers any more than all white men are good shots. The Bannocks say Kills Bear is the greatest tracker among his people."

Kills Bear was searching the ground but he was also thinking. It was not enough to simply follow the indications on the ground but the trail must be followed in the

mind of a man. From sign upon the earth one might learn
what manner of a man it is who is followed, and some indication of the pattern of his thinking, for only then
can a trail be followed with success.

This man knew he was pursued. By this time he knew
how many they were, and he had some idea of their purpose. Yet the white man had been going somewhere, changing direction as soon as he knew he was followed.
Therefore he did not wish to take his pursuers to his ul-
timate destination.

What could that destination be? It was not a lodge,
for no white men had lodges out here. There must be something else, something important which he wished them not
to find.

The white man would try to escape by tricks and devices, and if that failed he would fight. He would fight
as a lone man must, by surprise and escape, by taking a
shot here, another there, by whatever means he could find
for he was one and they were many.

The white man knew the country. For some time this
had been obvious to Kills Bear, hence he was leading them
somewhere of advantage to him, perhaps a trap for them.
Kills Bear considered the country that lay ahead.

Much of it was unknown even to him although he had
wandered farther afield than anyone of his village. It
was a region of wild snowcapped ridges and towering
peaks. Of deep, pine-scented canyons and rushing streams.
Not far away was the place the white men had called Col-
ter's Hell, a vast area of hot springs, geysers and fantastically colored rocks. It was a lonely, broken,
desolate area, but if one knew where to find it there was
game, and in some of the streams there were beaver.

The Delawares were on the trail again, moving
swiftly. He watched them go, then started after them, in
no hurry.

Higgins watched Kills Bear, making no effort to mask

the malice in his eyes. "He's got somethin' to learn, that young un has. I reckon I'll be his teacher."

Johnson glanced at Higgins. He was an ill-smelling, dirty man given to sly brutality, and Johnson trusted him not at all. There were men who might not have trusted Johnson, and with reason, but there are degrees in all things. He was suspicious of Higgins, wary of his plans. If they killed the man they sought there would be a reward from the Company. But how many would live to collect that reward? Had Higgins thought of that?

"Remember this, Hig," Johnson said, "we've got to trade with the Nez Perce, and the Bannocks and Flatheads are their friends. That Kills Bear is already a big man among them and his father was bigger, so be careful what you do."

From under his straight black brows Higgins shot Johnson a hard glance. "That's the joke." Higgins' grin was cruel. "Kills Bear doesn't know the man we're huntin' is his own father!"

CHAPTER II

Tom Patrick lay on a grassy hillside near a clump of aspens and studied the group through his glass. It had been a fortunate buy. A drunken steamboat captain had sold it to him in St. Louis on his last trip, and the captain himself had picked it up in New Orleans. It was battered and old but the lenses had been ground by a man who knew his craft.

He had lived in wild country too long not to watch his back trail, and he very soon realized he was followed. The presence of the four white men and the Delawares told him all he needed to know. These were Hudson's

Bay Company men, and the Company did not want anyone
trading with the Nez Perce.

Higgins he recognized with no pleasure. A thief and a
back-shooting killer who had been suspected of murdering
more than one trapper and stealing his furs. The others
he did not recognize but he knew that Company men had
seen him outfitting in St. Louis and he had worried there
might be trouble.

The Delawares he knew by sight. Their tribe had been
dispersed and many had come west, selling their skills as
hunters and trackers. The Bannocks he knew by their style
of dress and the only one who surprised him was the tall
young Nez Perce.

The Nez Perce were his own people and twenty years
ago he had left a wife among them. It had taken all that
time to get back as far as he was now.

Twenty years ago he had gone down the Missouri in a
hide boat with a fortune in furs. He reached St. Louis
after a bitter fight with Arikaras with his furs intact
but a festering wound in his thigh and another in his
side.

It had been almost three months before he could walk,
and then he had gone home. His parents were old, poor,
and times were hard. He bought them a small farm, some
pigs, chickens, a few head of dairy cattle as well as a
team of horses. By the time they were settled in the
house he built for them two years had gone by. He out-
fitted in St. Louis intending to return to the Snake and
Salmon River country.

There was trouble on the Missouri and the river was
low. It was a year in which few fur traders or free trappers wanted to attempt the long push up the Missouri. So
he had gone overland to Santa Fe, trapped successfully
and then had his furs seized by the governor and was
thrown into prison, a Yankee interloper in New Spain, a

foreign land. It had been another year before he was released and made his way back to Missouri minus his furs
and with no money for a stake.

The years that followed had been a brutal struggle
against impossible odds. Three times he lost his furs,
and twice the years were bad and he took few pelts and
those were of poor quality. Trying to return to the
Salmon River country he had started up the Platte with a
free company of twenty-three men.

Two were killed near the Sweetwater, another trampled
by a wounded buffalo, and they had fights with the Sioux
and the Crows. With only a few furs to show for their efforts they returned to St. Louis and there Tom Patrick
talked to a man who had recently come from the Yellowstone. His Nez Perce wife was dead.

Rumors abounded that the Hudson's Bay Company had ordered their trappers on the Snake River to kill every
beaver they found, not for their fur, but to keep Yankee
trappers from occupying land the Company considered its
private domain. There were fewer and fewer reasons to return to his adopted people.

Tom Patrick had gone west again, to California where
he remained several years. He fought the Modocs, traded
with the Choloquins in the Oregon Territory and returned
to St. Louis. And there he encountered a man just in from
the upper Missouri.

For hours they talked of trapping, of the Nez Perce,
and of their splendid horses, the Appaloosas. "Kills Bear
has become a great hunter and warrior. You would be proud
of him, Tom."

"Kills Bear?" He did not recall the name. "I should
be proud of him? Why?"

The trapper turned on him, astonished. "You mean you
didn't know? He's your son!"

Two days later Tom Patrick had started for the mountains with a party of free trappers and the Company men

noticed their departure, for they had spies everywhere.
Now scarcely a week's journey from the hunting grounds of
the Nez Perce the Company men and their allies were on
his trail and he did not want to bring trouble to his own
people.

For several days he had been playing with them, testing his skills against theirs. And Tom Patrick knew that
someone among them was a first class hand at reading
sign.

He looked again at the tall young Nez Perce. He studied the face through his glass. That young man could know
his son, could be his son . . . they would be nearly the
same age. Certainly, whoever he was, he was a splendidly
built young man and without a doubt he was the tracker
who held them to the trail. He was watching when he saw
him turn and point toward the saddle.

Tom Patrick slid back from his position and led his
horses down to the creek. Mounting up, he rode into the
water. It was a shallow stream and he walked the horses
down it for a mile, then turned up a branch that he remembered and left the creek at a shelf of rock where he
tied elk-hide moccasins on his horses' hooves and rode
with them for a half mile by a twisting, turning route
before dismounting to take the moccasins off. He rode at
once into the edge of a small lake and walked his horses
along the curving shore for half a mile, then up a deep,
sandy gully into the hills. This was all country he knew
and where he had trapped more than twenty years before.

The old trail was blocked by blow-downs but they were
young stuff and light. He dismounted, lifted the fallen
trees clear and rode his horse through, leading the pack
animals. Once through he walked back and shifted the
trees, like closing so many gates. He straightened the
grass where he could and taking up a handful of leaves he
let the wind drift them down naturally.

Only then did he ride on.

He had cut the odds. There were too many of them, but they were hunting him and he had no compunctions against what he intended to do. Only . . . he did not want to get into a shooting affair with any Nez Perce.

The young Indian seemed to be with, but not of, the party. Time and again he had held aloof, watching the others blundering about. Once he had seen Higgins seem-ingly have words with the Nez Perce . . . the young brave should be warned. Higgins was dangerous, a bitter and vengeful man who hated Indians of whatever kind.

Yet Higgins and the others were but tools. Tom Pat-rick knew very well the man who stood behind them. It was a dour and hard-featured Scotsman, a close-trading man and a cruel one.

Tom Patrick camped among the aspen where he could watch his back trail. With a few dry sticks he prepared a hot meal, ate it, wiped out the few signs he had left and rode on for another hour before camping.

At daylight he was up, chewing on a bit of jerky, and riding down to a rushing cold mountain stream. It was all of a hundred yards wide and deep, but he knew of a ford. Again he resorted to the moccasins and rode down to the ford before taking them off, then into the water.

He would never have dared enter such a stream with an Indian pony but his own horses were strong stock, heavier than most and accustomed to rough going. He crossed the stream, wiped out his tracks and disappeared into the forest where he wove a tricky way through the trees, dou-bling back from time to time. He had an idea he was not fooling that young Indian, but he had been thinking about that, too. Suppose it was Kills Bear?

Tom Patrick was worried. He dared not lead Higgins or those with him to his village. Unless matters had changed much over the years it was short on man-power, and Hig-gins and those with him were thieves and worse. Most mountain men were solid, hard-working men of above-

average intelligence. Often they were very shrewd busi-
nessmen who knew the quickest way for a man of small
capital to get ahead was by trapping fur or trading
for it.

Higgins was another matter. Without question he was a
skilled hunter and trapper. He was an excellent rifle
shot, and he often boasted of killing Indians. Every
mountain man had his brushes with Indian war parties, as
Indians did with each other, but when they killed it was
to protect themselves or those with them, who often
enough were other Indians. It was a custom as well as a
matter of survival for a mountain man to affiliate with
one or another of the tribes, which automatically made
their enemies his enemies.

He knew what he must do, and with the young Nez Perce
with them it would not be an easy thing to accomplish. He
must lead them into an area of little game, he must stam-
pede their horses, try to get their Indian allies to desert them. There was no time to waste.

The Nez Perce worried him . . . he did not want to
kill or be killed by anyone from his adopted tribe. Even
worse what if it was Kills Bear!

How much, if anything, would Kills Bear know of his
father? What if anything might be left of him in the
lodge?

Suddenly he remembered the scrimshaw and knots. As a
boy when he first left Ireland he had gone to sea and as
many deep-water sailors did, he took up the habit of
carving and making belts or ornaments from string, weaving them into all sorts of intricate patterns. Having
time on his hands, he had developed considerable skill.
He had made a belt for his wife of strings with stars of
red and blue. He had also made a sailing ship of string
and hung it on a tipi pole.

At daybreak Tom Patrick loaded his horses and started south along the Yellowstone. It was as beautiful a country as man could wish with the river running swift and clear over a mostly gravel bottom. There were springs all about and fine grass. "Someday," Tom Patrick said to his horse, "you an' me will come back here an' settle down." The horse flicked a doubtful ear and Tom chuckled.

He left the Yellowstone at what somebody had called Sixmile Creek and followed a dim trail along the watercourse to the high mountain that loomed against the sky. Skirting the mountain he camped in a lovely basin southeast of the peak. In the twenty years since his last visit it did not seem to have changed. He bedded down near a spring well back from the lake.

He let his horses graze until well after sundown when he brought them in and tied them in the aspen close by. He checked the load on his rifle with the ramrod, and pulled the old charges from his pistols, tightened their flints, and reloaded them. He got the shotgun from his pack and loaded it with buckshot.

They would find him, he was sure, but not yet. They would have trouble with his trail on the other side of the Yellowstone and by the time they worked it out his horses would be rested.

After he brought the horses in he prepared a good meal, hoisted what meat he had left high into an aspen where the bears could not get it, and relaxed by the fire.

To think, that after all these years, he had a son!

Never had he even dreamed of such a thing, and certainly if she had known, his wife had said nothing to him before he left. Suddenly, he swore, deeply and with feeling. To think of the years he had missed! Of the times they might have had together!

He lay back, supported by a log, and watched the slow smoke rise from the coals. His fire was dying, and he

would let it die. This was Crow country but he had seen
no Indian sign and for the moment he felt reasonably
secure . . . a dangerous feeling, he knew, for over-
confidence breeds disaster. Yet he needed these quiet
moments.

The trouble was people took too little time to savor
their existence, to breathe the cool air, to walk the
quiet ways, to enjoy the simple pleasure of living. The
Indian did this better than the white man although the
pressures, social and survival, were just as serious for
him. The fisherman, the shepherd, the sailor and the
wagon-men lived closer to nature, they had time to feel
the air, to know the stars, to live in their world.

The basin in which he rested was not quite a half
mile long and somewhat less wide, with a small lake from
which Bear Creek flowed steeply down to the Yellowstone.
He knew by the plant life around him that the altitude
was around nine thousand feet, and the peak behind him
went up a good fifteen hundred feet higher.

The last firelight flickered on the slim white trunks
of the aspen, overhead the stars seemed very near. He got
out his pipe and stoked it with tobacco. He rarely
smoked, and when he did it was beside a campfire.

Kills Bear . . . it was a good name, a strong name.
The bear was always big medicine. A noted warrior at
nineteen, that spoke well of him. Well, his mother had
been a fine woman, a woman with strength and pride and
hunger to know of the life beyond the mountains. A hunger
to know, to understand. It had been that as much as her
beauty and grace that had drawn him to her.

He smoked quietly, listening to the horses and the
night sounds, enjoying his recollections of the past. Finally, he knocked the ashes from his pipe and stowed it
away.

The moon was coming up, and the great peaks stood icy
clear against the sky.

Before the sun was warming the hills he was in the saddle, riding directly for the head of Bear Creek. He started down the trail then doubled back and took a dim path that curved above timberline and past the forks of Horse Creek.

It was sliderock country and his horses' hoofs would leave few tracks, nothing but here and there a scar upon a piece of rock already scarred by tumbling and falling. He found the trail in good shape as most of the higher mountain trails were inclined to be and followed it for several miles until he came to a still dimmer track that led north toward the head of Passage Creek. Leaving his pack horses he rode along that trail for perhaps a hundred yards, leaving tracks in a few sandy spots, then returning through the sliderock.

His pack animals in tow once more he rode on to the head of Grizzly Creek, following it down until it joined Hellroaring Creek which he crossed and started down the far side, putting the deep, narrowing Hellroaring Canyon between himself and pursuit.

The high, bare ridges lay above him now and from where he paused he could see anything that moved along the way he had come.

He built a small fire under a spruce where any smoke would be dissipated among the branches, and he made coffee and fixed a hot meal. There would be few of those in the future, he suspected.

From time to time he glanced up along the mountainside or studied it through his glass. There were several points along that trail where a rider must skirt close to the edge and at such times would be easily visible from below.

While his horses rested and grazed on the rich grass

and wildflowers, Tom Patrick dug through his duffel and
got out a ball of string.

He chuckled to himself. Oh, they would find him, soon
enough, but he'd lead them on a merry chase in the meantime. They would see some mighty fine country, climb a
lot of mountains and run into a lot of trouble, a part of
which he would cause. The rest would come naturally.

And if that was Kills Bear back there he would find
out soon enough.

CHAPTER III

Higgins reined in and looked down the slope ahead of
him. "Where the Hell is he goin'?" he demanded irritably.

Kills Bear was curious, too. An amusing idea had occurred to him. Was the mysterious white man they followed
taking them only to view the strange and beautiful? Or
was he leading them on, lulling them into over-confidence
until they fell into a trap?

Kills Bear knew something now of the type of man they
pursued and he was very careful not to be first in
line . . . nor last. Not being a regular member of the
party it ill-befitted him to take the lead, anyway. There
were times when it needed all his skill to pick up the
trail, and several times he let them wander astray when
he knew how they should go.

At least he knew where they were being led, for he
had twice been into this land of smoking ground. It was a
place bewitched where not many Indians cared to go, and
many refused to even look upon the land . . . but why was
he taking them there, of all places? And where had he
been going before he discovered he was being followed?

Higgins had grown more and more irritable. Kills

Bear, who knew enough English to understand, heard him grumbling to Johnson and the others. "Figured to be back afore this," he grumbled. "I figured to be back in St. Louis by now."

Shang Draper looked across the fire at him. "Hig, the way we're goin' it'll be months before we get back. Why don't we just forget it an' trap some fur? There's beaver all about here."

"You crazy?" Hig demanded angrily. "I was sent to kill a man and that's what I aim to do. He'll be trappin' our fur, gettin' the best of the tradin', buckin' those Canucks and the Company all the way. He's got to be got rid of."

Kills Bear understood the sense of what they were saying but cared little what white men did to each other, or why. He tired of the bickering and walked down to sit by the fire of the Bannocks. He listened to their talk with sympathy. They were growing weary of the protracted search and had bad feelings about the land into which they were going. They muttered among themselves and he listened with only part of his mind. He was thinking of the white man . . . where was he going? Why had he turned aside so quickly when he realized he was being followed? An Indian might do that to lead enemies away from his village but there was no white man's town except for the fort where the great west-flowing river ran into the sea, and that was many weeks of travel from here.

Kills Bear was himself feeling uneasy and he did not know why. It might be that he was putting himself too much in the place of the man they pursued. It was necessary to do this in order to read the trail at all, and it was such feelings as this that had helped Indians to identify with the wildlife that lived all about them.

He was dissatisfied with himself, also. He was accepted as a successful hunter within his small branch of

his people, and few surpassed him as a warrior and yet
his heart was not right. Perhaps it was what his mother
had told him of his father, or what Running Wolf had told
him. Running Wolf was also a white man like Kills Bear's
father, and he had been a prisoner of the Blackfeet when
Kills Bear had succeeded in freeing him.

"Don't know your pa," Running Wolf had said, after
looking over the books Tom Patrick had left behind at the
lodge, "but these," he tapped the books, "show he was an
educated man."

It was Running Wolf who taught him the little English
he knew. Few of the tribes knew any language but their
own, even that of others living close by, and Running
Wolf, whose name was John Ryland, did not expect Kills
Bear to listen, but he did, and showed an easy affinity
for languages.

Ryland read the books, reading some passages aloud to
Kills Bear, and explaining them. Much about them puzzled
him for their thinking was so different from what he had
known. Kills Bear said as much and Ryland agreed.

"Worries a body," he commented. "Here's two sets of
folks, my people and yours, each with different ideas and
different languages. I don't see how they will ever get
together. Even with the best intentions. The words may
seem the same but the meanings are different. When an Indian thinks of land that land is separate from him, its
own thing rather than a possession. It's an area to hunt
like a wolf or cougar or maybe a place to gather or
plant. A white man thinks of building or ownership,
clearly defined farms and towns. Both of them are honest
but they mean different things when they say 'em. In language there's the words and then there's the deeper meaning."

Kills Bear had puzzled a long time about that. Then
he tried even harder to learn the language for he had

heard the old men among both Nez Perce and Bannock talking of the increasing numbers of the white man. If they
were to deal with this stranger they must under tand him.

His father had become like an Indian, living as an
Indian and accepting the Indian ways. So had Running
Wolf, or Ryland, as Kills Bear now thought of him. Could
the Indian learn to live with the white man just as easily? He did not know.

At daybreak they were on the trail. At first it had
been clear enough, then they lost it many times, but now
the tracks were plain again. He was leading them south
and Kills Bear only occasionally took a hand in the
tracking, for he did not like the white men and was
thinking of setting off on his own.

They followed along the river of the yellow stones,
crossing and recrossing it, then they came near to a
falls, and went up among the mountains from which the
falls appeared and took a dim trail that led between that
river and the river of the yellow stones. The winding
trail took them higher and higher along the ridges until
suddenly there lay before them a vast basin more than
fifty miles in diameter and surrounded by peaks and
ridges. Far away the sun glinted from what must be a
large lake.

"Man, oh man, would you look at that!" Draper exclaimed. "Ever see such a stretch of country?"

"Smoke down there," Johnson said. "Somebody's got 'em
a fire."

"More'n one smoke," Draper agreed.

"Hot springs," Higgins said. "I heard tell of them."

They rode on, more cautiously now, through clumps of
scattered pine. There was much sulphur rock around and
Kills Bear did not like the odor. The tracks led straight
along, pointing toward the basin to the south. East was
the tremendous gash of the canyon of the river of the
yellow stones.

They had skirted a clump of pine and started down a
steep declivity when the horse of the Indian who was in
the lead seemed to stumble. Instantly there was a roar
and a rush. Kills Bear's horse leaped forward, frightened, and the horse of the Bannock who followed reared up
and turned . . . only just in time.

There was a rattle and rush of boulders and rocks
bursting across the trail and many of the bigger boulders
rolling and tumbling down the mountainside. There was a
moment of sound, a moment of dust and then silence. The
trail was blocked.

Perhaps three or four tons of rock and debris would
have to be moved as the cliff edge allowed no room for
skirting the pile.

"That was no accident," Draper said.

"A trap," Johnson agreed. "We've got to expect it
from now on."

"It wasn't much," Higgins scoffed.

"A warning," Kills Bear said. "He is telling us what
is to come."

Higgins' expression was unpleasant. "Since you know
so much, maybe you better ride up front."

Kills Bear sat very tall in the saddle and he looked
calmly at Higgins. "I tell you what I know. I am not pay
by you. I am Nez Perce."

Higgins' rifle started to move. Johnson put a hand on
it. "You shoot him an' they'll all leave. And like he
says, he's just along for the ride."

Kills Bear had not moved. For the first time Higgins
saw that Kills Bear's rifle, lying across the crook of
his elbow, was pointed directly at him, and Kills Bear's
hand was on the action. Higgins would have been shot from
the saddle before his rifle got into position. The knowledge infuriated him, yet he simply shrugged. "Forget it.
I'm gettin' touchy, I guess."

But he made up his mind . . . at the first chance he

would kill this Indian. The first opportunity when no one was around to pin it on him.

Dismounting they began clearing the rocks and debris from the trail. Draper scrambled up the exceedingly steep slope to see how the trap had been arranged. It was unclear, but somehow a thin piece of rawhide tied across the trail had triggered it. The lead horse tripped over the string, which had pulled a stick and that had caused the slide of rocks, no doubt already precariously perched, to come tumbling down.

An hour was lost before they cleared the passage, for as one boulder was moved another rolled into its place. Frustrated and angry, they mounted at last and started down the trail again, yet now they rode with caution, uncertain as to what might come next. This, too, slowed their pace. When they made camp at the head of a small stream that flowed toward the Yellowstone they had covered but a half dozen miles.

The ashes of old fires told them they were not the first to think of this as a likely place to camp. They staked out their horses on a wide, flat stretch of grass, and Higgins straightened up from his picket-pin to look toward Kills Bear. The Nez Perce rode a blue roan Appaloosa, a splendidly built animal that moved through the miles without effort, seemingly as fresh when the day ended as when it began.

Higgins wanted that horse, and he meant to have him. He said as much, low-voiced, to Johnson.

Johnson shook his head. "Hig, you better think on it. The Company wants the Nez Perce trade. Kills Bear is a big man among them, and if anything happened to him they'd be mighty upset."

"Who's to know?"

"Them Bannocks, for one thing. If he dies and you show up ridin' that horse you've got a problem. It ain't

only them, but what if the Scotsman finds out? And he
will. He knows everything that happens in these woods."

"It's the Injun's pa we're killin', ain't it? An' he
was a bigger man among them than his son. I'll just say
he found out who we were trailin' and I had to kill him."

"You want my advice, I'd say let it lay. Besides,
that one won't be so easy to kill. He moves through the
trees like a ghost."

"Uh-huh, an' I'm better than him. You'll see."

Kills Bear had known only a few white men and had
trusted but one. He had seen Higgins' eyes upon his
horse, and he knew about horses. Stealing horses was an
even quicker way to rise in influence in the tribe than
taking scalps or counting coup. Stealing horses called
for an inordinate amount of skill and among Indians it
was not accounted a crime or an evil thing, but a test of
ability as well as a means to wealth. Already Kills Bear
had over fifty horses, stolen from the Sioux, the Blackfeet and the Crows. Ryland had taught him something about
selective breeding.

"Don't let them all run loose," he advised. "Get your
best stallion and keep him up with your best mares. In a
few years you'll have the best and fastest horses
around."

Beside the fire Kills Bear listened to the talk and
then said to Black Beaver, "This one we follow. His medicine is strong. He understands much."

"We will find no more tracks," Little Hatchet said.
"He has brought us here, now he will go."

Kills Bear was making new moccasins for the ones he
wore would soon fall apart. "Where will he go?" he asked.

Black Beaver shrugged. "Where he was going. To your
village, I think."

Kills Bear wondered. What else was there unless the white man went on down the great river to the place called Astoria. But nobody went there. It was too far.

He glanced at the fire of the white men. Higgins was standing up and he had the coffee pot in his hand. He was talking.

Suddenly the pot seemed to burst, splattering him with hot coffee. The report of a rifle hung in the air.

Kills Bear was in the darkness, moving swiftly. The man they sought was near. He paused to listen. He heard nothing, but then he expected to hear nothing. He went to the horses and they were standing with their ears pricked.

He glanced back toward camp. The fires still burned but nobody was about them. He waited, watching and listening, but wherever the man was, he was far from here by now, or well hidden at least. To go seeking him in the darkness would be insanity.

When all was quiet again he went back to camp.

"Horses all right?" Johnson asked.

"Yes."

"Scared Hig," Johnson commented. "Never seen a man get himself lost so fast."

Shang Draper moved up beside them. "I was all fixed for some o' that coffee," he grumbled. "Now we got to do it all over."

"No," Kills Bear said.

"What?"

"He is still out there I think. I think no more hot meals by night. He will shoot."

Draper swore, slowly, viciously, "If I get my hands on that--"

"We got to catch him first," Johnson said, grimly. "Like lookin' for a single flea in a sand hill."

Higgins came out of the shadows and stood near them. "Injun," he said to Kills Bear, "you get me that man's scalp an' I'll get you a new rifle and a hundred rounds of shot an' powder. You get him, do you hear?"

A new rifle? A hundred rounds? It was a treasure. Yet he did not trust this man. He had never trusted him.

"Got me a brand new rifle right in my duffel. Ain't never been fired. Canucks give it to me for the man who killed this gent. You go get him an' the rifle is yours."

Kills Bear had seen the rifle, had looked upon it with envy, yet he hesitated. Elusive as the white man was, Kills Bear believed he could track him down, yet something within him shied from doing so.

Nevertheless, that was a beautiful rifle . . . a beautiful rifle.

COMMENTS: My father was a master of the device of having one character track another as a way to reveal a story. Other examples would include the short stories "Law of the Desert Born" and "Dutchman's Flat," and the novels *The Key-Lock Man* and *Last of the Breed*, to name just a few. I found it amusing to see Dad subtly extending the cast of characters from his Sackett series by using a Higgins as the heavy. In the Sackett stories, the Higgins family is often mentioned as being engaged in a long-running feud with the Sacketts, though this does not mean that all of his Higgins characters are portrayed in a negative light.

Dad wrote these chapters in the middle to late 1970s, during his second attempt to broaden his appeal and move away from constantly writing traditional Westerns. In this case, the time period is that of the true frontier, prior to both the Civil and the Mexican wars.

Early in the 1800s, what we now consider the Northwest United States was a territory disputed by the British and Americans. The Hudson's Bay Company administered the area for Great Britain and was concerned that more and more Yankees would be drawn to Oregon (which, in those days, was the name for quite a large area) by the agricultural possibilities in Willamette Valley and by the rich fur trade. The fear was that a critical mass of settlers from the United States would cost them control over the territory and, more important, over the rendezvous point for shipping at the mouth of the Columbia River.

The company used many tactics to keep interlopers out, including some of those mentioned in this story. At times there were worries that war might again break out between the United States and England. In 1818 and 1846, treaties were signed in an effort to resolve the issue, finally splitting the Western United States and Canada along the 49th parallel. I have always found this to be the most interesting time in the history of the West, the classic era of manifest destiny and of confronting many of the issues that created the modern United States.

BEN MALLORY

Seventeen Chapters of an Adventure Novel

CHAPTER 1

Sunlight and the shadow of trees lay across a road
that had never known a wheel. An ancient road, forgotten
in the passage of years by all but the people of the remote mountain villages, itinerant traders or occasional
pilgrims.

Over much of its distance the trail was a mere succession of stone slabs proceeding in single file through
the dark forests or along the brink of impossible chasms.
From time to time it mounted to heights shared only by
the wind or the Yeti, called in some parts of Tibet the
Migeu, and known elsewhere as the Abominable Snowman.

Occasionally, caravans passed along this road carrying goods from India, Nepal or Assam to the farthest
reaches of Tibet, Sinkiang or the region of the Tsaidam
marshes, just as they had for more than four thousand
years.

Upon this day among the trees flanking the road sat a
row of horsemen. At that point the trail lay along the
bottom of a narrow defile whose tree-clad slopes rose
steeply but not abruptly, and among the trees the bodies
of men and horses were dappled with sunlight and shadow
until virtually invisible.

Each rider held in his hand a rifle, butt resting
upon his thigh, muzzle pointed skyward at an angle from
his body.

The horsemen were dark and savage men with high
cheekbones and narrow eyes, most carrying the scars of
combat. They wore bulky knee-length sheepskin coats with
the wool on the inside. Each wore a bandolier of cartridges across his chest and carried a broad-sword slung
between his shoulder blades, the hilt in a position to be
grasped over the left shoulder. Many wore a pointed cap
with flaring ear-flaps.

The air, as is the case at such heights, was aston-
ishingly clear and there was nothing to be heard but the
sound of far-off wind among the trees.

The riders were motionless as stone-carved figures,
their eyes upon a Red Chinese soldier on the trail below.

The magnolias lining the trail were heavy with im-
mense purple blossoms, a variety rarely occurring below
8,000 feet. The soldier, unaware of their beauty, hurried
on, intent only upon some goal of his own. Over his
shoulder he carried a sack, in his hand a rifle.

He was obviously worried. This far from his command
he might be a deserter, but more likely was a scout or
forager who had slipped away from his detachment in
search of food or loot. From time to time he glanced over
his shoulder.

Suddenly, as if aware of some sense of danger, his
eyes swept up the slope.

Until that moment he had been secure, but that upward
flick of the eyes cost him his life. He came to an abrupt

halt, staring as if unable or unwilling to believe what
he saw . . . and then he broke into a run.

Mallory spoke then, and the rider at the end of the
line lifted his rifle, almost negligently. An instant his
aim held, and just as the soldier was about to disappear
around a turn of the trail, he squeezed off his shot.

The rifle seemed to leap in his hands and, caught in
mid-stride, the running man put down his stiff, advanced
leg and catapulted over it, falling on his face. He made
one lonely, involuntary movement, a dying spasm, then lay
still.

The report of the shot hung suspended in the still
afternoon air, then lost itself in futile echoes against
the surrounding hills. After it faded there was no other
sound, and for several minutes, no movement.

Mallory was a lean, powerful man with dark, weathered
features and green eyes. He spoke, haltingly but effec-
tively in the Go-log dialect, "I do not want him found."

Three riders detached themselves from the rank of
horsemen and walked their mounts to where the dead soldier lay. Bending over, the first rider hooked the fore-
sight of his rifle under the dead man's collar, lifting
him within reach of the second rider's grasp. Trotting
their horses to the rim of the gorge that flanked the
trail on one side, they dropped the body over the edge.
The third rider recovered the dead man's sack and rifle,
and then all three fell into place in the column now
forming on the narrow road.

Mallory lifted a hand and the column moved out in the
direction from which the soldier had come. Behind them
the ancient road lay empty once more, sleeping in sunlight and shadow. Only a single slab of rock bore witness
to their passing, for upon that rock lay the shadow of
war, the shadow of blood.

Thirty miles away and nearly a thousand feet lower, the defile down which the detachment of Go-log rode opened into a narrow mountain valley. It in turn descended into a deep gorge and thence to the Yellow River.

Near the opening of the defile stood an inn, if such it might be called in a land where such things are nearly unknown. Incredibly ancient, its buildings were a patchwork of addition and repair, surrounded by a rough wall. Massive wooden gates, closed except when admitting the rare traveler, gave access to the courtyard. There was but one other opening in the surrounding wall, this being behind the inn, and of a size to permit the passage of one man or one rider at a time.

The structure was low and rambling, seeming to crouch warily behind its palisade as if fearful of being seen. Nearby were a few acres of cultivation, and on the rich meadows along the stream two dozen yaks grazed in company with a few horses and fat-tailed sheep.

At one time the entire ground floor had been, as in most Tibetan houses, a stable for yaks and horses, but the demands of travelers in some far-off time had caused half the stable to be made into the inn. Within this ground floor a third of the area was given over to a k'ang. This was a raised portion of the floor, some three feet higher than the remainder, and built of stone slabs. On the exposed side were openings through which fuel could be thrust to heat the k'ang, and generations of travelers had slept upon it until their twistings and turnings had worn hollows in the stone.

The ceiling of the room was low, the huge, time-blackened timbers grimed with the smoke of centuries of cooking fires or charcoal braziers.

The k'ang was a relic of years when the inn had been occupied by a Chinese from Shensi, a Chinese who found the atmosphere less than congenial and abandoned the area

in the wake of a Chinese army badly used by the fierce
Go-log horsemen.

For many years the inn had not functioned as such,
being alternately occupied and abandoned, then finally
chosen by Mohammedan merchants from Kansu as a stopping
place. The Kansu merchants were a wild and hardy lot who
established a friendly relationship with the Go-log for
purposes of trade.

The trail that led past the inn joined with the main
caravan trail that led from Koko Nor, that fabulous blue
lake, crossed the Yellow River, skirted Tossum Nor on the
south and Oring Nor on the west, avoiding the vast
marshes of the Karma Tang to proceed westward by way of
Ulanergi to a crossing of the Yangtze at Baga Kokoser.

Of this ancient track no known map existed, although
upon some maps there were thin red lines that suggested
that the way might be traveled. Of the track coming up
from Choni to join the main trail there was not so much
as a suggestion. No record remained except that in the
memories of men.

Before entering the valley of the inn from the south
the trail mounted steeply for some distance, so the valley itself remained invisible until the traveler was upon
its very edge.

It was a place of quiet beauty, steep mountains lifting to high peaks where glacier-clogged hanging valleys
and cirques surrounded it and the mountains were clad
thickly with forest.

Renata Bernard, riding beside Marty Wells, drew up as
she topped the rise. Nothing on the road from the south
had quite prepared her for this, although there had been
much that was beautiful.

At the moment the valley was bathed in sunlight along
one side. In the green meadow yaks grazed beside the
clear mountain stream, the mountains soaring above in

snow-crowned serenity. At some distance the inn waited, a study of picturesque decay.

Dr. Martin Wells, whose somewhat boyish face belied the official title, reined his horse around. The view was beautiful beyond belief but he hoped any Red Chinese officials they met could read enough to comprehend the documents they carried. So far all had gone smoothly, guided and guarded by Gunther Hart's wealth and Gunther Hart's diplomacy, yet Marty Wells had found himself growing increasingly skeptical and increasingly wary.

"How can anyone think of war when there are places such as this?" Renata wondered.

"They don't all live in places like this, Nata. We haven't seen a human being for three days."

"I'm glad we're stopping here."

"We are?"

"There's an inn. A very old place. That must be it over there . . . across the valley."

"First I've heard of it. Of stopping, I mean. Hart never tells anybody anything."

The red and gold banner proclaiming in English, Chinese and Tibetan characters that this was the Gunther Hart Expedition to Tibet and Tsaidam was a good half mile behind them.

"I hope he really has it fixed. I'd hate to come this far and wind up in a Chinese prison."

"There's nothing to worry about, Marty. We're here, aren't we? Gunther is very friendly with many of the Red Chinese. He knows Chou En-lai himself. They were friends in Paris, years ago."

"I'd like to know who he knows in the State Department. How could he get permission to go into Tibet with things as they are?"

"Gunther went to school with the Under Secretary or somebody. But you should know that. He has friends everywhere."

"I'm still surprised. As for having friends everywhere, I'm skeptical."

"Marty!"

"I mean it. I've never known anyone less likely to
win friends. To influence people, yes. He has all that
money."

"He's a bit eccentric, I know, but he knows people
everywhere, and people know who he is."

"A Fellow-Traveler?"

"You've no right to say that. Once you get to know
him you'll change your mind."

"How long does it take, for God's sake?" Marty
shifted his seat in the saddle and looked back at the expedition which was slowly over-taking them. "He hasn't
said three words to me yet."

"He does keep to himself. He meditates."

Marty scoffed. "If you ask me, he sleeps. I still
haven't grasped his purpose. The rest of us are obvious
enough. We are all working scientists willing to risk our
necks to collect data. I will admit that without him
there might not have been another chance in this century
to get into this part of the world. That explains you,
your uncle, Roy and the rest of us. It does nothing to
explain Gunther Hart."

Renata hesitated, then said, "Marty, don't breathe a
word of this, but Gunther believes he can locate a great
store of manuscripts, Tantric manuscripts from the Bon
period . . . pre-Buddhist. He is quite sure he is on the
track of an important find, something to compare with
Stein's discovery at the Caves of the Thousand Buddhas."

Marty was silent. It could be the truth. He had seen
enough of Gunther Hart and heard him talk just enough to
believe it. The man claimed to be a Buddhist . . . well,
a pseudo-Buddhist, in Marty's books. The more he saw of
Hart the more he believed his old friend Doc Whiting.

"I had no reason to say the things I did," Marty

said, "and if he makes any kind of discovery at all I'll
be the first to say I was mistaken. I know you like him,
and you know him better than any of us. All I know is
pure hear-say, but in the past few days I'd come to believe most of what I'd heard."

"And that was?"

"That he was a pseudo-Buddhist, a pseudo-scientist, a
pseudo-philanthropist, and a pseudo-pacifist."

Renata's eyes sparked with anger. "You didn't have to
come you know."

"I was advised not to."

"You were? By whom?"

"Milne Whiting. He warned me that Hart was unstable."
She was surprised. "Milne Whiting?"

"He's a very good friend. Hart had classes with him."

They started on, and Renata was more disturbed than
she would have admitted. At twenty-eight, Marty Wells had
achieved a considerable reputation. He had specialized in
the search for useful and medicinal herbs, had written an
important paper on plant physiology, and another on the
occurrence of metallic poisons in plants. He had been one
of those consulted when soil from the moon had proved
toxic to some earth bacteria.

When the opportunity to accompany the Hart Expedition
to Tibet and Tsaidam had been offered, he had accepted at
once. Everyone agreed it was the chance of a life-time.
Everyone, that is, but Dr. Milne Whiting.

Marty was no novice when it came to investigating
wild country. At nineteen he had spent four months on the
island of New Britain off the coast of New Guinea.

He chuckled, remembering the expression of distaste
on Whiting's face when he informed him of Hart's proposed
expedition and his acceptance.

"It will be an experience," Whiting acknowledged,
"but you can have it."

"Do you know Hart?"

"He was in one of my classes, and the first time he submitted a paper, I knew I was in trouble."

After a moment, he continued. "It was written in long hand, script as precise as any machine, each line as if ruled, each letter of exact height, the grammar and punctuation faultless. Each point of argument was advanced in the most bloated and complex language imaginable. Yet, although you had to struggle to follow it, the logic was always impeccable. At first I wondered if he was having me on, but if it was a challenge to my intelligence or a joke of some sort there was never any indication. He seemed utterly devoid of humor, emotion or imagination."

Whiting was stuffing papers into his brief case as he talked. "My advice is to forget the whole idea. There will be other expeditions."

"Not to Tibet. And probably not in our life-time to eastern and northern Tibet. It may well be a generation before any western scientist enters the region again, and I simply can't afford to pass it up."

After a moment, he added, "It could be the beginning of a career!"

"Or the end of one. Oh, I'll admit if there was a chance to come up with some ancient Sanskrit or Karoshthi manuscripts, I'd be tempted."

"You're damned right you would."

"Tempted, I said. I did not say I'd go." Pausing on the steps outside the building, Whiting had offered one last bit of advice. "We've been friends a long time, Marty, so just listen. Don't ever cross him. Keep your opinions to yourself. Better still, don't let him even realize you have any opinions, and above all, don't get in his way!"

Marty was shocked. Milne Whiting was a scholar of international reputation, and a tolerant man. Admitting

Hart was an eccentric, it still seemed intemperate advice. If the man was eccentric it was his privilege, and by all accounts he could afford to be.

"Well, Hart may be difficult at times, but who is not?"

"I am not referring to day to day irritations, Marty. I believe the man is a dangerous psychopath."

"You can't be serious."

"But I am. Completely serious." Marty had no idea what to say. For the first time his respect for Whiting wavered. What was it with him? Was he jealous of the man? Gunther Hart had an international reputation for scholarship as well as for his wealth.

Whiting seemed to sense Marty's doubt. "For nearly two years I spent four hours a day with Hart. My opinion is based on an accumulation of details, few of which amount to much in themselves.

"Gunther Hart is an extremely egocentric individual who never, so far as I am aware, suffered the slightest frustration. His father died when he was young and his mother adored him and catered to his every whim.

"There was never any reason to give the slightest consideration to the rights and feelings of others. He was born with a gold spoon in his mouth and left it for an ivory tower of his own construction. He has a brilliant mind, but if he merely imagines something, he assumes it is reality.

"All you have heard is part of a carefully constructed public image that represents what he believes himself to be. Pay close attention to it, and remember that Hart is completely convinced of his own rightness on every score."

"But he was an athlete, Doc! There must have been some frustration there. He did compete, did he not?"

"After a fashion. His decathlon score was among the

best, and he won an inter-collegiate championship in boxing, but to understand that you must have the complete
picture.

"As a boy he wanted to be an athlete. He was naturally strong and active. His mother promptly hired the
best coaches, and believe me, I mean the best.

"He was beautifully coordinated, and they did their
job well. Every event in which he was entered was carefully prepared in advance. His coaches and trainers were
paid for results, so they found reason to enter him only
in events he was sure to win. When he was entered in the
inter-collegiate tournament it was only after his pro-
spective opponents had been well scouted and he had been
carefully trained to beat them.

"He was good, believe me. How far he might have gone
on his own it is hard to say. He was facing a bunch of
boys who had learned their fighting with busy trainers
with little time to spare for any one boy. His coaches
had trained the top professionals."

Marty had nothing more to say. He liked Whiting too
much to argue with him, and his own knowledge of Hart was
too limited to permit discussion.

Looking over the valley his thoughts returned to the
present situation. "Nata," he asked suddenly, "have you
looked at the maps? The government maps?"

"No. Not since we came into this wild country."

"That river down there is the Ba. It is a big river
and it flows into the Yellow not far west of here, but it
isn't even on the map."

"Gunther has a map. Marty, you should see it. I've no
idea where he got it, but it is very old, and very
strange. He told me once that most of the names on the
government maps are simply the names of monasteries or
sometimes only of temporary camps used by caravans."

"You've seen his map?"

"Not to examine it. It is like no map I ever saw, even in a museum. Nobody else has seen it, I'm sure. Unless it was Hank Carpenter."

"You can have him."

"Oh, he's all right, I guess. He's very efficient."

The sky was a deep, impossible blue. They drew up at the foot of the trail and waited for the caravan to catch up. Aside from the yaks, horses and sheep grazing on the meadow there was no evidence of life anywhere, and it was very still.

Now the sun touched only the high slopes of the mountains, for the valley was deep within the hills, and the day was drawing on.

"It has an eerie feeling," Renata said suddenly, "being so far from civilization. I wonder if anyone outside has any idea where we are?"

Marty shrugged his shoulders, then hunched them against a brief, chill wind. "If we do get into trouble there just isn't anything anyone outside can do. All the State Department could do would be to ask discreet questions. From all I hear even the authority of the Communists means little in some of these remote sections."

"There's nothing to worry about. Gunther has the connections to handle any sort of trouble, and Uncle Ralph and Dr. Penfield have friends everywhere."

Marty thought back to that first meeting with Gunther Hart at the Beverly Hills Hotel. The members of the expedition had been invited for a briefing, and it was a distinguished company.

Aside from Hank Carpenter, Hart's secretary, Marty knew none of them except by reputation.

Dr. Ralph Bernard, archaeologist, was a handsome, white-haired man of distinguished appearance, his skin darkened by the years of exposure to Middle Eastern suns where he had conducted digs or scouted areas for future investigation. He was the author of a half dozen books on

those lesser known cultures fringing the Fertile Cres-
cent.

Renata Bernard was his niece, with a growing reputation as an anthropologist whose most important work had
been a study of the Tochari tribesman.

Dr. Grant Penfield, accompanied by his wife, Mary,
was a noted physician and surgeon. He had contributed
time to the organization of a clinic for the Tibetan refugees at Mussoorie, and had organized medical research
projects in Vietnam, Tanganyika and New Guinea.

Of Roy Lewis, geologist, Marty knew nothing beyond
the fact that he had written a number of popular articles
on earthquakes, had photographed some hitherto unknown
ruins in Peru, and had conducted surveys for the government of the United States in various areas.

Others, not present at the briefing, had joined them
en route.

At the briefing no time was allowed for getting acquainted. No sooner were they seated than Carpenter arrived and presented the details. Whatever else might be
said, he kept the meeting moving. He presented a good
deal of information . . . and deflected many questions.

He would personally handle all luggage except carry-
on bags. He would handle passports, visas and clearances
of all kinds. If there were complaints or discomforts all
should be brought to him. Under no circumstances was Gunther Hart to be disturbed.

The briefing completed, Hank Carpenter stepped to one
side and drew a curtain, revealing Gunther Hart, seated
in profile, wearing the robes of a Buddhist monk.

They were allowed to study his profile in absolute
silence for a long, long minute. Undoubtedly, the profile
was magnificent. Then Carpenter spoke. "Sir? Do you have
any comments at this time?"

One might have counted a slow ten before Hart turned
to face them. He looked at them each in turn.

"You will be granted," as he spoke he arose to his full six feet and four inches, "every facility for the work you wish to do. If there is anything that would contribute to a better completion of your work, please speak to Mr. Carpenter.

"I have one small request. Interfere as little as possible with those among whom we visit, taking care not to offend their customs or religious beliefs.

"Above all I must insist there be no discussion of politics with the Chinese or other peoples with whom we come in contact." He smiled a warm, magnificent smile. "We must remember we are guests in their country, and we must act as we would wish them to act if they were guests in our homes."

"One question, Mr. Hart," Dr. Penfield asked. "We are entering a country that has recently been not on the best of terms with ours and there have been threats--"

"Have no fear, Doctor. None whatsoever. The way has been cleared for us and every facility will be granted.

"I would suggest," he addressed them all, "that you dismiss from your minds all you have heard of Red Chinese. You will find them warm and friendly hosts. Much of what you have heard was mere propaganda written by warmongers.

"There are those who consider the Red Chinese as potential enemies. I cannot allow myself to be guided by such prejudices." He paused briefly. "Mr. Carpenter will provide you with mimeographed instructions. Among other things you will observe that all statements to the press, under whatever circumstances, are to be cleared with Mr. Carpenter, and he is to be present at all interviews. Any unauthorized statement will lead to immediate dismissal."

He took one step back, bowed slightly, and the curtain was redrawn.

Carpenter resumed his place before the curtain. "That will be all--thank you for coming. We shall meet again at

the airport on the fifteenth. You may pick up your in-
struction folders at the door as you leave."

Marty recalled he had been amused by the so obviously
stage-managed meeting, but whatever doubts he had were
forgotten in preparations for the trip.

"What," Renata said suddenly, "are you thinking of?"

"Of that day in Beverly Hills when we first met
Hart."

"When you first met him, you mean. I already knew
him."

They started on. "I shouldn't be riding with you,
Nata," he commented. "I don't think he likes it."

"Gunther? Don't be absurd."

"No . . . I mean it."

Suddenly, as if played on a tape, Whiting's warning
sounded in his ears. "Above all, don't get in his way."

The man took himself very seriously, seriously enough
to think that the show he put on was impressive rather
than amusing. Back in California, Marty had thought he
was just an eccentric but now, off all maps and on the
other side of the world, he was beginning to realize that
Gunther Hart was a dangerous narcissist.

CHAPTER 2

Mallory squatted on his heels beside the small fire.
Built beneath a huge, wide-branching rhododendron, the
rising smoke was thinned and dissipated by the leaves and
branches until invisible but a few yards away.

He cupped a bowl of yak butter tea in his big hands
and listened to Gomba.

The sixty men of his command were scattered along the
side of a small ravine. All were hidden from observation
among the dense growth of trees and shrubs.

"I do not know him. Obviously, he flees from the Communists and from how he is treated it is plain he is of great importance, an Incarnation, I think. He has good men with him, but I am afraid he will not escape."

"He is an old man?"

"A young man. He speaks your tongue, it is said." Gomba spilled a little yak butter tea into a bowl, added a double-handful of barley meal, and mixed it slowly with his fingers. This was tsamba, the staple diet of Tibet and the lands adjoining. There had been a time when Mallory doubted his ability to swallow another mouthful, but he had come to like it as he did the yak butter tea. A lot of habits can change in ten years.

"They won't permit him to escape if it can be helped," Mallory said. "There is too much unrest as it is."

An Incarnation, such as this young lama reportedly was, would be too important for the Chinese to allow him to slip through their fingers. To control him would enable them to influence the Go-log, the Lolo, the Na-khi as well as other minor tribes along the difficult borderlands of Tibet, an area where the authority of China had always been doubtful, under whatever regime was in power.

"Do you think the Chinese will pursue him?"

"They will." He recalled the soldier they had killed. "They may already be here."

Gomba waited, popping a ball of tsamba into his mouth. Gomba had been a mere boy when Mallory first came among them but he remembered Mallory's father, too, and had seen the father win his way from abject slavery to leadership among the Go-log. Now he was curious, wondering what Mallory would do about the Incarnation.

"We must help him," Mallory said at last, "although it endangers our mission. Where is he now?"

"Tonight he sleeps at the Inn of the Three Hawks in the Valley of Pleasant Winds. The valley lies before us."

Gomba paused, then added, "His strength among us is equal
to the soldiers of ten thousand tents."

It was very cold. While the others slept, Mallory
huddled over the fire considering the possibilities, yet
even as he weighed the reasons for and against siding with
the Incarnation, his decision was a foregone conclusion.

The Go-log would say nothing, yet if he failed to attempt a rescue they would think the less of him. They
would follow and obey, but he would have lost prestige
among them. Besides that, his own inclinations were to
aid the escaping lama.

Already he was out of Go-log country as such, moving
into an area where they were both feared and hated. A
war-like, raiding people who had changed little from the
days of Genghis Khan, they lived by the sword, and their
neighbors had suffered from that sword.

He had proposed the trip to India, hundreds of miles
through some of the most forbidding terrain on earth,
much of it, for safety's sake, over trails unused a century or more.

The Go-log had fought the Chinese since before the
memory of man, and had held their homeland in the bend of
the Yellow River inviolate. They were a nomadic people
within their own vast area, but aside from their flocks
their chief source of income as well as their greatest
pleasure was in raiding caravans from China to Tibet. Now
the Communist Chinese were determined, better armed, better led than before, and they planned to put an end to
the independence of the mountain tribes.

Mallory argued the need for better rifles, grenades,
mortars and machine guns. He argued that if he could talk
to certain people in India he could arrange for periodic
drops of medicine, weapons and ammunition. Reluctantly,
they agreed. Their every instinct was to remain in their
own country, trusting to no one but themselves. He had
convinced these few otherwise. Now, to maintain that

trust, he must risk everything in an attempt to save a man he had not seen, a man who meant nothing to him.

If he succeeded in reaching India he anticipated no such easy time as he had led the Go-log to believe. The government of India wanted no trouble, and contacting the proper officials of either the British or American governments would not be easy.

He was considered dead, as his father had been. They must search their records to prove he even existed, and that would take time.

Yet in the back of his mind was the thought: this was his chance to escape.

He owed these people nothing. He had come into their country of his own free will and had succeeded in staying with them partly because of his own strength and will to survive . . . and the reputation his father had won before his arrival.

Mallory had been nine years old when his father's plane crashed in China while flying the Hump from India. Two years later there had been a rumor that some American pilots might be held as slaves among the mountain tribes. The Army investigated and, years later, stated it was untrue, but by that time Mallory had been reading everything he could find about the borderlands of Tibet and decided there was no way the Army could have been sure of that in the time their investigation team was in the area . . . or the out-skirts of the area.

He had grown up on a ranch in Montana, punching cows, hunting, and living a rugged frontier life. His mother had died when he was ten, and he had continued to live with an uncle, and together they whiled away many hours studying maps of China and speculating on his father's chances of survival.

In the back of his mind there had always been the thought: someday I shall go there. Someday I shall find out for myself.

He had gone and he had found his father alive and an important man among these people . . . but since his father had died he had continually thought of escape.

Once they arrived in India he would fulfill his promise. He would obtain guns for them and see them off for their homeland, but he would then be free. He could return to the States.

The home of the nomads with whom he lived was around a great mountain called Nyambo Yurtse, 20,000 or more feet in height, a lovely limestone range, honeycombed with caves and with several beautiful lakes fed by glacial waters.

For months following his capture by the Go-log he had slowly but steadily won a place among them, yet the event that finally freed him from servitude and permitted him to ride among them as a warrior might have turned out very differently.

From his boyhood he had known much about the handling and treating of animals and the horses he had ridden as a boy were bigger and fiercer than these. First, he had captured their admiration by riding an outlaw horse and next when he repaired a broken rifle, then a captured machine gun. But it was his single-handed taking of a Chinese truck containing food, weapons and ammunition that really won him his place.

He had seen the truck veer sharply from the road and disappear into the hills while another tribe of the Go-log were attacking the convoy. Following it, he watched for his chance. He had thought of the truck as a means of escape, so he came from the rocks and offered to help the four Chinese get their truck out of the sand.

They agreed, and he over-heard one Chinese say, "Let him help. Then kill him."

Which left him simply no choice at all.

The officer was in the cab with the driver. One man was behind the truck with Mallory, pushing. Another was

on the far side. As the wheels dug in and began to spin
Mallory slipped an arm beneath the chin of the man beside
him, and strangled him.

When the truck failed to move, the man at the side
came around behind and Mallory met him with a bayonet in
the stomach. The man screamed, and the officer and driver
leaped from the truck. Mallory was ready, and shot first.

Using their coats and some brush for traction, Mallory jockeyed the truck out of its hole and drove it
across country and hid it among the rocks. Armed with a
.45 Colt and a Russian sub-machine gun he returned to the
Go-log to bargain.

He made his point, but among the fighting, brawling
Go-log one victory was not an end. He had three brutal
fights before he was at last accepted as one of them. It
was only then that he learned that his father was alive,
with another band.

Now, while the others slept, he traced their route in
the sand and studied it. He was uneasy about their prox-
imity to the Inn of the Three Hawks. Their safety lay in
the fact that their presence was unknown, and Mallory
hoped to keep it so.

The man responsible was old Shi-lo. In his younger
years Shi-lo had been a trader, living his life along ob-
scure trails from the Tarim Basin to Choni, from Choni to
Darjeeling, from Darjeeling to Mount Kailas and Leh. It
was his knowledge of the ancient trade routes that en-
abled them to slip across the country like ghosts.

Yet there had been accidents. A few days earlier,
crossing the headwaters of a river, they had come upon a
Chinese patrol. Challenged, Mallory had attacked immediately, and the Go-log, always ready to fight, had cut
down the patrol to the last man.

The attack had been sudden, totally unexpected, and
the Go-log had suffered only a few minor wounds. The bod-

ies of the dead were dumped into the river after being
relieved of their weapons, ammunition and food supplies.

Of course, the disappearance of the patrol would
bring about an investigation. Forty men do not easily
vanish from the earth and no doubt some of the bodies
would be found down-stream. Twice, in the days following
the battle, planes were observed circling above the country, but each time the sound of their motors warned the
Go-log and they were swiftly under cover.

Mallory had taken time to eliminate what tracks they
had left, yet now they were nearing the Inn of the Three
Hawks and there was no possible way to avoid passing
through the valley unless some secret trail could be
found along the ridges above the timberline.

Assigning some men to this task, Mallory decided he
would take seven men and visit the Inn. If the Incarnation was there, as rumor had it, they would offer him
their protection and aid in escaping to India.

Mallory got to his feet. India! And after India,
Paris, London, and New York! Baseball, movies, the bars,
the restaurants . . . ten years was a long time to be
away, and aside from the fifty thousand dollars in gold
he carried for the Go-log, he carried evidence of his father's death and the twenty-odd years of back-pay that
would be forth-coming.

His excitement was touched with an odd reluctance to
think of it. He would be going home to his country, but
to nothing else. His uncle had died long ago, his brother
Tom had been killed in Korea.

The Go-log had no doubt he was returning with them.
That could mean trouble. He liked these people--his life
among them had been like an exotic dream, occasionally a
nightmare--but it was time to go. Whether they would understand or not he did not know, but once they were in
his world he had no doubt he could get away.

After the tents were pitched on level grass near the
Inn, Renata went inside the largest and set up her uncle's portable desk. Dr. Bernard had strolled away toward
the head of the valley to examine the step-like road.

Her conversation with Marty had brought into focus
her own doubts. They had been there from the beginning,
yet why should she be uneasy?

Gunther Hart was a striking figure, with a smile he
knew how to use, although he used it rarely. A romantic
part of her wanted to attribute his aloofness to an in-
nate shyness and reserve. The theatricality was something
else, something she didn't have an answer for.

Straightening from the desk she looked off toward the
Inn. Something about what she had just been thinking
bothered her. "A smile he knew how to use." Was that it?
That he used his smile instead of smiling because he felt
like it.

She had gone out with him but three times before the
expedition, and everywhere they were received with flattering deference. Gunther had few friends and no inti-
mates and by the third date she began to see how
completely he was insulated from all outside contact.
Sometimes she thought it was sad but it worried her that
he might actually like it that way. Certainly, no one
else thought anything about the multi-millionaire was
sad . . . in fact some of the scientists thought he was a
pretentious ass. Well, she had lived among scientists and
academics her whole life and she knew it took one to know
one.

Stepping outside she breathed deeply of the cool
mountain air. Beyond the gorge the mountain dropped so
steeply from enormous heights that it seemed impossible
anything could grow there, yet the entire face was covered with the deep green of forest.

Roy Lewis strolled over, taking out his pipe. "Gorgeous country. When I was a youngster I used to dream about Tibet, but never imagined it like this. Everything a man reads makes it out to be a cold, windy country, all high plateau, mountains and yaks."

"Pen says much of it is that way. He's learned a lot from treating his patients at Mussoorie."

Lewis was a well set-up man in his late thirties, with an open, pleasant face. "Let's walk over to the Inn? I'd like to see what it's like inside."

She glanced around. "Where is Mr. Hart? He might like to go with us."

"He's meditating. I spoke to Carpenter, but he just said 'The Master does not wish to be disturbed.' So I came away."

She glanced at him to see if any sarcasm was implied, but Lewis' features were innocent. "Let's go then," she suggested.

They crossed the spongy grass to the gate, which stood open, and for the first time she saw it was crowded with the horses and yaks of a caravan, as well as packs of goods and equipment. Lewis paused, striking a match to light his pipe, taking the moment to study the packs.

"Looks like company," he commented. "Somebody from up country."

"They might be going in, as we are."

"No. Those packs aren't from the outside. I am sure of that."

As they crossed the courtyard two wild-looking men emerged from the Inn. Both were armed. They glared and lifted their rifles threateningly.

Lewis stopped and took the pipe from his teeth. He smiled, but he lifted the hand holding the pipe and gently tried to push the muzzle of the rifle to one side. "It's all right," he said, "we're just going inside to look around."

A voice spoke from within and the rifles were lowered. Then in English the voice said, "Please to enter. I
am regretting my soldiers."

The room was shadowed and still, the only light that
which filtered through the open door and the reddish glow
from a charcoal brazier. On the k'ang, cross-legged, sat
a slim young man with a pleasant Asiatic face.

"Come in. Please do. I am Lagskha-tsang."

"Miss Renata Bernard," Lewis said, "and I am Roy
Lewis. We are with the Gunther Hart Expedition."

"You are British?"

"American," Lewis said. "Our mission is scientific."

"It is so? Forgive me. I did not think to see Americans in my country. It is an awkward time."

"Gunther Hart is a friend of Chou En-lai," Lewis explained, and then added, "Miss Bernard is an anthropologist. I am a geologist."

"Ah?" He indicated they should be seated. "I regret I
cannot invite. I am traveling now. My position is no longer official." He hesitated. "Many things have been
changed in my country."

He was wary, Renata thought, and since the mention of
Chou En-lai's name, a little less than warm.

"My uncle hopes to examine some of the ancient
sites," Renata said. "He is an archaeologist."

"We find few archaeologists in Tibet. I believe they
think my country too young." He glanced from Lewis to Renata. "It is very old, my country. Particularly the part
in which we now are."

He looked thoughtfully at Renata. "Your uncle is Bernard also? He is distinguished man."

"You know of him?"

"I see American journal." He smiled suddenly. "Very
strange. You come to my country, I go to yours."

"You are going to America?" She was surprised.

"I think yes. I like very much American music. I like American film."

Roy Lewis chuckled, and at Renata's glance he explained, "I was thinking of Hart. He despises American films and music, and the first lama with whom we come in contact likes them."

"You like films?"

"Very much. I am a regular fan."

"Fan? What is it . . . a fan? Is it not to brush air?"

"We use it in another sense as well, as someone who is very appreciative, and who knows a lot about the subject . . . movies, jazz music, rock and roll, baseball . . . whatever it happens to be."

"Good!" His grin was boyish and friendly. "I will be fan."

"You will have to talk to Marty. He knows more about films and music than any of us."

"He is with you also?"

"He is our expert on botany. He will be looking for useful herbs."

"Good! He will inform me of music and films, I will tell him of plants. It is my education to know such things."

He sat silent as a servant brought beautifully carved bowls of yak butter tea.

"This Gunther Hart. He is a Communist?"

"Gunther?" Renata asked. "I think it is unlikely though he may admire their goals. He is a very wealthy man--wealthy men are rarely Communists."

"So? It is different in America, then. In China some wealthy men become Communist to protect riches or power. They think to do so."

"Gunther Hart," Renata explained seriously, "is a very gentle man. He is a Buddhist. At least, he follows

the teachings of Buddha. To him this is a sacred pilgrimage. He comes to learn, to visit the shrines. He wishes
to visit Mount Kailas and Lake Mansorovar."

"These are sacred places. Much respected. Forgive me.
I did not know there were Buddhists in your country."

"There are few, I'm afraid," Lewis said, "although
there would be more if they understood what Buddha
taught. I know very little, but I hope to learn more."

"Is it a good time to come?" Lagskha inquired. "I
think there is much unrest."

"Gunther . . . Mr. Hart," Renata said, "wished to
come now. He . . . he is not a man to wait. He is impatient, sometimes."

"I should like to meet this man. This impatient Buddhist."

"We were fortunate to get the opportunity to visit
your country," Lewis said. "Hart is the man who has made
it possible."

"Yes, you are right. Who can know? The chance may not
come again." He smiled gently. "The Peking government
does not accept me into its confidences."

There was a stir behind them, and Gunther Hart spoke,
his tone deeply reverent. "Greetings. I hope my people
have not disturbed you, Master."

CHAPTER 3

Lagskha's face was innocent of expression. "It is to
my pleasure. I have much to learn."

"So have we all," Hart replied. "I come to your land
a pilgrim, seeking truth."

"The truth you seek lies within you."

Hart inclined his head. "I seek a guru, Master. I
seek one to lead me upon the Eight-Fold Path."

Lagskha's eyes were shadowed and his expression un-
readable. "My land is no longer free, Mr. Hart. You might
with better success go to India." His tone was edged with
bitterness. "Our great teachers do forced labor on the
roads, and many die. Often they are old men, unsuited to
such labor."

"I am sure," Hart replied smoothly, "the Chinese will
do what is possible to preserve the ancient beliefs."

There was a moment of silence, and then Lagskha said,
"Your journey to my land will no doubt prove informative."

He turned to Renata then, ignoring Hart. "Some of my
family have been fortunate. My sister, whom you shall
meet, has spent much time in Paris, London and New York.
She had sent me many films of your country, and much
music."

"Your sister is with you?"

"I am here."

She stood in the doorway, a slender, graceful girl,
eyes slightly oblique, skin a pale ivory, her face deli-
cately but beautifully boned. Renata Bernard, who had
been called a beautiful woman by many, felt suddenly awkward and plain.

She stepped into the room. "How do you do? Miss Bernard, I have read your paper on the Tochari. They are ancestors of ours . . . in part. It was very well done."

Turning her head she measured Hart with a glance. "I
am afraid my brother is much too polite, Mr. Hart. You
will find little of what you seek, and I know what you
seek. The only teachers who might instruct you in the
Tantric learning are hidden far back in the mountains
where we hope they will not be found."

"If you could tell me where I might find them . . ."

Her smile was brief and cool. "I would tell you nothing. I am afraid those who arranged your visit here are
not among those we can trust."

"You are abrupt," Gunther Hart said politely, "and mistaken. I am not what you would term political. The affairs of the world about us are temporary, transitory things. All this will pass. The eternal truths will remain."

"Nevertheless, this is a world many must live in. Your very presence in this part of China implies the permission of the Chinese government and permission implies recognition or friendship and that implies you are an enemy of our people."

She paused, ever so briefly. "If you will recall, Mr. Hart, our land was occupied by force of arms. Our leaders must flee or be used by those who have occupied our country. I am afraid you will find me neither a forgiving nor a tolerant person."

"If I am to incur dislike," Hart replied gently, "I should prefer it to be by a woman as lovely as yourself. At least, you are not indifferent."

"You are mistaken, Mr. Hart. I am completely indifferent!"

His face stiffened a little, but he turned to Lagskha and bowed. "If there is any way in which we may be of service, feel free to call upon me or any of my people."

Hank Carpenter appeared in the back of the room. "Sir? There's a party coming down the trail. I don't like their looks."

The sister of the Incarnation moved swiftly to the door. She shaded her eyes, looking toward the mountains.

"Who are they?" Carpenter's voice was sharp.

"No reason to get the wind up," Lewis prodded, "they are probably just bandits."

The Incarnation's sister spoke quietly. "I would suggest you be very, very careful. I have no idea how they come to be in this place, but those men are Go-logs."

"What?" Hart's tone was high. "What did you call them?"

"Go-logs." There was a kind of triumph in her voice.
"And they are savage, completely without mercy. They come
from the big bend of the Yellow River and are nomadic
herdsmen and yes, they are often bandits."

"What are they doing here?"

"That," she admitted, "is a very good question. They
are farther from home than ever before."

"How can it be that I have never heard of these . . .
these Go-logs, as you call them?" Hart inquired.

"A question I cannot answer, but there are people in
both Tibet and China who have never heard of them.
They've lived off the beaten tracks of history and they
prefer it so. They permit no travel through their country, and when China has sent armies they either found no
one or were sent back bloody and beaten."

Lewis touched Renata's arm. "Nata! The man on the
black horse! I'd swear he was a white man!"

Mallory drew up some hundred feet off, and instantly
three men broke away on either side to ride around the
Inn and make sure there was no ambush. He was, however,
expecting no trouble. The Inn had been watched for several hours.

Two parties were in residence. The Incarnation had
but six Khambas as escort, and two dozen others handling
the yak train. Of the Gunther Hart Expedition he knew
nothing, but there were several women along and they did
not at all resemble an armed party.

"Gomba," Mallory said, "my compliments to Lagskha-
tsang and request permission to approach him."

Gunther Hart stepped out, a tall, arresting figure.

"How do you do? Do you speak English?"

Mallory swung down. "I speak American, if you call it
English. You picked a lousy time to come into this country."

The sister of the Incarnation spoke from the gateway, using the Lolo dialect. "I am Brikhuti, the sister of the Lagskha-tsang. Be careful of what you say. I do not trust this man."

Mallory looked at her again, feeling a flush of warmth at the very sight of her. "I know who you are. Tell your brother we are going his way. I will gladly escort him . . . and my people wish it."

"Thank you. I shall speak to him." She hesitated an instant. "Major Mallory, whether you realize it or not, you have become a famous man."

Mallory started for the gate, rifle in hand. Hart spoke, his tone brusque. "Look here, my man. I asked you a question."

"And I answered it. What more do you want?"

"I want to know who you are, and just what you are doing here. I know of no one . . . no one, you understand . . . who has permission to be in this area."

Mallory merely looked at him. "Looks to me like you missed something somewhere. If you don't know about me maybe I'm not even here, so forget about it. You ignore me and I'll be glad to ignore you."

His riders dismounting, he strode into the Inn. Roy Lewis looked after him, his eyes alive with curiosity.

There was no nonsense about the Go-log. One rider raced off in the direction from which they had come, another toward the road up which the expedition had marched. The others dismounted, several taking the horses to water, the others clustering about the gate.

Gunther Hart had not moved. Then he started after Mallory, his face flushed and angry. He motioned to Carpenter. "Hank, I want to know who that man is and all about him. I want to know at once, do you hear?"

"Yes, sir. At once." Carpenter hurried away and Hart turned sharply away and walked to his tent.

"Well," Lewis commented mildly, "he could've asked me."

"Do you know who he is? How could you?" Renata said.

"When Hart gave me the chance to come with him I went to the library and read everything I could find. There's a lot published in magazines and newspapers that never got into the books."

"During World War Two a number of flyers were reported to have crash-landed while flying the Hump. Some were reported held as slaves by various peoples that border on Tibet.

"About ten years ago there was an article about a young fellow who went back in here looking for his father. He never came out. He served in Korea and then was among the first advisers sent to Vietnam."

"You believe he is that man?"

"Who else?"

"He rides well," Renata admitted.

Mallory paused inside the door to let his eyes grow accustomed to the deeper shadow within. Outside the last of the light was fading and the stars were out. Brikhuti came up beside him. "Major Mallory, we believe Marshal Chu is not far behind us."

"We killed a Red soldier up yonder. He could have been one of Marshal Chu's men."

He indicated the courtyard. "What about them?"

"The tall man is Gunther Hart. He is the leader of a scientific expedition. I know some of the people by reputation and they are well-established in their fields. Dr. Penfield has done a great deal of work among the Tibetan refugees, so we have a particular interest in him.

"Hart is very wealthy and he is used to getting what he wants. The geologist said Hart was a personal friend

of Chou En-lai." Her fingers touched his sleeve. "Major,
we need help. Help to get my brother out of this country."

"That's what we came for. The Go-log have great respect for him, and that's saying a lot. I'll do whatever
I can, but that means we haven't much time. We've got to
get out before Chu's men get here. And soft pedal that
'Major' bit. I'm no major and never have been."

"That's what they call you."

"Forget it."

"The trail is open . . . the Americans came in over
it."

"No good. They'll have planes scouting that trail."
He looked down at her. "Ma'am, I've got to see your
brother."

The k'ang was empty. Brikhuti disappeared up the
stairs, returning after a moment. "He is meditating and
we cannot disturb him."

"All right. Be sure that your people eat something,
and without making any fuss, have them ready to pull out."

"I never thought to see a foreigner win a place among
the Go-log," she said. "They are a difficult people."

"I like them."

He seated himself on the k'ang. He had some meditating of his own to do. He had learned much since coming to
the borderlands of Tibet, and one was to exclude all else
from his mind but the problem at hand, and he did that
now.

He and the men with him had slipped through the country unobserved until now, but their efforts were to be
rendered useless by this American expedition, whose people would surely talk.

The trail up which Gunther Hart had brought the expedition was out of the question. It was vulnerable to attacking aircraft, offering no concealment. They must
continue along the ancient tracks, even if it meant rebuilding them in places.

In recent years most travel was by well-known routes, and many of the old ways had been left out of use. At the end that might lead him through Bhutan or Nepal, and neither country was eager to incur the displeasure of the Chinese.

One by one he examined the possibilities, and one by one he tested the problems offered by each. He avoided no issues, thinking ruthlessly, favoring no idea, allowing himself to be convinced by none of them until he had studied their every aspect.

A trail must be found, and they must move by daylight, if at all possible. Every instant of delay brought added danger.

Renata and Dr. Bernard entered the room. Renata glanced at Mallory, then said, "If I were you I'd not make an enemy of Mr. Hart--he might be of help to you."

"We do not need his help."

"He has great influence."

"Obviously."

Renata flushed at his sarcasm but Dr. Bernard said, "If you have the time I would enjoy discussing the Go-log country, and the country you crossed in getting here."

"It's rugged." He paused. "I wish, Doctor, you could have the time and the opportunity to investigate the situation here. The country we passed over shows indication of very ancient habitation.

"There are caves in the mountains of the Go-log country where grain has been stored from very ancient times. I have seen characters carved in rock, almost obliterated by time, and these are often in sheltered areas."

"That is very interesting. I have suspected something of the kind."

"What are your plans now?" Renata interrupted.

"To get away from here before your friends close in on us."

Renata stifled her anger. "If you refer to the Red

Chinese as my friends, I suppose you are right. They have done nothing to cause me to regard them as enemies."

"Not being a Tibetan, I suppose that may be true. You must forgive them if their reactions are somewhat different. After all, they have been a peace-loving people for more than a thousand years and did not wish to be invaded."

"This lama is making a mistake. He should remain with his people."

"His people," Mallory replied brusquely, "have been forced into a way of life they did not want. They have been killed, enslaved or have escaped into the mountains to fight. The Incarnation of whom you speak will be of much more use to his people on the outside. Here he would be held in restraint, bulletins would be issued in his name, and he would become a puppet of a regime he does not admire."

"I cannot accept that," Bernard replied.

"Nobody asked you to. A question was made and replied to. You can believe whatever you damn please."

Renata was furious. "You are not polite."

Mallory smiled without humor. "It is simply that I have a quaint, old-fashioned idea that a people should be allowed to choose their own government, and to make their reforms in their own time, in their own way."

"You do not believe that China can help?"

"If you were a Tibetan at this moment, Doctor, you would either have become a mouthpiece for Chinese policy or you would be doing hand-labor on the roads, working in all kinds of weather, regardless of your age or health.

"China can best help Tibet by leaving it alone. I have every respect for the Chinese but they have problems enough in their own country."

"You do not deny they have made great strides?"

"Compared to the period before World War Two? Absolutely. Almost anything would be better than that sort of

anarchy, communism included. When several hundred million
people are organized into labor units they can accomplish
a great deal, even if enthusiasm is lacking. That is
their business and I wish them luck. However, Tibet did
not have the same problems and I know few Tibetans who
would choose to be like China, let alone be a part of it.

"Make no mistake. The Chinese are an energetic people, a great people. No man on earth admires them more
than I. But their present methods I admire not at all."

"Perhaps it is as well that you are leaving," Renata
said, coolly.

Roy Lewis had come into the room with Marty Wells.
Both sat on a corner of the k'ang, listening without comment.

Mallory glanced at them. "Either of you guys a baseball fan?"

"I'm a Dodger fan myself," Lewis said, "but since
Koufax quit we haven't had much to yell about."

"I've had a short-wave radio," Mallory explained,
"but the only baseball news we got was an occasional
Armed Services broadcast from Vietnam. Most of what we
picked up was from China, India or Japan."

Mallory glanced at Renata. She was a damned pretty
girl. Too bad they'd gotten off on the wrong foot. It was
almost like old times to see an American girl. He'd lost
touch with women and how to converse with them, and he
wished these people would stop talking to him and talk
among themselves. He could learn more that way. He found
himself grasping for words . . . his English had grown
weak over the years.

He had a few books and he often read aloud just to
hear the English words. The Go-log respected that, oddly
enough. They believed he was making magic. Only priests
read, so far as they knew.

Gomba entered and whispered to Mallory. Mallory
glanced over at Bernard. "Take a tip from me and get back

down that trail fast. The Red Army has sent a detachment
after the Incarnation."

"I am sorry for him," Bernard replied, "but that cannot affect us."

Mallory shrugged. "Better tell Hart, anyway. It's
your funeral."

"You don't seem to understand," Renata said. "We have
personal letters from Chou En-lai."

"Bully for you," Mallory said dryly, "and where is
Chou En-lai?"

"In Peking, I expect."

"Exactly . . . and he might as well be on the moon.
If anything happens to you up here nobody would ever know
or care. When you're in this country you're clean off the
map."

Mallory walked out and stood for a moment in the
gateway. Too many memories were aroused by hearing their
voices and he was uneasy. A premonition of danger? He had
learned, like a wild animal, to trust his instincts.

His countrymen were fools to come here at such a
time. Command decisions were made here, not Peking. Marshal Chu was a soldier first, a Communist second. He
would do what was necessary to survive and prosper polit-
ically, and whoever or whatever got in the way would be
brushed aside.

Mallory considered the situation. His knowledge of
trails across Tibet was limited, and so far he had gone
by what he had picked up and by what Shi-lo had told him.
Lagskha might know more. His ties with the old Bon religion were as close as with Buddhism. He was an Incarnation and few secrets would have been kept from him . . .
if he had ever found reason to inquire.

Mallory's father had told him over a campfire, when

they had one of their few times alone, about the old monastery and about the secret trail, an ancient trail used
by Bon monks in traveling to Kashmir and India before the
time of Buddha.

Ten years of discreet inquiries had brought him little knowledge. Some said the trail had not been traveled
since used by Kesar of Ling, the great Tibetan folk hero.
Padma Sambhava and Sambhota were said to have traveled it
in coming to Tibet from Nalanda.

Rumor had it that the trail was beset with traps for
the unwary, and that it was a way known only to the Bon
priests. Mallory discounted much of this, but over the
years many trails had been abandoned due to slides,
changing river courses and other reasons.

Yet legend said there was a trail, and if Mallory had
learned one thing in his life it was that most legends
contained a core of truth.

He must talk to Lagskha, and to Brikhuti.

There was no time to be wasted.

CHAPTER 4

Cook fires blazed at the two camps, the camp of the
expedition and the smaller camp of the Go-logs. No light
showed from the Inn, squatting as it did behind its palisade.

Brikhuti crossed the grass to the Go-log camp. "Mallory, I must talk to you."

He stood up. The Go-log looked at her, their cold
faces showing nothing. "I was coming to see you, and your
brother."

"The geologist . . . Mr. Lewis . . . told me you had
some word of the Chinese."

"They are near. I'm afraid whatever is done we must do quickly. We should leave before daylight . . . if possible."

"We will do it." She looked at him. "You do not need to help us."

"Six Khambas? They are good men, but not enough. I can help your brother, but I need help also. That trail," he indicated the way the expedition had come, "is a death-trap for either of us, but there is another."

"I know of none."

"I was hoping your brother did. I know a little, but not enough. It is an ancient trail, no longer used."

"I suppose there are old trails," she was dubious, "but my brother is not widely traveled. I am not sure he would know much."

"This one he might know."

She looked at him suddenly. "But that's just a legend! That is, if you are thinking of the one I am. You mean Kesar's route."

"It has sometimes been called that."

"I don't know. I don't believe he knows anything about it." She accepted a bowl of tea from one of the Gologs. "You say you do?"

"I know where it begins. I know a little of the way it follows, but there are said to be traps, places one cannot pass."

"I will ask him."

"I had heard Lagskha had a sister who lived in Europe. It was you?"

"Yes. My father wanted his children to study there as well as at home. He saw conditions were changing, and he wished us to be prepared, yet I was the only one who had the chance to go. I am afraid I was gone too long. I am more of a European now."

"Your name is a famous one."

She was surprised. "You know our history?"

"I remember Brikhuti was the Nepalese wife of the king who brought Buddhism to Tibet."

"He had two wives. The other was Chinese and also a Buddhist." She looked at him curiously. "Do you miss your own country? All this is so different, so strange to you."

He shrugged. "I don't know, really. I have no idea what I'd be doing if I was back in the States. Ranching, I expect. I hadn't made up my mind when I went into the Army, and of course there was always that obsession to find out what happened to my father. I was afraid I'd find him somewhere, crippled and helpless."

"But you did not."

"No, he'd made a place for himself with the Go-log. God knows what he must have gone through first."

"But you went through it also?"

"Some. They knew I was the son of my father long before they let me know he was alive."

"I liked the West . . . loved it. Capri, St. Tropez, Deauville, Cannes, Paris, Acapulco, Mexico City, New York . . . it was exciting at first, but there was always so much to learn, and it was so . . . different."

"I knew nothing of such places. I ran a trap-line from the time I was ten. I punched cows and I went to school."

"You can go home now. When you get to India, what is to prevent you?"

"Nothing . . . I hope. But I've come to love this country. There's so much of it unknown to the world outside. There's been a few plant-hunters in here, but not many. I hear the Lolo country is lovely, too. There's a valley over near the Min-shan somewhere, it's called Choni . . . I hear it is close to paradise."

She gestured toward the tents of the expedition. "What do you think will happen to them?"

"Who knows."

"They have faith in Gunther Hart," she commented.

"He'd better live up to it," Mallory said grimly.

They walked back to the courtyard. Large as it was, it was crowded now. The yaks lay with hoofs doubled under calmly chewing their cuds. The only brightness came from a little thread of light around the door.

Lagskha was seated on the k'ang in the lotus position when Mallory entered. Facing him from a dozen feet away in Buddhist robes was Gunther Hart. The others from the expedition were gathered around.

Mallory and Brikhuti entered. Renata glanced at them, then away. They seated themselves just as Hank Carpenter entered. Mallory noticed that . . . where had he been? At the tents? Mallory had seen nothing of him as they passed.

"If you wish," Hart was saying, "you may come with us, under our protection, but I am sure your fears are without foundation. The leaders of the new China would welcome you among them."

"I am sure they would," Lagskha quipped.

"And you would be assured of your position," Hart added.

"It is not my position that disturbs me, Mr. Hart. It is the position of my people."

"I believe your fears to be without base. These men are striving to rule China with science and intellect, the best choices made by experts for the benefit of all. Naturally, there will have to be some reorganization at the labor source, but your religion will remain undisturbed. Chou En-lai himself assured me of it. After all," he added, "I am a practicing Buddhist."

There was a very long moment of silence during which Hart's ears began to grow pink.

Dr. Penfield broke the silence. "I have heard stories about you but know little for certain. Do you come from Lhasa?"

"I was there briefly, Doctor, as a very small boy. I know of your work at Mussoorie, and am deeply grateful. My people are lonely, Doctor, and they know not which way to turn. Their homes are gone, their herds are taken and their temples have been bombed."

"Come with us," Hart insisted. "Then if you wish to leave, I will arrange it."

"You are confident," Lagskha murmured.

"Mr. Hart," Brikhuti interrupted, "you do not know what you suggest. If he went to Lhasa he would be imprisoned or killed . . . or held in what is termed 'protective restraint.'"

"You need not be alarmed. If you are under my protection no harm will come to you."

Mallory put down his bowl. "That," he said emphatically, "is a lot of damned nonsense."

There was a startled, unbelieving silence. Before Hart could respond, Hank Carpenter leaped to his feet. "You will apologize to Mr. Hart, or leave the room."

Mallory ignored him, taking up his bowl and sipping tea as if Carpenter had not spoken. Carpenter gestured, and on the far side of the Inn a huge man got to his feet. "I said," Carpenter repeated, "you will apologize or leave the Inn."

"Oh, sit down!" Mallory said tiredly. "If you don't like my being here you're free to leave. Hart was talking of something he doesn't know the least bit about. Obviously, he is accustomed to having his wishes respected. He had better begin to realize he is a long way from home. In a democracy people might listen; here they do not."

"You do not understand," Dr. Penfield said. "Gunther Hart has a clearance from Chou En-lai. You may be sure his wishes will be respected."

"Not by me," Mallory replied cheerfully, "or by anyone unless it suits their purpose. You've much to learn,

gentlemen, and what happens in these mountains need never
be heard of outside them. All your influence isn't worth
a plugged nickel unless the officer in command is amused
by it.

"Chou is a very competent man, and has a greater understanding of world power relationships than any of the
others. But he and Mao have a . . ." American English was
coming back to Mallory. ". . . a 'good cop, bad cop' routine going. And when they are not busy playing their
power games, he's as worried about getting stabbed in the
back as anyone.

"I also know a good bit about Marshal Chu, who is in
command in this area. He is a tough, competent soldier, a
military man first, last, and always. No matter what regime is in power, Marshal Chu will be listened to and respected. His mission is to bring this area under control.
For that he needs the Incarnation under his control so he
can issue orders in his name. The Dalai Lama got away and
they'll be damned if they let it happen again!

"Anybody who creates trouble will likely be killed,
and if it happens to be your expedition he will simply
eliminate all of you, report you had been killed by bandits or wiped out by an avalanche, and who is to say he
is wrong?"

Carpenter faced Mallory. "You have one minute to
apologize or leave the Inn. If you do not you will be
thrown out bodily."

There was a murmur of protest, but Mallory merely
smiled. "You wouldn't try that yourself, would you?"

"I wouldn't soil my hands." Carpenter stepped aside,
gesturing to the big man who had come up behind him. "He
will do it for me."

Pulaski had been a professional football player until
recruited by Gunther Hart. He weighed in at two hundred
and sixty pounds, in condition.

Mallory ignored him. "I was under the impression you good people did not believe in violence. Particularly Mr. Hart, who is a practicing Buddhist. Can I be mistaken?"

"You are not mistaken." Hart spoke sharply. "Hank, tell Pulaski to remain where he is."

"Don't disturb yourself." Mallory had not even looked up. "He isn't going anywhere."

Pulaski was standing rock-still, his face an ugly white. Three Go-log stood around him, sword-points denting his flesh.

"The Go-log," Mallory explained, "pride themselves on disemboweling a man with one twist of the blade. Pulaski is in an excellent position to put the matter to a test."

Mallory lifted his bowl again. Hart had made no move to stop Pulaski until it was obvious the big man would have been killed had he moved. Was the delay deliberate? Or had Hart been distracted by their argument?

"Mr. Hart's protection means nothing at all here," Mallory continued calmly. "Administration is at the field level, in the hands of field officers. Whatever report Chu turns in will be accepted in Peking."

"You under-estimate me," Hart said mildly.

"Actually, I am not concerned with you. Anybody fool enough to come _into_ this country at this time cannot concern me. However, Lagskha-tsang and his people want to get _out_ and so do we. If he wishes, he may accompany me."

"He will, of course, do as he wishes," Hart replied. "I want nothing but his safety and happiness."

Mallory was tired, tired as a man can be. For days they had followed dim trails through the roughest country on earth, traveling often by night and in the worst possible weather, yet they must move on at once. He had an uneasy feeling, a premonition of trouble.

Carpenter worried him. The man was cool and efficient. Admittedly, he was secretary to a man of power and

influence, but there was still something more. Gunther
Hart might be guilty of fuzzy thinking. Hank Carpenter
would not.

He got up, took his bowl of tea and walked outside.
To the Go-log on guard he said, "There may be trouble."

"The more who come," the Go-log said, "the more we
will kill. Let them come."

He handed the bowl to the guard. "I will ride now."

"A horse stands ready."

Mallory gathered the reins and stepped into the saddle. He turned toward the upper end of the valley to
check the guard there. He had an instinct for the night,
and knew that in these gorges there could be no movement
without sound. He drew up, hearing a rider coming up behind him. It was Renata Bernard.

"Do you mind? I wanted to ride."

"If you wish."

They rode on in silence, and after a bit she said,
"You talk very little."

"I have lived with the Go-log. They speak when there
is something to say."

"That would be dull. Don't they ever talk for fun? I
love to talk, and to listen to people who talk well."

He offered no comment, but she persisted. "You could
be more diplomatic, you know. After all, why antagonize a
man like Hart?"

"I don't trust him. He's a poseur and I think he's
going to get you and maybe me in trouble."

Renata rode on in silence. She wanted to retort, but
was bothered by the similarity of Mallory's comment to
that Marty Wells reported made by Dr. Milne Whiting.

"He has his own way of doing things, I expect. He is
a multi-millionaire and has always been wealthy."

"That explains a lot but excuses nothing. In any
event he's not a topic I would choose on a night ride
with a pretty girl."

"I wasn't aware you'd noticed."

"It's obvious, isn't it? Not that it matters, because
you are riding into Tibet and I am riding out. If I decide to return there's small chance of our meeting, even
if you are alive."

"You're not very cheerful."

"Only honest . . . and if I come back I'll be fighting, helping the Go-log or somebody."

"Is that all you think of? Fighting is brutal, dis-
gusting, and cruel. I should think a man of your intelli-
gence--"

"Don't give me that. You've no idea whether I am intelligent or not. Fighting is all the things you say, yet
the world isn't going to change . . . or stay the same
because some professor wrote a critical essay. Would you
even want to live in a world where people believed in
things so . . . lightly that they wouldn't risk everything for what they cared about? You couldn't talk freely
if men hadn't bought the right with blood and death. They
can't do that here . . . not even someone like your Mr.
Chou En-lai."

"Gunther Hart doesn't believe that way; neither does
Dr. Penfield or my uncle." After a moment, she added,
"Neither did Mahatma Gandhi."

Mallory snorted. "The Mahatma used violence more in-
telligently than any man in history, he just used it on
himself. The British, who for all their faults have an
ingrained decency, couldn't take it. He confronted them
with their own hypocrisy and they blinked. More power to
him.

"Had he been non-violent against the Nazis, the Impe-
rial Japanese, or any one of fifty governments of the
time or of now they would simply have shot him or thrown
him into prison and he wouldn't have lasted long enough
to be known to anybody but his mother. I'll bet this
country has seen fifty Gandhis in the last fifty years

and none of them lasted long enough to speak out more
than twice!"

"I believe Mahatma Gandhi was a great man," she insisted.

"So do I. I merely maintain that he was fortunate to
live and protest in a country, and against an empire,
that would listen to protest, and where there were enough
people willing to hold back those who wouldn't.

"Just be careful. The only thing between you and disaster is good fortune and whatever flimsy influence Hart
is supposed to have."

"I have seen what his influence can do, Mr. Mallory,"
she said stiffly.

"Just remember, his influence is in banks, in trust
funds, in stocks or real estate, and all that is far
away. Little of it could even be used if it was
here . . . we are in the feudal borderlands of a Communist country. You can still buy influence but you have to
do it with what you have today . . . they don't take
checks. If you want to impress them you have to talk in
terms of gold or yaks or horses or sheep, or the number
of rifles at your command."

"You believe we really are in danger?"

"In danger? Right now I'd say you've one chance in a
hundred of escaping death, ransom or a local prison somewhere."

He turned to her. "What does Hart want, anyway? Why
did he come here? I can understand the rest of you--
a scholar in pursuit of an idea will go where a normal
man wouldn't dream of going--but why Hart?"

"Why, to learn! To study! He wishes to know something
more in the field of yoga."

"Lady, with a very few exceptions, the greatest masters are refugees in Kashmir or India."

"What does that mean?"

"You're being led down the garden path. The purpose of the expedition is something else entirely. Or else--"

He stopped, startled by the thought that came to him. "No . . . no, that's unlikely."

"What?"

"Oh . . . just a random thought, but don't forget what I told you."

They had come to the end of the valley. A Go-log emerged from the darkness, and Mallory conversed with him in low tones.

"We have to walk," he said. "Horses' hoofs make too much noise on rock slabs."

She fell in beside him. He carried a rifle and he walked easily, as a woodsman walks, rather than a rider. When they had walked about a half mile from where they had left their horses, he whispered, "Stay here on that slab. I want to look around."

He moved away from her and disappeared into the dark, then she saw the outline of him at the rim of the gorge and off the rock-slab trail. He knelt and seemed to be touching the ground. Behind them the whole valley lay open and she could see a faint glow from a light within one of the tents.

Then he was beside her again. "You won't have to wait long to see what the Red Chinese are like," he said. "There was a small patrol here, just about sundown."

"How can you tell?"

"Horse tracks. Mud that fell off their shoes is still soft. They picked up that mud crossing the stream about a hundred yards back up the trail. They stood there looking down toward us and some of the mud fell off while the horses were moving about. The cold stiffens the mud, and by midnight it would have only a soft center."

"What will you do?"

"Wait until daybreak. I'm stretching our chances but my men are tired, and so are their horses."

"And if they come before then?"

"You'll have a chance to see what war is like."

As they rode up to the Inn gate a dark figure materialized before them. It was Gunther Hart.

"Renata," his tone was cool, "I do not like this. Your safety is my concern."

"It was my idea, Gunther. Mallory had left the Inn. It was a beautiful night for a ride, so I followed him."

"Nevertheless," Hart's voice lifted, "I will not have it. The behavior of this group is my responsibility."

"Don't worry," Renata replied, "I shall do nothing to embarrass you or the expedition."

Suddenly furious, he held his tongue, his eyes following Mallory as he walked away. When he spoke again his voice was calm, reasonable.

"He is not important, Renata, except that his presence endangers us all. He is an enemy of the people, and if our hosts believe we were consorting with him our invitation might be withdrawn.

"I am sure," he added, "the others would not appreciate that. Their work has been planned for months."

She was contrite. Gunther was perfectly right. Mallory infuriated her but there was something electric about him, something that demanded one's attention.

She returned to her tent. Her uncle, beyond the canvas partition, was asleep. The only tent now showing a light was that of Marty and Roy.

Mallory found Lagskha seated on the k'ang; the only light was from the brazier. "I have waited," the young lama said. "You have a plan?"

"To leave before daybreak. You must be away from here, Your Eminence. You must escape."

"You go to India with Go-log? That is curious."

Mallory lowered his voice. "They will fight, as you know, so I will try to arrange an air-drop of guns, machine guns, recoilless rifles, grenades."

"You will return?"

"They expect me to. They even might kill me if they believe I will not return. I do not know. I am alone here."

"You have no woman?"

"No. At first I was a slave. My father was with another tribe. To have gone among the Go-log women when I was a slave would have meant my death. Since then I have been wary. I like them, but . . ."

"You would be missed."

"Maybe. I think of staying sometimes but the world has moved on and maybe I'm kidding when I pretend their problems are my own."

"What of the Americans? Will they aid us?"

"Officially, no. Unofficially, perhaps. Some fear involvement, some believe in diplomacy. But diplomacy only works if you have something to trade . . . or if you are backed up by active force."

"Our people were unprepared to defend themselves against a modern army. Had we begun preparing earlier nobody would have risked invading our land."

Fire-light played on the time-stained walls, and the Incarnation studied Mallory with thoughtful eyes. "You have lived many lives . . . even in this one life you have lived many lives. You are a trukka, one of those who reached the threshold of eternity but chose to be reborn, to live on among men. Will you return to your Montana?"

"Where can a man go who has been dead for ten years? I have nothing there . . . nothing here. I have to figure it out . . ."

Mallory and Lagskha talked a bit longer. Mallory felt himself strangely drawn to this troubled young man, scarcely more than a boy, wise beyond his years, yet eager for the things any young man would have wanted.

Lagskha returned to the upstairs room and Mallory rolled up on the k'ang, his rifle beside him, a pistol-butt within reach of his fingers.

Long after he fell asleep, he awakened briefly, hearing the distant rumble of an avalanche.

And then, for a long time, there was silence.

CHAPTER 5

The Valley of Peasant Winds offered no other sound to the night. Mallory, lying on the k'ang, felt the urge to change position and sat up. Except for the faint crimson glow from the brazier, the room was in darkness. The Inn offered faint, old-building creaks, but there was no other sound until just as his eyes began to close he became aware of a sporadic, metallic tapping. After a moment it stopped . . . and then began again.

He swung his feet to the floor and tucked his pistol behind his belt. Taking up his broad-sword he moved toward the sound, on tip-toe to the foot of the stairs. The sound seemed to come from behind the steps.

From a crack in the wall came a suggestion of light. He peered through.

In a cubby-hole of a room, his back to Mallory, a man sat at a radio; there were headphones covering his ears and he was working a Morse key. He began the pattern of taps again--evidently he was calling a station.

Mallory felt for a door but there was none--the wall was bare except for the crack where age had crumbled the mortar between the stones. But beyond the man at the

radio Mallory could see the edge of a door evidently
opening to the outside. He turned quickly, his eyes seeking the front door to the Inn. The darkness, even after
the dim light that came through the crack, was profound
and in his haste, his elbow touched a bowl left on the
edge of the stairs and it fell with a clatter. Swearing
under his breath, Mallory ran through the door to the
yard, out and around the building.

The wing of the building extended far to the side and
by the time he rounded it the small door stood open, the
room empty. Both the man and the radio had vanished.
There was a thin smell of smoke and a glow of red from a
recently blown out lantern wick. The rarely used gate at
the back of the Inn yard was open, and Mallory ran to it.

The meadow was empty. He went through cautiously.
Nothing lay beyond but the dark, silent tents of the Hart
Expedition.

Sword in hand he crossed to the tents, and hearing a
movement within one, he ripped back the flap.

Renata Bernard stood before him, in a negligee. Startled, her eyes went from the naked blade to his face.
"Really, Mr. Mallory, isn't this a bit much?"

"Did you hear anyone? Anything? I am looking for a
man."

Roy Lewis emerged from the next tent, buckling his
belt. From another tent, Gunther Hart emerged. "Just what
is going on here?" he demanded.

"Somebody was operating a radio at the Inn. He got
away."

"And why shouldn't he? Whoever he is? I don't understand what disturbs you."

"Don't act the fool. The only thing the Chinese would
like better than to wipe out my people and me would be to
take the Incarnation. I can permit no communications that
would endanger our security."

"You are mistaken. No message can be sent from here

without my authorization and I have not given it. Now
have the goodness to put that . . . that . . . object
away."

Mallory checked their feet. All wore slippers or un-
tied boots, or were bare-footed. None showed any indication of a run through wet grass. Yet Bernard, Carpenter,
Penfield and his wife were missing.

"Do you have a radio?"

"Of course. We maintain communication with New Delhi,
Hongkong and Peking."

"You are sure no message was sent tonight?"

"Our radio has not even been set up. You may see it
if you wish."

"All right."

The set was larger, more powerful, altogether a better outfit than the compact set he had seen. And it was
still packed for travel.

Nothing was to be gained by delay. The set he had
seen must be carried by someone who had slipped into the
abandoned storage room to send out messages unheard by
the people in the tents.

Lagskha-tsang was sipping tea when he re-entered the
Inn. "We must go," Mallory said, "there is little time."

"I know." He put down the bowl. "I think even now it
is too late."

There was a rush of hoofs, a shout of warning, and
the Go-log from the entrance to the valley rushed in.
"They come," he said, "they come quickly."

"How many?"

The Go-log grinned. "Only ten fours," he said. "We
can beat them."

"Do not fire. Let us see what talking can do."

The sky was turning gray, the mountains were deep in
shadow. He could see the column of horsemen but could not

make out their number. They rode smartly, a tough, disciplined lot of men.

Mallory called out to Bernard. "You had better come inside the wall. All of you."

"We have nothing to fear," Hart said.

Gomba had moved up beside Mallory. "The rifles! Look at them! Shall I ride for the others?"

"Wait."

"But we can have their guns!" Gomba protested. "If we get the men from the hills--!"

"Wait. We must think of the Incarnation. Close the gate and stay out of sight."

The first troops in line headed at once for the lower end of the valley. Now both ends of the valley would be blocked . . . did they know of the other route?

These were no raw recruits. These were soldiers. As for Marshal Chu, he was no commissar, no bureaucrat, no party functionary. He was a fighting man. Accompanied by two soldiers he was approaching the Inn. It was apparent that he anticipated no trouble, which meant that he knew nothing of the presence of the Go-log.

Gunther Hart, in his robe, stepped away from the tents and walked out to meet him, a tall, austere, and impressive figure. Bernard and Penfield walked beside him, Wells and Lewis remaining near the tent, with the woman. Suddenly a tent flap was pushed aside and Hank Carpenter emerged. He went quickly to Gunther Hart and stood a half-step behind him.

Chu drew up before the closed gates, glanced toward the tents, finally at Hart.

Hart stated his name as one who expects it to be known, and so it was, over much of the world. Chu merely glanced at him, then at the closed gate. "I want that gate opened," he said.

"We have nothing to do with those inside," Hart replied, "except for the lama. He is under my protection."

Chu was a stocky, well set-up man of forty, every inch the soldier. He looked at Hart again. Slowly, carefully, he looked him up and down, then at the others.

His eyes rested on Penfield. "Who is in there?" he demanded.

"A lama, whose name seems to be Lagskha-tsang. Also, there is an American named Mallory and a party of Go-logs," Penfield replied.

"Go-logs? Here?" Chu was startled.

Hart tried once more. "Marshal, I am Gunther Hart. This is the Hart Expedi--"

"Be still!" Chu said impatiently, then to Penfield, "They cannot be Go-logs . . . not here."

"They are Go-logs," Renata said. "I know their physical type, their dress, their customs."

"Miss Bernard is an anthropologist," Carpenter explained.

Chu looked thoughtfully at the palisade. No sound came from it, no evidence of movement, yet Chu was disturbed. At such point-blank range he could be killed. "How many are there?"

"Ten?" Penfield suggested. "I don't know. There might be less. They scattered out very quickly, and I was not counting."

The palisade, old as it was, patched though it might be, was still strong. Anticipating only the capture of a fleeing lama, of a religion that did not advocate fighting, he had brought only riflemen. No rocket propelled grenade launcher, nor machine gun, or mortar. The weight would have slowed him down on the steep, narrow passes, and no need for them was foreseen.

Hart started to speak again, but Chu pushed his horse past him, brushing him aside. "You I will talk to later. Stay out of the way." His eyes swept the tents. Roy Lewis had come forward with Renata and his eyes slid over him, paused on Dr. Bernard, then returned to the palisade.

"You have seen the lama?"

"He is there," Carpenter said.

Marty Wells threw Carpenter an irritated glance. Why help him? Let Chu solve his own problems.

Chu turned to the soldier nearest him. "Open the gate," he said.

The soldier hesitated the merest second, then strode to the gate and grasped the handle. The gate opened easily. The soldier leaned to peer inside . . . and disappeared. Then the gate closed, and again there was silence.

"Open that gate and release that man!" Chu shouted. "Or I'll break it down!"

Mallory appeared on the palisade near the gate. "I wouldn't try that. You haven't men enough."

"Come down here! I want to talk to you!"

"It will be my pleasure, Marshal Chu," Mallory replied, "but if you move out of your tracks before I get back inside the gate you will have six bullets in your belly."

The gate opened and two Go-logs appeared, each armed with a Soviet PPSh machine-pistol. Chu's glance identified the weapons and his manner grew more cautious.

"I want the lama who is inside. Give him to me and go your way."

"You are amusing yourself, Marshal. If you consent to ride out of here right now we will let you go."

"I did not come to joke," said the Chinese. "You have ten minutes."

Mallory stepped forward. "You'd better reconsider. If you try to signal your men you will be shot to bits. The truth of the matter is, Marshal, we've got you."

Chu's features revealed nothing. In a career that began as a child on the Long March, continued in warfare against the Japanese, then against Chiang Kai-shek and finally in Korea, he had faced many difficulties.

He had no intention of allowing himself or any of his men to be killed to no purpose. The weight of power was on his side and the escape route to India was long. Peking did not appreciate failure and he did not permit failure to himself nor was there need to think of that now. He had six hundred men within call and, within hours, his radio could bring planes to strafe any escaping party.

His mission was to capture the Incarnation, for that young man had already given evidence of judgment and intelligence far beyond his years. Moreover, his name carried great weight among the hill tribes, never subdued under any Chinese government. He could be a powerful weapon in the hands of Mao but if allowed to escape he could become a formidable propaganda tool.

The presence of the expedition was an annoying complication, for if the Incarnation was not captured, he must be killed, and there must be no witnesses who could take the story to the outside.

Undoubtedly, the expedition had come with official sanction or they would never have gotten this far, but what were they doing here? This was no known route. In fact he himself had known nothing of this inn until forty-eight hours before. Their presence was one of the things that had thrown him off guard.

Chu had not met the Go-log before, but he knew all about them, and had a wholesome respect for them as fighting men. This Mallory . . . he did not look old enough to have been here for nearly twenty-five years but his name had been known that long.

"Do you mind if I smoke?"

"Suit yourself," Mallory replied.

Chu took a cigarette case from his pocket but took his own time in lighting up. "We are at a stand-off, my friend. You have me but I also have you. No doubt you can order me killed, but you would never escape alive."

Hart interrupted. "Marshal, this man is no concern of ours. He arrived after we did. We have a permit from Chou En-lai and--"

Chu spoke directly to Mallory. "These civilians will be killed if I am killed. You would not want that on your conscience?"

"You trust to my conscience?"

Chu shrugged. "You Americans are sentimental people. Conscience is important to you. To me it is nothing. I think of results."

"I have read Confucius," Mallory said. "He was more ethical, I believe."

"But scarcely a Marxist, would you say?" Chu was enjoying himself. "I respect Marx but when it is inconvenient, I ignore him. I don't care that men are taught to think the right thoughts, I just want them to obey and help me carry out my orders."

He drew on his cigarette. "Let us make an end to this. I do not know what you are doing here, nor do I care. I am a single-minded man and my problem is that young lama. You can surrender him and ride away freely, or you can try to help him and all die together. It is as simple as that."

"Chou--" Hart began.

Chu glanced at Hart with contempt. "Comrade Chou is a very important man for whom I have great admiration. He also has many duties. If you interfere with me I will have you shot and then I will explain my actions. He will be understanding, particularly as I am in a position to be very useful to him, and a dead American, even several dead Americans, means nothing to anybody."

Chu turned in his saddle and spoke to the soldier beside him. "If that man," he pointed at Hart, "speaks again, strike him in the mouth with your rifle butt. After you do it, if he has any teeth left in the front of his face I will have you shot."

Dr. Bernard spoke, "Sir, Mr. Hart wishes to cause no trouble. We are concerned with the welfare of the People's Republic of China, and came here to study the ancient life of your country, its plants and its geology. Our reports will be submitted to Peking, and are looked for there. We are, sir, men of peace. Hence Gunther Hart was concerned that our expedition not be confused with whatever Mallory and his men are doing."

"And what is he doing?"

"I . . . I don't actually know, sir. We have had no opportunity to talk."

Chu's expression was icy. "But time to use a radio? There was time for that, was there not?"

"Radio? I do not know. Mallory was very concerned about somebody using a radio. I believed it was a mistake."

"It was not a mistake. A radio message was sent . . . or attempted . . . just recently." Chu looked over at Mallory. "You know something of this?"

"You're damned right I do. Marshal, if a message was sent from here it was somebody with a hidden radio. I do not believe more than one of this expedition knows anything about it but I could be wrong."

"It was sent by one of them?"

"Unless there is somebody here whom none of us know. I believe that message was being relayed to Peking . . . or Moscow."

"Ah?"

Chu considered the matter. He was not surprised. The Party had its people everywhere and they could be reporting his actions. He had friends in Peking but enemies also. He was not sure who all of those enemies were but they were concerned with his growing strength, his autonomy.

The leaders were old, none of them in the best of health, and soon there would be changes, new faces. Mar-

shal Chu had long had it in mind to be one of those new
faces. A radio message was not only possible but probable. His own operator had picked up a signal, and from
its strength it could have come from nowhere else . . .
in this area there simply wasn't anywhere else. Of
course, it might also be an agent of the imperialist
West.

Even as he used the phrase he rebelled at it. He was
a party member in good standing, but that did not say he
accepted all the pap used for propaganda purposes. The
Party had been an effective means to seize control and if
some of the older members and young idealists still clung
to the vision of International Communism, it was their
privilege. For himself, party slogans were simply a means
to seize power and to hold it.

He was quite willing to deal with the so-called capi-
talist powers but he wished to deal from strength. And,
soon enough, there must be such deals; there must be ar-
rangements. They had much China needed and could get in
no other way except through Russia . . . and there had
been enough of that. His eyes shifted to Mallory, weigh-
ing the man. This was the one with whom he must deal,
this was his enemy, and yet he was the man Chu respected
most.

"You can hold me, Major Mallory, or release me. It
grows late and I am tired. If you intend holding me, by
all means let us go inside. If not release me to return
to my command."

"We shall go inside, of course. Come, Marshal Chu.
Will you be first?"

Chu hesitated only a moment. "Not first. If my men
decide I am a prisoner, they will attack." He smiled. "I
have a second in command who is very ambitious, Major."

CHAPTER 6

Marty Wells walked back to the tents. Chu had gone inside with Mallory, walking side by side as if they were old friends, but that was window-dressing for any of his men who might be watching.

Renata had started toward the tents but she waited for Marty to over-take her. "You're worried?"

"I'm scared."

"Of the Chinese? Gunther will manage. Just wait and see."

He gave her a sour glance. "Chu couldn't care less about him, or about us."

"Wait. Gunther will be in touch with Peking and Chu will get his orders."

Marty glanced at the mountains. "I'm still trying to figure out where Gunther Hart was going. He was never very explicit, you know, except that we should be in eastern Tibet, perhaps the Upper Mekong area or the sources of the Huang-Ho, but all that covers an enormous stretch of country. People outside do not realize the vastness of all this. Tibet is about twice the size of Texas, and this area . . . some of it used to be Tibet . . . is almost as large.

"Hart is using a map that we have never had a chance to examine. When we were permitted to come here we were given a prescribed route to follow. That was part of his agreement with the People's Republic of China. I heard him discussing it with Hank and Hank was very upset when Hart turned off the designated route."

Lewis joined them. "I like this man Mallory," he said. "He doesn't take any guff from anyone." He glanced at Wells. "How'd you come to make this trip, Marty?"

"A friend of mine recommended me to Hart. Of course, I jumped at it. This area has been gone over lightly . . .

I say this area, but I mean this part of China. Ward covered some of it further south, and Wilson, Forrest and
Rock worked through here some, but none of it has been
done as thoroughly as one would like.

"There have been some old documents turning up
lately, their origin is uncertain, but they are extremely
old. The thing is they describe plants quite accurately,
some of which we know, and some we've never catalogued."

"When you say 'old' what do you mean, Marty?"

"Renata, I simply mean old. You know about the Bower
manuscript, of course? These were similar except the thin
strips of wood on which they were written had been
treated with some kind of preservative."

"Didn't you have a carbon-14 reading on it?"

"That's just it. And the man who did the reading was
one of the best, but he flatly refused to issue a statement on it. He said the reading had to be wrong . . . it
was far too old. He believed the way the wood had been
treated had made a difference in the reading."

"Who knows?" Lewis said. "They've just found some
rice in Thailand that proves man was cultivating grain
long before anybody dreamed they could.

"There's been too much of a fixation on the Near and
Middle East, Egypt, Sumer and all that. Most of the studies have been made there and without anything more than
that many European scientists jumped to the conclusion
that those were the first civilizations.

"Most of the money goes into the Mediterranean area
or Sumer. We know damned little about the rest of the
world. It's fairly obvious there was a great belt of civilizations stretching across the great land masses from
the Sahara through Egypt, Sumer, southern Arabia, Dilmun,
the Indus Valley and Southeast Asia. I believe trade and
travel were as active as in Europe of the Crusade period."

"I wonder what's going on inside?" Marty suggested.

"Let's go see," Renata offered.

Lagskha-tsang sat on the k'ang, Brikhuti beside him. Mallory and Marshal Chu faced them with Gunther Hart and Hank Carpenter at one side.

"You would be wise, Your Eminence," Chu suggested, "to return with us. Your former position is assured. You may be sure your opinions will be listened to and respected."

"And ignored?" Lagskha asked.

"The Dalai Lama is no longer in Tibet," Chu suggested suavely. "It is important your people have someone to speak for them. By leaving the country he has, in effect, abdicated. It is important he be replaced by someone suitable."

"Ah? That is a possibility I had not considered." Lagskha's face was innocent of guile. "I must have time. I must meditate. For such a decision . . . I must have a day and a night."

"Of course. Shall we say twenty-four hours? I regret I can allow no more time but my government is impatient. Someone is needed in Lhasa, someone with authority."

Lagskha frowned thoughtfully. "Yes . . . yes, of course. You understand, however, that a Dalai Lama cannot, as you put it, abdicate? He is an Incarnation, and the only way such a man can abdicate is by dying. He is not the first Dalai Lama to leave his country temporarily. Such a decision has been forced upon several . . . all have returned. I think the people understand very well why he left, and in fact, they tried to persuade him to leave long before he finally did. And a Dalai Lama cannot be appointed by Peking."

Chu smiled. "We understand, Your Eminence, that a Dalai Lama is born . . . a regent is not. In his absence, the government must continue, conducted by a regent."

"Yes, of course. That might just be the thing.
Twenty-four hours, please?"

Marshal Chu turned to Mallory. "You will abide by his
decision?"

"Of course. I have no interest in kidnapping. He will
do as he sees fit."

"And you, Major Mallory? What will you do in that
case?"

Mallory smiled. "I want to settle down with a good
bottle of bourbon and a cigar. You can have this country." His words were calculated to disarm Marshal Chu, as
much as he might be disarmed, but Mallory had spoken with
the awareness that few of the Go-log could follow the nu-
ances of the conversation. Only a couple of his men understood more than the most basic Mandarin Chinese. It
always came as a surprise to Europeans or Americans that
so few people in the outlying portions of China actually
spoke Chinese.

What he needed was time, and if Chu believed he was
leaving, he might not be so quick to follow unless he
discovered Lagskha had gone with him. Chu was a pragma-
tist. To capture or kill Mallory and his Go-log was a
possibility, and a desirable one, yet if Mallory would
leave of his own accord, Chu and China were well rid of
him, and without him the Go-log might never get back to
their own land in the bend of the Yellow River.

To attempt a capture now would mean a battle, the
loss of time and undoubtedly many casualties . . . one of
whom might be this young lama that Chu was so interested
in. That fear might work to all their benefit, Mallory
thought.

"All right," Mallory said, "you can go. I have no
idea what the Incarnation wishes to do. He will make his
own decision."

"My interest," Chu said bluntly, "is only in him." He

smiled. "As for the Hart Expedition, they are Comrade
Chou's problem. Not mine."

Nothing was to be gained by holding him. That he had
an ambitious second in command was probably true, and
such a man might be likely to precipitate a fight. What
Mallory needed was time, and Chu was confident enough to
give it to him. After all, did he not have both ends of
the valley blocked?

When Marshal Chu had gone Mallory immediately dispatched a rider to get word to the rest of his men, holed
up in the mountains only a few miles away. He had a feeling he would need them all, and the time was near when a
move must be made. Both of the armed camps would be gathering reinforcements. In the short term the numbers favored the Go-log, but that could not last. As soon as
Marshal Chu felt he had the advantage the truce might be
over.

There was nothing for it but to attempt the secret
trail, hoping he would be able to find his way.

Renata was awaiting him inside. "What will you do?
You realize, of course, that anything you do will involve
us?"

"I am not concerned with you. My only interest is
getting to India with my men. You are Hart's problem."

He went on up the stairs after the lama. Renata
looked after him. "He's trouble, Marty," she said wryly.
"I wish he had never come here. We're going to be in all
kinds of trouble."

"That's one way of looking at it. Personally, I wonder if we're getting a last chance to get out of here
while the getting is good. Gunther was so sure of himself, but the Marshal obviously didn't care who he was or
what connections he had. What they say is true. Peking is
a long way off."

At the top of the stairs Lagskha awaited him. Mallory
seated himself. Brikhuti appeared, offering them both
bowls of tsamba.

"Do you trust the Marshal, Mallory?" Lagskha asked.

"No."

"Nor do I. I am afraid you are better at what comes
next, Major. I place myself in your hands."

"Chu's men bar the way on the traditional route. If
we broke through, Chu could call upon planes to bomb and
strafe the road. The route through the valley is wide--we
would be an easy target for aircraft."

Lagskha waited, his eyes bright and attentive.

"There is another way. I believe you know it, and I
do not. At least, I do not know all one needs to know." He
paused. "If we could vanish in the night . . . suddenly."

"You talk of miracles."

"I talk of a road. A secret road."

"It is not possible. We would be leading them--no, it
cannot be done."

Brikhuti started to speak, then was silent. Her
brother spoke then. "This way you speak of . . . how do
you know of it?"

"I found a map on the wall of a cave temple. A very
intricate, difficult map, by the way. It was like nothing
I had ever seen, but then, quite suddenly it began to
look familiar and I recognized it for what it was.

"Marked on this map was a road, beside the road a
monastery, further along a temple and a fort. There was
even a city, hidden among the peaks."

"Who has seen this map?"

"So far as I am aware, only myself. It is hidden beyond finding. In the land of the Go-log."

"He is one of us, My Brother," Brikhuti said, "is
that not plain enough? This must have been the cave of
Kesar . . . and who could find it was he not guided
there?"

"I know the way is a sacred way, but you are an Incarnation, so what better use for such a road?"

"Give me time. I must think of this."

Mallory got to his feet. "Between this time and the
noon sun, I must know."

Brikhuti followed him down the stairs. "He will go. I
know it. But you must tell me how you found the cave."

"It was an accident. I was climbing in the mountains."

"I do not believe in accidents. You found it because
you were meant to find it."

"Well, you may see it as some sort of destiny. I'm
just happy to have a way out . . . and to have someone
who understands at least some of the path and can help me
follow it."

Her eyes were dark and lovely. Mallory found himself
groping for words. How did a man talk to a woman? It had
been so long, and this girl was infinitely more lovely
than any he had known. "You'll be going back to Europe?"

"Wherever we must. I hope so, however. I love the
cities, the music, the gaiety . . . and the books."

"Books?"

"Here there are so few, and I like to read.

"What of you, Major Mallory? That is your world,
too."

"I am not so sure. I fear I have become a savage."

"A savage who reads the Upanishads? Perhaps not so
savage as you would have us believe."

He looked at her quizzically. "Now who could have
told you that?"

"You have been too long among the mountain people for
there not to be stories, and you are a curiosity. Many of
the people you've met had never seen a European or an
American before.

"Long before I went away to school there were stories
about you, how you rode like a demon and fought like a

tiger. A Bon priest stopped at our house for a few days and he told us about the mysterious white man who reads books. He said you were a man of great wisdom."

"That was my father. But a man does need exercise for the mind."

He was tired, tired as ever he could remember. He wondered about Gunther Hart. The man was accustomed to authority. How would he react when his word was no longer obeyed?

"Stay with your brother," he told her. "If there is trouble, call me."

After she had gone he finished his tsamba, drank another bowl of tea, and looked up as Roy Lewis came in.

The geologist sat down. "I hope I am not disturbing you, Mallory, but you know this country. Why would Hart choose to come into this valley?"

"Hasn't he told you?"

"We were told nothing. Renata was the only one who knew he planned to stop here for a few days."

"He had planned to stop here?"

"So Renata told Marty Wells. He's off the route prescribed by Peking."

"He's taking a chance. When the Chinese give you a route you'd better stay with it."

Lewis shrugged. "You've been out of touch, Mallory. Gunther Hart has a name for doing what he damn well chooses and with his money and his connections he gets away with it. He is a heavy contributor to both the Republicans and Democrats and nobody wants to cross him. He has the reputation of being a bad enemy."

Mallory stretched out on the k'ang and clasped his hands behind his head.

"He must be looking for something and I suspect he knows a lot more than he's letting on," Lewis said. "The man values his life as highly as anything. I'll bet he's not taking this risk lightly. I heard he has a map. Could

he be looking for something archaeological? The Bernards
were brought in on this thing very early."

"That depends on where he looks. In most of the high
plateau country he will find little, but in the valleys
. . . there are places here, Lewis, that are older than
man's measurement of time.

"It is very easy to lay down rules for the ages of
history when you examine only one small corner. It is
quite another thing when you look further and dig
deeper."

"Just this afternoon I was saying something like
that. We must have a talk."

"It would be interesting," Mallory said, closing his
eyes, "but I'm headed out of here as soon as I can figure
out how."

Roy Lewis walked from the room and Mallory lay one
last moment awake, staring up at the smoke-blackened
beams. This inn was more Chinese than Tibetan, an odd
thing, at this remote place. And it was old, so very,
very old.

He closed his eyes again. The inside of his lids
seemed raw from sleeplessness, yet they remained shut,
and in a moment, he slept.

CHAPTER 7

Over the Valley of Pleasant Winds there was an avenue
of stars, and within the valley there was silence. The
lights in the tents had gone out and within the Inn men
slept upon the k'ang in the faint red glow of the charcoal brazier.

Back in the lost canyons of the mountains there were
the small, lonely sounds of the mountains breathing, and
of the forest. A rock fell, gravel trickled after it, and

the contraction of cold caused a branch to creak. Here and there some small nocturnal creature rustled among the leaves of the rhododendrons.

Here in these lonely peaks, these dark, mysterious canyons, here on the edge of the vast, grassy plains of the Chang-tang, here begin several of the greatest rivers on earth, all finding their sources within one comparatively small area.

Out of great gorges in the mountains flow the Yellow, the Yangtze, the Mekong, the Salween, the Brahmaputra, the Irrawaddy . . . and others, all with names like incantations.

In her tent Renata lay awake, staring up into darkness. She, who always fell asleep easily, was sleepless, and it was not the altitude, for they were but little higher than yesterday.

Was it fear? She searched herself and found nothing that resembled fear. She admitted she was no longer so sure of Gunther. Chu had brushed him aside as though he were an annoyance rather than anyone to be considered seriously.

Mallory was the disturbing element. She was not accustomed to such a completely masculine man, and with it was the realization that she seemed unable to reach him, to affect him in any way. He was single-minded to a degree to which she was unaccustomed.

Men had always been attracted to her physically, and had come to respect her intelligence later. If Mallory was attracted it did not seem to matter very much, and as for intelligence, he simply took it for granted if he realized it at all.

She had been immediately aware that Chu respected Mallory, and vice versa. The two men were enemies, but in a sense they spoke the same language, and had come to an immediate understanding, yet she was quite sure each of them was now planning to out-wit the other.

What had they gotten into? For the first time she began to realize the vast distances involved here, and her total irrelevance as a person in the light of international complications. For the first time it dawned upon her that this whole venture had been foolish. Scientists too easily considered themselves, or perhaps their work, to be the center of the universe.

Gunther Hart moved in such an aura of his own that he had seemed immune from the petty bickerings of nations. Now she began to wonder if he was inconsequential once removed from the world that his money and influence had built. Well, he still had the radio with which to communicate to the world outside. He could put himself in touch with Chu's superiors if he needed to.

Yet what if the rules were different here even if they were able to speak with Gunther's connections? What if Chou En-lai or his lieutenants behaved differently now that Gunther was in their world? They might seem more than polite and helpful when Gunther Hart was treating them to dinner in the West but what would they be like when Hart started asking them for favors here . . . in a place where he might not know the rules? Just what could Gunther mean to them, anyway? Could a Communist in a land of Communists be seen to allow a person whose position was based on wealth to influence policy or goals?

They were a long way from home. Lhasa, the capital of Tibet, was at least four hundred miles away from their present position. On horseback, in this country, that could be a trip that took weeks. The nearest Tibetan city, if such it could be called, was Chamdo, several days travel from where they were now.

Moreover, Gunther Hart, on some mission of his own, had taken them off the designated route. This in itself was enough to land them in prison in any Communist country where travel was restricted.

Worried, she remembered Carpenter telling Pulaski to

throw Mallory out. It had been a hasty, ill-considered
action, and suddenly she was trembling, remembering that
naked display of power when the three Go-log had moved so
quickly with their blades. An instant more and if there
had been no word from Mallory they might have killed
Pulaski . . . would have killed him. Mallory and the Go-
logs, even Lagskha and his sister, were armed and their
survival was threatened. Her people must not forget that.
Academics often chose to live in a world of abstractions,
but here life could be terrifying and immediate.

A long time later she fell asleep, and it was not
until day was breaking that she awakened, suddenly. For
an instant she lay still, hearing low voices outside,
then the swish of feet through the grass. The tent curtain drew back and Mary Penfield came in.

"Now they've done it." Mary's hands were shaking as
she tried to light her cigarette. "Somebody got into the
packs last night and smashed the radio . . . smashed it
to bits."

Renata sat up, her mind blank. She could only stare.
Realization came over her slowly. The radio smashed! Then
how--?

"Oh, Mary!" she whispered. "The radio! What will we
do?"

Mary drew on her cigarette and glanced at her, then
smiled, wryly. "Make friends with Mallory. What else?"

There was a scratching at the canvas. "Come in," she
said, and Marty lifted the flap and stepped in.

"It's early but you'd better get dressed. Somebody
got into the supplies, smashed the radio, stole some
extra batteries, and Hart's fit to be tied."

"We'd better pack up and get out," Mary commented.
"At least back to a city or town where there are communications."

"That's a good idea," Marty agreed, squatting on his
heels, "but we've come a long way to quit so quickly.

Why, I haven't done hardly anything, and I'm sure nobody ever worked this valley before. Or the country around here, for that matter."

Marty Wells left and she dressed quickly. Marty was waiting outside with Dr. Penfield and Renata's uncle. The morning was bright enough, but the sky was not the clear blue she expected.

"The weather's changing," her uncle said. "I think it's going to rain."

"Have you seen Gunther?"

"Only for a minute. He's been talking to Carpenter." He glanced at her. "He's not going back, if that's what you are thinking. He's going to send a man out with a message. He'll have an air-drop of a new radio . . . two of them in fact."

"A messenger? Where to?"

"I don't know. He didn't say."

"Why, he would have to ride for days!"

Mallory opened the gate and stepped out, looking around. His Go-log had returned only an hour before, having made contact with the rest of his command in the hills. Chu had attempted to prevent anyone from leaving the valley but most of his soldiers were city men, unused to the ways or the skills of the Go-log. His messenger had slipped by within a few feet of a watching soldier, and returning had done the same thing.

"If you like," he said to Mallory, "I bring them all in . . . every one. These are stupid."

"Don't take them lightly," Mallory advised. "They aren't hunters and woodsmen, but they can fight, and they will. They also have damned good weapons."

"Which we will have soon," the Go-log said grimly. "I have seen them." He slapped his long Mosin Nagant rifle. "But I prefer this."

Roy Lewis walked over. "Know anything about Tantric Yoga?"

"A little."

"I think that's the bee in Hart's bonnet."

"Well, if he's looking for a teacher he'd do better to look somewhere that isn't in so much conflict. These gurus up here are independent. They don't care who you are or what you are, and they will only accept you as a student if they feel the urge. That is if they haven't fled or gone into hiding. He's going to a Hell of a lot of trouble if he's not looking for something in particular."

"Those Go-logs of yours," Lewis said tentatively. "Old enemies of the Chinese, are they not?"

"They are enemies of almost everybody. Aside from their raids on Tibet to China caravans, they want to be left alone."

"I've heard they hit the Reds pretty hard, even shot down some low-flying aircraft. Is that true?"

Mallory glanced at him. "The Go-logs mind their own affairs, and so do I."

Lewis chuckled. "No offense intended, Mallory. I am interested, however. I was just thinking how lucky it is that these Go-logs don't have modern equipment. With somebody to instruct them they could be welded into quite a force. Something the CIA might appreciate . . . even pay for, if the situation was right."

Mallory stretched. "You know something, Lewis? I'm going to get some breakfast."

"Why not join us? Hart might be more willing to listen to reason now that his radio is busted. We can offer you bacon and eggs, good coffee--?"

"I'll take it," Mallory said. "The change might do me good." He turned back into the gate and conferred briefly with the Go-log sentry. "All right," he said to Lewis. "I hope Hart doesn't resent my coming."

"Talk gently," Lewis advised. "After all, why antagonize the man?"

Renata watched Mallory talking to Roy Lewis. How
strong he was! It was a strange face, a brooding, unre-
vealing face. It was the face of a man who had lived with
mountains. She irritably pushed the thought away; some
part of her mind seemed bent on making him seem more attractive than he really was.

Brikhuti came up beside her. "Without him," she said,
"we will die here . . . all of us."

"You are mistaken." Renata lifted her chin. "Our expedition need have nothing to do with him. Gunther Hart
will communicate with Peking and everything will be all
right. Another radio will be flown in, and perhaps an official to act as an intermediary."

"How strong is your Mr. Hart when he faces adversity?
How would he react to a knife? Or a gun?"

"Gunther Hart," Renata replied coolly, "is not my
man. As to facing a knife, I doubt if that will be necessary. He is a man of peace."

"To be a man of peace is very easy when one is protected. My country was a land of peace, yet we have been
invaded several times, and now we have been enslaved, our
homes and our religion destroyed. Would it have been so
had we been better armed? Had we had alliances with other
countries? Your country, perhaps? You have an example in
your own world . . . the Swiss. They are men of peace,
but every Swiss has a rifle in his home, and he is prepared to use it. Other nations know this, and know the
cost of invasion would be too high. In being so prepared
the Swiss have no need of greater, more immoral, weapons."

Brikhuti smiled slightly, at Renata. "I saw how you
looked at Mallory. He is very much a man."

Renata felt herself tense. "I really wouldn't know,"
she said politely, "he isn't my man. Is he yours?"

"Like you, I never saw him before yesterday, but I've
heard of him, of course."

Renata was eager to hear what Brikhuti had heard, but
could not bring herself to ask. The morning was very
still. The yaks grazed in the meadows and all was peace-
ful. Above them the mountains towered, the peaks icy and
alone, the sunlight sparkling on their snows. She could
hear the rustling of the water in the small creek that
crossed the meadow.

Brikhuti held out her hand. "I have enjoyed the chat,
Miss Bernard. You know, if you want him you will have to
fight, because I want him, too!"

CHAPTER 8

Breakfast was a pleasant meal, served in a long tent,
and at a long, folding table. Gunther Hart was already
seated when Mallory entered.

"Mr. Hart," Lewis said, "I took the liberty of invit-
ing Mallory to join us."

"Of course, it will be our pleasure. Will you be
seated? I am afraid our menu is somewhat limited, but
from all I understand yours has been even more so."

"You're right," Mallory said, "and an American style
breakfast will be a treat."

"In fact, we could spare you a few odds and ends, I
believe." He turned his head. "Hank, see that Mallory has
a few jars of marmalade from our supply, will you?"

"Mallory," Marty said suddenly, "I don't suppose you
are a botanist, but you undoubtedly are familiar with a
lot of the plants. Can you tell me anything about them?"

Mallory watched his coffee-cup filled, then said,

"This is the Chala Shan where we are now . . . shan meaning mountain range. I think you'll find it listed among
the unexplored areas, if at all. As near as I've noticed
the growth is somewhat similar to that in the Yunnan
mountains.

"From seven thousand feet to ten thousand there's a
variety of trees and shrubs, many fine hardwoods, and the
lower-level types of rhododendrons. Many of them are
fair-sized trees, and not just the shrubs you've probably
seen.

"Above ten thousand feet is mostly evergreen, several
varieties of pines, for example, and delphiniums, anemo-
nes, and the usual plants you find growing at that altitude anywhere. The best stuff for you will be found above
twelve thousand."

"Are you as familiar with the local history?" Hart
asked. "I mean the very ancient history?"

"You're in the midst of it, Hart. This inn has been a
stopping place for centuries. Before it was an inn it was
a farmhouse, before that a minor fort or castle.

"This trade route that runs through here, part of
which you followed coming in, and all of that you would
follow if you continued on, is thousands of years old."

"Thousands?" Dr. Bernard asked.

"I know. The usual story is that Tibet began when Ru-
pati, a Kaurava prince or commander, escaped here after
the defeat of the Kauravas by the Pandavas in the great
war in northern India. But it is foolish to talk of beginnings.

"Whenever one tries to find a beginning, one finds
there was still something before that and Tibet has been
no different in that respect than others. There is a
place not far from here where long ago the river cut deep
into the hill that supported a deserted monastery . . .
a very old one, dating from the first years of Buddhism
in Tibet. That bank reveals seven layers of habitation,

Dr. Bernard, with a three-foot-thick bed of silt between
the fourth and the fifth layers."

"Could you take me to that place?"

"Another time." Mallory smiled thinly. "When it won't
cost me my life. There are ancient places all around you.
If you live long in this country and are of a curious
mind it does not take long to understand how much has
taken place here.

"Major trade routes from India to the Tarim Valley
led across Tibet not far from here. In those days there
was a great civilization there--"

"You have some basis for this?"

"Observation, careful listening . . . I'm not trying
to prove anything or threaten anyone's theories. There
were trade routes that led from here into Burma, and others that went into Thailand. Our world is old, Dr. Bernard, so much older than the caution of scholars will
allow them to admit."

Gunther Hart studied Mallory thoughtfully as Mallory
talked, and after a moment, he said, "These old monasteries . . ." He paused. "Are any of them left? Wasn't this
area a stronghold of the Bon religion?"

"It was." Mallory refilled his cup and waited a moment. Then he said, "It was also a stronghold of the belief from which the Bon religion derived. Unfortunately,
all religions eventually end in superstition, losing
their purity with time and with the ignorance of the followers. What became the Bon religion grew out of something infinitely stronger, deeper, and more real than
what preceded it. Are you familiar with the logical theories of Dignaga and Dharmakirti?"

"No."

"They had some similarity to ideas of Bergson and
Leibniz. I'm not an expert but they seem to share something with contemporary physics. In part those ideas are
very ancient, such as the theory of instantaneous being,

the idea that change is constant and immediate. Our
senses betray us in being unable to record the changes
rapidly enough to perceive the alteration that has taken
place. Therefore we speak of things as being the same
when they are no longer so. Every minute is lost in that
minute."

"What you are suggesting," Hart said, "is a civilization advanced enough to conceive of such ideas, a civilization of which we have no record."

"We had no record of the Indus Valley civilization
that any scholar would accept until about 1928, and it
was one of the greatest of the ancient civilizations. Actually, most of the work there has been done in the past
ten to fifteen years. Are we constantly to assume there
is no more to be discovered?"

"I had no idea you were a scholar, Mr. Mallory," Renata said. "You surprise me."

"I am not a scholar, but I had ten years with several
hours of each day, and sometimes months, with no demands
on my time, no interruptions. I had very few books, but
the ones I had were excellent, and I had access to the
old men, and the old men love to talk, and I to listen."

Mallory got up. "Look, this is all well and good but
it is not worth our lives. There isn't much time, so let
me make you an offer. Come out of here with me. Come
now . . . you may not have another chance."

Gunther Hart shook his head. "No, Mr. Mallory. We
will persist. We are not frightened. You see, I suspected
something might happen and I have arranged for planes to
scout certain routes. One of those planes will be coming
soon. We can make our wants known with ground signals."

"Very well then." Mallory paused in the opening. "Be
sure you do not miss what you came for, Mr. Hart. It is
easy to be blind, very hard to see clearly."

He went out, and Renata looked after him, watching
him cross the meadow toward the Inn.

"Well," her uncle said, "we have a philosopher among us!"

"Words come easily to some," Hart replied carelessly. "If the man had anything, would he be wasting it here?"

Mallory crossed the meadow, mentally cursing himself for a fool. He had no business making such an offer, for the last thing he needed was to be saddled with a party such as this: scientists who would find fifty reasons for stopping by the way, and coddled Western women.

Speed was the essence of escape, speed and the immediate necessity for covering their tracks. He need not worry about the lama or about his sister. They were Tibetans, accustomed to travel under much worse conditions.

Yet one thing had happened in there, for even as he talked he had made up his mind. He would go today . . . within a few hours. He would not even wait until night.

They would be suspecting nothing now. After dark tonight, as his time was growing shorter, they would double the guards. With any luck by night he would be on his way and moving fast but to do that he was going to need a lot of luck.

At the gate he turned and let his eyes sweep the meadow. Gomba moved up beside him. "Tell the Khambas to drive their yaks to water." He pointed. "Over there where there is low ground along the stream. Drive them slowly, let whoever is watching see them go down to the low ground; after they've had a drink, bring them back up on the meadow, but close-herd them, understand? Later, drift a couple of them down to the low ground, then more, and more.

"I want them to disappear. Now in the Inn there are several yak hides. Kick some brush together or find standing brush and drape them with the hides . . . while the yaks are feeding.

"The soldiers watch from a distance. They will know there is low ground along the stream, and hopefully, they will think nothing of it when a few yak drift off to drink."

He scowled suddenly, remembering the radio. If Hart knew who that operator was, he wasn't saying, but Mallory had a hunch he did not know.

And somebody had destroyed Hart's radio--nine chances out of ten that had been Chu's men. Whatever Chu had to do now he would do himself; he wanted no interference. Once it was all over others could say little, but he obviously wanted no one talking to Peking, providing ammunition for his enemies there.

His thoughts returned to the conversation at breakfast. Gunther Hart was fishing for something. He wanted information but he was reluctant to come right out and ask yet something had brought him here in the first place.

Lagskha came down the steps, Brikhuti behind him. "Mallory?" He paused on the lowest step. "I have decided. I shall go with you."

"It will be very hard."

He shrugged. "When was travel not hard? At least, the cold will not be so great as on the Chang-tang." He seated himself on the k'ang. "If anything happens to me, Mallory, you will care for my sister?"

"I will. With her permission."

"Thank you. What do you think of the man Carpenter?"

"Very cold, very intelligent, very dangerous. He is not to be trusted, never, not under any circumstances."

"I agree. And Lewis?"

Mallory hesitated. "We'll wait and see. I am not sure about Lewis. He was suggesting a drop of guns and ammunition might be helpful."

"Was he fishing?"

Mallory considered that. "Maybe. And perhaps he was just talking. Lots of men do. Or--?"

"Yes?"

"Suggesting. That might have been it. He might have been seriously suggesting."

"You spoke of a way out of this valley, Mallory? Do you know it?"

"The general direction, but what I do not know are the problems peculiar to that trail, the special problems there might be. The stories of those who have traveled the route might save our lives."

"I shall be of little help, I am afraid. Mallory, do you have any idea what it means to be an Incarnation? My studies began when I was very young. Each day there were many hours, and some lessons I learned very well, and some not so well. Do you remember all you learned in school?"

"Very little, I'm afraid."

"It was the same with me. I am afraid I liked the stories best, and stories of Kesar of Ling, of Dikchen Shenpa, his minister, and of Kurkar, his enemy. I also liked the stories of Chang Shambala." He chuckled. "My sister told me you have a story of it, too?"

"Yes, Lost Horizon. A very popular novel--there was a film made of it, which was also very good. Only they called it Shangri-la."

"A good name. Do you believe that story, Mallory?"

Mallory shrugged. "We all like to believe such stories."

"Some say Shambala is only in your mind," Brikhuti said, "and it is just as well if that is so."

"The map in the cave of Kesar, Mallory? Did it show the way to Shambala?"

"I don't know. The map was very intricate, not like any map I ever saw."

A Go-log came in with tea. Mallory sipped his, waiting for a moment to feel the warmth of it in his stomach. And then he said, "This afternoon, Lagskha."

"All of us?"

"Your people and mine."

"And the Hart Expedition? Do we leave them here?"

"It is their choice, and anyway, I do not think we could all go as we are going. It will have to be done as a magician does it, distracting attention and then disappearing before their eyes."

"I do not like to leave them. They are very innocent, I think. They have not seen blood," Lagskha said.

"They will. This is not a land in which one keeps one's innocence. They have heard of violent things, evil things, read of them, but it always occurs somewhere else, happens to somebody else. They have been protected by traffic lights, curbstones, policemen and soldiers for so long they scarcely believe them necessary."

"Is that the way your country is?"

"That depends. The world of academics and the wealthy is often very protected . . . they go to great trouble to insulate themselves and then they forget what they wanted protection from."

"Yes. I understand. In Tibet we did that too."

They were quiet, drinking their tea. Then Lagskha said, "Mallory? The way the map showed? Where did it end?"

"At the sea?"

"No further?"

Mallory hesitated, then reluctantly he added, "At an island in the sea."

CHAPTER 9

The Chinese had a saying that he who could concentrate upon any particular problem for three uninterrupted minutes could rule the world. Mallory didn't believe it

was true but he had at least learned to focus his attention upon one problem at a time.

Now with a bowl of yak butter tea, he sat on the
k'ang, and considered the problem before him. A problem
well-stated was a problem half-solved and his problem was
simple indeed.

He must move approximately thirty people and as many
animals from under the eyes of watching guards in broad
daylight.

With luck, his method would work, but he must consider alternatives, sudden changes that might be necessary, and the probable moves of the enemy. Two things
were in his favor. The natural negligence of any kind of
a guard, and the sheer unexpectedness of attempting an
escape at such a time.

The moment he had seen the yak hides he had realized
their possibility, and they could be carried into the
fields on the backs of yaks, draped over shrubs or rocks
when the yaks went to drink. Each time some of the yaks
went down to the creek, some would be allowed to wander
back, but those belonging to the train of the lama would
remain hidden.

Three of the Go-log and two of the Khambas who accompanied Lagskha had been in the creek bottom since his
order. It was they who after allowing them to drink,
carefully led the lama's yaks away into a hidden hollow.
All of this movement was barely out of sight behind the
banks of the small stream.

Another advantage was that ever since the Hart Expedition arrived there had been a constant movement around
the tents, into the meadows, back and forth from the
tents to the Inn. The attention of the soldiers on guard
would be naturally drawn to the Hart Expedition. First,
their activities, clothing, tents and all connected with
them were strange, even extraordinary by the standards of
Chu's troops. They would be distracted and exactly which

horses and yaks belonged to the scientists and their por-
ters, which belonged to Lagskha, Mallory, and the Go-
logs, and which were the property of the Inn would be
hard to determine.

The guards would also be watching the women. Renata
and Mary Penfield wore clothing strange to them. Brikhuti
wore the clothing of a Tibetan woman traveling, and that,
too, they had seen many times. It might work, and it
might forestall a fire fight.

Marshal Chu, encamped near the head of the valley,
emerged from his tent from time to time to watch the activity. All was normal. Possibly, he reflected, they were
trying to put him off guard before an attempted escape
under cover of darkness. More likely they had simply
given up.

"Could it be anything else?" Colonel Shih was a young
officer, but very stiff, very correct, very much a party
man. "How could they escape?"

Marshal Chu glanced at him, his expression bland. "Do
not under-estimate the imagination. A man of imagination
is a dangerous antagonist."

"The American? Bah! He is as weak and degenerate as
all of them! Why else would he be in such a place, living
with animals?"

"Animals who can fight, Colonel. Our armies have been
defeated in their country, many times. Or when they go
into that country they find nothing . . . simply nothing
at all!"

In the late morning Marty Wells rode up to the tent.
Chu stepped outside at the sound of the horse's hoofs.
"Sir? Mr. Hart presents his compliments and wishes you,
and any of your officers who are free, to join him for
lunch."

"Yes, of course. You may tell him we will be there."

Wells lifted a hand, and turning his horse rode away.
"You are going?" Shih said, lifting an eyebrow.

"I am going," Chu said quietly, "and so are you. It
is your duty," he said, "to know the enemy. At his meals
he is often off guard. You will come with us, Colonel."

Mallory was pleased. The invitation could have come
at no better time. Dinner, for example, would have been
fatal. Lunch gave them a chance to appear casual, unwor-
ried, unhurried.

Lagskha was seated on Hart's right, Chu opposite him.
Brikhuti was seated beside Chu, Renata beside the lama.
Dr. Bernard and Dr. Penfield faced each other across the
table, and Mallory was seated opposite Mary Penfield with
Lewis, Shih and Wells close by. Hank Carpenter sat at the
foot of the table.

Mary Penfield looked across the table at Mallory.
"There are stories about you, Mr. Mallory. When we were
working with the clinic in Mussoorie I heard things that
sounded like pure fantasy."

"No doubt they were," he said, "or perhaps some of
them were actually about my father."

"You must know a great deal about this part of
China."

"Ten years is nothing, even ten years in the saddle.
The country is too big, too diverse."

"We are building roads," Colonel Shih said. "Soon
there will be good roads everywhere. Soon the entire
country will be working as one toward the great goal of
communism. It will be an example to all but especially
you in the imperialist West."

"I'm sure everyone appreciates these advances," Mallory said. "Lucky for you that China's enormous size has

been achieved through something other than imperialism.
How astonishing, when one recalls that China was once
only a tiny nation on the Yellow River."

He turned to Mary Penfield. "Are you interested in
poetry, Mrs. Penfield? The Chinese poets are as eloquent
as their historians. Some time you must read 'The Chari-
ots Go Forth' by Tu Fu. It is very informative. There was
an emperor of China named Wu-ti, also. A very interesting
man. His armies spent a great deal of time in the Tarim
Basin protecting trade routes . . . or something."

"That is part of China," Shih said stiffly.

"Well, perhaps you are riding on the coat-tails of
previous empires. Still, perhaps they should be able to
choose independence."

Mallory looked away and taking up his cup said, "By
the way, Mrs. Penfield, where was your home in the
States?"

Shih had started to speak but the abrupt change of
direction stopped him.

For several minutes they talked of Texas, California
and New York, but Mallory's attention was only half present. He was picking up the discussion between Hart and
Chu.

The food was good, and he ate as he listened. Colonel
Shih seemed to have nothing more to say to him and Mary
Penfield talked, lightly and easily, of many things. She
was a charming woman and she knew how to make conversation.

"You speak Chinese, Mr. Mallory. Did you learn it
here?"

"In Montana. When I heard my father was lost over
China when his plane crashed, I told myself someday I
would come here.

"There was a small town near our ranch and there was
a Chinese restaurant there. I used to drop in quite
often, drink coffee, and get them to tell me about China.

Most of the Chinese in that part of America are from Canton or its environs. But this family spoke Mandarin. They offered to teach me.

"In the winter I delivered newspapers in the town, and I started dropping in every night after I'd finished my paper route. By the time I was twelve, about two years from the time I started, I could speak enough to be understood. Because of that, the Army put me in a crash course for officers headed for Korea."

"Did you know anything about this part of China?" she asked.

"I'm afraid I got over into Mr. Wells's field. I found some of the best books were written by plant-hunters. I also read Ssu-ma ch'ien's history, The Art of War, and some of the Chinese novels, The Dream of the Red Chamber, The Scholars, and of course, The Romance of the Three Kingdoms."

Chu glanced down the table. "And Chin P'ing Mei?"

Mallory smiled. "Yes, that, too."

He took his time eating and with his coffee, yet inwardly he was eager to be out and going. From time to time through the tent door he saw somebody cross the grass walking toward the creek. Most of the Khambas and many of his own men would be ready.

Yet the most important, the most noticeable ones were trapped here keeping up the illusion. He must not be the first to leave the table, yet Lagskha could do that . . . he had his own ritual of living and none of those at the table were familiar enough with his life to guess what was his custom or was not.

A slow half hour went by, with talk that moved from archaeology to Tibet to China proper. "The Tsinling Mountains," Marshal Chu suggested, "are the least explored area in China."

"Where are they exactly?" Marty Wells asked.

"In Shensi, near the border of Kansu. Very rugged.

Once, as a boy, after the Long March, I had occasion to
be in that area. Even the people who live nearby know
little of them."

At last Lagskha excused himself, and rising from the
table, started back for the Inn, accompanied by his sister. Shih, obviously impatient with socializing, also
arose and left, accompanied by Chu's aide. Chu lingered,
dawdling over his coffee.

Mallory refilled his cup, sitting back in his chair
as if time were the least important of all things. Yet
even now he knew his men would be moving the stock away;
only the Khambas would be waiting in the hollow near the
stream for the lama to join them.

It was growing darker, clouding over a little. He
glanced outside. "Looks like rain," he commented.

"This place you mentioned," Dr. Bernard said suddenly, ". . . could you guide us to it?"

Mallory chuckled. "Now, Doctor, our very civilized
meeting here at this table is one thing but that is quite
another. I'd be glad to show you . . . some time.

"You see," he explained, "when the Incarnation an-
nounces his decision, the good Marshal will no longer
have to restrain himself. A party can escort Lagskha
toward Chamdo and the Marshal will still have a considerable number of soldiers left. I think he will make a move
to detain us, to restrain our movements. He would like to
have me for a prisoner . . . or dead . . . and the same
for those men with me.

"Marshal Chu is a gentleman, and conducts himself as
such, but he is also a soldier. In his place I would do
as he will do. I am afraid, Doctor, that you and your
friends are about to see what war is like. It will be a
small war, but the Go-log do not surrender and neither
shall I.

"None of us wish to endanger the Incarnation but when
he is safely off the stage we all know what will happen

here. I suggest you all keep down and out of sight. A
bullet doesn't care who it hits."

"I am sure you exaggerate," Penfield protested.

"Major Mallory could surrender," Chu suggested. "If
he would surrender, I do not think his Go-log would last
long."

Mallory chuckled. "You know I'll not surrender, Marshal, and I shall not suggest that you do so."

"I?" The Marshal was suddenly wary.

Mallory smiled. "Your position is but little better
than mine. Even, if I may say so, a little worse. You
have a career at stake. I do not.

"The trail out there, it runs two ways, north to the
Magnung Chu, and south along that stream to the Yalung
River.

"Now if the Marshal takes Lagskha and retires without
any fanfare, he has every chance of making it back to his
headquarters at Chamdo. But supposing he decides to move
against me?

"My men are few, but they are very tough men. They
are well-armed and determined . . . even eager. The Marshal is going to have to pursue us down the trail your
expedition came up. It is a very difficult trail, ideal
for a guerrilla action.

"I am sure as distinguished an officer as Marshal
Chu, and as high in the ranks of the followers of Mao, is
familiar with his maxims for guerrilla war? I say 'his'
advisedly, for the principles have been known and used
for years.

"Now I suspect the Marshal is an excellent chess-
player. As he knows there is a point in every game where
further moves are useless . . . but there is always another game. Especially when he has gotten what he came
for, the Incarnation. He can return to headquarters a
success or with a devastated command and little to show
for it beyond what he would have anyway."

"You are right, Mallory. There is always another
game. My only regret is that you are not Chinese, Major
Mallory, we have so many ideas in common."

He got to his feet. "Mallory, you pleased me very
much a little earlier when you mentioned Tu Fu's poem.
Colonel Shih is a very efficient man, a very excellent
soldier, but he should also paint . . . or write poetry.

"Did you know, Mr. Hart, that many of our greatest
military men were poets? I understand that your own General Patton was also. That he wrote at least two volumes
of poetry. It develops the imagination, opens the avenues
of thought.

"I particularly like that part of the poem that is
something like this: 'Today they send me again to the
wars, Back to the north frontier, By whose gray towers
our blood has flowed In a red tide, like the sea--And
will flow again, for Wu Huang Ti is resolved to rule the
world.'"

Chu paused at the opening of the tent. "I will return
in the morning for our lama's decision and I will watch
closely by night." He walked swiftly away, and Bernard
looked after him. "An interesting man," he said, "a very
interesting man."

"And a dangerous one," Mallory said. "Anyone who
under-rates him is a fool."

"What do think he will do?" Renata asked.

Mallory shrugged. "Probably he will do the unexpected. He might gracefully pull out, taking the lama
with him, knowing, as I suggested, that there is always
another day. He is shrewd enough to retreat from an un-
tenable position.

"What is even more likely is that he will seem to re-
tire, but will actually detach a portion of his men to
destroy us." Mallory smiled then. "And he will probably
offer Colonel Shih the command."

CHAPTER 10

Mallory paused on the grass, glancing toward the Inn.
All was quiet.

Lagskha and Brikhuti were strolling together upon the
meadow, Brikhuti pausing from time to time to pick a
flower from the thick grass.

Mallory hesitated a moment longer, then strolled
after them. In the distance thunder rolled, and Lagskha
turned as if to start back for the Inn, but his sister
tugged at his sleeve.

It was as beautiful a bit of impromptu acting as Mallory had seen, and he smiled as he walked, yet his mouth
was dry, his heart was beating heavily. If they were
stopped now--

But nobody did stop them and the rain that might have
ended their little performance held off. They paused on
the bank of the stream, then walked down into it.

Mallory, who had gained on them, followed.

The moment they were hidden below the bank, which was
scarcely high enough to conceal them, both started to
run.

Lagskha gathered up his robe and ran well. They
paused to catch their breath, and Mallory over-took them.
"It's now or never," he said. "The horses are right
ahead!"

Six Go-log awaited them with their horses. They all
rode into the water and swiftly along the creek bed. But
Mallory knew that despite all the stories one read, running water would not immediately wipe out the tracks of
horses or men. The water was crystal clear and the inden-
tations of the hoof tracks would remain an hour or more.

For a half mile they followed the stream, then Mallory led them out at a low cut where formerly another

stream had joined this one. The surface was rock, and
they rode up the small draw and into the mountains.

The ancient stream had cut down to bed-rock, leaving
no soil. Here and there leaves had fallen, and there was
much scattered debris of rock, small slides, dead
branches. Here they paused a moment to listen.

"Nothing yet," he said, at last. "Now follow me." The
banks of the stream were high, and here and there an old
slide permitted a climb up the steep, tree-clad hill.

Turning his horse suddenly, Mallory rode up the bank,
and ducking his head under arching rhododendrons, disappeared. They all followed.

"Keep on along the trail," he said. "You'll catch up
with the yaks soon." Dismounting, he walked back. The
horses' hoofs had torn the earth of the slide, so using a
branch he loosened more dirt from the slope above and allowed it to cascade down to the water's edge.

The dim trail was heavily shadowed by the trees and
brush. Riding swiftly, Mallory over-took the convoy and
with Brikhuti beside him, rode swiftly ahead. Gomba
looked at him curiously. "It is not old," he said, "old,
but not yet that old."

"No." He pointed back down the way they had come.
"Hundreds of years ago a slide washed down there, wiping
out the road, turning the stream. This is a cut-off. You
will see."

He led the way. There were no tracks on the trail.
The canyon was narrow, thickly covered with trees, and
the trail would be invisible from the sky. Only one could
go at a time, except in rare places where two might ride.

The trail dipped down between two massive boulders
allowing scarcely room for passage. The trail kept on,
but Mallory, consulting notes he kept in an inner pocket,
turned sharply right and scrambled up a rocky trail that
showed no evidence of passage. Riders and yaks followed
him.

Not even a mountain goat can excel the yak as a climber. Huge, long-haired and horned, but sure-footed, the yaks with their packs followed him.

Soon it began to rain. At first a few big scattered drops, then a down-pour.

From time to time through breaks in the trees they could see towering snow- and ice-covered peaks looming before them in a gigantic wall. "We aren't going over that?" Brikhuti exclaimed.

"Through it," Mallory said, "but not yet."

They emerged from the trees and before them lay slopes covered with alpine grasses and flowers. More and more their movement made breathing a conscious action. "We'll walk now. This altitude is too much, even for these horses."

The rain fell steadily then turned to snow, gathering in a thin white sheet over the rocks. For a little way he held to his upward course, then turned sharply right and eastward along the flank of the mountains.

Vast drums of thunder rolled in the canyons, and lightning leaped from peak to peak. By the time darkness began to close in they had traveled nine miles since leaving the Valley of Pleasant Winds.

Mallory led them down into the trees and into a hollow among some rocks. There were wind-hollowed caves there, not deep, but shelter of a sort. "We'll camp here."

Lagskha turned in his saddle, concerned, "It is soon to stop, if it is for me or my sister--"

"We can't see in the dark. I'm guessing the trail from here on is a nightmare."

"You mean this one hasn't been?" Brikhuti looked down at the fire a Go-log was kindling. "How much of this do we have?"

"Weeks, perhaps months. It is a long way to India."

They sat together in the shallow cave and watched the

gray curtain of rain slanting down, metallic and cold.
Mallory held the bowl of tea in his hands, enjoying the
warmth. When he had first come to Tibet he had been astonished at the capacity the Tibetans had for tea, drinking as many as thirty bowls in a day . . . and often even
more.

A Go-log came in, a slender, powerful man in a
weather-darkened sheepskin coat. The man spoke rapidly.

Mallory said, "This man says there is a place nearby
where one can see the trail far, far below. Would you
like to come?"

The caves where they had taken shelter were just
below timberline, and leaving them they climbed up between some boulders to the alpine meadows which slanted
away for miles upon miles toward the south, the icy gray
peaks and ridges rearing proudly up on their left.

A few dwarfish, wind-barbered trees straggled up the
slope, then even these disappeared. They walked on, following their guide for nearly a hundred yards, then went
out on a rain-wet rock, and their eyes followed the Go-
log's pointing finger.

Far below, caught in a momentary island of slanting
sunlight, they could see the shine of the rain-wet inn
roof, the white of the tents, and the distant sheen of
the stream in the meadow.

"Do you think they have found our trail?"

Mallory had been wondering about that. "I don't know,
but they would have to look. The dry creek bed up which
we came is over-lapped by the mountain. From the valley
one cannot even see that an opening exists. They would
have to ride up the bed of the stream, as we did."

He waved a hand. "All of this is unexplored country.
Tomorrow morning we will be riding the old trail, but
don't expect much. So far as anyone knows it hasn't been
traveled in centuries.

"I said earlier that we would go through those moun-

tains. You see, far ahead of us this range jogs somewhat,
and in that jog there is a saddle. The old trail went
over that saddle and follows down the back side."

Mallory went out into the night and moved away from
the small sounds of their camp. Despite his doubt that
Chu had so quickly located their line of flight, he dared
not risk the possibility that the contrary was true.

It was very dark, and in the silence of the mountains
he could hear only the whisper of the rain. He walked
among the horses, talking to them gently. He was uneasy.
Brikhuti's presence was distracting, and now, if ever in
his life, he needed to concentrate. He was under no illusions as to what lay before them. Aside from the pursuit
which would soon be augmented by aircraft there were all
the risks of travel in the high country. At this altitude
even their rough mountain horses must be handled with
care. He had seen passes but little higher than this
marked with the bones of animals that had died in the
crossing.

The trails would be bad. Never very good, they had
been untraveled in many years, and undoubtedly other ways
must occasionally be found or repairs made. Yet within a
few days their only way would lead them down from the
peaks. They must cross the Yalung river, and it would be
necessary to get additional horses at Dzogchen Gompa, one
of the largest monasteries in this part of Tibet.

Without a doubt Marshal Chu would anticipate both the
crossing of the river and the possibility they must pass
by Dzogchen Gompa. He would have troops at both places,
or spies, at least. And they could expect troops eventually.

On the other hand the grape-vine would probably alert
the monks at Dzogchen to the fact that the Incarnation
would be coming their way. With luck they would be ready
to help.

Both the Incarnation and his sister seemed strong,

and so they must be. The march ahead was to be desperate
and grueling.

When at last he returned to the caves, all were
asleep. He added a few heavier sticks to the small fire,
drank one more bowl of tea, and thought longingly of the
coffee enjoyed with Hart's expedition. He also thought of
Renata, the American girl. She was very lovely . . .
well, no matter. They had little use for him. To them he
was a renegade, a drifter whom they were better off without.

The night wind moaned in the trees, and slow drops
fell from the drooping branches of the evergreens. He
finished his tea and went to his bed, rolling up in a
couple of yak hides to sleep until morning.

A time or two he awakened, as always, to listen to
the night, but there was only the whisper of rain, the
falling of an occasional drop into the coals, and a faint
stirring among the horses or yaks. Again he slept.

CHAPTER 11

Renata Bernard was awakened suddenly by a thunder of
hoofs and angry shouts. The canvas flap of her tent was
ripped open and a soldier rushed in. She got to her feet
and, prodded by a rifle, was driven to the main tent.

Hart was already there, his face white with anger.
Dr. Bernard stumbled in, a cut over one eye, and then
Marty Wells. Of them all, only Hank Carpenter and Roy
Lewis seemed calm.

In the other tents there was shouting and confusion.
Horses raced by, and then Colonel Shih entered the tent.

"Where are they?" he shouted.

"Where are who?" Hart's manner was icy.

"The lama!" Shih shouted again. "Where have you hidden him? Where is Mallory?"

"I assure you," Hart said calmly, "I have no idea what you are talking about. I have seen none of them since lunch . . . when you were present as well."

"Lies! Lies! You are all together in this!"

"What has happened?" Hart asked. "If you could tell us then we might be able to help you."

"You know what happened!" Shih's tone was ugly. "They are gone. Gone!"

"How can that be?" Dr. Penfield said. "Haven't you guards at both ends of the valley?"

"They saw nothing," Shih said irritably. "They heard nothing. They are fools."

"As I explained to the Marshal," Hart said coolly, "their activities are no concern of ours. It merely happened that they arrived here at the same time we did. We entertained them, as we did you."

"We will find them," Shih threatened, "and in the meantime you may all consider yourselves under arrest."

"I am afraid that Chou En-lai will not appreciate this," Hart said calmly. "I shall have to notify him of my treatment."

Colonel Shih turned very slowly, measuring Gunther Hart with a careful glance. "Do you know Chou En-lai?"

"Of course. We are good friends. He was the one who arranged for our permission to enter this part of China."

"I see."

The change in manner was subtle, but it was there. The anger went from his tone, and Hart, who could see the obsequiousness in a man quicker than most, recognized the tone for what it was.

"Chou En-lai and I were friends in Paris," Gunther Hart said quietly, "and I have been able to be of some small aid to him from time to time. You know," he sug-

gested, "how it is. One man can often help another in
reaching the seats of power. There were occasionally people whom Chou wished to talk to off the record. I was in
a position to arrange this.

"When all communication is through military or political channels a very competent man can often be prevented
from doing those things he is best able to do. Take yourself, for example," Hart said suavely. "I doubt if the
reports of your efficiency and skill always reach the
ears of your superiors."

He paused. "I am always glad to recommend those who
help me. And I have been a good friend to the People's
Republic of China." He smiled his beautiful smile. "If it
were not so, would they permit me to come here?"

"I am ordered to find the man Mallory and the monk."

"Of course. I hope you do find him, but I assure you
we have no knowledge of his whereabouts. As you may have
heard, Major Mallory and I were not friendly."

"I have been ordered," Colonel Shih said, "to place
you under arrest. You are not to attempt to leave this
valley. These are my orders, do you understand?"

"Of course, Colonel Shih, and we shall do our best to
obey. When you again see Marshal Chu I wish you would
give him my respects and suggest that I should like to
talk to him. In the meanwhile, the best of luck to you.
We must talk again, Colonel, but if there is anything I
can do to help, would you tell me? I would take it as a
favor."

When the Colonel departed, Hart suggested, "My advice
would be for us all to dress, as promptly as possible."

"But how could he have escaped?" Carpenter protested.
"There is no other way out!"

"For a clever man, there might be--also for a man who
knows much of the history of this region. My friends, I
have erred. I should have cultivated the acquaintance of
this man Mallory. I think he knew the very thing I wished

to know . . . I had some inkling of his knowledge
but . . . well, there simply wasn't time."

When they were back in their tent Mary Penfield said,
"Gunther Hart isn't the only one to miss their chance."

"What do you mean by that?"

"If I'd been a single woman I'd never let the most
exciting man I ever saw slip through my fingers. And now
look what's happened. He's off on a long trek through the
mountains with another woman."

"I had not thought of him in that way," Renata said
primly.

"You're a liar, Nata," Mary said cheerfully, "or woe-
fully under-sexed. Any red-blooded woman who could look
at that man . . . well, honey, had I been your age I'd
have moved in . . . fast."

"I wonder how they got away?"

"Talk to Jalu about it . . . you know, the herdsman.
The Doctor and I were talking to him last night . . . he
knows a thousand stories about your man Mallory. Jalu
says he can walk over mountains . . . or through them. He
says this is enchanted country. Most outsiders won't even
think of coming here, and as far as going back into the
Chala shan, forget it."

Renata dressed hurriedly and met the others outside.
Marty was waiting for her, Roy Lewis beside him. "Roy
suggests we not stray away today and I think he's got
something, although I do want to work the banks of the
creek."

"I'll come with you."

"Just don't get out of sight," Lewis warned. "Just
because Hart soft-soaped the Colonel doesn't mean we're
off the hook."

"I'm armed," Marty said. And Renata glanced at him,
surprised.

"Don't use it or even show it unless there's no other
way," Lewis warned. "No matter what Hart says or does,

Chu is in command here. He can issue any kind of a report
he wants and spin any kind of a story. He could shoot the
lot of us and merely say we were trying to stir up a
counter revolution."

Marty Wells and Renata walked toward the stream. The
rain of the previous night had ceased but lowering clouds
shrouded the peaks. They walked along the banks of the
stream but the plants he saw were ones he had previously
collected or which were well known . . . he would note
them in his journal for the trip but there was no need to
collect.

They had almost reached the mountain wall when Marty
stopped. What he saw was an odd color on a white-flowered
gentian, and a closer look showed him the petal had been
bruised. He squatted on his heels, looking carefully
around.

The growth along the opposite bank was willow and
birch; farther back the birch was mixed with juniper. Two
kinds of willow . . . he got up and moved along the bank.

Renata, who was picking flowers, turned to watch.
"Found something unusual?"

"It isn't the plant," he said, and the tone of his
voice brought her to him.

"What is it, Marty?"

He had picked the bruised flower. "This," he said.

"It's been stepped on or something."

"Exactly . . . by whom?" He walked along the bank and
discovered a place where a little gravel had been caved
off. He looked at it, then along the stream toward the
mountain. "Well, I'll be damned!"

"What is it?"

"Don't you see? There's a break in the mountain,
right where the stream curves."

"I'm not sure . . . it may be the way the light
falls."

"No, there's a break. This near wall over-laps the
other and from a few hundred yards you can hardly see it.
I'll bet there's a water-course there . . . run-off from
the mountain. And that's how they got away!"

"Marty? Don't tell anybody."

He looked at her. "Glad you feel that way. I wasn't
going to." He glanced at it again. "That must be the old
route they were speaking of."

"We'd better start back--they'll come looking for
us."

When they had walked back a little way Marty said,
"Nata, the way I see it, let the lama make up his own
mind. If he wants to stay, he will. If he wants to go, it
should be his choice."

"Did you ever talk to him about music? Brikhuti said
she brought him a lot of records--jazz, swing, rock and
roll . . . even the classics. But he really likes the
modern stuff."

"Sure. We talked about an hour the other night. What
he really likes is country-western. I was telling him
about Johnny Cash."

They were silent. The night had become suddenly dark
with the heavy clouds over the tight little valley. A
light glowed through the canvas of the tent Lewis shared
with Wells, and they could see him moving about. Then another man entered the tent. Marty hesitated . . . the
head-gear the newcomer wore looked like the ear-flaps the
Khambas wore.

A Khamba visiting Lewis? It was unlikely. So far as
Wells knew, none of them spoke English.

Gunther Hart was standing outside when they approached, and he glanced from one to the other, no pleasure on his face. "A moment," he said, "before you go in."

They paused. The man in conversation with Hart was
Dr. Penfield. "In the old stories," Hart said, "they

called it a council of war. Keep yourselves prepared for
a quick move. We may be forced to take a page from Mallory's book."

"What has happened?"

"Nothing . . . yet. I shall speak to Marshal Chu tomorrow and request permission to go forward. He will tell
me I cannot go forward and so we will go back."

"Back?"

Gunther Hart smiled. "At least as far as that monastery we passed by on the way in. We will go into the
hills from there, but I want no talk of this.

"I believe Chu wishes to be rid of us, and he will
be, but not by our leaving the country. Once on the hill
trail you shall study and research to your heart's desire."

He looked at Renata. "Did Mallory give you any idea
which direction he was taking? Did he speak of a way
out?"

"No . . . no, he didn't. Actually, I talked to him
very little."

Mary Penfield was combing her hair before Renata's
mirror. "It's better than mine. Do you mind? Your uncle
was working in the main tent, so I took the opportunity."

"Come any time." Renata sat down, her hat in her
hand. She should be doing the work her uncle was doing
for himself, but she had been unable to settle down to
anything. And now they might move again, at any moment.

"I'm worried," she said suddenly. "Sometimes I wish
we had listened to Mallory. Gunther is conniving to use
Colonel Shih to circumvent Marshal Chu in some way. I
don't like it."

"Neither do I. Shih isn't shrewd enough to match wits
with Chu and neither is Gunther. Well, we're here. All we
can do now is sing the song the way the notes read."

Dinner was a silent meal. Gunther Hart had little to

say, eating and retiring to his own tent to dictate to
Hank Carpenter.

Lewis and Wells stayed on in the main tent. Of them
all, Bernard was the only one excited. "I've been checking the Inn . . . you know, Mallory made some comments
about the age of it and he was right.

"There's a part of the wall on the far side . . .
a whole corner, in fact, that is very, very old. But the
stones themselves are even older. I can just make out
some inscriptions . . . no language I could recognize,
but I'm sure the inscription was turned on its side.

"Obviously, that stone was taken from some older site
to be used in this building. The place is a patchwork . . . a regular cross-word puzzle of a building, and
I never saw so much material from different periods put
together into one structure.

"Back about two hundred yards behind the Inn there's
an old stone water-trough they use for washing
clothes . . . not too often, I'm afraid.

"It stands on the edge of a tilted stone platform,
tilted by some upheaval in the earth, I imagine. A
shrine, perhaps, or a part of a fort or castle such as
the ones mentioned by Mallory."

They sat over their coffee and talked until nearly
midnight, discussing mutual problems and points at which
their various disciplines might be of service to one another.

"I never thought of it as anything but an exploration," Bernard said. "There's been no serious work undertaken in this area. Not even a good canvass that I'm
aware of. I have no doubt there were trade routes of a
sort . . . even the American Indians had them . . . but
not to the extent Mallory implies."

He smiled suddenly, a little embarrassed. "You know,
a good many years ago . . . oh, twenty-five, perhaps

thirty years ago, I stumbled on a translation of a book
by a man who claimed to know something about the Tantric
beliefs. It was a wild, unbelievable sort of account,
purporting to be the truth.

"He told of the track, route or trail, whatever you
wish to call it, that could be followed only by those of
particular courage or virtue, a route beset with dangers
. . . all manner of evil . . . but which led to ancient
monasteries where the old secret knowledge was still
studied by people who came there from the ends of the
earth . . . chosen people.

"Oh, it was a ridiculous story but I loved it. I had
less discrimination then, and that book was something
right out of Rider-Haggard or Pierre Benoit."

He stood up. "It is late. I think I shall be off to
bed."

Lewis stopped him. "Doctor? Who wrote that book?"

Bernard paused, frowning. "You know, I've been trying
to remember. It has simply escaped me."

He shrugged into his coat. "You know how it is when
one is young. The imagination is there and anything is
possible. It was my dream then . . . I really think it
was what got me started in archaeology . . . it was my
dream to follow that road. To find it, no matter how, and
follow it."

"You may yet, Doctor Bernard." It was Gunther Hart
standing in the opening of the tent. "You may yet, indeed."

CHAPTER 12

Among the icy peaks and across the alpine uplands
there was silence. Only the soft hoof-falls of horse and
yak, only the creak of saddle-leather and occasionally

the moan of the wind. Mallory rode ahead, his rifle at
hand. Occasionally he looked back. There was nothing. But
he knew they were not alone, for no matter what else was
back there, his Go-logs would be following, the band that
he left in the hills when he went down into the Valley of
Pleasant Winds. They would follow and they would also
form a rear guard, maintaining a moving ambush for any
who pressed too closely.

The travelers talked little, for the silence about
them bred silence within. Something seemed to listen . . .
and they listened in turn.

Now, from time to time, they found artifacts. An ancient fire circle, and once a magnificent axe-head shaped
from obsidian, beautifully worked and polished. And here
and there the trail, brief sections of it that even the
snow, ice and wind of these altitudes could not erase.

"How high are we?" Brikhuti asked, during one pause
for rest.

They were almost two miles ahead of the slowly plodding caravan. The yak moves at a speed of a camel, about
two and a half miles per hour, when on long treks. This
allowed time for Mallory or one of the Go-log, usually
Gomba, to ride on ahead and scout the trail.

He glanced around, then shrugged. "One can usually
judge from the plants, although I'm not Marty Wells. The
tree limit is about twelve thousand feet, and vegetation
of all kinds except moss and what they call cushion herbs
disappears at about sixteen thousand.

"I'd say we were around fourteen thousand, maybe a
little less." He pointed. "I've seen those red poppies
growing on up to almost fifteen thousand feet, and that
dark blue, purplish flower . . . I don't know what it
is . . . grows in the scree up to well over fifteen."

He indicated the raw-backed peaks above them. "They
probably aren't over sixteen thousand, but I'd be guessing. This is all new country to me."

They huddled together at night in a rock basin, a
kind of miniature cirque hollowed by a glacier. There was
water from melted snow, and timberline, with a straggling
growth of cedar lying not far below. Two of the Go-log
took a yak and went down into the juniper for fire-wood,
returning with ancient juniper logs and chunks from dead
growth, of which there was plenty.

They were settled down around their cooking fires
when suddenly there was a shout and the Go-log scattered
into the rocks, rifles in hand.

"What is it?" Mallory asked.

Gomba pointed across the alpine meadow. It was not
quite dark, and out of the shadows came riding at least
fifty horsemen.

They were obviously Go-log, wild, fierce horsemen
carrying thirty-foot lances as well as their rifles and
broad-swords. But they were not the men of his group;
this was a raiding party of the Ri-mang, largest of the
Go-log tribes, whose home-lands were east of the Chala
Shan and south of the Yellow River.

They drew up in a tight line, lances gripped in their
fists.

Mallory and Gomba walked out to meet them. Speaking
quickly, Mallory asked who they were and where they were
going.

Their leader looked down at him coldly. "We have
heard of you. You are the foreigner who rides with the
Khang-rgan."

Mallory had lived too long among the Go-log not to
know that when no one else was available, they fought
among themselves, and he had neither the time nor the men
to waste in fighting for sheer glory.

"I am that foreigner. I ride with my people on a far
mission. I escort the Lagskha-tsang and his sister, who
go to India."

The Go-log respected few things, feared nothing. They

were considered Buddhists, though religion sat lightly
upon their hard shoulders.

"Not far behind us," Mallory continued, "are fifty of
the Khang-rgan who will soon join us. And," he added, "in
the Valley of Pleasant Winds are six hundred soldiers of
China . . . unless they are following us."

Several of the Go-log had come down from the rocks.
They also knew the temper of their people, and each carried his machine pistol in plain sight. The weapons were
better than any the Ri-mang carried . . . at least, in
this group. Some had modern rifles, some only had old
match-locks.

"The soldiers of China have good rifles," Gomba suggested slyly.

"We will see," the chieftain said. He started to turn
the horse.

"One moment," Mallory lifted a hand. "How is the
road?"

For a long moment there was silence, and then the
chieftain said, "For some it is not bad, for others not
good. We did not travel far, coming up from Ch'ang-
ning-ha." A kind of ugly smile came to his lips. "Ride
carefully, Foreigner, this is not a road to be easily
traveled."

And then they were gone, a clatter of hoofs, one last
derisive yell, and the sound faded.

They returned to their fires then and Brikhuti handed
him a bowl of tea. "You know," she said, "I have lived
away from my people so much that I feel a stranger. So
much of this is new to me . . . or just barely remembered
from when I was a child.

"When I came to Europe there was so much I did not
understand, and I felt I must know something of their
history, so I began to read. I already knew English . . .
I had learned it at home from a teacher who had lived in
Sikkim.

"I read a book called When Knighthood Was in Flower, and then Ivanhoe. The ceremonies and the tourneys were so much like those in my country that I was astonished. Do you know our Festival of the Great Prayer? When there are horse races, foot races, wrestling and all? It was like that.

"My father was an official, so we had to send many horsemen to the festival . . . all in armor just like in the Middle Ages in Europe.

"I remember, my father often would ride himself to demonstrate. They would charge down a course at full gallop, shoot at a white disk hanging about five or six feet from the ground, then put the rifle away, and shoot at another target with a bow and arrow. Father was very good, and he rarely missed. There were booths where one could buy food or something to drink, and it was fun.

"The Go-logs have such games, too, but theirs are rough. My military training was pretty easy when compared to what they think is fun."

The fire dwindled. The Go-log had gone to sleep except for one man, who was on guard.

Mallory added a few sticks to the fire and walked out into the night. It was very still but the guard moved over to him as soon as he appeared.

"We are watched," he whispered. "There is something out there."

"What have you heard?"

"Nothing . . . only, I know. There is something there."

"Go get some tea. I will watch until you have finished."

Mallory moved out a little farther from camp. The moon was rising and the shoulder of the mountain lay in vast tilted ledges, grass-covered except here and there where they were exposed . . . great smooth, almost polished white ledges, shining in the night.

After awhile his eyes became accustomed to the night, and he could see more clearly. The moon lifted higher, and the great flat shoulder of the mountain stretched away into an infinity that ended in darkness. There were shadows here and there . . . had the Ri-mang come back? He doubted that.

Yet he felt it, too. There was something out there in the darkness. Behind him the camp was hidden. From here there was not even a glow of the fire, for they had chosen their site well. He put a hand into the folds of his shuba and touched the butt of his gun, to make sure it was ready to hand.

He waited . . . he thought he detected a sound, but it was not repeated. He strained his ears to hear, and all was quiet.

A yeti? He had heard the stories of the mountain creatures but he had never seen one. Many of the Go-log had . . . he no longer doubted the existence of something though he would not speculate on what it was. After all, who should know better? A scientist who spent a few weeks in the mountains? Or the people who lived there?

There had been a time when he spent nearly a year in the desert without ever seeing a rattler. Of course, he knew they were there and the Indians had told him so . . . then, on his last day, he saw three. Yet anyone coming into that desert might have gone away and said there were no snakes because that person had not happened to see one.

The people of eastern Tibet had known forever of the giant panda, but it was not until about forty years ago that the first was seen by a white man.

He moved out into the night. If the yeti lived in the mountains there could be no better area than this . . . lonely as it was.

He heard and saw nothing. Like his guard, it was rather something that he felt. Something intangible,

elusive . . . yet perhaps it was simply the loneliness,
the emptiness, perhaps some primitive suspicion that
there ought to be something out there. Man had always
peopled his wilderness with shadows, werewolves, gnomes
and the ghosts of things departed.

Was thought only a mechanical function of the brain?
Or could it become, under proper guidance, a tangible
thing bringing tangible results by its very being? By
some force within itself?

He shook his head irritably; he was tired and he
wanted to sleep. He hadn't the capability of solving such
problems--he'd be lucky to avoid a bullet in the back.
Looking out over the moonlit wastes, he thought that the
Buddhists were right. Each instant lives only in that instant. Out there before him nothing could be in any two
successive minutes the same.

The Go-log returned, moving silently. "You have listened?"

"Do not sleep, my friend. We live in a world of darkness and enemies."

"I shall not."

Mallory pushed the charred ends of a few sticks into
the fire and loosened his clothes for sleep. There could
be no thought of undressing. Not upon this night.

The Ri-mang were gone . . . but what else remained?

Were the shadows in his own mind? Of his own creation?

He hunched his yak-skin about his ears. He would
think of that in the morning.

Only he knew he would not, for morning brought san-
ity, or at least freedom from the imagination which loved
to create monsters in the shadows.

He slept . . . and long after the moon had passed behind the mountains something came silently out of the
night and squatted by the fire, watching him.

CHAPTER 13

By daybreak they were moving again, Mallory in the
lead. Until now the ancient trail had been vague, often
broken, and sometimes faded out entirely. Far ahead he
could see the break in the line of the ridge that was the
pass toward which they were headed.

They rode across a vast slope of the most impossible
green. The alpine grass was thick with wildflowers, for
the ridge was high enough to catch a few extra rain
clouds . . . perhaps the last gathering of moisture before the great desiccated bowl of Central Asia.

Here and there the ice of winter had polished the
limestone ledges until they were smooth as glass and
white as marble. Overhead the sky was a dark blue and the
sun was warm.

From time to time they drew up to let the horses
breathe. Accustomed as they were to high altitudes, this
was higher still and the horses could suffer and die if
not handled with extreme care. The air was very clear and
sounds carried for great distances.

Brikhuti came up beside him. "Mallory, did you say
you had more men?"

"They are behind us. We will await them before we
cross the pass."

"You are not worried? I mean by what we might find on
the other side of the range?"

"Mountains do not worry me. People do. When I am sad
or in trouble, I always go to the mountains. We had a
poet in the United States named Robinson Jeffers, and he
said, 'When the cities lie at the monster's feet, there
are left the mountains.' I believe that."

He thought ahead to the river crossing. If only there
were another spot, some place not known or no longer

used. But an unknown crossing was unlikely in an area
where travel was thousands of years old. He checked his
notes and tried to recall the details of the map, closing
his eyes to bring the picture into focus. The river
crossing on the ancient and forgotten trail they traveled
had seemed to be at the same spot where the main trail
crossed, but was that true? Might there not be some older
or more difficult crossing that had fallen out of favor?

He was dreaming. The Go-log might know of such a
place. They often raided this area, and if anyone knew,
they would.

Lagskha-tsang rode up beside them. "This I like!" he
said with enthusiasm. "I envy the man with sheep! He
lives always among the high mountains!"

Brikhuti talked for awhile with her brother, in Tibetan. Mallory rode on ahead, swinging his horse this way
and that, checking every available place for tracks. Much
of their travel was over stone, where no tracks would be
left, but there was much also of grass and some spots of
soil. Yet he found no tracks.

Marmots whistled from the rocks nearby, and a kite
soared lazily overhead.

Tomorrow they would make the pass . . . and after
that?

In the Valley of Pleasant Winds, all was still. The
soldiers were gone and the way of departure was open, yet
Gunther Hart made no move to leave.

Today he had gone out alone, on horseback, refusing
company. Renata watched him go, watched him as she typed
her uncle's report on the Inn and the stone ruins behind it.

Hart circled around toward the gorge and rode along
its edge. Was he looking for something he expected to
find? The way taken by Mallory, for example? Or was he

looking for something he had known of before he came to
the valley?

Marty had gone into the hills searching for samples.
Roy Lewis was writing up his notes on the geology of the
region and her uncle was off across the valley, casting
back and forth to see if there were any other remains or
surface indications.

Renata had done a little work of her own. She alone
had come along with no definite project beyond that of
learning all she could of the myths, legends and mysteries of the Sino-Tibetan borderland. Hart had been pleased
at the thought and had promised her some rather spectacular results. Her own wish was simply to gather what information she could. She hoped to contribute something to
the origin of the Tibetan people through a study of those
myths she was seeking.

She had discovered that the easiest way to learn was
simply to ask, to ask anybody, everybody. One never knew
who possessed the information she needed and the idea
that such information could only be obtained from officials or scholars was mistaken.

To learn the plants, the animals, the geology or the
stories in an area, ask the man who lives there. Invari-
ably in each village or area there is one man who has
specialized in its history, or one man who is the storyteller.

In the Valley of Pleasant Winds she had talked a little with the inn-keeper, who was manifestly impatient
with the whole idea. He was worried about his unexpected
guests, about the Red soldiers, about Mallory and his Go-
logs. The old stories, he implied rather definitely, were
for women and children. Men had no time for such things.

But on the day that Mallory departed with Lagskha-
tsang, another man appeared in the valley.

He was a slender man, of indefinite age, yet obviously no longer young. His face was European rather than

Asiatic, but that was a quality she was accustomed to, for many of the Tocharis appeared Caucasian, as did many of the Lolos. The old man had sat alone on the k'ang, talking to no one, ignored by all. The inn-keeper avoided him. The old man seemed to have no place to go or at least no particular time in which to get there.

Now, as she turned to look for Hart, she failed to find him. Instead, she saw the old man coming toward her across the meadow from the Inn. He paused a short distance away, obviously listening to the sound of the typewriter. She spoke to him, and he smiled slightly. "It is a good sound," he said.

She was astonished. She had no idea the man spoke English, but she said, "I had not thought of it in that way. It does get the work done."

"Yes. Of course." He paused a moment. "The stylus was much slower."

In spite of herself, she laughed. "I should say it was. Thank Heaven, I don't have to do all this on clay tablets!"

"They had one advantage," he said quietly, "that your paper lacks. They lasted. They did not crumble away; the writing did not fade."

"You speak excellent English."

"No . . . not excellent. It is a language I acquired long ago, but seldom use." He gestured to the empty chair where her uncle had been sitting earlier in the day. "May I sit down?"

She was embarrassed. "Of course. Please do."

He seated himself and she typed on to the bottom of the page. As she was placing her carbons for another page he said, "I heard you asking about the old stories, the old legends. You are doing a paper on them?"

"If I can gather enough information. My uncle and I are working toward the same end from two different direc-

tions. We are interested in the earliest history of the
Sino-Tibetan borderlands."

"Ah, yes. It is a place of much history. Your uncle
is Dr. Bernard? The man who was studying the ruins of the
temple out back?"

"Temple or fort. He is not sure."

"Temple. The fort is further back and higher up. If
you would like I could show him."

"You are a Tibetan?"

He hesitated. "I have lived here many years, but I
was born in Swat." She typed briskly for a few moments
and he sat quietly, and then he said, "Mr. Hart looks for
something?"

She paused before replying. Was he a spy? She was
wary. Yet she felt drawn to the man, he was friendly . . .
but so would a spy be friendly.

"He leads our expedition," she said. "I believe he is
very interested in all our projects, and in China as
well."

"And Mallory?"

Again she paused, "We met him only briefly."

"A very unusual man. You know that some of the Go-log
believe him to be the incarnation of Kesar? The story is
that when he came among them he did everything better
than they. He rode their wildest horses, was an expert
with all manner of weapons. You should hear the stories."

They talked quietly, and of many things. Suddenly, an
idea occurred to her. "Would it be possible for you to
work for us? I mean, as a guide, adviser, interpreter?"

"Of course. If Mr. Hart is interested. It is a pleasure to use English again." He watched her typing. "I was
employed for a time by the British government as a car-
tographer."

He got to his feet, easily, gracefully. "I am called
Muhsin."

He walked back toward the Inn and Renata looked after him, very puzzled. It was a little too opportune, his sudden arrival, his knowledge of English, of history . . . where was he going? Who was he? And how did he happen to appear here just at this time?

His questions had been few, and discreet, yet she was unaccountably worried.

Suddenly she was aware of Hank Carpenter. "Who was that?"

She shrugged. "A traveler. He speaks excellent English."

"How odd . . . in such a place as this."

It was exactly what she thought but somehow she was annoyed. "Well, there is an inn here."

"What was he asking you?"

Renata adjusted her carbons. "Asking? He was interested in my uncle's researches. He offered to show him the site of a ruined fort. He was very considerate and helpful."

Carpenter walked away, and after awhile Gunther Hart rode up and dismounted at his tent, then he walked over to where she was seated.

"Renata, why didn't you tell me about the other trail out of the valley?"

"Trail?" She glanced up. "Oh, that? I wasn't sure it was a trail, and then if that was the way Mallory disappeared, I did not want to mention it when Chu was still here. In any event, I am not sure there is any trail, properly speaking."

He asked about Muhsin and she explained briefly, adding a bit more than she had told Carpenter. As she did, she realized she had liked the man.

"He could be useful to us," she volunteered, and then added, almost as an after-thought, "He knows a great deal about the old history. He offered to show Uncle Ralph where the ancient fort was."

Hart turned away as Carpenter approached. Before Hank could speak, Hart said, "That man . . . Muhsin. Hire him."

"But--!" Carpenter started to protest, then stopped. "Sir? He may be a spy."

Gunther Hart merely glanced at him. "And what do we have to fear if he is? He speaks English and he knows the region. Hire him."

Gunther Hart walked away without even glancing back, and Hank Carpenter stared after him. Renata, catching his expression, was amused.

CHAPTER 14

Twice in the past few days they had seen tracks, the tracks of one man, and he was traveling on foot. In each case after following the trail briefly he had come upon a flat surface of exposed rock, and after that, simply nothing. Mallory was tired and worried. Both were a result of the altitude, he was sure. He had seen men become irritable before when traveling in high altitudes and thin air.

The pass lay just before them. He looked up at the high saddle in the ridge with no enthusiasm. He had never climbed mountains just to be climbing, but always for what lay beyond. In this case it was unknown, supposedly unexplored country.

They camped before approaching the pass. Lamlung Pass, some fifteen or sixteen miles to the south, was over fifteen thousand feet. This one was higher.

Gomba came and squatted near him. "What about the horses?" Mallory asked.

Gomba shrugged. After awhile he said, "They are Golog horses, they will cross over."

They rode to the foot of the pass in the fading afternoon and bedded their yaks where the grass grew tall,
and their horses where a watch could be kept. A long wind
blew cold off the snow peaks, and westward beyond where
the Yarlung River flowed, there was another snow-crested
range. Beyond that in another far-off valley was the
Yang-tze-kiang, or as they called it here, the Dre Chu.

Mallory looked again at the saddle where no snow lay.
They would cross over tomorrow into a land as wild,
lonely and unknown as the craters of the moon.

A wild land lay before them and a wild land lay behind. In the fading light he looked again upon the hills.
Brikhuti came and sat nearby.

"Is that it? Is that the pass?"

"Yes."

He was thinking of her. Scarcely six weeks ago she
had been living in Europe.

"You like it, don't you?"

He looked at the pass. "Men come to places like this
for places like that. There's nobody waiting over there
with a cold drink, and there isn't any place a man could
take a hot shower. We may be riding into a little corner
of Hell, but it will be a new Hell and a place we've
never seen."

"I've forgotten so much. When I talk to my brother I
know I have changed; now it feels like I've stepped
across some boundary into another world." She looked up
at him. "What do you believe, Mallory?"

His eyes showed amusement. "If it is a god or gods
you are talking about, I live with them . . . or him.
There's no fit place in the world for a god these days
but right where we are, up here, among the high peaks.
Each meadow is a cathedral. A man who lives high and
lonely doesn't have to talk to God . . . they understand
one another."

"And what about death?"

"It's right here . . . right at one's elbow all the
time. Anybody who thinks otherwise is a fool. It may come
one way or it may come another, but it is never far
away . . . nor is it important.

"It's like moving picture film, you know. The still
pictures give the sensation of movement to the characters. Life is like that, and death the intervals between
pictures."

"Then you believe as we do? In reincarnation?"

"Voltaire said something to the effect that it would
be no more surprising to be born twice than once, that
all nature was resurrection."

"Have you thought any more about going home, Mallory?
I love the United States."

"So do I . . . but you yourself have found how difficult it is to return. As I understand it you've been away
at school most of twelve years . . . well, I've been away
ten.

"I can go back, but will I have come home? The sights
and sounds will be different than I remembered, the people will have grown older, settled into new patterns of
living, they will have relationships and memories that I
cannot share. I suppose after awhile one settles into the
routine again, but I am not sure I could.

"And I'd miss all this . . . the wild country. I'd
miss the unexpectedness of it, the finding of an old
trail, a ruined fort or shrine . . . the sudden coming
upon of some isolated village where they have no idea
there is a London or a New York, and care less."

He was watching the slope of the mountain near the
pass. Something had moved up there . . . the distance was
too great to make out what it was. A bear? Too high for a
leopard . . . even a snow leopard. Possibly a goat.

"Do you know Colorado?" she asked suddenly. "When at
first I grew very lonely I used to go there."

"To ski at Aspen?" His tone was ironic.

"Yes, that, too. But I loved it. It was like my own
country."

By daylight they were mounting the pass. Mallory led
the way, walking ahead of his horse. The wind was raw and
cold, the trail, if such it could be called, was narrow.
In many places there was scarcely room for a horse to move
and, in this altitude, they were having a bad time of it.

Mallory took two steps, then paused, and after the
time required for at least three steps, took two more.
His heart hammered, his head was light. The yaks plodded
along, heads down, unconcerned by the troubles of men and
horses. On the highest passes their handlers would open a
vein if they carried too heavy a load, reducing their
blood pressure.

A few flakes of snow fell and the top of the pass
seemed even farther away. In places the trail was almost
blocked by falls of granite, fractures had split the
granite into blocks and at the base of the cliff masses
of boulders had accumulated. Several times all the Go-log
had to come forward and help in rolling a boulder from
the path. Even they were breathing hard, sucking at the
thin air.

There was almost nothing in the way of vegetation as
they climbed higher. The rock looked gray and cold, here
and there were streaks of frozen snow, the snow which was
falling had turned to tiny particles of ice that stung
the exposed flesh.

The clouds thickened and the wind blew a gale down
the pass. Mallory leaned into the wind. Once he slipped
to his knees and staggered erect just as a lumbering yak
came abreast with Brikhuti clinging to its long hair.

The yak's pace on level ground is about two and a
half miles per hour; up hill and against the wind it was
less than a mile per hour. The snow thickened and began

to drift. Not far ahead they could see a long patch of frozen snow that extended diagonally across the pass.

The snow bank was an icy berm. Mallory stabbed at it with his wooden staff but it skidded off, making scarcely a scratch. Feeling his way through the blinding snow, he worked his way along the bank until he had almost reached the far wall of the pass. There it was lower, less than two feet deep and not over a dozen feet across.

Helping the Go-log they got the first yak started up. Its hoofs skidded, then fought for a foot-hold, and miraculously, they gripped into the ice and the yak scrambled, half-falling, over the snow bank. The others followed, each one churning the snow a little until the following horses had an easier path.

By the time they struggled to the top of the pass the wind was blowing a gale, and the pass itself, only a few hundred yards across, was swept clean. With ice crystals slicing at their cheeks, they fought their way over and started down the far side. Twice horses fell and had to be helped up, yet Lagskha-tsang walked steadily, head bowed into the storm, plodding along as well as the toughest of the Go-log.

The wind howled, lashing at them in fury, and nothing could be heard above its howling. Mallory, who was walking ahead, slipped and fell to his knees. Struggling against the wind he put his hand upon a boulder to push himself up.

His fingers gripped, felt, then he bent his head to peer through the snow. It was a shaped stone! Not a common boulder, but a stone shaped by men. He got to his feet, staring into the blinding snow.

At first he could see nothing, then during a momentary break in the blowing curtain he saw another tumbled block on the slide of talus beside and above the trail.

Through the snow he glimpsed a massive tower . . . a wall.

He caught the first yak and stopped it. The Go-log
came up beside him and he grasped the man's arm . . .
there was no way to make him hear above the storm . . .
he pointed at the wall, then at himself and again at the
wall. Then he motioned for the Go-log to stay.

The bank was steep and icy, but he climbed from rock
to rock until he found himself at the wall. It was massive, built of carefully cut stones but in various shapes,
all fitted neatly together. Feeling his way along the
wall, he came to the tower. Below it the cliff fell sheer
away, how far he could not determine. Turning he worked
his way back, beyond the point at which he had climbed,
and when he had followed the wall for sixty steps it
turned sharply. Before him was a massive gate, and inside
it an impressive courtyard. The floor of the court was
paved, and along the far side a series of stone buildings.

There was shelter here, from the wind. To go on in
this storm, along a trail steadily growing worse, might
mean the loss of both animals and men.

He retraced his steps to the gate, then followed a
trail that slanted down to the one upon which the caravan
waited. He came down almost abreast of one of the last
animals. The Go-log saw him through the snow and reached
for his broad-sword, then recognized him.

Catching his arm, Mallory pointed up the trail, and
the Go-log turned, leading his horse. Those behind him
followed, and Mallory struggled along the trail against
the blinding snow, turning each man and beast back toward
the roadway to the fort.

The wind ripped at his clothing, and when he turned
to face it, drove the breath right back in his throat.
Bowing his head he pushed on, up the steep bank to find
the fort. At last they were all within the shelter of the
walls. He loosened his collar and ear-flaps and looked
around.

What he had taken for a tower was actually a corner

of a flat-roofed building, several stories in height. The
building was a typical podrang, a fort built in a square
around an open court. What he had first seen was simply
the outer wall of the structure, which had long been
abandoned and was slowly going to ruin.

Gomba came to him, gesturing. He followed and the Go-
log led them into what must have been a vast hall. Part
of the roof had fallen in, and snow had drifted through
and frozen into ice, but it was still more sheltered
there. He noticed some of the long dried yak chips, or
argols, indicating that others had sheltered here at some
time.

He started toward them to kindle a fire when Brikhuti
caught Mallory's arm.

He stared. Firelight flickered on a stone wall down a
corridor. Motioning to the others to stay back, he walked
that way. Two of the Go-log, sensing a fight, were quick
to follow.

It was a square room. Once there had been wooden columns to hold up the roof; now they had fallen, but the
roof remained in place, scorning any need for pillars. At
one side of the room, in a crude fireplace built into the
floor, a fire was burning.

There was no one there. All was silent but for the
distant sounds of men and animals, the moan of the wind,
and an occasional crackle from the fire.

There were no packs, no men . . . only weird shadows,
dancing along the wall.

CHAPTER 15

Mallory looked at the fire, the fuel stacked neatly
nearby, and then his eyes slowly circled the room. Nothing could be more empty. And it was old, so very old.

"It is for you." He turned to Lagskha. "The fire is for you."

The Incarnation stared at the flames, then looked over at him. "Or for you, Mallory. Had you thought of that?"

Mallory shook his head, not knowing what to think. He dispatched two Go-log to search the compound and the surrounding area. As hospitable as the fire might be the mystery of it was a potential threat and he would rest better when he knew the answer.

They settled in. The howl of the wind was a remote thing, wild and lonely, but outside. When is comfort greater than when one sits within walls and listens to the wind outside? A wind that whines like a wild, feverish thing in a broken voice?

"We will stay throughout the storm," Mallory said. "I must see to the men, and the animals."

He went into the courtyard knowing the Go-log needed no seeing to. This place disturbed him. It was opportune, but it left him uneasy. He wandered through the freezing rooms, many still retaining their flat roofs, some lying open to the wind and snow, scattered with broken rock and ancient timbers. All were icy and still. And then in the snow of one of them he found a track, half a track, actually, of a large bare foot.

Brikhuti sat by the fire when he returned. Lagskha was bundled in yak robes and asleep.

"You should rest," he advised. "It has been a long day."

"Do you think of her?"

"Who?"

"Of the American girl."

"There is nothing of which to think. I do not know her; I'm unlikely to see her again. We have many other things to worry about."

"That is true but she was yours if you had reached
out. I could see it."

He shrugged. "Renata Bernard," he commented dryly,
"is a young lady of some importance in her world. She is
obviously well off. In the States I am nobody, just a
former soldier who worked on ranches."

"A man is what he wishes to be."

"You've lived in the States. You know how it is
there. It is a world of accomplishment, of achievement.
One is either doing something or has done something, and
even if he has done something he must be on the verge of
doing something else."

"Your country is changing. There are increases in
crime, and the rioting?"

"I haven't been home in a long time. But we Americans
love to exaggerate. We build up our problems enormously
and then argue over how to deal with the situation. There
has always been violence and turmoil . . . the Copperhead
riots during the Civil War period or what happened in Europe before the Second World War . . . or in 1848. If one
wants to fear there is always something to be afraid of,
and there are always people aching for a chance to run,
scream and tear their hair. Television and the newspapers
have given them a chance to wet their pants in public,
that's the only difference.

"And there's always been people ready to use that
fear to their own ends. The only thing we have to fear
is over-reaction, the people, some of them well meaning,
who think that in order to be against one thing they
must join its opposite. One doesn't have to become a
fascist to fight communism or a Communist to change
capitalism . . . in fact, it's vastly less convincing.
It's an over-reaction born of weakness. The strong, those
who don't need to be told who they are by others, stand
in the middle."

Outside the cold wind moaned, and even as he talked he was wondering about that fire. Was it built for them? Or for someone else who fled on their arrival?

"I wish whoever built this fire," he spoke loudly, "would share it with us. The night is cold."

Brikhuti said, "I think they have gone. I think they ran when we came to this place."

"Whoever they are, they are welcome. We are friends to all who would be friendly."

When Brikhuti had fallen asleep, Mallory replenished the fire from the argols stacked nearby, then went to the courtyard where the animals were huddled.

It was cold and bleak. Two of the Go-log in their conical hats, ear-flaps tied down against the cold, sat by a small fire. Glancing at him as he approached, they returned their attention to the brewing tea.

Outside the open gate the snow swirled. It was black out there, and a blizzard was blowing. At least, they would have called it that in Montana. He need not warn them to be alert, for a Go-log is always alert.

Returning to the building he wandered restlessly from room to room, most of them great, drafty halls. Despite the ruined condition of the building its pattern was obvious. Whatever else it might have been it had been a monastery as well. The outer yard where the animals rested and the Go-log were on watch had been a court of cells, for all about it were the tiny cubicles where monks had lived. The room where Brikhuti and Lagskha slept had been the refectory, or dining hall, with a steward's room adjoining.

Alongside of it was the kitchen, and beyond that the Hall of Assembly. Above and on a higher level of the mountain were other rooms, perhaps the place of residence of a higher lama, the abbot of the monastery or whatever.

The pattern was the usual one of monasteries in India, many had begun as monsoon-shelters for the wander-

ing almsmen, or bhikkhus. Although the bhikkhus lived on
donations from those who wished to contribute, they were
not classed with ordinary beggars. Their begging was the
outward manifestation of the fact that they had given up
the things of this world, that they had become homeless
wanderers. Yet with the coming of seasonal rains it was
no longer practical to wander. Roads became sloppy with
mud, rivers flooded the country around, and travel became
virtually impossible. It became the custom for the wandering also to find a rain-retreat or shelter during the
monsoon. Often they built such shelters themselves, and
occasionally they were the gift of a donor, a wealthy
merchant or prince.

Hence it became the custom when the monsoon approached for the wanderers to congregate at such a place
for the vassa period. Soon some of these wanderers ceased
to wander and became permanent residents and the monasteries as such had begun. This was the way it had begun
in India, although the custom was very old, and was ancient before the Buddha began his own wanderings.

The first teachers from India to Tibet had brought
the pattern of the monastery with them . . . or perhaps
it had, in a measure, preceded them. This building was
built much as many had been in India.

From the Hall of Assembly he glimpsed a narrow stair
mounting to a higher level. A moment he hesitated. He was
beginning to feel like sleeping, and further exploration
of the building could wait. Tomorrow the blizzard might
hold and they could not continue, and the building could
be explored then. Yet the temptation of the stair was too
great.

He had a flash-light, a bit of loot from his last
successful raid on a Chinese convoy, and another fifteen
minutes without sleep would do no harm.

Turning into the narrow opening he started up the
steps. Here and there stones had fallen from above, and

the steps were littered with fragments. Despite the fact
that two walls protected the stair, it was bitterly cold.

He climbed, and the steps became shorter and steeper.
Emerging from the stair-well he found himself on a roof
or terrace, and across it was a small, low-roofed house
or apartment. Leaning into the fierce wind, he struggled
across to the door, dropped a hand to the latch, and
lifted it. The door opened . . . the air was warm, but
the room was dark. The air smelled of smoke. Someone had
been here. Had his Go-log missed this place?

He searched the room with his flash-light, but it was
bare and empty. In the corner of the room was another
door, a closed door. Mallory hesitated, and then with a
tentative touch of his pistol-butt he crossed the floor
and opened the door.

On the far wall, dimly lighted by the red glow from
two charcoal braziers, was a part of a painted tapestry,
a thanka, showing the tree of great masters through whom
learning is transmitted. Before it, wearing a gown of
reddish purple trimmed with skin of the snow leopard, sat
a man in the lotus position.

"How do you do, Major Mallory? Will you sit down?"

Mallory hesitated, his eyes sweeping the room. There
were several bundles of carpet nearby, nothing more.
There was no one else in the room. It was warm, almost
hot. The air was a thin haze of scented smoke.

"We were wondering who made the fire down below; we
are grateful even if it was not for us." He seated himself on a pile of carpet. He could see the face of the
other man but dimly. He appeared to be a Tibetan.

Mallory glanced at the man's feet. He was not bare-
footed, but wearing red-leather boots soled with white
yak hide.

"You ride a strange trail."

"Yes."

"How do you know of this track? It is upon no map."

"Your Eminence is wise . . . but there is a map. I have seen it."

The man was surprised. Mallory could sense it rather than see it. He sat very still, waiting, and listening.

How did this man come to be here? No means of transportation had been seen, and the clothing the lama wore at this moment was not fit for travel in such weather. Incense or something in the close air dulled his senses. He shook his head--he was tired . . . that must be it.

Mallory waited and his ears searched for sound. There must be others. This man could not be here alone. He remained where he was. Let this stranger play his cards, then he would do what was needed.

"I did not know of such a map. It is very old?"

"Undoubtedly."

"This track is shown . . . is there more?"

"Much more."

How old was the man? Mallory found himself unable to shape an opinion. He might be thirty, forty . . . or seventy.

"I should like to see this map."

"It is far, far from here. In a secret place." Mallory hesitated, and then said what he was not at all sure was true, but he needed help, all the help he could get. "It was in the place of Kesar."

"Ah!"

He remained quiet for a moment, and then said, "Of course. It would be so." He raised his eyes and looked directly at Mallory. "Is it true then? Are you the incarnation of Kesar?"

"I am Mallory. If I am an incarnation of anything I am unaware of it."

"The lama you have with you? He is Lagskha-tsang?"

"Yes . . . and his sister."

"You have very few men."

"More will come. We were to rejoin at the pass." Mallory paused a moment. "The way ahead? Is it open?"

"It is difficult. A man may have traveled it from time to time. I do not believe animals have crossed it in many years."

"We must cross the Yulang. Is there another crossing than that near Dzogchen Gompa?"

"I have heard of it. Does not your map show it?"

"The map was very old. If another crossing was close by it might have been the only one known at the time."

"From the crossing, where will you go?"

Mallory smiled. "Where the Lord wills. We will follow the Way."

"Ah? You do not trust me?"

"I trust my sword. It was made by a smith who knew a true edge and a thin one. As for you, Your Eminence, there has not been time to trust your temper or your interests."

"What of the Americans? What is their purpose here?"

Mallory was surprised--the Hart Expedition was days behind them. This man had good information, information that might help him in the coming days. He explained briefly, and added, "I do not know Gunther Hart. He may have other reasons for coming. Hart and his people are not the only ones we left behind."

"Marshal Chu is very angry that Lagskha-tsang escaped him. He will have men sent to the crossing of the Dzogchen Gompa. There will be a fight, I think."

"We shall see."

"Marshal Chu has troops at Kantse. He has men at Paan, which we used to call Batang. There are men waiting at Chamdo. If you go west toward Chamdo, those forces at Paan will move north, and those at Kantse will come up behind you. The Marshal had planned to intercept the Incarnation, but did not plan on you. Now, however, he has radioed his troops and they know what to expect. You must cross rivers, and the tracks through the mountains are few. He has many soldiers."

"We will avoid them; if we cannot avoid them, we will fight, but when we fight the ground will be of our choosing." Mallory paused a moment. "I do not think the good Marshal's men will like the kind of country where they must go to capture us."

"The map you spoke of? In its secret place? It is in Go-log country?"

"Yes."

"Ah . . . well, I should like to have seen it." He stood up. "You will need sleep. What we can do will be done, Major Mallory, although I fear it will be all too little. It is up to you, and those who follow you . . . if it can be done, you will do it."

Mallory descended the steps through the howling wind and the blown snow. The man, lama, whatever he was, was not an enemy, and there might be help along the way. The people of the mountains might help if they could, but he must plan without them.

Outside the wind howled with a blizzard. In Montana such storms often lasted three to four days. If this one lasted that long they might never escape.

There had once been the story of an island in the Indian Ocean peopled by enchanters who could control the winds. No ship could pass without stopping to trade, and if they attempted it they encountered adverse winds.

"I could use them," he said, half-aloud, "I could use them now. I must have a good day tomorrow, a good day for travel."

CHAPTER 16

When the morning came there was no wind. The icy
peaks held still, the air silent . . . nothing moved.

It was cold . . . bitter cold. On the peaks and the
high levels of the mountain there was no softness in the
snow. Gray hogbacks thrust upward, their raw flanks blown
clean by the wind, looking colder than the ice that lay
in their crevices and shadowed places.

Lagskha-tsang was ready to travel. Brikhuti warmed
her hands at the fire. The Go-log huddled over their tea,
waiting. "We will go," he said, and they got up and went
out to the horses and yaks.

Mallory climbed the icy stair. The lama's rooms were
empty, cold, just the rugs and the smell of smoke. He
could almost believe it had been a dream. In the light of
day the place was in considerably worse shape than it had
seemed last night--there was dirt piled in the corners
and spider webs connecting ceiling and wall. Where had
the man gone and how had he done it without raising an
alarm? More than that, where was there for the man to go?

From outside Mallory could see his men readying the
animals. He headed back down the stairs.

Tibetans are born to travel, and within minutes the
caravan was strung out along the faint track. Where they
now must ride the track lay open upon the flank of the
mountain. Anyone coming up from behind could see them
from miles away. He hoped that his rear guard hadn't been
stopped by the storm. He felt exposed, but there was no
other way.

He glanced back at the ruin, but there was no movement around the roof-top apartments. How had the lama
come to that place? He had come, and now he had
gone . . . how? The fact that there must be another trail
disturbed him. If one man used it, another could.

He dropped back, detailing four Go-log to hold back
and watch their trail. All morning they followed the
flank of the mountain. There were no trees, no bushes,
only the snow and the out-croppings of granite.

They moved slowly. There could be no question of
hurry on such a slope. The mountainside grew steeper;
occasionally juniper appeared, and some scattered brush.
Once a flock of snow partridge flew up, almost from under
their feet. Even at this altitude there were insects.
Wolf spiders were frequent. Mallory had seen them above
nineteen thousand feet and suspected they went even
higher. He did not plan to look.

Several times, riding on ahead, he studied the track
with binoculars. The trail followed a slope that grew
steeper as they progressed, and seemed to enter a gorge a
few miles farther along. The track that lay between was
only occasionally visible due to the twists and turns of
the trail as it followed the mountains. The slope was now
cut by water-courses or wide swaths where avalanches had
swept down taking everything before them.

A rider clattered up from behind. "They come! Our
people come!" he shouted.

They had entered upon a wide place before the mouth
of the gorge, and Mallory gestured. "Tea," he said. And
as Brikhuti joined him he said, "There may not be a place
to stop once we're in that," he indicated the gorge, "and
I want to hear what our friends have to tell us."

The caravan bunched around him, gathering fuel for
fires. Mallory watched them, noting the argols were dry
and old. A few sticks could be found, and there were several half-dead junipers on the slope to provide fuel.

Far below he could hear what must be the sound of
rushing water. He listened, watching the Go-log ride into
the open and step down from the saddle to gather about
the fires.

Marshal Chu, they reported, left the Inn immediately

and moved south. Undoubtedly he was even now approaching
the crossing toward which they were headed.

"And the Americans?"

"They waited a day, then followed Chu."

"Followed? Why, in God's name?"

Nobody could hazard a guess. Chu would be annoyed and
suspicious when he found they had followed him. They had
been let off the hook, free to go where they wished, and
they chose to follow him.

His reactions would be obvious. He would have cause
to wonder if they were not simply spies, or allowed to
come to the Tibet area by those in the Peking government
who would discredit him.

In any event, it was no business of his. They had
come into this country of their own choice, and if they
chose to follow Chu, that was their business. Mallory had
problems sufficient for the moment.

The track now descended steeply into the black opening of the gorge, winding along the sheer face, and in
some cases, simply chopped out of the cliff itself. Far
below the water rushed in a torrent, and far above was
the sky, a mere slit between towering black walls.

Nowhere was the trail more than four feet wide and
the yaks walked the very outer edge to keep their packs
from brushing the wall. Mallory remained in the lead, and
he saw no tracks. If the trail had been traveled in recent years it gave no evidence of it.

Rounding a slight bend, he drew rein. The trail ahead
was covered with a mass of debris: logs, heavy boulders
and earth. The slide had started on the face above, and
most of it cascaded over into the gorge, but it had left
enough behind to block the trail.

Mallory swung down, very carefully, for the edge was
near. For a moment he stared at the heap of rocks and
earth with disgust. Stopping, he picked up a rock and
threw it over the rim, and then working steadily he went

at the pile. Several of the Go-log edged along, squeezing
past their horses to get into position to help. Using
the limb of a juniper they pried a larger rock loose and
it fell, taking a few inches at the edge of the trail
with it.

For more than an hour they worked, and then Brikhuti
edged her horse past him, and slowly the others followed.
His own horse had gone on, following that of Brikhuti,
and Mallory donned his shuba, waiting for the others to
pass. Each time one neared the trail's edge a little more
fell off until at last they were all gone, and only he
remained.

He stood alone, listening to the retreating footsteps
of the caravan. Somewhere ahead they would wait for him,
but he was not concerned with that. The track along the
wall of the cliff was now just more than two feet wide.

Taking up the stick that he had thrown down after
prying a boulder loose, he stabbed and pried at the remaining earth until much of it had fallen off into the
chasm. Then he threw the stick over and started on, after
the caravan. If anyone was following they would not find
it easy. The trail could be repaired, but it would require time and tools, and every minute gained was important.

Already the riders had disappeared around another
bend in the trail, yet there was no chance of their getting far ahead, and he was content to be alone. It was
utterly still. As he looked up he could see that the sun
was declining, and the darkness would come quickly in
this deep place.

For the first time in many weeks he was alone, and
the feeling brought a sense of freedom and freshness. The
Go-log were a somber people and not at all easy to be
with. Lagskha and Brikhuti were friendly and he enjoyed
talking to them but what he needed now was time to think.

The lama at the ruin seemed friendly, and yet he had

not made himself known to the others, and even Mallory
had discovered the man only by exploring the building. He
had seemed helpful, and undoubtedly there were many people in Tibet who were willing to help Lagskha escape the
Chinese. There were also sure to be a few who would be in
the pay of the Communists, and who would do anything to
assist in the capture of either Lagskha or himself.

Despite his ten years in the area there was much that
went on of which he knew nothing. There were old jealou-
sies, old hatreds and rivalries, and there were secret
societies as well, men banded together in ancient orders
with purposes of their own.

There were sects of the Red Cap monks such as the
Zek-chenpas or the Dogpas with no reason for loyalty to
Lagskha, and much reason for hating all he stood for.
Weird stories were told of them and their secret rites,
of their seeming ability to appear or disappear at will,
and their practices that smacked of devil-worship. How
much of this was idle gossip he did not know, but they
were feared by many, and in an area of which he knew
nothing his way was to walk softly.

What worried him most was that someone was aware of
what route they had taken, knew exactly where they were
when he had hoped to vanish completely.

Overhead the light was fading. He heard no sound from
the caravan. Here and there pines grew from the walls of
the gorge, and gnarled juniper clung to the ragged edge
of the trail. The way descended steadily, growing colder
by the moment.

The track along the cliff seemed without end, winding
steadily on, revealing no more than a few hundred yards
at any one time. Eventually he came to a place where the
trail ceased, and the builders had carried it around a
great rocky shoulder by sinking timbers into the rock
wall.

Mallory hesitated, looking into the blackness below, yet the caravan had gone on, so he did, walking around the face of the mountain on a platform suspended over darkness. On the far side, and some distance below, he saw a gleam of fire. They had stopped then. They had found a place.

It was just light enough to see a dozen or so yards, and the track widened and Mallory saw before him, perched precariously above the gorge, a tiny village, a mere cluster of houses, most of them in ruins. Beyond the village, there was a small meadow. On it the yaks and the horses were grazing.

Brikhuti came to meet him. "I was worried," she said, "but they were not."

He glanced at the houses. "Is anyone here?"

"I looked into some of the houses. I think they have been deserted for a long time."

Death had come to this village, death and something else . . . Mallory walked to the fire and extended his hands to the flames. They turned their heads to look, some of them, but already they were bedding down, for they knew the day would bring another trail.

Mallory lifted his bowl to them. "May there be a road!" he said, and several who still drank repeated after him, "May there be a road!"

"We will have trouble tomorrow," he said.

Brikhuti turned her dark eyes to him. How could a woman still be beautiful after such a day of travel? Yet she was . . . very beautiful.

"Somebody knows we are here, and that may mean that others do too." He did not want to tell her of the sudden feeling he had, a cold whisper of warning.

She looked at him, then finished her tea. "You will bring us through," she said positively.

He chuckled, without humor. "I wish I was as sure."

"If you were sure, I would be less sure. It is well to be afraid."

She looked around slowly. "I wonder about this place. Why did anyone build here? Was it only a resting place? How could these people exist?"

Gompa had come up to them. "It was a place of the Dogpas," he said. "They lived in this village, and before them devils lived here. Kesar drove them out."

"He came to this place?" Brikhuti asked.

"Upon his magical horse, Kyang Go Karkar, he rode here, where enemies waited, but his horse smelled them out, and he destroyed them. He turned them into great stones and rolled them into the gorge. My father knew the words, and often he sang the song of Kesar."

Gompa looked at Mallory. "That is why the black spirit-shadows do not frighten us. Because you are here."

"Do not make up stories . . ."

The Go-log shrugged. "Who else would know of this track, Kushog, that we who live near did not know? And of this place? For who else are the fires lighted?"

"Fires?"

"A fire burned before we came. There was fuel. There was tsamba."

CHAPTER 17

Nor was the fire all. Beside it, and awaiting Mallory, untouched by the Go-log, was a large kettle of djo, a very pleasant dish of curdled yak's milk which had been put on the fire and stirred briskly while boiling, then slightly sweetened.

Mallory invited Brikhuti and Lagskha to share it with him, only regretting it was insufficient for all. Yet the

Go-log urged him to eat, protesting that it was his, and
his alone.

The wind was cold and a light snow was falling. The
houses of the ruined village were close by, but Mallory
preferred the open air. He could hear better, and see
farther. He trusted none of his surroundings, and had no
idea whether the food he was given was not merely bait
for a trap to be sprung farther along . . . yet the djo
was no casual dish. This had been very specially prepared.

"You are favored," Lagskha remarked, smiling. "They
are sure you are Kesar. There are many who believe this
was the route he chose when going to attack Hor. Do you
know the stories?"

"Some of them. Kesar of Ling, I believe, was the
great Tibetan folk hero. He was said to have been born
into the world to bring order, to suppress violence and
evil, and he rode a magical horse and could perform
magic, himself, although occasionally he was the victim
of the magic of others. I've heard the stories sung in
the tents of the Go-log in several versions."

"I have read that your scholars believe the legend
dates from the seventh or eighth centuries," Lagskha
said, "but some of us believe they are much, much older,
and were known to the Bonpo."

When morning came the wind blew cold along the
ranges, whispering where the pines grew, for now the
track emerged from the gorge and wound once more along
the flank of the mountain.

Mallory resumed the lead, riding on ahead, studying
the trail, scanning the mountain, eyes alert for whatever
might be there.

The gorge they had followed, Mallory saw, had taken
them through the Kuo-Lo Shan, a range of mountains that
joined the Chala Shan at right angles. Looking back, he

could no longer even see the mouth of the gorge, and unless he had known it was there he would not have believed
that such a pass existed.

On his left he could now look out over a vast sweep
of country: rugged mountains, canyons, all unknown and
unexplored. In the distance he could see a river or what
appeared to be a river that was probably the She Ch'u.
Closer to him there were several gorges, each with a
river that must form the headwaters of the Ta To Ho. The
Ta To Ho eventually joined the She Ch'u, but not the Yarlung, for a mountain range divided the two rivers.

Mallory saw the tracks of several large bears, and
judging by the size of the tracks and the length of the
stride the animals must weigh seven or eight hundred
pounds. Once, some distance off, he saw one eating a dead
yak. He pointed, and handed the glass to Brikhuti.

"They are very fierce," she said, after a glance.
"They have killed many hunters."

"I wouldn't doubt it," Mallory replied dryly, "seeing
the kind of guns most of them have. It takes a good
weapon to stop a bear that big."

Before them was a ridge, and Mallory slowed his pace,
approaching with caution. Slowly, he edged his mount
closer to the rim until he could see beyond. He was looking into the valley of the Yarlung, and beyond it another
snow-topped range, which seemed to end not far off.

Lagskha rode up beside him, pointing. "Dzogchen Gompa
is there, and the crossing is of the Den Chu, then we
cross it again, and work north in a great loop and back
south to the crossing of the Yarlung. It is a track much
used, and the soldiers of Chu will be there."

He turned in his saddle. "The crossing is for those
traveling to or from An-ch'e-k'o-mao, but is little traveled until the crossing of the Den Chu, when it joins the
caravan route from Kantse."

The situation was not a happy one. In a land of riv-

ers and high mountains the available routes are few, the
passes known. To strike south to another crossing would
mean nearing troops stationed at Kantse, undoubtedly
in greater force and alerted to be on the look-out for
them.

The crossing must be here. A river crossing was always dangerous, and Marshal Chu would appreciate his advantage. A shrewd and capable man, he would not risk his
soldiers until the situation was favorable, despite the
fact that he out-numbered them ten to one. If Chu could
catch them crossing or on the far side, he might wipe
them out.

"Mallory," Lagskha suggested, "Kesar's route may have
used another crossing."

Mallory shook his head. "I hate to gamble on it, but
from this moment on we must play it by ear."

The descent toward the river was gradual, the ground
beneath them mostly broken up mica-schist and slate, yet
surprisingly, the route was hidden, twisting and turning
to utilize every projection of rock, every boulder. There
were occasional junipers, and some of them left the impression that they had been planted, scattered along to
conceal the trail they followed.

After two hours of slow descent a track broke off
from the one they followed and descended into a hollow, a
notch in the mountain with a sandy floor and a small
spring.

Near the spring was a crude circle of rocks, blackened by fire, and near it a stack of argols and some
pieces of dead juniper. Also, piled nearby and in plain
sight were a dozen sacks.

Gompa rode swiftly past, dropping to the ground near
the sacks. "Barley!" he said, after a swift examination.

The Go-log went to their packs and got out copper
pans and began to parch the barley for use in making
tsamba. It was obvious that the people of the area were

not going to let them starve. Probably they did not appear because of their fear of the Go-log, known far and wide as robbers and raiders.

Atop one of the sacks was a sheep's shoulder blade, and Gompa called Pagyar. "It is for you to read the future!" he said.

Pagyar was a noted soothsayer, a teller of fortunes, a reader of the past, present and future. The people of Kham are known to be gifted in this way, and magicians from Kham were always present at the ancient courts of the emperors of China.

When tea had been prepared and the embers pulled aside, Pagyar put the sheep's shoulder-blade in the embers, leaving it there until charred. Removing it, he studied the cracks made by the heat. The longitudinal cracks represented the way they pursued, the horizontal ones what would happen en route. The color of the bone fore-told the weather they would encounter.

Pagyar studied the cracks with care, and Mallory watched him curiously. Many times before he had seen this done, as well as divination in other forms, and he was convinced from what he had seen that the cracks actually were only something on which the soothsayer concentrated, that what he foretold came from his own intuition, clairvoyance or ESP or whatever one wished to call it.

Mallory was not a skeptic. He had witnessed too many strange things, had seen too many prophecies come true, but he knew the power such prophecies had over the minds of their followers. He suspected that Pagyar, as many of his kind, relied as much on exceptional knowledge as on what his clairvoyant powers revealed. Most such men were the confidants of hunters and travelers, they heard much, and remembered most of it. Coupled with their divination was a knowledge of trails and conditions that far exceeded that of the average traveler.

"There will be war," Pagyar said, "there will be war

and blood. Men will fall, and others will flee, scream-
ing. There will be the sound of guns and the clash of
blades, yet we Go-log will win through."

He bent over the shoulder blade, the fire-light dancing on his narrow features. "There are dark shadows upon
the road, shadows through which I cannot see, but there
is blood again and there is mystery . . . always and forever mystery, veils of darkness are drawn across my eyes,
but we will win through because Mallory leads us, and because Kesar rides beside the Incarnation.

"The white men and women will be among us again, they
will come fleeing in terror from they know not what, but
from what they know, also.

"In the end there will be the death of a prince, and
good fortune that will come late, after much trial. Marriage vows will be spoken between a man and a maid under
the shadow of fear when death is all around."

He sat on his heels and looked all around, but mostly
at Mallory. "You will fight to the death," he said, "a
bold fight, a strong fight."

Brikhuti looked at him, her face pale. "He did not
say whether you lived or died, Mallory. Will you not ask
him?"

"No. He trusts in his divination. I trust in my
sword."

When they had finished their tea and tsamba they
mounted again. With each minute they drew nearer to the
place where they must cross, nearer to where the enemy
lay, and at last they camped, ready to see what tomorrow
might bring. Before they bedded down, Mallory called two
of the Go-log to him. "Sleep," he said. "At midnight rise
and ride into the valley. See where the crossing is, and
if our enemies are there. Meet me here," he drew with his
finger in the dust and showed a place where the track
came near the stream, "but go quietly and no fighting unless you must."

Brikhuti came over as he sat on a rock away from the fire-light, listening to their snores. "Will they be safe?"

"With any luck. They are like ghosts. Their only enemy is their bravery. Too often they would rather simply fight than choose their battles with an eye to victory."

The wind from down the ridges blew cold, it stirred the fire with tentative fingers and the flames fluttered and bent low above the coals. Mallory filled two bowls with tea. One he handed to Brikhuti.

"You were safely away from all this. Did you come back just for Lagskha?"

"My brother is a gifted man, Mallory, very gifted, and very important to Tibet and to our enduring culture. The Communists will try to destroy that culture, they will stamp out any diversity in the name of the universal man. We must be sure that what we have will not die. Lagskha needed to escape. From outside Tibet he can work, even as the Dalai Lama does, to improve the lot of his people and to prepare for a day of freedom."

"It could be a long time off."

"We will do what we must. Our roots are here, our memories are here, and the places of our religion are here. No people has the right to decide the destiny of another."

"Tibet is strategically important, Brikhuti. It sits at the peak of Asia, with all of Asia lying in a circle about it. The nations of the world have been slow to grasp that fact, but China has not.

"Tibet opens a door to India, to Pakistan, to Kashmir, to Central Asia . . . even to Iran."

They talked long into the night, and then Lagskha awoke and came to join them. He sipped his tea, then glanced up at Mallory, who stood across the fire, listen-

ing to the night. "The river crossing is dangerous, is it
not?"

"Very. I am hoping there will be another, further up
or down stream. If we could cross before they found us,
we'd have a fighting chance."

"Could we swim?"

Mallory shrugged. "I have not seen the river at that
place, but most of these rivers run strong, the current
is too swift." He thought about it. "There was an American who swam a thousand head of cattle across the Missis-
sippi where it was a mile wide. I suppose it might be
done if the water is not too swift or too cold."

Later he walked out to look down over the valley. He
could hear no sound but the wind, no stirring, no warning
from the night.

COMMENTS: Mentions of this novel crop up in Louis's journals and
letters in 1962, 1967, and again in 1971. The subject of Communist
expansion into the western regions of China proper had already figured in Dad's work; he explored it in "May There Be a Road," a short
story that he wrote in 1960 (though it was not published until 2001),
and touched upon it also in another short story, "Beyond the Great
Snow Mountains."

By '62, Louis decided he wanted to try something bigger on the
subject, and by 1967 work on this project was begun. I am not sure
how far he got at that time, but the book was jump-started again in '71
when a mutual friend put him in touch with the deputy private secretary to the Dalai Lama and, through him, with the Dalai Lama himself. This was no more than a brief and superficial correspondence,
but they did arrange for their Information and Publicity Office to
keep Louis abreast of events in Tibet and its borderlands. They also

suggested some books to help with research, though Dad was already pretty familiar with the terrain—familiar enough to mention the following in his journal:

> Have Army maps of Tibet and Sinkiang. Very inaccurate. The Ba Chu (a river of some size) [empties] into the Yellow in the area of which I am writing, and it is not even on the map. The gorge of the Ba is over a thousand feet deep near the Yellow. The place called Rircha Gompa is in the wrong position, much too far north, and that's the wrong name, anyway. Should be Rag-grya Gompa, or something akin to that. Many of the places marked on the map are mere campsites which the uninitiated might take for towns or monasteries. Several mountains are wrongly placed.

It is unclear how Louis knew these maps were wrong (or even if they actually are). There are stories of him traveling in China but, while my research shows that he was there, the amount of time he would have needed to journey so far west makes his having done so extremely unlikely. Probably he was comparing the maps with accounts of others or comparing the 1940s-era Army maps to older ones that he considered to be more accurate.

Soon after Dad restarted work on the book in '71, we received what he described as a "good omen." One morning, after my mother had driven my sister and me to school, she returned home to find that a white dove had flown into our garage. She left the door open for a few hours, but the bird seemed content to stay. Eventually, my mother went and got an old hamster cage. Dad held out a pencil and the bird hopped onto it and he placed the bird in the cage. When my sister and I returned from school . . . we had a new pet! We named the dove Rama and he lived with us for nearly thirty years—probably some sort of record, since he was mature when he arrived.

Little did we know the dove's incessant cooing was to plague many who called us on the telephone. I can't count the times people

Rama in his temporary cage.

asked, "What in the world is that noise?" It was always kind of surprising, because we had spent so long around Rama that no one in our
household really noticed it anymore.

In its early years, this story shared the title "Journey to Aksu"
with my dad's other central China story, the fragments of which are
published in the first volume of *Louis L'Amour's Lost Treasures*. Louis
often had trouble coming up with titles, so he may simply have been
recycling this one for convenience. Unless something goes terribly
wrong, I can't imagine either Mallory's or Hart's group ending up in
Aksu or anywhere near it. Nevertheless, there do seem to be some
other similarities.

Gunther Hart may be searching for a special place, a monastery
perhaps, that contains some sort of secret knowledge. Both the hidden
map that Mallory has seen, and the knowledge Brikhuti and her
brother may have, seem to indicate a hidden or ancient city, a place to
which the Tibetans definitely do not want to lead Marshal Chu. All of
this is, of course, similar to the City of the Blue Wall in "Journey to

Aksu" and the repository of information for those who have "arrived," or become aware of their past lives, in "Samsara," another section of *Volume 1*.

There are a few other hints here that might link these three documents. The most amusing of them is Doctor Bernard's account of the manuscript he once read:

> ". . . twenty-five, perhaps thirty years . . ."
> before. A book that was ". . . something right out of
> Rider-Haggard or Pierre Benoit." And had to do with
> an ancient track, a ". . . route or trail, whatever
> you wish to call it, that could be followed only by
> those of particular courage or virtue, a route beset
> with dangers . . . all manner of evil . . . but which
> led to ancient monasteries where the old secret
> knowledge was still studied by people who came there
> from the ends of the earth . . . chosen people."

This sounds suspiciously like Louis might have been thinking of his own, unfinished manuscript, the first version of "Journey to Aksu," which was the story of the mercenary Paul Medrac and the City of the Blue Wall.

There is also the moment when Renata runs across Muhsin, the man she thinks could help the Hart Expedition as a guide or interpreter. After she makes the offer to employ him she has second thoughts:

> He walked back toward the Inn and Renata looked
> after him, very puzzled. It was a little too oppor-
> tune, his sudden arrival, his knowledge of English,
> of history . . . where was he going? Who was he? And
> how did he happen to appear here just at this time?

That feels a bit like the scene where Medrac hires Serat, the mysterious Ladakhi with the pockmarked face in the original "Journey to Aksu." Even more familiar is Marshal Chu, who seems to be the very same character Louis wrote about in "Aksu," just revived forty years later and with only slightly different politics!

Here are two pages of Louis's handwritten notes for the "Ben Mallory" story:

Moving on, it is interesting to watch Louis have some fun, making the character of Gunther Hart share some of the attributes of so many in the pretentious "Hollywood" culture that surrounded us in those years.

Here's a scene from Louis's notes that he modified somewhat before he put it in the final manuscript:

Hart enters, expresses a wish to see the lama;
Brikhuti is there, a beautiful attractively dressed
girl. "He cannot see you now." Hart merely glances at
her. "He will see me." He instructs Carpenter to tell
the lama he is present. Carpenter is stopped by two

powerful guards. Brikhuti tells Hart, "If you wish to
see him, I will try to arrange it."

"You know him?"

"I am his sister."

Tibetan assistant of Hart explains about lama: he
is very hip; his sister has studied in Europe; is
known at Cannes, on the Costa Brava, on the ski
slopes.

She also knows Hart, is not impressed.

Marty Wells, later, is playing a folk song on his
harmonica when the lama enters. He is young, attractive, very interested. Hart enters, is offended that
the lama who would not see him is now talking to a
member of the expedition. The lama tells him he would
be happy to see him later . . . if there is time.

Hart tells the lama he is Gunther Hart, but the
lama knows nothing of him. Brikhuti smiles.

And then a last note about Hart:

Realization of inadequacy and his resentment creates desire to destroy those who exposed him, not
only to others but to himself.

Louis also played around with having Lagskha, the young lama,
act as literary critic. He experimented in his notes with the following
paragraphs:

So many of your literary magazines amaze me.
They view the world with so much immediacy . . . none
seem to have any perspective. They are obviously
written by intelligent people, but they wail, one and
all, about the end of civilization without seeming to
realize that what we have now is much what we have
always had . . . the only difference is that more

people care, give to charity, protect the environment
and support the rights of others . . . what could be
better than that?

I miss the stories of character. I find no
Shakespeare, Dickens, Balzac or Dostoevsky anymore.
No one interprets character anymore, not from their
own experience. All have seized on the misguided Mr.
Freud, who seems quite a bright man, really, but so
obsessed with his own problems that his spectacles
became fogged.

Your best writing that I have seen comes from
journalists. They see much more clearly than novelists. The novelists no longer are story-tellers, they
are [so] obsessed with being considered "important"
that they become bogged down in causes that are so
temporary that a later generation will not be able to
comprehend what all the excitement was about. They
have forgotten that the story is man himself not the
passing fads of politics.

It seems very likely that these lines were opinions Dad considered placing in Lagskha's mouth. They were just notes, but the last
one is sort of ironic in that Louis was writing what was, at least for
him, a political book. I also want to be cautious, however, because I
believe it is a mistake for readers to assume that they know the difference between the voice of an author and the voice of a character. Dad
tended to jot stuff like this down and, occasionally, he'd even talk like
this in an interview. But he almost never expressed himself privately
in the manner of these experimental quotes. I guess that raises the
additional question of the difference between an author's personal and
professional voice!

At one time I considered expanding this story fragment into a
complete novel but eventually decided to put off that decision. Though

Louis wrote many chapters, and there may be indications of what he intended to do hiding in "Journey to Aksu," "Samsara," and his short story "Beyond the Great Snow Mountains," I am still considering whether or not to proceed. It is quite likely that even he didn't consciously know where he was going to take the story next. However, that was always the situation that excited him the most.

THE DEATH OF PETER TALON

The Beginning of a Western Novel

CHAPTER 1

When I glanced back over our trail there was blood on
the snow, blood from ice-cuts on our horses' hoofs.

The snow was a foot to two feet deep and a few days
back it had warmed enough to melt the surface, then frozen again into an icy crust. Often when our horses' hoofs
broke through that ice cut like a knife.

We had been nine hours in the saddle, riding in the
bitter cold. The horses were struggling now and Charlie's
gelding had gone down once. We were hard put to get him
back on his feet.

"We got to get under cover." Charlie's voice was muffled by the bandanna tied over his nose and mouth.

"This here's a trail of some sort," Burt said. "I
seen a wagon track back yonder where the snow had blowed
off."

Luckier than the others, I had a wool muffler tied

across my face, knitted for me by a girl whose name was
Mary. I never expected to see her again but she'd left
kindly thoughts in my mind. That muffler was a od-send
and I'd have given plenty to be putting my feet under her
table.

I squinted through the slowly falling snow at the
bulk of the mountain ahead, and the way the trees climbed
its side. I'd never been to this part of the country before, so why should it seem familiar?

Like that big old oak tree where we'd camped last
night? And the spring where I'd dipped up water.

"Fence," Charlie pointed.

Sure enough, there was the corner of a split-rail
fence just off the road; the fence running alongside the
road as if to hold back the trees.

"Thank God!" Burt said. "There'll be a house and a
fire!"

We needed it. We just weren't going much further. The
cold was intense, night was coming on and our horses were
played out. Three days we'd been riding now with mighty
little rest.

The trees ended at the edge of a small meadow covered
with snow. Up the road a ways we could see a gate, and
back against more trees was the house. There was a barn
and a corral with a big stack of hay alongside. No smoke
came from the chimney.

"It will be shelter," Charlie said. "There's got to
be a fireplace or a stove."

"Let's hope there's wood, too," Burt said. "I ain't
in no mood."

The gate was closed and Charlie leaned from the saddle to slide back the bar. Glancing up at the sign arching above the gate, it took me a moment to read it: The
Burning Lamp.

Burt, he stared at it, too. "Now what the Hell does

that mean? Anyway, I'd rather it was a burning fire in the stove."

Me, I didn't say anything. I took another look then pulled my chin back behind my coat collar. Something about that sign made me feel all funny inside, and that was foolishness. The Burning Lamp, what did it mean, anyway?

No hoof marks or those of sled-runners. No smoke from the chimney. We waited while Charlie closed the gate. No ranching man ever leaves a gate open that he finds closed, and habit was stronger than the cold.

We rode up to the house. Snow all over everything. Heavy on the roof, on the porch. Snow blown against the shutters leaving white lines like bars.

"Hello, the house!" I yelled.

Wind blew a whiff of snow off the eaves, and a dry branch scraped against a roof-corner. One of the horses stamped impatiently. Burt turned his mount and walked him toward the barn.

Stepping down from the saddle, so stiff I could only fumble at the front door. It was locked. The porch and the steps creaked when I left them to walk around to the side of the house.

"We'll have to break in," Charlie suggested.

"Let's try the back door first," I said. Cold or no it went against the grain for me to break into anybody's house. Although Western folks usually expected people to stop by. All they wanted in return was to leave things as they were found.

There was a stack of wood, as much as two cords of it, stacked alongside the house, and in the shadows of the covered back porch I saw an axe, and a cross-cut saw.

Stepping into the cold stillness of that back porch, I tried the door.

Locked.

On a hunch I looked up along the door frame and saw a
key hanging from a peg. Not a nail, but a peg. Well, a
lot of folks used pegs. Nails were scarce.

Unlocking the door, I pushed it open. It was a small
kitchen, oil-cloth on the floor, a big old kitchen range
and some pots here and there. The wood-box was filled.
There were a few dishes on the shelves.

Charlie went back for the horses and I stepped into
the next room.

There was a pot-bellied stove, another full wood-box,
and some pitch-pine slivers laid out ready to start a
fire. Standing in the icy stillness of that empty room, I
stared at those slivers of pine. I said, "I'll bet the
fire's laid, too."

Opening the stove, I peered in. There it was, some
crumpled bark, some small twigs, slivers of pitch-pine
and heavier wood. Squatting before the stove I struck a
match. It flared up and I leaned in, touching the match
to a thin, curled edge of bark. It caught, crept along
the edge, showing a tiny blue flame, then it gathered
strength and reached hungrily for the twigs. I closed the
stove door and stood up.

No sound. Only icy stillness. An empty house can be
the coldest place in the world. Slowly, I let my eyes
take in the room.

Two doors opened into other rooms or closets. The
floor was well-made, the planks tightly fitted. No rugs
on the floor but there had been rugs, for I saw a dark
stain, straight along one edge as though something had
spilled partly on the rug, partly off its edge.

I shivered. What was it about this place?

The room was dim with only a little light filtering
through the shutters. On a small table there was a coal-
oil lamp, half-filled with oil. I crossed the room,
struck a match and lifted the lamp chimney to touch the

match to the wick. Then I replaced the lamp chimney and
blew out the match. Adding fuel to the fire which was
blazing up, I crossed to the nearest door.

A bed-room, bed built against the wall. A home-made
bed with leather straps for springs. No mattress now.
Pegs on the walls for hanging clothing, one picture I
could not make out in the darkness. Leaving the door open
to warm the room in case somebody decided to sleep there,
I went to the other room.

The second room was smaller, but there were two beds,
pegs on the walls here, too, and an old trunk between the
beds. When I turned around I noticed there was a bar for
the door, a bar on the inside.

"Odd," I said aloud.

The stamping of feet on the porch brought me back to
the living-room. "Took care of your horse," Charlie said.
"Took the gear off and rubbed him down a mite. There's
plenty of hay and whoever built that barn, built it tight
and strong." He glanced around. "Same as this house."

They walked to the stove, peeling off their gloves to
extend their opened fingers to the heat. "Man! That
surely feels good! Didn't take you long to get a fire
goin'!"

"It was already laid."

Burt glanced around at me. "Grave out yonder." He
gestured toward the woods near the barn. "Seen it when I
was gettin' hay."

Burt was a big, quiet man, a top-hand on any outfit,
and older than Charlie and me. Burt was out of Arkansas
by way of Texas, and he'd been up the trail to Kansas a
time or two. Easy-going man, but no nonsense about him,
either.

"Good place," he said, looking around. "Makes a body
wonder why they left it."

"Trouble in the family," I said. Indicating the sec-

ond door I said, "Whoever slept in there had a bar across
the door. Ain't likely a man would want to keep anybody
out, so it must have been a woman."

"Pretty bad if she had to use a bar," Burt said. He
was opening his pack. "Seen a skillet out there, and I'm
goin' to fry up some bacon." He glanced around at me.
"Any of that bread left?"

"Most of one loaf, all of another. And I've coffee.
We'll make out."

Burt left the room and we heard him moving around
outside. When he returned he had a bucket of snow which
he placed beside the stove to melt. "Pump's froze," he
explained.

Uneasily, I looked around. There was something about
this place--"Be glad when we can get back on the trail,"
I said.

Burt glanced at me. "Have you looked outside? We'll
be lucky if we can move out for days. She's comin' down
pretty good out there. Anyway, it's snug and tight in
here and it ain't likely we'll find anywhere else."

"Our horses are done in. A few miles further and we'd
have been afoot. We were shot with luck when we come up
to this place."

From the wood-box I added sticks to the fire. The
room was warming up.

"I'll bring in some more wood," I said, and went to
the door. Burt was rinsing out the frying pan with melted
snow-water.

Outside the snow was falling faster, and so thick I
could no longer see the gate. Gathering an armful of wood
from the pile I brought it inside, then followed it with
two more.

Charlie was squatting near the stove when I came in.
He was a thin, tall man with a drooping yellow mustache
from which the ice was melting.

"I'd have lost my horse," he commented.

"Burt's right," I admitted. "We should hole up here a couple of days."

Charlie and me met up when we were punching cows on the Slash Seven. He'd been there just a few days when I hired on and we made a team of it. He was a good man with a rope and he tied fast. Me, I was a dally man, myself. Just take a turn around the old horn when I latch onto something.

For a few months there we rode some serious country together, gathering strays out of the canyons and working the rough string. When you said rough string on the Seven you meant it. Some of those horses were rounded up out on the mesa from wild stock and they'd been rode mighty little. I was a fair hand but Charlie was better. Burt was the best rider of us three but he wasn't hunting any bad ones. "You kids can have them," he said. "I cut my teeth on wild mustangs and they've jounced me around enough."

We'd been riding together, Charlie and me, for eight or nine months when we met Burt.

Burt was down in a buffalo wallow with a dead horse, and he was smoking it out with a bunch of Arapahos. He'd been burned by a couple of rifle shots and he was down to his last four cartridges.

When we showed up we taken the fun out of it for the Indians and they taken off waving their hands and slapping their behinds at us.

Burt stood up and says, "You boys come along at the right time. I'd just a few beans left in the mill." That was when he showed us the four cartridges he had left.

"You nailed one of them," Charlie said.

"That was right off. I never did get a good shot at anything after." He glanced down at his horse. "I surely do hate to lose my outfit. I've set astride of that old saddle across some rough country."

"You can ride with me," Charlie said. "My horse can carry double. Copper will take your gear."

It was forty miles to town, a settlement gathered around a box-car that doubled for a railroad station, general store and saloon. There were some loading-pens and four or five dry farmers, bucking the odds and the dust storms.

At the bar where he taken us to buy a drink, this gent looked over at us and said, "I'm Burt Hoogan."

Charlie, he just nods, so I say, "They call me Copper, because of my hair."

My hair wasn't red, just about the color of dusty copper. My folks said I taken after a woman who married into the family. She was my great-grandmother or something of the kind.

Charlie never said what his other name was and nobody asked him.

"Glad you boys come along," Burt said. "I was fixing to get almighty lonesome, and them Injuns wasn't much comp'ny."

After that the three of us rode together and when the Seven let us go for the winter we hit the trail together.

Burt was slicing bacon into the pan when I came in with the last armful of wood. He glanced at me. "That grave I seen . . ." he said, "I went over and taken a look. Eleven years old. That was all. Name of Peter Talon."

Well--

Burt, he looked at me again, mighty sharp. "What's wrong? Copper? What's the matter?"

"That kid . . . Peter Talon . . . I think he was my brother."

CHAPTER 2

They stared at me, and then Burt said, "You mean you know this place? You _lived_ here?"

"I never saw it before. I've never even been in this part of the country. If this is the place I heard about I think it is my pa built this cabin, with ma helping. The Talons were mostly builders, and he took after them."

"What happened to your ma?"

"Last I heard she was in Kansas, and Petey was with her, but they were headed west.

"She an' pa had been out west and they'd built a cabin, but when she was fixin' to have me they went back east where she could have care. Pa, he left her there and guided a wagon train west and he did some more work on this place, fencing it, and the like. He put in a crop, bought some cows, and then he came back east to be with ma.

"After I was born pa was building a bridge and so he stayed by. Then he got another job working on a fort the Army was building, and then as a teamster with the Army. That took him right where this place was. So he stayed on awhile, fixing things up and building the barn. Then he came back.

"We moved from Tennessee to Missouri. Petey was born after a bit, and all they did was talk about their place out west. It was like a dream to them. Pa taken sick and died. He caught pneumonia. He was all strong and happy like, then he was down in bed and then he was gone. I don't recall the years. Pa left ma with a little money and she taken care of us, but she was scared.

"You know how those days were. Missouri was wild. There was a lot of bad blood over the War, and occasional shootings. There was several men wanted to marry ma, but she shied away from them. Then this one man came around and he sort of warned the others off. He was a strapping

big man, handsome, and better dressed than most. Ma
thought he was like pa, but he surely wasn't.

"Once they were married he began to ask questions
about the place out west and about grandpa. I used to
hear them talking, and I knew ma couldn't make head or
tail of it, and he would get mad. He thought she was hiding something from him when she just flat didn't know
what he was after.

"I knew, and one time when he was down to the saloon,
I told her. It was that ol' treasure story. Pa told it to
me like he told me a lot of other stories, and he didn't
think there was anything to it, and it wasn't grandpa at
all, but much further back than that.

"Even before they were married my step-father had
been curious about a medallion my mother wore. It was
gold and it had funny markings on it. Pa said it was an
heirloom from his family and wanted my mother to have it.

"Maybe Pa had never told her the story, thinking it
fanciful, but I was a little boy and him hard put to come
up with fresh stories for me, he told it to me.

"An ancestor of his, away back, had been a pirate.
Not in Jamaica and those islands like you hear, but off
in India somewhere. I don't know much about that over
there so all the names and places were strange to me, but
I recall they had wonderful sounds.

"Pa talked of places like Madagascar, Coromandel,
Zanzibar, Borneo and such-like. Anyway, this ancestor of
his was the one who first took the name Talon, took it
because he'd had one arm cut off and a claw to replace
the hand. An old devil by all accounts.

"He'd raided and marauded and captured ships here and
there and finally sailed back with four big ships, heading across the Pacific. By the time they came to the
shores of America, and that was some time in the 1600s,
they were in bad shape.

"They had to abandon one vessel, and as they were all

heavy loaded, they buried that treasure. Millions, they
said.

"They were attacked by Indians but got safely off
after losing a few men. Further south they had a fight
with a Spanish ship and it crippled another one of
theirs, so they buried what they had from it and what
they'd taken from the Spanish ship.

"They sailed around the horn with just two ships
left. They were taken with scurvy and some died, and some
were lost in storms so when they finally came into harbor
on the coast of Canada, a place called the Gaspe, later,
they were short-handed.

"That first Talon, he chose to stay right where he
was, and some stayed with him. Some stayed, some went.
Those who went were given shares of treasure but of
course, they wanted more. At the end they sailed off,
then came back to seize the rest, but the old man was
waiting for them. There was a mad fight there on the
shore and some men died and some lived. That time when
they sailed off their ship exploded. Blew right up, and
some do say the old Talon rigged it so.

"Anyway, some carried the story that a Talon knows
where there's treasure, hidden somewhere in the West.
Where there was one story there's now a dozen, all different, and treasures hid in places no Talon ever was,
but folks will believe what they wish to believe."

"What about the loot buried on the West Coast? From
that first ship?" Charlie asked.

"She's still there, wherever that is. So far as I
know the Old Man told nobody. Maybe he went back and got
it. He had ships there for awhile, and he did what he
said and gave land to those who stayed with him.

"Anyway, that heirloom ma wore, that was supposed to
be a gold piece from the treasure, handed down in the
family. This man who married ma, he heard the name Talon,
and he'd heard the story before. Talon had been set on

going west, had a place out there, somebody said. Somehow
he got it in his mind that where the cabin was, that was
where the treasure was.

"She didn't even know what he was talking about until
I told her, then she told him it was all nonsense. He
couldn't accept that. To believe that he had to admit he
was a damn fool.

"He'd talked mighty big about all he was going to
have, and now he had nothing. Instead he was spending
what he had taking care of us. Only he took what ma had,
too, and when I went to work, he took what I earned, little as it was. He drank more and more and he beat us more
and more. He couldn't give up on the story but I don't
know if he believed it anymore, either.

"He got me to one side and tried to get out of me
what I knew. I told him the only treasure I heard of was
buried afar off, at sea. He whipped me for that. If I
hadn't run off, he'd of killed me. Now I'm wondering what
happened to Petey."

"And to her," Burt said, "to your ma."

The idea chilled me. "I've got to find out," I said.
"I've got to find out what happened."

"There's that trunk," Charlie suggested.

"There's another place, too," I said. "There's our
secret place back in Missouri where Petey and me used to
hide. Ma knew of it, and she left notes there for me,
time to time, warning me when he was drinking and such,
so's I could stay clear. She used to leave grub for me."

"Your pa ever look for that treasure?" Burt asked.

"I asked him that, and he says, 'Look where? Two
places in maybe three thousand miles of coast? I wouldn't
even know where to begin, nor would anybody else. The
whole story may be a pack of lies. I don't know. It's
just a good story, that's all. If there's any proof it's
true or not it's right back there on the Gaspe, where the
Old Man lived . . . and died.'"

Burt fried some bacon and made coffee. "Beats me why they'd leave such a snug, warm cabin," he said. "Your pa was a sure enough builder. Look at how those corners are fitted. Ain't a chink nowhere, and the window sashes fit. I tell you a body doesn't often see work like this."

"Ma loved this place," I said. "I can't figure why she'd leave."

"Maybe after her other boy died there was no reason to stay."

We sat up to the table and made do with what we had and when I was washing up after I turned to them and said, "Boys, I've got to quit you. I know we figured on going out to the Nevada country but I've just got to find out what happened to ma."

Charlie lay back on the bunk where he'd spread his blankets. "You just do that. Burt an' me, we ain't in no hurry, and she's mighty cold in the saddle."

"Nevada will look a whole lot better in the spring," Burt agreed. "If we lay in some grub there's no better place to last out the winter. A snug cabin, good stove, and plenty of fuel."

Charlie slept in the main room and Burt took over one bed-room and I slept in the room which had the bar on the door. That, I figured, might have been ma's room. She must have slept here with Petey in the other bed.

First, I lit the coil-oil lamp and then I rustled around for some paper. All I could find there at first was a couple of old envelopes.

With a stub of pencil I sat down and looked at the back of those envelopes. Some folks think well in one way, some in another. I like to get something on paper where I can look at it, study it and add a thought here and there. Tracing in the dust with a twig or scratching on a piece of bark is nigh as good.

This was pa's place out west. That was why that oak tree where we camped had seemed familiar. He had told me of camping there. Ma had come here with Petey and that man . . . my step-father. Petey had died here. Ma was gone.

That man . . . Frank. Somehow I even hated to say his name. Frank had expected to find something and he had found nothing. So what would he do?

He wouldn't believe it. He couldn't believe it. He had his dream, too, of easy money, somebody else's money. People hunting treasure are mighty unreasonable people as a rule. You can prove to them there isn't any gold and never was any, and they simply won't accept it. I'd seen that before.

He would think there was something. He would think ma knew and just wasn't going to tell him.

COMMENTS: Like the first fragment in this collection, *The Bastard of Brignogan*, this piece contains a good deal of information on the progenitor of the Talons. Not all of the material in these fragments is completely consistent; if you read carefully you can see Louis trying out slightly different versions of the Talon backstory to see which one he likes best. More about the family can be found in *The Ferguson Rifle*, *Rivers West*, and even a bit in the Sackett novel *To the Far Blue Mountains*.

While there are quite a few coincidences in Louis's fiction, this character accidentally winding up in his own family home is a whopper! I've never been quite sure why coincidence plays such a big role, but, though I'm fairly critical of my father's work, I'm left with the feeling that it wasn't laziness. The concept of synchronicity or connectedness between people was such a powerful force in Dad's imagination that he devoted his first novel, *No Traveller Returns*, to that very theme.

We should also remember that the world was a smaller and more compact place during his formative years. The population was less than half of what it is today, and with class and race barriers being what they were, connections between people who were very much alike may have been significantly more common. Dad transcended more of those barriers than many of his time, working as a laborer alongside people of all races from all parts of the world, and then living as a celebrity under conditions where people sought him out to remind him of their connection to his life. It all leads me to wonder if there may have been fewer degrees of separation between the people of his era than we tend to think.

This story was created late in Dad's career (1986 or so), and in his journal he revealed that he got the idea from a picture on a postcard. Wanting it to develop differently from other stories, he had chosen to "start it earlier in the story to get the full effect of the men lost in the snow storm and finding the cabin." This refers to him not starting at some high-stakes moment, which was his usual modus operandi. His notes included the following brief description of the story, which will give you some clues as to how a slightly different version of it evolved:

```
     A cowboy, drifting with two buddies, and broke,
comes to a ranch gate with a sign over it THE BURNING
LAMP. It gives him a twinge . . . long ago his Ma had
said she'd keep a lamp burning in the window for him.
He rides into the gate and they come up to a deserted
ranch-house, an empty barn. They go in and he finds
things that tell him this is, indeed, the place where
his mother and sister had once lived. With his little
brother, too. And another girl, taken in by them when
her folks were killed.
     They warm themselves in the cabin and he putters
about finding a fragment here and one there, he re-
members the last letter he got, worn almost away in
his pocket and the trouble facing them.
     He had run away at his mother's urging when his
stepfather threatened to kill him. His sister had
```

added a note to the last letter telling him of her
"secret place," a hollow in the old tree where she
kept her diary. He starts to ride away in the morning, then on a chance, turns back to the tree and
finds her diary and the last, sad days. Under the
trees he finds his brother's grave.

He begins a lonely trail and at the end when the
conflict comes to a head his two old trail partners
join him in the shoot out. They just couldn't see him
face it alone. Build into this all the charm of an
old folk song, even the rhyming words, a line here
and there until the song is ended.

THE JADE EATERS

A Treatment for a Motion Picture

COMMENTS: Of all the movie treatments in the Lost Treasures project, this is the only one that actually made it into the development process that might have led to its becoming a feature film. Dad kept careful files of his contracts, and *The Jade Eaters* appears here with the permission of (and special thanks to) Universal Studios.

As many feature film projects tend to do, *The Jade Eaters* dragged on interminably. A producer optioned the raw idea, some notes describing the narrative were set down in this treatment, but then the time came for another option payment to be made to Louis. The producer, typically, begged poverty, and Dad allowed him to keep trying to sell the project for free for a while. Amazingly, he eventually succeeded: Universal purchased the concept, and, in the best of circumstances, that would have been the start of a process where the story was discussed and perfected and a screenwriter was hired. However, for one reason or another, the project was abandoned. The number of stories that disappear into the black hole of studio "development" is astounding . . . some time ago the odds against a project's ever being completed were rather generously considered to be around 30 to 1.

The majority of correspondence about this project is dated 1956, and, having compared several sets of records, I believe the treatment reprinted here is actually an early draft. What was delivered to the studio may well have been a later and possibly more sophisticated version.

You will notice that character names are capitalized the first time they appear. That is a convention in the film business intended to allow a quick assessment of how many actors are needed and how to schedule them. The other stylistic aspect of a film treatment is that it is supposed to be written in the present tense. As a writer of traditional prose, Louis had a difficult time with this when he would write a treatment, and so, along with a few other corrections, I have converted this entire document into past tense . . . the way Dad would have been most comfortable telling this story.

It is important to remember that a treatment is really just a testing ground for ideas, an attempt to interest a buyer, and a point of departure for the continued development of the story concept. Even in this early phase it is interesting to see Dad playing around with ideas much more esoteric or even occult than those usually found in his published stories. As with some of the other Lost Treasures material, there are aspects of the narrative suggesting that James Hilton's *Lost Horizon* and possibly the work of Talbot Mundy were of greater influence on him than his writing in the Western genre would suggest.

Unlike many of the other stories in this collection, this manuscript is missing its first page rather than its ending. Page two begins in the midst of describing the protagonist, BEN STROUD, and his wife . . .

. . . RUTH, the daughter of a client, and had two years of married life before leaving for Korea.

His background fitted him perfectly for what he be-

came: one of the war's most successful combat patrol
leaders. Twice recommended for decorations he never received, he had finally been cut off with his company, and
had brought them out with the loss of but one man after a
harrowing retreat.

Awaiting him was news that Ruth had been lost in a
plane crash over southern Mexico. She had been visiting
her sister in Jamaica, and had started back with friends
in a private plane, planning a stop in Mexico City.
Caught in a storm, the aircraft disappeared over that unknown, unexplored area of Mexico where the three states
of Oaxaca, Chiapas and Veracruz come together.

Search planes had flown over the area and, when not
socked in with clouds, the few glimpses showed only an
unbroken jungle into which no known man had ever pene-
trated. An expedition starting in on the ground had come
to an area where nothing lived. No bird, snake, animal or
insect. The expedition doubled back, finding nothing, and
in a hurry to get out.

Ben Stroud could not accept the idea that his wife
was dead. Once before, in their first year of marriage,
they had gone hunting and she had fallen over a cliff
into a tree. Below her lay two hundred feet of sheer
rock, and the slightest move might have caused her to
fall. Later, after he had found and rescued her, she told
him, "I wasn't worried, Ben. I knew you'd find me and get
me out."

Discharged from the service he had gone at once to
Mexico, and when he had spent his savings in flights over
the jungle and mountains, he turned to free-lance photog-
raphy to make a living and continue his search.

Twice he was able to get into the area on the ground.
He found tapir, wild boar, jaguar, deer, and other life,
but no people. Yet there were rumors, queer stories of
people who had lived unmolested in the forest since before the time of the Maya, of a people who retreated

there to escape conquering tribes and had never emerged
nor come in any contact with civilization. There were rumors of strange creatures, half-man, half-animal, and
myths that the water-filled caves were the portals to
Hell.

Stroud believed none of it, but he did know that people are strangely resilient creatures with a great capacity for survival. He knew that Ruth had both hunted and
fished from the time she was a small girl, and she was
more than ordinarily practical and intelligent. If she
had emerged alive and unhurt from the crash, she would
have at least a fifty-fifty chance of survival.

Everybody advised him to let go. There was no chance
that anyone had survived. The area was trackless jungle,
drenched by torrential rains, haunted by fever. And then
he met ERIK PLATTNER.

He disliked Plattner from the beginning, but Plattner
had money and a willingness to go into the jungle. He was
a commercial explorer searching for medicinal herbs and
rare orchids, all the while keeping an eye out to find
gold, diamonds, or an ancient ruin filled with priceless
antiquities, of which he was a good judge.

Plattner introduced him to DR. TITUS SHAW, half-
Mexican, half-American, and a distinguished archaeologist
who divided his time between the United States and Mexico. Dr. Shaw had theories about the Lost Jade Mines of
Mexico. Strange theories.

They had formed an expedition, each with their own
agenda for exploration yet all looking for something in
the same intractable wilderness. The last to join them
was JANINE, Titus Shaw's daughter. After setting up a
base of operations in the village of Chimalapa and stock-
piling supplies, Ben made the run back to civilization to
pick Janine Shaw up at the muddy, seldom used airfield.

It was immediately obvious why Erik Plattner was
willing to have her along. She was young, attractive, and
seemingly not put off by the mud, heat, and mosquitos.
Gathering her bags, Ben had loaded the jeep and started
back to Chimalapa.

Tooling the jeep over the muddy, deeply rutted road,
Ben Stroud remembered what Plattner asked him on the
first day.

"Ever hear of the Indian jade mines?"

"I know they carved jade down there, and that's all I
know about it."

"Much of it was of high quality, fabulously beautiful
and extremely rare. The Conquistadores could never find
where it came from, nor has anybody else."

"Well, maybe someone will know something. We can always ask around."

"Unless they were afraid to talk . . . unless somebody has reason to keep them from it."

"You sound like you know something about it," Stroud
suggested.

"The Doc's heard some strange rumors and I . . .
well, the Chinese believed jade contributed to health,
they even believed that ground up and mixed into a drink
it would enable a person to live forever."

"Sounds like a lot of malarkey."

"Who knows? We live in an age of miracles, and we are
using a drug now called rauwolfia, and we refer to it as
a miracle drug, yet it has been known and used in India
for 2,500 years."

"So?"

"So how many other things did the ancients know that
we've forgotten? What of the tens of thousands of books,
many of them on medicine and science, that were destroyed
in the library at Alexandria in Egypt? And the libraries
right here in Mexico destroyed by Bishop Landa?

"Who knows but what the Chinese were right? They were

a thousand years ahead of us with vaccination for small
pox, and even so simple a thing as the wheel-barrow they
had for a thousand years before Westerners did."

"But that jade business doesn't make sense. It sounds
like a quick way to get kidney stones," Stroud laughed.
"I mean, if a man lived beyond a hundred years, everybody
would know it."

"Not if he did not want it known. Suppose only a limited supply of jade was available and those who knew
wanted it all for themselves?" Plattner had ended the
conversation abruptly.

"Anyway, don't mention jade to anyone, d'you hear?"

The jeep pushed its blunt nose up a small slope and
straightened out onto the longest stretch of road they
would travel all day. Far ahead of them an old peon stumbled along in the night and the mud. Thunder rumbled in
the far-off mountains and there were flashes of lightning.

"Look!" Janine touched his arm. "That old man fell
down!"

"Some old Indio with a skin full," Stroud suggested.

"I don't think so. I believe he's hurt or sick."

The old man had gotten to his feet, but managed only
a few steps before he fell again, and as the jeep drew
abreast of him he struggled to rise.

Ben Stroud brought the jeep to a halt and studied the
jungle with suspicion. Such a trick had been used by bandits in the States and might be used here. He reached inside his shirt which he wore with a button unfastened and
eased the Smith & Wesson .44 magnum into a better position. Then he got out.

Again he swept the jungle with hard, probing eyes before taking the old man by the arm and helping him up. He
was amazed at the fragility of the man. Lifting him as he

would a child, Stroud put him on the baggage in the back
of the jeep. As he put the old man down the aged eyes
flickered open. "Gracias," he whispered. "Gracias."

"Chimalapa?" Stroud inquired.

"No." In an area where few people spoke Spanish, but
mostly Zapotec or Quiche, this old man suddenly spoke
English. "The Rancho Encantada."

"Never heard of it. Anyway, we're only going as far
as Chimalapa."

"It is before Chimalapa. It is four . . . perhaps
five miles. At the Place of Nawales."

"Nawales?" The name was unknown to Stroud. He picked
up his map-board from the front seat. "Show me?"

The old man placed a fingernail upon a spot on the
map not far ahead of them. Obviously, he was no stranger
to maps. "There! Will you take me there?"

Stroud stared . . . the fingernail that indicated the
spot was manicured! Neatly tapered, perfectly polished,
and with a straight white scar across the brown finger
below the nail.

He lifted his eyes to Janine's and she was staring at
him. She had seen it too. He lowered the curtain and
walked around the jeep and slipped into the driver's
seat. "Bad road ahead," he commented, then added, "No
telling what we're getting into."

"Encantada," she mused. "It is a beautiful name. It
means enchanted . . . or haunted."

"I've been over this road several times, and I didn't
notice any turn off."

Thunder grumbled in the far-off peaks. If it rained
again before they reached Chimalapa the road would be im-
passable and they would be bogged down for the night. Yet
he could not put a sick old man out on the road in
weather like this. Wherever he was going they must take
him . . . and, wherever that was, there might be shelter.

He could hear the old man's heavy breathing, but

whether he was asleep, unconscious or merely breathing
badly he did not know. He had taken the old man's pulse
after placing him in the back of the jeep. It had been
frighteningly weak.

He glimpsed the opening suddenly. Narrow, scarcely
more than a game trail, he saw a faint, almost obliterated track running deep into the jungle. The trail was so
narrow leaves brushed both sides of the jeep. He twisted
and touched the old man's shoulder. "Is this the place?"

Struggling, breathing in short, hard gasps, the old
man sat up, blinking his aged eyes like an owl in a sand
storm.

"Si!" he gasped. Then from his pocket he drew an iron
key all of seven inches long. "Here."

They coasted down a small incline, splashed through a
pool that was hub deep, and then struggled up the slip-
pery slope beyond. For a mile farther they twisted, doubled and turned along the trail until suddenly mounting a
rise they found themselves stopped by a massive iron gate
with a huge, old fashioned lock. The key opened it easily
and after closing the gate they drove on.

The road was smoother now, and suddenly striking a
place where water had washed away the sand or earth,
Stroud saw the track was paved, with a width of seven
feet and the pavement of stone blocks, perfectly fitted.

"Father should see this," Janine whispered. "He believes the civilization they call Olmec originated near
here."

"I've seen some of the carved stones they left behind. Strange things, just big heads with no body."

"You're interested in archaeology?"

"All I want is to find my wife and get out of here."

"How long since she was lost?"

He said nothing for a moment, peering ahead through
the rain, which was beginning again. Then he said, "Three
years."

He knew she believed him a fool. How could he hope to
find her alive after so long?

They emerged from the jungle into a ranch yard. Before them was a long low building with boarded up windows, a barn, pole corrals, but no sign of life.

Pulling the jeep up close to the over-hang of the
porch, he got out and banged on the door. The sound re-
verberated emptily within. He waited and tried again,
pounding with his fist. Just as he was turning away he
heard a vague sound from within, and then the door was
unlatched. A big Indian in a serape and wide hat stared
out at him. Briefly, he explained.

The Indian carried his lantern to the jeep and held
it up as Stroud drew back the curtain. Instantly, the Indian handed the lantern to Stroud and lifted the old man
gently in his arms, then taking the lantern went inside
and closed the door after him. They were left alone in
silence and the falling rain.

It was impossible to go on. He knew the road before
them too well, and he also knew there was no other shelter, anywhere. They were going to remain here if they had
to sleep in the barn. Returning to the door he pounded
and pounded, but there was no response, no movement or
sound within.

He walked back to the car and got the key the old man
had given him. From the looks of the lock on the door it
would work here as well.

When the door was open his flashlight showed him a
very large and very empty room that showed no evidence of
occupancy for many years. Three doors opened off this
room and behind the first he found two carefully made
beds, one of them in a small alcove out of sight of the
first. This room was neat, clean, and seemed to have been
used more recently than the outer room could have been.

Behind the next door was just a bare, empty space
containing nothing but dust and cobwebs. The third door

opened into a large area that might have once been a
kitchen. There was no furniture, not even a bench, but on
the coals of a dying fire was a large, blackened coffee
pot. He hefted it--there was coffee.

On the floor near it was a spot where water had
dripped from clothing . . . or something.

Where a man had waited, perhaps? Waited for the old
man to come home? Waited for a peon who manicured his
fingernails?

He had opened three interior doors and there were no
more. Where, then, were the two men? They might have gone
through the back and outside again but there was nothing
visible in that direction but dense forest.

Janine glanced at him, "Ben, it gives me the shivers.
It's . . . it's like they were ghosts."

"Maybe they were, but if this coffee is any good
we're going to have some. I'll get our stuff out of the
jeep."

He moved their gear into the bedroom, and then they
returned to the fireplace with two cups. The coffee was
scalding hot, black and strong.

"We're staying here?" Her eyes searched his.

"Unless you're afraid to sleep in the same room as
me."

"I'm not afraid," she replied coolly.

He tried a sip of the coffee. "You probably think I'm
crazy to go hunting for Ruth after so long a time."

"You must have been very happy with her."

"I don't know. I used to think I was. Now, I don't
know. Ruth was a great pal, but she . . . well, she
wasn't very affectionate."

"But you're looking for her."

"I just keep thinking she's back there waiting for me
to come and get her."

"She must have great confidence in you."

"Maybe . . . I guess so." He got up. "We'd better get

some sleep." He glanced at her. "Are you nervous about staying here?"

She got up with him. "I carry insurance," she said coolly, and drew a compact .32 automatic.

He grinned at her. "It looks like a good policy."

He removed his boots, jacket and shirt, then stretched out on the bed with his pistol under his jacket and close to his hand. After a moment he got up and taking his duffel bag placed it on the floor just inside the door where anyone entering would be likely to trip over it. Then he went back to bed.

He awakened suddenly, his hand gripping the Smith & Wesson. The door was opening . . .

How long he had been asleep he did not know, but the light in the room seemed faintly gray.

He watched the widening crack of the door but was not worried. He knew what that .44 magnum could do. There was a muttered exclamation as someone stumbled against the duffel bag.

In the darkness Stroud could see it was a man and he carried a tray. The gun muzzle, still concealed by the jacket, covered every move as the man approached the bedside and placed the tray on the table. Then the figure retired softly and drew the door shut after him. Stroud sat up.

"What was that?" Janine asked from her bed.

"Breakfast," he said, seeing a coffee pot, two cups, some small cakes and fruit on the tray. "Come and get it before the genie takes it away."

He turned on his flashlight and found a candle on the tray, and some matches. He lit the candle.

She joined him and they ate a quick, silent breakfast. "I'd like to see that man we picked up," Janine said. "I wonder how he is?"

"We should get out of here. I fear somebody is trying to speed the parting guests."

The house seemed as deserted when they left as when
they had entered it and the mystery only deepened.

They were nearing Chimalapa before Janine spoke of
their experience.

"Ben, that was very strange but I don't think we
should let Erik know we spent a night in the same room."

He had been thinking the same thing. He wanted no
complications on this trip. As far as he was concerned
there was only one thing he wanted . . . get into the
jungle, find the plane, find Ruth if he could, and get
out. And he wanted no trouble with Erik Plattner, who, he
was sure, was a man it would be easy to have trouble
with.

"I'll tell dad," she said, "but I'd rather nothing
more was said of it."

"All right." He swung the jeep into the narrow street
and scattered chickens in every direction, then braked to
a halt before the cantina.

Plattner and Shaw emerged at once. "Get caught by the
storm?"

"We were lucky enough to get through at all. When do
we leave?"

"We don't . . . not for awhile anyway. We've lost our
guide."

The guide had disappeared. Chimalapa was a very small
village but the ALCALDE could not help them. He offered
one suggestion . . . why not give it all up? There was
nothing back in that jungle, anyway. Nothing at all. Ben
Stroud, hanging back and allowing the others to do the
talking, got the idea that the alcalde knew all about the
missing guide.

Stroud didn't think that the guide sounded like much

of a loss and when the argument died down he said so. Nobody, according to the <u>alcalde</u>, knew anything about the jungle, anyway. Stroud felt himself to be as good with a map as anyone the Army ever taught, Plattner was familiar with the wilderness and Dr. Shaw had done his bit of exploration. They had their supplies and permits and were as ready as they were ever going to get. Given the situation, Stroud told them, he was ready to proceed without a guide.

The <u>alcalde</u> vehemently protested, arguing that their well-being is his responsibility. But none of the Americans had trusted him from the start and so they made their plans to depart the next day.

Erik spent a good deal of time with Janine. To Stroud their relationship appeared to be more than casual and yet they were not truly a couple either. He made sure to carefully avoid them. Whatever the situation, it was none of his business.

They met in the <u>cantina</u> to eat, and as they sat over the remains of their meal Ben noticed an OLD INDIAN who stood nearby, seemingly very drunk, yet the old man was obviously listening. During the course of the conversation Ben stated that all he wanted to do was find his wife, and those words seemed to attract the attention of the Indian.

Titus Shaw told them of an old legend to the effect that South America's fabled Andes highway, built long before the days of the Aztecs, had actually originated somewhere in the north, near here, at the Place of Nawales. Janine shot Ben a startled glance and Erik, though quick to see it, said nothing.

Nawales, Shaw explained, means "wise old ones," but exactly what this "Place of the Nawales" was he did not know unless it referred to some temple where priests had once stayed.

After more than a year in Mexico, Ben's command of

the Zapotec tongue had become more than sufficient for
ordinary purposes. Leaving the others to talk he wandered
over to the bar and bought the old Indian a drink. The
man was a Zapotec, once a chicle hunter, and Stroud's
comment about searching for his wife caught his attention. "I never knew what an angel my first wife was until
I remarried!" the man said.

Then he leaned close to Ben's ear and whispered that
even he, a poor Indio, knew something that might help.
Beyond the village called Potrero there was a deep cut,
marked by a huge cypress tree. If one was to go down that
cut he would come to an ancient road, paved in stone,
that would take him far back into the jungle. It was the
ancient route to the mountains.

Ben walked to the door, looking out into the night.
From the shadows he heard the sound of a scuffle and a
cry for help. He stepped down into the street. TWO MEN
were struggling with the old Indian. He leaped into the
fight, and knocking a man down, was struck himself. By
the time he managed to get to his feet the two men had
run off and the old man was dead . . . knifed.

The townspeople were suspicious, but Plattner told
them that he was watching Stroud when he heard the cry,
and saw Stroud rush out to save the old Zapotec only
after the attack had begun. Another man from the cantina
eventually agreed; this was what he saw also. As he said
this a boy of fourteen slid into the room and stood
against the wall, listening carefully.

Ben had the strange feeling the locals were less interested in finding out what happened than what he might
have seen. Who, then, were the killers? And had the man
been killed because of the information he had given to
Stroud? Or was it because of something more that he might
have said?

Stroud discussed these points with Janine and the
others. As he did so, he noticed the boy hanging around

in the background. His attitude was seemingly dejected
yet he was focused intently on Stroud and his party. Ex-
cusing himself, Stroud strolled across the street letting
the boy follow. When they were together under the trees,
the boy introduced himself and explained.

His name was MIGUEL. The old man was his grandfather.
He had no other family, and Stroud had gone to help the
old man. So now that the old man was dead, if Stroud
would have him, he, Miguel, would be their guide, saying
he knew where the old road was, as his grandfather had
shown it to him.

Despite the protests of the alcalde, they decided to
leave, taking the muddy road toward Potrero. If they
could find the track of which Miguel and his grandfather
had told them then they would be on what could be called
the North American stretch of the Andes road and might be
able to drive far back into the jungle.

Twelve miles out, and several hours later, they were
forced to camp because of the bad road conditions. They
were directed to their camp site by a rider they met beside the trail, a man obviously of some education, wearing neatly pressed clothing, and riding a fine-looking
horse. The man introduced himself as SENOR DE MORLA, and
explained that he happened to live at a nearby hacienda.
He then asked if they would join both him and some of his
neighbors for dinner. There were, he said, few visitors
and so company was always welcome.

Plattner's group agreed with little discussion, the
prospect of learning more about the country from the people who lived there enough to get their promise, and De
Morla rode away.

Plattner looked after him curiously. "Nice looking
man. How old would you say he was?"

Stroud was suspicious, and said so. Shaw was skeptical and Janine amused. Only Plattner was silent. Stroud
and Janine walked back to where the rider had been stand-

ing as they came up the road. From the tracks it was obvious the horseman had been on the spot for quite awhile, for the horse had shifted his feet many times. In other words, they had been intercepted . . . but why?

"Too much coincidence," Stroud told them. "I think somebody doesn't want us to go back in there, not at all."

"You could be right," Plattner suggested. "If I knew where there was a jade mine, I don't think I'd tell anybody, myself."

The hacienda was an ancient but well kept place; its fortress like lines had been softened by gardens and many flowers. Stroud noticed that several large trucks were parked in the mud to one side of the house. He wondered if someone was in the process of moving in . . . or out. Three of the trucks were heavily loaded ore carriers, yet there were no indications of any sort of industry or agriculture nearby.

Their host met them at the door in a white dinner jacket, and the woman with him was very attractive but . . . strange. Her features were young but her eyes were old as the ages.

"Welcome. It's a bit of a going away party but we are glad you could join us."

Ben Stroud followed the others inside, and they were offered drinks. The house was beautiful, comfortable, and well decorated. Shaw gasped. He crossed the room to stare at a vase, frankly astounded. It was, he explained, a museum piece.

De Morla smiled. "Naturally, being on the ground, we have opportunities others do not. I could show you more but we are in the process of--um, moving north for the season."

Later, Shaw whispered to Stroud and Plattner that there was at least a million dollars in antique pottery and stone carvings within the room and the bar adjoining.

There were a dozen people present, several of them having strongly marked Indian features. Only one of them might be called young. She was introduced to Ben as EL-VIRA DE LEON, the daughter of a man who owned another ha-cienda not far off, DON JUAN VELASQUEZ DE LEON.

Her father was a tall man of commanding physique and a neatly trimmed Van Dyke beard. Elvira carried herself beautifully, and had fair skin and dark hair. Their name rang a responsive chord in Ben's mind though he could not remember why.

De Morla drew Dr. Shaw away from a hallway lined with cartons and suitcases. "Are you the Dr. Shaw, the archae-ologist? It is fortunate you have come at this time. We have just located a ruin just north of here that has never been examined by anyone. Would you like to be the first, Doctor?"

Dr. Titus Shaw was a short, stocky man of great en-thusiasms, boundless energy and perpetual good humor. He was also a man utterly without suspicions, devoted to his work, and without interest in financial gain other than that necessary for the continuation of his research.

Throughout the evening there was a casual but none-theless persistent effort to convince Stroud, Plattner and Shaw that going south into the jungle would be a waste of their time. They were told there is nothing to the south, and there never had been. Yet there were many unexplored ruins close by.

Leaving the conversation to the others, Stroud strolled around, looking at the art objects, some of them fantastically carved, and eventually he wandered out onto the terrace.

He found Elvira De Leon there, alone, and for the

first time he saw that suspended from her throat was a
jade pendant. Intricately carved, it was a tiny figure in
a wreath of strange characters. Stroud froze, flat-footed
with shock, his eyes riveted on the pendant. As he recovered his composure her lips twitched into an amused
smile, obviously mistaking his interest in the pendant
for interest in her obvious physical attributes.

She was a beautiful woman but there was another reason for his shock. The last time he saw that pendant was
when he put it in a box in Japan and mailed it to his
wife, Ruth. In fact there was a companion piece which had
been made into the setting for a ring which was even now
in his pocket.

Stroud's mind worked swiftly as he talked. Ruth must
have survived the crash . . . or at least, the plane had
been found and the pendant recovered from the wreckage.
So why was the finding of the crashed plane not reported?
And did it not also mean that somebody had been back into
the jungle?

Somebody obviously did not want that jungle examined.
The killing of the old man in Chimalapa and this party
were examples of the lengths to which they were prepared
to go.

This beautifully appointed home, miles from anywhere,
was more than it seemed. The gracious smiling people
about him seemed to be suddenly filled with menace. Instinct warned Stroud that an outright question about
where the pendant came from might cause trouble, and he
was prepared to wait.

"The girl with you . . . she is beautiful."

"Janine?" He shrugged. "I suppose she is."

"Strange . . . that one should be so preoccupied as
to ignore a beautiful girl. It is not flattering, Mr.
Stroud."

"I'm not the flattering sort of guy," he said, "but
that's a beautiful stone you have there."

She lifted the pendant and glanced at it. "Yes, our people do lovely work . . . it is very old, I think."

She changed the subject. "The tall blond man? What does he do?"

He explained about Plattner, then commented, "Do you travel very much? I'd think you'd like Paris, Rome, perhaps the Far East . . . but you probably know all those places."

"I have not been away for a very long time. Now, it seems that I shall have a chance . . . to leave home after a long time, it is a challenge."

"I'm sure you will enjoy it; there are so many places for us to see . . . you know, before we die."

Her expression changed and her face seemed to stiffen. For a moment she looked almost gray, old. "Do not talk of death." Then she tried to smile, "You know, you never think about it, then suddenly . . ."

"I hope that doesn't mean anyone you know is ill?"

"No, no. We are well, um . . . provided for."

Feeling that her answer was somewhat odd, Stroud walked to the edge of the terrace and leaned on the balustrade. Possibly her choice of words was just that English was not her principal language.

The jungle was no more than a hundred feet away. A solid mass of foliage, just beyond the lawn. In the shadow of the trees he could see the faint outlines of an ancient stone wall. He had seen that wall as they arrived; it completely surrounded the place and, old as it was, must still form a protective barrier.

"I am puzzled," Elvira leaned on the balustrade beside him, "as to why you wish to go into the jungle. It is a frightful place . . . like another world. If you go in you may never return."

"Don't let it worry you," he said quietly. "If we go in, we'll come out."

He glanced back into the room where Shaw was in ani-

mated conversation with several men, and Erik Plattner
was talking to Janine and an older woman. He was conscious of his own rumpled whites, which looked sad beside
the smartness of Erik's dinner jacket.

He felt a hand on his sleeve. "Mr. Stroud, you must
not go. We are the closest thing that you could call civilization for many miles. Within a day or two most of us
will be gone and there will be no one to help your expedition. I fear if you go into the jungle only disaster
can come of it, disaster, destruction and death."

"It can't be that bad," he said. "Men have been going
to difficult terrain the world over and, most of the
time, they have come back."

She was impatient. "You are an attractive man, Mr.
Stroud, but you are also a fool."

He reached out, lifted the jade pendant and turned it
in his fingers. "Beautiful," he said, "really beautiful."

On the back, etched into the gold, was the Chinese
character tao . . . the way, the path.

He remembered the man who had given him that jade. It
had been for bringing his child out of a battle ravaged
town in Korea, and he remembered the old Chinese who had
set it for him. Now here it was in Mexico, half way
across the world.

She looked at him coldly. "You are familiar, Mr.
Stroud. I do not like that."

His smile was equally cold. "You've convinced me of
one thing," he said. "I'll find what I'm looking for."

Turning away, he walked back into the living room.
Plattner left the people to whom he was talking and
crossed the room to him. "Ben," he whispered, "we've
walked into something."

Stroud waited, listening.

Plattner lowered his voice. "Shaw was right. Look
around the room--there's easily over a million dollars

worth of artifacts here!" He paused. "Do you know what
this means?"

"You tell me."

"It means they've found something, a ruined city, a
cave or tomb or a dozen of them, something no archaeologist knows anything about. If we could make a find like
that we could become rich, all of us."

"We'd have to get whatever it was out of the country.
Mexico won't allow antiquities to be taken out, and I
don't blame them."

"You leave that to me."

"If we found this site, and there was anything left
for the taking, do you suppose they would just let us
walk in and help ourselves?"

Plattner smiled. "Ben, why do you think I wanted you
along? Because of your beauty? I wanted you because you
were a trained, intelligent, fighting man."

"How do you know that?"

"I checked your background." He nodded at a gold mask
on the wall with garnets for eyes. "Look at that, the
finest example of Zapotec gold work I have ever seen."

He lowered his voice again. "Ben, there's something
they don't want us to find, and you know something else?
We're going to find it."

"Erik," he said quietly, "you're right about them not
wanting us back there in that jungle. They don't want
anybody back there, including searching parties. They
found the plane, Erik. Elvira De Leon is wearing a pendant I gave Ruth."

Erik shot him a swift glance. "You're sure?"

Ben Stroud took the ring from his pocket. "They were
twins, made by some artist during the T'ang dynasty."

"I'll be damned!"

"What about Shaw? How far will he go?"

"To find a ruined city nobody ever saw? To find arti-

facts like these? To be the first scientist on the ground
in such a place? Believe me, Ben, Shaw would do anything
short of murder, and he's a good man."

The dinner was excellent, conversation light, casual
and amusing until at the end, over coffee, De Morla suggested Dr. Shaw investigate the temple they had found,
"older than Monte Alban. It is to the north. I could mark
it on a map."

Thoughtfully, they drove back to their camp. Miguel,
their guide, was nowhere to be found. Stroud faced around
sharply, concerned and ready to act. "Doc, I think we
should break camp now, right now."

"And fail to examine a temple older than Monte
Alban?" He shook his head. "It would be criminal!"

"If we don't move now, and fast," Stroud said, "I
don't think we'll get out of here at all!"

Shaw shook his head, and they argued. Stroud was impatient, and worried. Miguel's grandfather had been
killed in Chimalapa, and the discovery of Ruth's plane
seemed to have been covered up. There was no telling what
was going on or how far these people would go. Some or
all of them had seemed to be moving or leaving but he
couldn't be concerned about that; several seemed to be
important individuals and they had a number of trucks
full of possessions; they couldn't easily disappear.

First, he must find the crash site. If he found that
and got out safely, he would have an argument for the authorities, enough to ask for an investigation. Then he
could smoke out De Morla and De Leon if he had to. But
first he needed proof.

Shaw had been impressed by his new friends and would
hear no argument against them. It was ridiculous. They
were wealthy people. What reason could they have for
keeping a scientific expedition out of the jungle?

Stroud walked out of the tent into the night, and after a minute, Janine followed. "What's the matter, Ben? You're behaving very oddly, you know."

"Something's bugging me. Something's all wrong around here and I'm trying to put my finger on it."

He explained about the pendant. Janine had noticed it and recognized the ring as the twin of the pendant.

"She's either dead," Stroud concluded, "or a prisoner."

"That's absurd . . . isn't it?"

"Erik has some ideas that make a sort of logic . . . he believes they have something to conceal. I think so too. Even though they seem to be leaving there is something they want to hide. I think the further we get away from here, and the faster we leave, the safer we'll be and the closer we'll get to whatever it is."

"I agree, senõr. We must go now!"

They turned swiftly to see Miguel standing behind them. There was blood on his head and face, and his white trousers were covered with swamp mud.

"They shot at me," he explained, "with a gun that made no sound. They could not find me in the swamp, but for a long time I was lost."

After they left Miguel had been prowling about, worried about his new friends, and curious about this _haci-_ _enda_ of which he had heard much. There was a place near the swamp where a gate had been standing open. He had approached from that angle, and had been shot at. He fell, hit his head, and ran away. But before that, he had found there was a branch canyon behind the house with a well travelled road leading into the mountains. It was also a very old road, but in better shape than the one he knew of.

Shaw was adamant, wanting to stay for a few days, but both Erik Plattner and Stroud insisted on pulling out before their hosts could turn violent. Stroud got out a

rifle and loaded it. Swiftly they bundled together most
of their possessions, and leaving the pyramidal tent
where it was along with some of the bulkier baggage, they
took off.

Stroud and Miguel rode in the first jeep. In places
the road was rough, and at all times it held to its width
of seven feet, but they sped along through the night with
the canyon slowly narrowing. At daybreak they pulled off
to the side of the road and in the first gray light of
dawn, they made breakfast.

Stroud kept a restless watch on the road. It was
doubtful that the people from the hacienda realized their
party was gone, yet it would not be long, and they must
make time while they could. How far had they come? Was it
forty miles?

He felt like he had when on patrol. There was real
danger here, he was sure of it. The place where they had
stopped was silent and eerie. Prowling about, he walked
among some boulders and suddenly found himself standing
at the edge of a tiny and long-abandoned graveyard.

There were a dozen graves without markers, perhaps
more, but there were at least six with stones carrying
inscriptions. Curiously, he walked over to the nearest
grave and squatted to read the inscription.

He looked, then looked again to make sure he had seen
aright.

Xcumane
1497-1911

It was absurd, on the face of it. If those dates were
correct then the man Xcumane had died when he was more
than four hundred years old!

He checked the stone beyond it, a stone that had
tipped sidewise and was half-covered with earth. He studied the date and name.

Francisco de Torres
1457-1890

It was ridiculous, but there it was again. He checked
three other stones and then got to his feet. "Dr. Shaw!"
he called. "Will you come here, please?"

Shaw came through the boulders followed by Erik and
Janine. "What is it?" Shaw asked as he approached.

Stroud indicated the dates. "You give me an answer."

According to the stone markers not one of these people, if the dates were to be believed, had lived less
than three hundred years.

"It's some sort of a joke!" Janine protested. "It's
ridiculous!"

Dr. Shaw was silent. He studied the stones and the
patina of years that smoothed their sides. He walked
thoughtfully around the graveyard. He did not smile.

Erik Plattner walked close to Stroud. His voice was
excited. "Ben! This is it! Remember what we heard about
the jade? That people who drank powdered jade might live
forever? Well, they are apparently doing it!"

Silently, they walked back to the jeep and loaded
their few belongings. Without a word said by anyone, they
started off again.

He had thought it ridiculous, and yet . . . was it?
What was ridiculous, and what was not? Was it not ridiculous to cut open a man's heart to save him? To see a picture on television taken hundreds of miles away?

And what of the stories in the Bible of men living
hundreds of years? Were they merely fable? Mistakes, ex-
aggerations, or differences in counting time?

Suppose those people back there had antiquities because they had always had them, or because they knew
where all the lost cities were because they had known of
them before they became lost?

When he had been speaking to Elvira, he had asked

what was important to her, and she had replied, "To live, and to go on living."

Wouldn't someone who had lived a very long time in good health want to protect their life at all costs? Those who are safe and secure tend to become more and more fearful, while people who live in tough conditions and with their lives in jeopardy are more ready to risk everything. He had seen it over and over in Korea.

Dr. Shaw spoke suddenly. "I have seen no sickness since we left Chimalapa."

"You haven't seen many people," Janine objected.

"I was not thinking only of people, but even plants. I have seen no disease . . . the air is fresh from the sea, drawn inland up this long canyon from the coast. It is high, for we must be almost a mile above sea level."

Stroud saw a trail of smoke above the trees. He swung the jeep over and lifted a hand. Erik stopped behind him and Miguel, who had been riding with Erik since the last stop, walked forward.

"There's a fire," Stroud said. "Wait, I'll have a look."

He returned with the information that three men with rifles stood guard at a cross-roads a hundred yards farther along. Through the glass they looked like tough, competent men, and were obviously Indians. Beyond them the valley widened out and there were cultivated fields; as near as he could make out there was coffee, cacao, yams and some citrus fruit. There were men at work in the fields.

"We've come sixty miles," Shaw said thoughtfully, "and this is supposed to be wild country."

"There's an old road off to the right," Stroud suggested, "and with luck we might cut around through the jungle without being seen."

"Any sign of buildings?"

"Yes . . . there's a ruin in the distance--it looks
like a very large one."

Successfully they skirted the guards and got to the
old road. It showed no signs of recent travel, and they
sped on.

Ruth might be ahead somewhere. Suppose she was alive?

The mountains loomed above them now. From time to
time, climbing some knoll to look around, they could see
miles of cultivated fields behind them. And the ruined
city, which they approached by a roundabout route, was
drawing nearer.

At one of their stops, Janine came close to Ben
Stroud. "I'm scared," she said frankly. "I'm scared and
yet somehow it's all so amazing I can't believe it is
happening. I just can't."

"I want a look at that ruin," Plattner said. "Do you
know of anything like that around here, Doctor?"

"Nothing . . . we've come upon something unknown to
the world outside."

"We'd better take it easy," Stroud advised. "From now
on we're heading into trouble."

"Or it may be nothing at all," Shaw said uneasily.
"We may be building danger when none exists."

They pushed on, more slowly now, with frequent stops.
Miguel was wide eyed with curiosity and apprehension, and
Janine sat quietly beside Ben, saying nothing. At each
stop the second jeep drew up alongside the first, so they
could talk.

The road dipped down and they drove through a small
village to the outskirts of the ruined city. There were
chickens, pigs . . . but there were few people around.

"They seem frightened," Shaw said. "Probably they haven't seen any strangers in years."

"I don't think they know we are strangers," Plattner said. "I think they have a reason to fear people in vehicles."

The road dipped into some brush and climbed a low hill to the edge of the ruined city. Beside a tumbled wall they looked out upon the broad expanse of a plaza. Ben got out of the jeep and mopped his brow. Upon both sides of the valley towering ranges lifted into the low-hanging clouds, and beyond the city with its massive ruined buildings, its pyramids and columns, the valley cut back still deeper into the mountains.

Plattner climbed a wall to look around and Dr. Shaw disappeared behind a building, studying the inscriptions. Miguel and Janine stayed close to Stroud.

There was no sound, and the very silence was disturbing. They walked out into the great plaza and looked toward the village. Suddenly there was a call from Plattner and he came down the wall, running, scrambling, finally jumping to the ground.

"Two vehicles are coming in from the west down a mountain trail, and another group from the north. I think they are hunting for us."

Stroud shouted for Dr. Shaw but he was preoccupied and merely waved a hand. They piled into the jeeps and swung by, getting him into the jeep with Plattner. Stroud led the way toward the upper end of the ruin, racing the jeeps across the plaza and dodging from sight. It took several minutes before they could find the road again, and then it was only a dim trail. Stroud braked around a narrow bend and saw before him another ruin, and beside it a jeep with four riflemen and De Morla.

De Morla advanced to meet them, pistol in hand. "I am sorry," he said coolly. "You could have gone north and found many ruins. You have chosen the wrong direction."

"What seems to be the trouble?" Plattner was walking
calmly up the road, his vehicle stashed somewhere in the
shattered walls and foliage behind them. "Are we tres-
passing?"

"Unfortunately, yes. And we must take you back. Now!"

"This is ridiculous, senor!" Shaw protested. "I have
a permit from the government for archaeological exploration. It covers this area."

De Morla shrugged. "Unfortunately we do not recognize
this or any other government of Mexico." His smile was
not pleasant. "We manage our own affairs. In fact, we do
not recognize any government at all."

"Nor the laws of humanity."

De Morla turned his eyes on Stroud. "What was that?"

"You don't report plane crashes," Stroud said, "but
you do rob the victims."

"Rob? What kind of talk is that? We rob no one. Why
should we? We have the wealth of ages at our fingers.
Nonsense!"

"The jade pendant Elvira De Leon is wearing belonged
to my wife."

De Morla was obviously surprised. "You are a fool.
Such a thing could not be."

"I identified it by the character <u>tao</u> placed on the
back of the setting. It was put there in my presence."

"So?"

"Where is my wife? Where is Ruth Stroud?"

De Morla turned sharply away. "Bind them," he said,
"and bring them in. We must return to the <u>hacienda</u>. We
have a day, no longer."

Ben Stroud was ten feet from the edge of the jungle
and when the guard was between himself and the rifles of
the others he turned nonchalantly toward him. The rifle
covered him, held waist high, but moving swiftly he
grasped the muzzle from underneath with his right hand,
and stepping in, grasped the action with his left and

ripped the rifle from the guard's hands, then hit him on
the jaw with a smashing butt stroke. Reversing the
weapon, Stroud shot at the next guard and then lunged
into the brush.

The entire action had taken no more than a split second. He hit the brush, dropped to a crouch and ran at
right angles. Bullets cut leaves where he had entered the
jungle, then swung to follow the sound of his movement.
He came to a game trail and stopped, holding low and
waiting for the shooting to cease. Then he went on, but
silently. He ran along the narrow trail, vaulted a ruined
wall, and crawled in among some rocks.

Behind him there were shouts, then a piercing whistle. Stroud lay still, panting.

He could hear the searchers, but his hiding place was
secure. A huge slab of rock was above him and the hole
into which he had crawled was small.

Ben Stroud waited. He kept telling himself they would
not kill the others until they had him, for as long as
the others were still alive they could always talk or
bribe their way out of this.

The shadows were growing long; it had been some time
since there had been any movement at all, and then he
heard a faint rattle of gravel and something moved below
him. Something moved down there, very quietly, something
that could be a man . . . or a jaguar.

Whatever it was stopped and stood still some distance
away. He crept close to the opening and looked down. For
an instant he did not believe what he saw, and then the
head turned . . . "Miguel!" he whispered.

The boy turned and looked up the slight rise to the
ruins of the building where Ben Stroud was hiding among
the rocks. Then the boy scrambled up the slope. "I look
for you," he gasped. "I get away, too!"

In a few minutes he had explained. The others had
been taken to the temple, which was also something of a

fort. And in the morning there would be more men and they
would make a careful, painstaking search. The men from
the <u>hacienda</u> were very frightened of something that was
about to happen. They wanted to be far away but they also
needed to remove any potential witnesses . . . the question was, witnesses to what?

Scrambling out of his hole, Stroud came down the
slope. His wrinkled whites looked ever more shabby now,
but he felt good. He had the rifle and there were still
four shells in it, and he had the Smith & Wesson with a
full box of ammunition.

He led the way into the jungle. They were higher now,
and once away from the ruins and secondary growth, they
came into a forest that was almost without brush, just
huge trees. They walked on and in the distance a great
wall could be seen. Overgrown with vines and brush, its
ancient stones closed off the upper end of the valley.
Finally they paused near a stream.

"You know the people down there?" Stroud asked, gesturing back toward the ruined city and the fields.

"I do not know them. I think no man knows them. My
grandfather, he says they were evil . . . they are men
who never die, but evil, not like the good ones?"

"Good ones?"

"The Nawale." Miguel pointed up the canyon. "They
live in the forest beyond the wall, and they are good
men. My father has seen them, and once when he was bitten
by a snake, they cared for him. They do not like Senor De
Morla and those Indios with him."

They started on with the first gray light. The boy's
story gave him some hope. Ben Stroud had an idea of what
he could do, but first he would need help. If the Nawale
would help him, then something might be possible.

They walked into an open area. Stroud caught a move-

ment from the corner of his eye and wheeled, raising the
rifle. Before them a tall man with dark hair was standing. He wore a white robe with braid around a square cut
collar.

Miguel tugged Stroud's sleeve. "The Nawale!" he whispered. Stroud lowered his rifle and walked forward to
greet the old man. He spoke in the few words of Quiche
Maya he had picked up, but to his surprise, the old man
replied in English.

"You have found trouble?"

Ben Stroud's explanation was brief and to the point,
and the old man listened attentively.

"I cannot help you," he said finally. "We do not par-
ticipate in the violence of others, but your friends are
in more serious danger than you suppose."

The old man explained then that a rebellion was
planned by the workmen from the fields and the jade mine.
De Morla and his associates had enslaved many of the
local Indians, and even some of the Nawale who had not
yet fled to the forests. These workers also drank the
powdered jade and within a generation the older ones were
reliant upon it to keep their youth and strength, for if
it was not administered regularly, the aging process returned with devastating results.

Addicted to this drug they were trapped, doing the
work so that a small community of Spaniards and aristo-
cratic Indians could live in comfort and wealth. But now
there was little of the jade left and De Morla and De
Leon had kept it a secret just how much or little they
had stockpiled over the years as the miners searched for
a new deposit. The time period between treatments with
the jade had been stretched to the maximum and the day
was coming when they would simply cease giving their
workers the needed dose.

"Are all those people going to die?"

"Yes." The Nawale nodded. "And De Morla is foolish,

for it is not the jade that has kept us alive these many years, but a quality in the jade . . . a substance that is veined through it. It actually takes very little to prolong life. They have trapped themselves here for centuries and are now convinced that they are doomed."

Suddenly, they heard the baying of hounds. But at their eagerness to go the Nawale was only amused. He took something from his leather purse and scattered it upon the ground. "This will stop them," he said.

"Is it a magic powder, Nawale?" Miguel asked eagerly.

"It is a magic powder that once changed the world's history," the Nawale said, smiling. "It is pepper . . . red pepper."

He took them to a place near a gate in the great wall that shut off the valley. Beyond that, he explained, was their home. There was no friendship between them and those below, who were late comers.

"Late comers?"

"We of the Nawale came long ago, when Kukulcan came, and we have preferred to live here. Once we occupied much of the land you have crossed, but when the Spanish and their allies, who were northern Indians, came we retreated into these mountains.

"You have met De Morla. He was one of them. Juan Velasquez De Leon was another. Both were listed as missing by Cortez and were believed killed, but both took Indian wives and preferred to remain here, where there need be no death."

"Suppose they follow us?"

"They will come no further. They will be angry, but they will come no further."

"How is it that you speak English?"

The Nawale explained that from time to time men from their valleys went out into the world, on pilgrimages, or to find books or supplies they needed. There were men among them who spoke many languages. They went out, but they always returned; sometimes, but rarely, they communicated with scientists or physicians.

Stroud waited in the shadow of the wall, but the pursuers evidently lost the trail for the dogs failed them and the sounds of pursuit died out. The morning wore on, and he became increasingly worried. Despite himself he kept thinking about Janine.

He asked the Nawale about the plane crash, and discovered that only one had survived . . . a woman, a young woman. She had been found and taken away to the settlements below. "But she tried to escape and was killed," the Nawale explained.

"Who killed her?"

"It was De Leon . . . who was the Conquistador. When he first came he was one of the best, but endless life does not always make one a better man. He is corrupt, Mr. Stroud. Long life has corrupted him."

Ben Stroud grew restless and finally he got up. The Nawale glanced at him. "Yes, it is time. They have gone back, the searchers have, and they will not come again. But you must hurry if you would save your friends.

"You will find them," the Nawale continued, "in the temple. Approach it from the rear and there is a way through the ruins. But you must hurry; they distribute the jade at sundown and when it is discovered there is no more there will be a rebellion. The Conquistadores will need to flee and they will allow no one who could identify them in the wider world to live."

Ben Stroud picked up his rifle and started down the hill. He did not wonder at what the Nawale knew, nor did he doubt any of what he had heard. Perhaps it was nonsense, perhaps it was not, but what he wanted to do was to get back and get his people out of there . . . fast.

Crouched among the ruins at the edge of the huge
plaza they looked toward the temple. Beyond it there were
scattered groups of the workers who shouted to those in
the temple that it was time, time for the jade that kept
them young and strong. Tools and a few weapons were bran-
dished and several of the hacienda's jeeps had been over-
turned; one was burning.

Then De Leon appeared on the steps and yelled back.
Stroud could not distinguish the words but Miguel told
him that De Leon was telling them they must wait, and
they were shouting that they could not wait, that it must
be now. Suddenly the knots of men grouped together and
began to push toward the front of the building. De Leon
lifted a pistol and fired downward. A man fell, but the
rest rushed and as several others fired at the guards De
Leon ducked back under cover.

Circling behind the building Stroud found the door
he'd been told of. The thick wood was shaped and bleached
to look like stone, and the two of them entered. There
was a short, walled passage, and then a room.

Only one man was on guard and he whirled in surprise
at their approach. Stroud was in no mood to stop--he
smashed into the man, knocking him down, then covered him
with the rifle. Gleefully, Miguel grabbed the guard's
rifle and rudely jerked the bandolier from the man's
shoulder. To their angry demands he could only gesture
toward the interior of the building. Stroud shoved the
man outside and advised him to run for it. He barred the
door behind him.

From in front of the building there were shouts and
yells. The people were attacking. There was a rattle of
gunfire. Ben Stroud lifted a curtain and peered into an
inner room. There, against the wall, stood Janine, her

face stiff with fear. She looked at him, then glanced quickly away so others would not be drawn to him by her gaze.

Dr. Shaw was on the floor and there was blood on his head, dried blood, from a blow some time back. Erik Plattner was there and he was talking.

At first Stroud could hear nothing, and then he caught the words.

". . . you've lost unless you listen to me. You can keep them out, keep them out until they die out there. But what of you, De Morla? You intended to be long gone by now. What of De Leon?"

"I have a jeep hidden away. I can take you to it. I can save you. But I want the contents of the room back there at the <u>hacienda</u>. I want everything that's in it."

Stroud shifted his position. He could see no one but Janine and Shaw because the others were near the door, and he could not take a chance on stepping in the room to face them for they would have the advantage of position . . . and if they fired at him Janine and her father would be beyond him, in the direct line of fire.

De Morla growled, "I won't kill you if you tell me where it is and give me the keys. If you are lucky they won't kill you either."

"Trust a dying angry mob? Forget it. Without a vehicle you'll never get away!"

"I do not trust you. Once away from here your group will not keep our secret." Turning, De Morla raised his voice and called out, "De Leon! Get ready--we are going to attempt an escape! We don't have much time!"

"Just take me," Plattner argued. "You can make me one of you. I am just one man--give me the jade like you did for them." He gestured to the mob outside. "You know you can trust me if I need the jade!"

Janine was staring at Plattner, shocked.

De Morla hesitated.

Stroud gripped the rifle in both hands, ready to take a chance. From the front of the building there was another out-burst of rifle fire, and the sounds of a struggle.

"They might get in." Plattner was calm. "And even if they don't, they can hold you here. They may die, but you will die also. I am your only hope."

De Morla suddenly agreed, then added, "But the others must stay." At that, Plattner merely shrugged. He started for the door and De Morla turned his pistol on Shaw.

"Hold it!" Stroud stepped into the room, his rifle high.

"We are going out the back," Stroud said, "and you two are coming with us." Stroud jerked the barrel toward Plattner and De Morla. "At least as far as the door."

Plattner hesitated. "Ben," he said, "we can walk out of here. We can make a deal."

"I only want to walk out of here," Ben replied shortly.

Janine helped her father to his feet. Stroud demanded to know where De Leon was. The firing out front had stopped, and there was no sound. Neither De Morla or Plattner would reply.

Stroud began to back down the passage, his rifle on Plattner and De Morla. He directed Janine and her father to go first but to keep to one side of the passage and out of the line of fire.

"You go out there," De Morla snapped, "and they will kill us all."

Stroud refused to listen. He had seen the jeep parked just off the road, and he knew what he was going to do. There was nothing here for him. Ruth was dead and De Morla knew of it, but it was De Leon that he really wanted, and wanted badly. With any luck having De Morla hostage would allow him to get close to the other Spaniard.

"Stroud," Plattner said, "I've made a deal. Everything in that room back there, everything, and all of it
for us. And the secret of the jade."

"There is no secret," Stroud replied, "except the
something that even he," indicating De Morla, "does not
know. It's not the jade. There's another substance, found
within it. When refined it actually takes very little of
it to have the same effect."

De Morla was pale. "What do you mean?"

"I talked with the Nawale. They know. It's never been
necessary to mine jade in such volume."

De Morla's lips worked. "You're wrong. You must be
wrong!"

"Neither one of you is going to get what you want but
maybe we can get out of this situation with no more
bloodshed. So, shut up and get moving!"

They left the building by the wooden door and Stroud
started for the jeep, forcing them to follow. Shaw
reached it and was helped in, managing to start it. If
they were to escape now it must be quickly. If they
didn't get away the angry mob was apt to tear their op-
pressors apart and any strangers along with them.

He did not know exactly how long a man could live
after the time came for the drink, but from the way these
people were behaving he suspected it was not long. He was
sure now that the man they had picked up on the road to
Chimalapa had been such a man, one of those who had been
searching for other deposits or a Nawale returning home
after his supply of the purified substance ran low.

Stroud crouched on the tailgate of the jeep, rifle in
one hand, the other clenched around one of the canvas
covered ribs. "Take it easy until you're in sight of
them," he warned, "then gun it."

As the jeep rounded the front of the temple the workers started forward in a ragged line. There was a shot
from De Leon's defenders and a man fell. That was fol-

lowed by sporadic firing from the crowd. Stroud glanced
toward the fighting and in that instant Erik Plattner
swung a back hand blow that knocked the rifle from his
hand. The jeep lurched and his grip was torn loose and he
fell.

Bullets smashed into the pavement beside him and the
jeep was tearing away. Janine, who had grabbed wildly at
him, had fallen also. Coming to his feet, Ben Stroud
caught the girl and, running, they reached the shelter of
the temple wall again. They hugged it closely as bullets
raked past them. The gunfire had not been from the mob,
but from the temple top.

Running, they ducked back into the door from which
they had come only a short time before. It was but temporary shelter, yet any move to leave it might expose them
to fire from the top where De Leon and some of the guards
were waiting.

From inside the temple there were running feet. Flattened against the wall, Stroud shucked the Smith & Wesson. A guard came into sight and he fired. The heavy slug
hit the man and knocked him back onto the steps from
above, the concussion of the big pistol loud in the narrow passage.

Then there was a noise of a door scraping open from
the passage behind them. Stroud started to turn, but was
stopped by a cold feminine voice. "Drop the pistol or I
will shoot you both."

It was Elvira.

He dropped the pistol.

De Leon came running down the steps with two men at
his heels and a sword raised to strike.

"Now!" Janine said, and shot Elvira with her hidden
.32 automatic.

The woman fell, with a low, moaning cry of horror,
and De Leon lunged. Ben Stroud turned on the ball of his
foot and knocked the blade aside with his left forearm.

The man reversed and cut viciously and as Stroud backed
into Janine, he tripped, and the two of them went down.
One of De Leon's guards grabbed the arm of the Spaniard
and pulled him out the door and toward the plaza.

Stroud scooped up his fallen gun and followed Janine
from the passage. They headed for the ball court across
the plaza. The jeep wheeled into sight with Erik Plattner
and De Morla. It jerked to a stop near De Leon and there
were a few hurried words as De Leon piled into the jeep.

Ben Stroud paused on the rubble strewn slope of the
court, taking cover and gasping for breath. Janine, still
clutching the .32, held his arm.

"You all right?" he asked.

"Yes."

They were looking for a better place to hide when the
jeep ground to a halt below them. Some of the workmen who
had scaled the temple walls were shooting down at it.
Their bullets caught one of De Morla's guards and he
fell . . . but then, without any of the men in the jeep
returning fire, one of the marksmen collapsed, another
went to his aid, but then it seemed as if neither could
arise.

"We have to go. Now! Get back in the truck and
drive!" De Morla ordered.

But Erik turned and ripped the pistol from De Morla's
hand. Flipping the gun around he shot the other guard in
the back of the head. He then turned the pistol on De
Leon.

"Hand it over!"

He surrendered his weapon. "Just help us get back to
the hacienda!" De Leon begged. "You can have what you
want but we must get back to have our potion. If we do
not our fate will be the same as these peons."

Erik came out from his cover behind the jeep.
Stroud's gun was thrust into his waistband but his hand
was hooked in his belt and he turned slowly.

Stroud hesitated, catching his breath. "If I shoot,"
he said to Janine, "run."

"Without you?"

"I'll be right behind you."

Plattner walked to the side of the court. "Ben," he
said, "why don't you join us? You know too much; you have
to be in this thing or out of it, and there's nothing
waiting for you on the outside.

"You can run this end of things if you want. We can
get this stuff out of the country and in the States it
will make us rich. They've got a stash of the jade back
at the hacienda. If you're right we'll be rich enough to
figure out exactly what it is that creates the longevity.
What d'you say?"

"Where's Shaw?"

"We dumped him back yonder."

"Alive?"

"Sure . . . we just didn't want him around for
awhile. Later, we can use him. He knows how to dig, and
how to preserve what we find."

"I want no part of it. I'm clearing out."

"That is not an alternative. This is your last
chance!"

"You're going to work with them?"

Plattner smiled. "I'm where the money is, Ben, you
know that." He grinned and while Stroud didn't doubt that
he had just heard the pitch Plattner had given De Morla
and the others, he knew that in his case it was just window dressing--the man was going to kill him no matter
what he said.

Ben Stroud saw the movement of Plattner's shoulder
that brought the gun up and he yelled, "Run!"

The gun had fairly jumped from Stroud's waistband. He
fired from waist level, knocking Plattner back against
the jeep. De Morla twisted, whining like a sick dog and
tearing at Plattner's coat and Stroud realized he was

trying to get the keys to the jeep from the dead man's pocket.

De Leon struggled to get out of the vehicle and then tumbled headlong to the stone.

Juan Velasquez De Leon, the man who had been one of the trusted captains of Cortez, got to his feet and started toward them. Then he seemed to stagger and he stopped, peering up at Ben Stroud as if staring into the sun.

Stroud paused, gun up, but holding his fire. All sound had ceased.

De Leon advanced another step and then seemed to crumble as his knees gave way and he fell. De Leon tried to rise, then lay back.

Gun ready, Ben Stroud descended several steps, then froze. The face of De Leon was that of a wizened, dried up old man . . . or a mummy.

Ben Stroud looked beyond him to the still twitching body of De Morla; the face up-turned to the last rays of the sun was monkey-like with age. The clothing sagged about the shrunken figure.

There was no more shooting, no sound from the crowd of mine workers, nothing. He turned and started up the steps toward Janine.

"What is it?" she asked. "What's happened?"

"Let's go find your father," he said. "There's no more to do here."

They descended the steps. In the distance, far back of the plaza they could see Dr. Shaw picking his way through a maze of bodies. His clothing was rumpled and dirty, and his face and head were bloody, but he was all right.

"Mr. Stroud?"

They turned . . . it was the Nawale. Though exhausted, head ringing from gunfire and emotionally spent,

Stroud noticed his hands. The carefully groomed nails,
the scar on his finger.

"Do you still have the key I gave you?"

It took him a moment to remember. Their night in the
mysterious house seemed such a long time ago.

"Yes."

"It works on the gate in the wall also. Come if you
wish, Mr. Stroud. We would welcome you among the Nawale."

He turned and started off.

"Throw it away," Janine said, "it frightens me."

He paused, key in hand, ready to toss it into the
ruins. The Nawale was far off now. Ben Stroud weighed the
key in his hands, glanced at it, smiled, and slipped it
into his inside coat pocket.

THE END.

THE FREEZE

The Beginning of a Science Fiction Story

There, now . . . a fire going. A few dead branches
from the lower part of that tree, some bark from the
under side of the big log . . . drag that dead-fall
closer. It's going to be a cold night.

Nothing looks so good as a fire when a man is cold,
or when he is hungry . . . or alone. Stirs memories,
too . . . takes a man back . . .

Cold . . . and rain. Setting in for a miserable
night. I'd better lace the branches tighter, pile on some
more evergreen boughs. I'm not feeling too good . . . not
so young as I used to be.

How many fires? How many lonely fires? And each one I
have built with careful hands, with tender hands. Fire is
a precious gift, a sacred thing . . . the first step Man
made in his march upward from the beast.

The shadows play, the wind touches the fire and it
ducks its points of flame and gives a gusty sigh . . .
a stick falls and the sparks fly up . . . I add another

stick and another . . . now let it blow and let it rain,
I have my fire.

Black are the columns of the trees . . . black are
the masses above where the wind plays tiny violins among
the pine needles . . . and off there a bare tree chafes
its branches together . . . a cold sound, a lost sound.

How many miles did I make today, I wonder? Miles have
lost their meaning, of course. If I could find a car . . .
but there would be small chance of that. In a city I could
find many things lost, useful things to me.

I feel the cold more now, even though it is growing
less. This year the ice melts a little at noon. It is a
sign, but a small one. I think the dust is going away and
someday we will have the sun again.

The sun . . . how long since I clearly saw the sun?
It was the day I started to return, coming down the
river. It was about ten degrees below zero that morning,
but bright and cold . . . and then it happened.

We should have known, all of us. It had happened before and there was nothing to prevent it happening again.
We had the evidence . . . mammoths or bison had been
found frozen and completely preserved, even with green
grass in their stomachs. The last time it had happened, a
chap from Columbia University had established the time by
carbon-dating . . . 28,000 years ago.

A sudden deep freeze, everything alive frozen in
their tracks. Killed . . . dead . . . wiped out, just
like that.

What had caused it? Nobody speculated very much. The
theories of cataclysms were out of fashion right then,
and scientists, creatures of fashion as are we all, carefully avoided any facts that seemed to controvert their
pet theories.

A mammoth with green grass in his stomach . . . obviously frozen very quickly . . . a perfectly preserved

ancient bison . . . the last was in Alaska, the former
in Siberia. But there were a few vague theories about
interstellar dust clouds shutting off the heat of the
sun . . . and it happened again, in April 1954.

More fuel . . . the appetite of a fire is amazing
. . . the tongues of flame lick the chill from the dead
branches. More fuel here now than there was twenty years
ago. Two or three days more and I should reach the site
of Palm Springs. What would they think at that once desert resort to see it now? All the northern Mojave and
most of the old Colorado deserts have been sprouting pine
forests for the last several years.

Snow falling . . . the rain is changing to snow. It
is May if my calculations are right. It was seven years
ago this May that I saw my last human being . . . it was
a woman, she was dying. Dying when I found her.

Starvation . . . cold . . . exhaustion, and loneliness. She had nothing. Had seen no living human being in
four years, she said.

It had come so suddenly there was no chance to prepare. Somewhere some scientist may have recorded the temperature. My own thermometer showed minus 30 Fahrenheit
before it went out of whack. The temperature might have
fallen to 60 below zero. Possibly colder . . . my advantage was simple. I was coming back from a year in the Arc-
tic, taking the route up the Mackenzie River, and I had
plenty of warm clothing and was conditioned to great cold.

At a trappers cabin I holed up, and the snow buried
it except where I kept an opening. It snowed for more
than a month, but the winds blew, and sometimes I could
get out for more fuel. There was food, so I stuck it out.
It was more than a month before I appreciated what must
have happened.

After awhile the food got short so I loaded the rest
on a hand-sled I found near the cabin, loaded up a little
dry fuel, and struck south. By that time I was ready for

the cold. My body had adjusted itself to a degree. I was
always cold, but I survived.

Three Indians were living at the trading post. They
let me have a few more supplies, and I continued on. But
after that one city . . . after that I learned to avoid
them.

The cold had struck at the end of winter and fuel
supplies had been low. A rail strike, for reasons I never
understood, meant food supplies were depleted also. There
was open war in the city, bitter fighting over food, and
ransacking and looting of houses and stores. Thousands
had died in the first awful weeks of cold, many of them
trapped in apartments that, without electricity, were
their only shelter.

It had been a warm spring in the States. The cold had
struck with daytime temperatures in Minnesota, the Dako-
tas and Maine cascading downward from the middle 70s to
below zero within a month.

The human body is amazingly tough, and amazingly ad-
justable to change . . . only it requires time, and there
was no time.

Twenty-four, that's what I was, just twenty-four
years old, with all my future before me, before my whole
generation. But it was neither my education nor my training that saved me, it was my hobby . . . Hunting, tracking, living off the country. I knew how to survive.

Got to move, getting stiff. That's the penalty of
growing old . . . and I'm old now, although in good shape
from activity and out-door living. Got to get more fuel
before I settle down, and some snow to melt for water.

One thing about cold . . . it preserves. My advantage
was that I was away from cities, that I knew what to eat,
and where to find it, and that I avoided civilization and
the chaos it created.

It is probable that thirty percent of the world's
population died within two months of that April.

Others died within subsequent days, and then still others in the struggle for existence and in fighting over food, clothing and fuel. Here and there small groups organized and worked together for mutual benefit. These groups made out best of all, some to finally die, but often to survive on down the years.

COMMENTS: This is likely Louis's earliest attempt at writing science fiction. Though later in life he would occasionally buy a sci-fi novel, most of it was foisted upon him by me. I was an avid reader of the genre, and, while he liked it too, Dad was never entirely at ease with the idea of creating his own SF stories. He preferred to have more of a foundation in reality. He was, however, continually fascinated by the possibilities and by the "frontier" aspects of the genre. Because of a connection facilitated by a friend of mine, composer Fred Paroutaud, Dad eventually joined Dr. Thomas Paine, head of NASA during Apollo, when he formed the National Commission on Space. It was an incredible opportunity for my father to discuss a good deal of the science without the fiction.

While the cause of the sudden cooling of the earth in this story seems to be an interstellar dust cloud, the mid-1950s was a time when a new ice age was considered a real possibility. Fears of global cooling—caused by space dust, the humidity from a warming trend creating more snow and glaciation, increased volcanic activity, or nuclear war—lasted through the 1980s.

In this case the direct inspiration seems to be the mystery of the "Berezovka Mammoth," which had been discovered in Siberia around the turn of the century. The Berezovka Mammoth was found with grass in its teeth and mouth, suggesting that it had died and been frozen fairly suddenly. Dad mentioned this connection, and his ongoing interest in it, in the following journal entry from October of 1986:

People wonder how I write so much. I wonder why I write so little. People suggest stories when my brain is loaded with stories . . . and [I] would be telling them by the roadside if not with a typewriter . . . my study is filled with fragments of stories. I have just read one, a few pages written long ago of a man who survived a terrible disaster to the earth, something like when the mammoths were frozen, some with grass undigested in their stomachs. This man was in the far north and survived, stayed away from cities. Good story there, may never find time to write it.

It's interesting to see Louis make a stab at a postapocalyptic tale. With its emphasis on man-against-nature survival, if he had ever found time to return to it, "The Freeze" might have been right up his alley.

Being from North Dakota, Louis was more familiar than he wanted to be with cold weather. For a short time he trained soldiers in winter survival and tested newly developed gear in Michigan's Upper Peninsula.

BEN MILO

The Beginning of a Crime Story

When Ben Milo returned to his cabin he put on the
coffee pot. That was pure habit, of course, the ingrained
pattern of years. Then he stood in the middle of the room
and tried to think it out.

He had seen the car come bounding and plunging over
the desert as if driven by a madman. Certainly, nobody
who knew this country would drive like that, or even venture onto his old trail in anything without four-wheel
drive. It was a burro trail, not a highway.

A few years back he would have waited cynically for
them to come, wiry, able, confident. But his mind worked
a little slower now and arthritis had stiffened the hands
that had once handled a gun with deadly speed. Ben Milo
had been born to hard country and rough living; however,
that was eighty-six years ago.

Ben had been an outlaw for too many of those years
but his lawless deeds lay buried in the graves of his
generation. If anyone suspected him now it was that young

highway patrolman, Jim Garrity, who was always asking
questions about the old days.

Ben Milo liked Garrity. He was a salty youngster, fit
to have walked with the old breed. They had worked together a time or two . . . like when that Prescott youngster was lost over east. Ben's eyes were not much for
reading print, but he could still read sign. They trailed
that youngster nine miles over the badlands before they
found him.

Three times since then Garrity had called on Ben to
lend a hand and each time they had found what they went
after. Old . . . yes, Ben Milo was old, but he could
still walk twenty miles in any kind of weather and over
almost any kind of country.

When he first saw the car he had stopped to watch. It
was shining and new, but when it hit the wash below his
place it stopped as he knew it would. By direct travel,
up and over the hillside, the wash was only ten minutes
from his shack, but by the trail it was a good hour of
walking around the rocky backbone of a mountain that
thrust up boldly from the desert.

He knew that wash, and nothing short of a tractor was
likely to get them out of it. He had stood listening to
the roar of the motor and the spinning of tires in loose
sand, heard the swearing as they hurled blame back and
forth, and then they came up out of the wash pushing the
girl ahead of them.

There were three of them, boys or young men, and they
wore city clothes and one of them was carrying a suit-
case. Another one carried some kind of a weapon, too
short for a rifle, but obviously heavy. Might be one of
those tommy-guns he'd seen at the picture show. They were
packing no grub and not one of them had a canteen.

Ben backed off the ridge and returned to his cabin.
When he had the coffee pot on, he gathered his canteens

and water sacks and hid them away. Had it not been for
the girl he would have gone back up in the rocks and
waited them out, and Ben was an Indian when it came to
waiting.

That girl . . . she was in real trouble, and in Ben's
day even an outlaw would go out of his way to help a
woman. It looked like she might be a hostage. Certainly,
that outfit was on the dodge. That suitcase now, it might
be filled with loot.

He must be careful. The last thing he wanted was a
shooting. Folks asked too many questions these days, and
they pried into a man's past. It was best to let the dead
past remain dead.

Ben was a hard old man whose life had been lived
among hard, fiercely independent men. The law was often
too far away to call, even if a man had been of a mind
to. A man fought his own battles back then; most of the
time he didn't have a choice.

His baptism of fire . . . at least familiarity with
it . . . came one evening when he was a youngster playing
in the street back at old Fort Sumner . . . that was in
'81. He had seen Sheriff Garrett come up the street with
his deputies, John Poe and Tip McKinney, and stop at Pete
Maxwell's place. The deputies sat down on the steps and
Pat walked back to the room where Maxwell lay in bed sick.

A few minutes later he saw Billy come out of Deluvina
Maxwell's adobe, and he heard her say, "There's a side of
beef hung up on Maxwell's porch. You cut yourself a steak
and I'll fry it for you."

Ben had seen Billy start for Maxwell's place and he
called after him, but Billy had just waved a hand . . .
and a minute or two later there were two gun shots. One
of them had killed Billy, the other they found years
later, embedded in the bottom of a wash stand. Garrett
had fired and thrown himself to the floor. His second
shot missed by nine feet.

Only a few of the old breed lived on. Wyatt died in '29, George Coe, Jeff Milton, Chris Madsen and Dee Harkey in the 1940s. The old ones were like that. They lived on hard work, beef and beans and if you didn't shoot them they'd live forever.

That outfit coming up the trail. They weren't going anywhere, they just thought they were. Why didn't they learn about the country before high-tailing it off into the desert that away? They must have spotted this trail and turned off into it to hide . . . or to cut across country to the other highway. They had ridden into a death trap, but the trouble was it could mean death for Ben Milo and for that girl, too.

He could see them come up the slope to the bench where the old mine was located. The cabin where he lived, a ramshackle sheet-metal shed and the gallows-frame over the shaft were all that remained except for a few foundations. Nobody had tried working the mine since 1905. Long after it was abandoned, Old Ben moved in, filed on several claims, and did the assessment work.

The tall one had his shirt out of his pants and he carried that tommy-gun. He was tall, but thin. The second one was thick-set and the third a gangling youngster of sixteen or so. The oldest could be no more than nineteen.

The girl? Well, say seventeen . . . and mighty pretty.

She took a quick look around when they reached the bench, and he would have gambled it was not the first such lay-out she had seen.

Ben Milo stepped into the door. "Howdy, folks! Glad to see you! Coffee's on!"

The gun muzzle lifted and the stocky one started his hand toward his waist-band. So he had a gun, too.

"Coffee? On a day like this? You got a beer?"

"No ice." Ben's eyes went to the girl. The utter despair in her eyes had changed to hope. A body would think

he was four men, the way she looked at him. What could he
do? What chance did he have? "No electricity," he added.

"No telephone?" The tall one seemed to be the boss-
man. His eyes swept the area. "You've got a radio? TV?"

"Nothin' like that away out here." Ben's eyes sur-
veyed them mildly but shrewdly. "Like I said, no electricity."

The tall one gestured with the gun. "Stand aside, Old
Man. Buzzer, you go inside and have a look-see."

Ben Milo moved aside, careful to make no sudden
moves. The tall one with the tommy-gun had a shoulder-
holster beneath his shirt. It was open far enough to make
grasping the gun a simple thing.

Buzzer went up the steps and into the house. A moment
later he appeared. "Nobody here."

"There's coffee," Ben suggested mildly.

"What else have you got? To eat, I mean?"

"Beans . . . I live mostly on beans and rice. Time to
time I make myself a batch of sourdough bread."

Buzzer stood aside as they entered. "Crumby lookin'
shack. On'y two rooms. This'n and the bedroom behind the
blanket."

Ben Milo walked to the cupboard and took down cups
and saucers, then poured the coffee. He had just enough
cups to go around. They needn't have said it was
crumby . . . as desert shacks went, it was mighty neat.
He always liked things kept in order. Took after his ma,
that way.

"How far to the highway?"

"Quite a piece. I never go that way myself. I usually
go up to Blythe." He paused momentarily. "Or east."

"East?"

"To the river . . . the Colorado."

It was a critical moment. Old Ben Milo wanted to get
them off his hands and east would be the way if they
would take the bait, but it was a slim chance. He had

been reading men too long to doubt the sort of man this
tall one was . . . he would kill quickly, heedlessly, almost without thinking. Killing would be his first solution to almost any problem.

The one called Buzzer now . . . he was the tough one.
A bad one he might be, but there was a deep toughness of
fiber built into him. He would take a lot of punishment,
a lot of killing.

The kid . . . there was a weak link. The kid had
stumbled into more than he bargained for.

The easiest way out was the way they had come, and
there was small chance of their making it out alive by
any other way. But they were running from something and
going back was probably not an option.

"What's on the river?" Buzzer asked.

"A few fishermen, maybe. They camp along the river
sometimes, launch their boats off the banks. Otherwise,
there would be nothing. Just Yuma . . . and Mexico." The
idea was planted now. He could not raise it again without
causing suspicion.

"Fix us something to eat." The tall one slouched into
a chair. He glanced at the girl. "You help him."

She came over to Ben obediently and he showed her
where the plates were. They were gray enamel dishes, the
simplest kind of eating ware a man could buy. There was a
big pot of beans, some rice, the remains of a loaf of
sourdough. There was also a comb of honey he'd robbed
from the bees in the wash over east.

With a queer certainty Ben Milo knew he was not going
to get out of this alive. They would want no witnesses
left behind to say where they had gone.

They did not yet realize the situation they were
in . . . maybe the girl did. Young as she was, she had a
knowing way around a desert cabin and around a mine. He
had watched her, and there was a certain air of familiarity in her way of doing things.

He considered the possibility of a shoot out. He
could have a try at it. His guns were cached and if he
could lay a hand to one of them he might nail at least
two of them before they got him. Coolly, he judged his
chances and knew they were good. He was a dead shot . . .
a little slower than of old, but once he lifted a gun he
hit what he aimed at.

Only that tommy-gun would spray lead all over the
cabin. He didn't trust a gun like that and he didn't
trust the man who held it. If something happened at the
wrong moment the girl was almost sure to catch some. Reluctantly, he yielded before the realities. Without the
girl he might have tried it.

The tall one sat down astride a chair with the tommy-
gun across his lap, his arms on the back of the chair. He
turned his blue eyes to Ben Milo. "You live here all the
time, Old Man?"

"Thirty years."

"Thirty years? You must be nuts." He turned to
Buzzer. "You hear that? He's lived in this god-forsaken
desert for thirty years!"

"It ain't so bad," Ben said quietly.

This one thought he was tough, and would be likely to
try to prove it somehow. The other one . . . Buzzer . . .
he was the toughest of the lot. His eyes shifted to the
third one . . . he didn't belong. He shouldn't be here at
all.

The cool, tough ones a body could figure out. You
could study on them and come up with an answer, but the
hotheaded, rattle-brained types were dangerous to themselves and everybody else.

COMMENTS: Looking at Louis's life, there's a good deal of familiar territory covered in these few pages. The mining claim the old man lives on is similar to several Dad worked in his youth, though, as far as I know, none were so far south. I believe he set this story somewhere southwest of Blythe for reasons relating to the plot, so that his criminal characters can be tempted by the idea of getting to Mexico via the Colorado River. The story of the death of Billy the Kid is also something out of Louis's past. He worked for Deluvina Maxwell one summer in the 1920s and heard her, as well as others who had actually been there, tell the story of Billy and Pat Garrett.

Though I have labeled this a "crime story" it is really a Western, contemporary to the time, probably the 1950s, when Louis wrote it. A twentieth-century Western, it contains classic Western genre elements, like commenting on the passing of the frontier era and on the conflict between generations. In this case the commonly used twitchy kid-with-a-Colt type character has been replaced by a juvenile delinquent with a sub-machine gun.

The Death Valley mine where Louis worked in the 1920s. He was
forced to walk from the mine to Barstow, California, a distance of over
a hundred miles, when the owner failed to pick him up.

IN THE MEASURE OF TIME

A Complete Adventure Story

Black was the sea and dark were the skies above, low clouds bulged with rain unspilled. Morgan looked at the sky and at the sea and knew in his heart he was frightened.

He was alone on the wide Pacific and the skies turning to storm. He watched the mountainous waves and tried to recall the lore picked up in many ports or read in books. His tiny craft was tossed along like a scrap of paper before the gale. He, a merchant seaman from the great iron ships, was a man used to oil or coal, not a handful of wind caught in a few yards of fabric.

Then, from the sea there was a quavering cry, and he saw a raft, and clinging to it, something that might have been a man. His only hope for life was to hold his course, hold his bow into the storm . . . a thin and lonely chance.

Yet out there was a human being and it was not in him, who needed hope, to deny it to another. He looked

upon the black water and was shaken by fear, but he let
the boat lose way until near the raft.

It was a dark skinned old man with the look of the
islands, a rack of bones that held a child. Morgan saw a
great sea rise, and then the raft lifted and he took from
the scrawny arms the child, and reaching for the man,
caught a frail wrist.

He clung to the hand and the old man's eyes looked
into Morgan's . . . and then the sea lifted the man and
Morgan drew him aboard.

He shared with them his water, and he held to the
tiller until muscles ached and his body yearned for
death, but he fought the sea and a day came when haggard
and beaten he lay across the rail and the ocean around
them was still.

As if to win where the sea had lost, the sun came
out, and the fresh water dwindled. The man raved against
god and challenged the elements to destroy him . . . and
then a fresh wind came and he lay in the boat's bottom
and the naked brown child looked upon him with ancient
eyes.

And one day the boat came to a still lagoon where
palms leaned over a beach, and the old man lifted the
child and said to Morgan, "Come. Come with me."

Somehow he found strength and followed through a wood
to an ancient square where grass grew among the stones
and vast temples opened their halls to the sky. And the
old man took leaves and ground them to powder and filling
a pipe, said, "Smoke this," and Morgan did.

He smoked and darkness fell, though it was mid-day,
and he was no longer at the temple but running, and in
his hands he held a rifle, and was pursued by Asian soldiers in rough uniforms.

Suddenly in a hollow of ground was an ancient temple,
something incredibly old, beyond the count of years, and

in the temple was an idol, like no other he had seen, but
he ran behind it and pressed a flat stone, and the stone
moved, opening a space, and suddenly he was drawing a
girl into the space with him and the opening closed and
they clung together in darkness.

Morgan was a tall young man with humor in his eyes,
and he told the story and people smiled at the delirium
and mariners said there were no such islands, not upon
the sea where he had been.

"Though," a geographer said, "there are legends. A
Portuguese sighted them in 1533, and they were seen by a
whaler in 1840, but no, not in reality were there such
islands. The seas were thoroughly mapped."

"The native," they asked, "what did he say?"

"Only that the child was the last of his race, the
son and grandson of a thousand generations of priests."

In the passing of years Morgan read of lost conti-
nents and Easter Island with its heads of long-lobed
ears, of the gigantic helmeted heads of stone found in
Central America with features blunt and powerful, of the
strange city of Nan Madol in the Carolines and roads that
came out of the sea on Malden Island, and a fallen mono-
lith on Vanua Levu, covered with hieroglyphics. But he
found no clue to the island of the ancient man and the
child with the eyes old beyond their time.

The Red conquest of China caught him unprepared. His
friends helped him along country roads to a tattered
fragment of an army, valiant fighters who did not flee to
Formosa but remained to fight. On the Mekong River they
found refuge and gained strength. Skillful at war, Morgan
joined them.

Returning from a raid he found a girl in the door of

his quarters, smiling. "Are you the American? I'm Lori King."

A theatrical unit playing for French troops in Indo-China had flown in to do a show for the tiny Chinese force. She was a tall girl and blonde, and they were much together. The plane of the unit was damaged, and departure delayed.

"You'll return soon," he said. "I'm sure they'll get it fixed."

"And you?" she asked.

"I have no one to go back to," he said.

Her head was near his shoulder. "I'd like you to come back," she said, and meant it.

"I'd want you with me then," he said, "and it would not be easy. I've never made much money."

"I'd be with you."

The Mekong rustled along the bank, chuckling with age-old humor. Beyond the river there were temples, their history forgotten, their beginning beyond time. "I'd like to see them," she told him, watching moonlight on the walls.

"There's a patrol to the villages tomorrow, just going for food. Come with us."

The morning was bright and there was laughter in the trees. Morgan walked to the village with Lori, and they talked with the women there, and looked into the round faces of the children. At the edge of the village the people said, "Do not go . . . they are strange temples . . . the ancient ones have left their spirits there."

Then men were coming toward them on the double and a mortar bomb exploded, and suddenly the village was a flaming nightmare of exploding shells and death.

Troops wearing the Red Star burst into the upper end of the village, and there was sporadic firing. Then he and Lori slid down a muddy hillside into a canyon and were running . . . running . . . running . . .

Their breath came in gasps, torn by fear they climbed among the ruins. Behind them was a shout, then a shot, another. Before them in a grove was a temple. Its roof had fallen and great stones lay upon the floor. There were high walls and deep shadows, stones that dripped with jungle, and a floor deep in the death of centuries.

"They are coming, Jack!" Lori whispered. "Oh, Jack, I--"

And he looked into her eyes and saw there all the love, all the promise, all in this world that any man could ask.

"Come on," he said.

One man with thirty rounds . . . against fifty men?

They ran through an ancient door, behind them a shout, then Morgan stopped and his face was white and he stared around him. He knew this place . . . he knew . . . There came to him then an odor, pungent, intangible, drifting.

"Lori!" He grabbed her hand. "We're safe!"

Astonished, she looked at him, but he caught her hand and went through the door to the inner room where stood an idol, incredibly ancient but he did not stop to look but ran behind it and pulled aside the vines.

"We're safe, darling," he said, and pressed hard upon a flat stone. It moved under his hand . . .

COMMENTS: Strange, yes? Digging deep in my memory I believe I heard something about this piece. Louis once told me of a very short story that he banged out in the middle of the night in response to a dream. In the morning it wasn't a tenth as brilliant as he had thought when he was writing or dreaming or whatever state he was in when he created it. I'm sure we've all had moments like that.

I include this story here because, as has been obvious, one of the interesting aspects of *Louis L'Amour's Lost Treasures* is the amount of mysticism that shows up in Louis's unfinished or unpublished work. This story has a dreamlike quality and may well have been written in what was nearly a trance state. The rapid yet oddly smooth shifts in time and place and the reoccurring use of words like "and" and "then" make the narrative seem very much like a dream. Louis very rarely wrote when he was tired—he was much more of an early morning sort of guy. It is also interesting to note that this may be the only case in his career where he has a principal character using something like a hallucinogenic drug.

There are a couple more interesting points; Louis includes this line:

```
and followed through a wood to an ancient square
where grass grew among the stones and vast temples
opened their halls to the sky.
```

This sounds a good deal like the same place he described in *Jeremy Loccard* in *Louis L'Amour's Lost Treasures: Volume 1*, a place in the East Indies that Dad might have read about or even visited. In the notes following *The Bastard of Brignogan* in this collection, Louis, again talking about a character traveling in the Indonesian/Malaysian area, writes:

```
. . . Finds Neolithic settlements . . .
```

I'm guessing it's the same mysterious spot he's either imagining or referring to.

The other issue is Dad's interest, which we've seen in a number of stories, in the Chinese interior and in the Communist revolution in that country in 1949. He was certainly fascinated by China and the role that it would play in the future of our world. Some of that may have stemmed from his own travels in Asia many years before, as well as from the experiences of his brother Parker, who briefly served with the American diplomatic mission to China toward the end of WWII.

When I first read this story I was tempted to joke, "What was Dad smokin'?" But I really think it was fatigue and the vague edge of some not quite articulated or resolved idea that spurred this odd little story into existence.

THE PAPAGO KID

The Beginning of a Western Novel

CHAPTER I

A sudden rush of rain-drops did quick finger-taps on
my hat, living up to the promise of the bulging clouds
that hung low above the desert. Reaching around, I pulled
the draw-strings holding my slicker and shook it out.

The first rush of rain went off across the desert,
stirring dust as it fell. Shrugging into the slicker
brought an end, for the moment, to the rain. A last few
reluctant drops falling, amused by my struggles.

Well, I was ready. If it was going to rain, let it
come.

Along the horizon mountains lay like a heap of rusty
scrap-iron and the nearby desert was salmon-pink dotted
with sage-brush gray and the shabby green of greasewood.
Under the low sky the wide valley before me lay empty and
still. Hugh had certainly known what he was talking about

when he told me I'd meet nobody on this route . . . he
knew I wanted to avoid travelers.

The only spot of real green anywhere in sight was the
sharp, strong color of pines showing from a notch in the
rust-red mountains, and that was the place I'd come from
Texas to find.

This was where I could hole up and rest until Hugh
Taylor sent word for me. It was something great to have a
friend like Hugh to give you a hand when the going was
rough. When I returned from Mexico to find myself a fugi-
tive from justice, he had been very quick to offer help.

It was like Hugh Taylor to know of such a place as
this. He had taken off from home when only a youngster,
riding far and wide upon the land and he seemed to have
connections everywhere.

The drops came again, and then a rushing downpour
that made me turn up my collar and tug down on my hat.
This looked to be settling in for a hard, long rain.

Rowdy, my big black gelding, was beginning to feel
the rough going of the past few weeks. It was the first
time I had seen the big horse even close to weariness,
but it was no wonder. We had come out of Dimmit County,
Texas to the Apache country of Arizona, and the way had
been long and hard.

The trail puzzled me. It was rough, but many Western
trails were, and it was too good a path not to be better
known or traveled. In three days of riding I had seen nobody, not a person, not a ranch, not a mine shack. Most
trails led to towns, to where people were, but not this
one.

The camps were good, and they were spaced right for a
hard riding man. At every camp there was grass, water and
fuel. At every camp there were signs of occasional use,
horse droppings and the ashes of fires, often places
where small herds had been held.

There were no tracks of wagons on any of it, and no

recent travel. The trail held to low ground, winding among buttes, up dry washes, an easy route on the whole, and a hidden one.

Several times I pulled up to study the lay-out of the country. It was not the first time I had ridden such trails, nor probably the last. Most of them were made by Indians who did not want to be seen, and were traveling only from water-hole to water-hole.

The red rocks of the mountains began to take on form and line, to shape themselves from the stuff of distance. Here and there were the raw cancers of washes that ate into the face of the plain, and the deeper scars of canyons. Here or there lines of gray or green climbed along creases in the rock, evidence of underlying water or of gathering places for run-off from the higher peaks.

The trail curved north, skirting mountains toward the waiting pines. "Ride right to the Tin-Cup Ranch," Hugh Taylor had said, "and ask for Bill Keys. He'll be in charge, and he'll take care of you until this blows over. I am sure we can get this straightened out, and you'll be free to come home."

Suddenly the mountains seemed to crack wide open on my left, and the trail went gently up a slope into the pines and along the side of the canyon. Blue gentians carpeted both sides of the trail and crept almost up to the trees in a mass of sky blue. The trail was faint here, rarely used, but two riders had gone ahead of me not long ago, headed right into Tin-Cup Canyon.

It was a time to be careful. This was the kind of country frequented by outlaws, and even honest ranchers were suspicious of strange riders coming in out of wild country. Nothing in my years had bred carelessness in me, so I drew up in the deepest shadow and waited, listening.

And then I heard a shot.

It rapped out, a sharp, bitter sound, ugly in its finality.

A single shot, then silence.

My rifle rode right ahead of my right leg. I was doing no roping on this trip so I carried that rifle where I could draw it almost as fast as a six-shooter. It slid into my hand, and I waited.

Rowdy knew what a shot meant as well as I did, and he stepped forward, light and easy, ears up, nostrils wide. So it was that we first looked down into the little hollow that was the Tin-Cup, a stone barn, a stone house and two pole corrals adjoining. Near them were two riderless horses.

Then I saw them. The air was clear and they were not more than two hundred yards away. There were three men, but one was sprawled on the ground near another horse.

The man standing over the body turned it with his boot toe and I heard him swear. Then he yelled at the other man, who waited under the porch. "No, it ain't him!"

And then they both saw me.

Panic must have hit them at the same instant. One made a break for his horse, the other for his gun. Honest men do not start shooting when a stranger rides up and my rifle was ready.

The nearest man fired. I was not worried as the action must have been sheer impulse and he was much too far away for accuracy with a pistol.

He sprang for his horse and I waited until he was down in the saddle. He lurched like he was hit and I saw his six-gun fall into the rocks, and then both of them were getting out of there. Holding my fire, I let them go.

Rowdy was not gun-shy. With me in the saddle he had no cause to be for we had been through a lot down Sonora way. That had been part of my life that even Hugh knew nothing about, and to him I was just a quiet kid he had seen grow up on our uncle's ranch, the XY.

We had always been friendly, but Hugh was not a man
with whom one became close. He was handsome, fine looking
in every sense, and he carried himself well, but he did
not confide in me and did not invite confidence. Older
than I, he had been a fine horseman, a good hand with
cattle, and good enough with a gun for most purposes.
Often when he wanted to ride off to town to see some girl
or other I had done his work as well as my own, but never
minded. I admired him, and he knew it.

Occasionally, he brought me presents. A fine new hat,
a pair of boots, and another time some Mexican spurs.
Whenever I tried to thank him or pay him he just brushed
me off saying, "Oh, forget it, kid! You've done a thing
or two for me."

With the two riders gone I rode up to the man on the
ground and swinging down, felt his pulse. He seemed to be
dead, all right, and I had guessed as much before I got
down from the saddle. No man with a hole in him of that
size was going very much farther.

Two holes . . .

The first shot was a little high, and there had been
some interval between shots for the blood around the
first wound had coagulated.

A horse's hoof clicked on stone, and I turned to face
them. My rifle was in my hands but you don't try anything
fancy when you're facing four men at that range.

"What did you kill him for?" The speaker was a squat,
broad-chested man with a square red face and hard blue
eyes. He looked as tough as a long winter in the mountains, and at least two of the riders with him looked
just as mean.

"Don't jump your fences, stranger. I didn't shoot
this man, and I don't even know who he is. When I rode
into The Cup two men were standing here, and one of them
right over him. They took a shot at me and then high-
tailed it out of here."

"We heard shootin'," the square-faced man said. "He's dead an' you're here."

My eyes went over them, sizing them up. Nobody needed to burn any brands on this hide for me. Here I was on the dodge from one killing, which I had not done, and now I'd run into another. Nobody had seen the other riders but me, so a lot depended now on who and what these men were.

My quick glance at them told me only one of the four would be inclined to believe me. He was a nice-looking young fellow with brown eyes and dark hair. He looked smart and he looked honest, although a man can be fooled on both counts.

That square-built man who had started the talking seemed to be the man in charge, if there was one. "Who are you," he demanded, "and what brings you here?"

Something in the way he asked that question decided me that I had better be careful. I was downwind of an idea that had not quite come home to me. The last thing I intended to tell them was that I was Wat Bell.

"They call me Papago Kid," I said. "I'm from down Sonora way.

"As for what brought me here, it was this black horse and a lot of trails strung together. I've been a lot of places before this, and when I decided to ride out, nobody stopped me."

He didn't like that. This was a man who liked riding rough-shod over things. His lips kind of thinned down and the look in his eyes was not a pleasant one, but suddenly I wasn't feeling worried anymore; I should have been. A man ought to think of himself in a spot like that, but something about trouble makes me light-hearted.

This man believed he was tough. He wore a gun and he was prepared to use it, and I was a stranger and fair game. Yet when I told him my name a funny thing happened to his eyes and I had the feeling he had expected to hear another name. The idea was there and ready for branding, and it slowed him down a little.

The truth of the matter was that in Dimmit County, Texas, I was Wat Bell, and in Sonora I was the Papago Kid. The first name I'd been born to, and the second had been sort of tacked on me during some scuffles down yonder.

The young man interrupted. "Lynch, let's get in out of the rain. I liked Tom Ludlow too much to see his body lying there like that. We can just as well talk over coffee, anyway."

Lynch had no liking for me and was itching for trouble, but he shrugged, and turned to the others. "You two pick up Tom's body and carry it to the stable. Better put the horses up, then come on in." He paused a moment, then added, "Don't leave anything undone, Bill."

When I heard the name a suspicion stirred, but I did not look up or give any sign that the name meant anything. Of course, Bill was a not uncommon name. Still--

My question was answered almost at once when one of the men took the dead man by the shoulders. "Grab his feet, Keys."

Lynch led the way to the stone house, and I followed with my horse. There was no talk in the stable, and I gave them no chance to have a look at my outfit. Taking my horse into the stall I put down some hay for him and then taking my rifle and saddle-bags I followed them into the house.

Lynch had removed his slicker and I got a shock. He wore a badge.

"The coffee was your idea, Dolliver," Lynch said. "You want to make it?"

Dolliver agreed, glancing at me. He had noticed my reaction to the badge and was obviously curious. He turned to the shelves and began taking things down like he knew the place, and in the meantime I was doing some fast thinking. It was time to scout my trail and figure out what kind of situation I had gotten into.

Hugh Taylor had told me to ride to the Tin-Cup and ask for Bill Keys. Yet when I arrived there was a dead man who wasn't Bill Keys but who was apparently the owner of the ranch. Keys appeared to be riding for the sheriff, for what reason I had no idea.

The cabin was neat as an old maid's boudoir and the smell of coffee that soon filled the room gave it a warm, cozy feeling. The fireplace was huge, the copper utensils all bright and well-polished.

Dolliver was quick and sure in his movements, but he was missing nothing, either. Taking off my slicker I hung it over a chair within easy reach of my hand. I had not unsaddled, nor had any of the others. Obviously they were going on, and what I would do remained a question.

Lynch had dropped astride a chair and started to build a smoke, but when I took off my slicker his fingers stopped dead still for a moment. I was wearing two guns . . . not a common thing, one being expensive enough, and something about me disturbed him. It was not the guns, and he was not afraid. It was the fact that I was wearing them that seemed to bother him, not what I might do with them.

"You call yourself Papago Kid?" Lynch's question was sharp.

My eyes held his. Lynch and I were not going to be friends. For some reason he was distinctly irritated, and with me. I had the feeling he had expected to find some-body here, and that I did not fit the picture of the man for whom he looked.

"I've been called that, sheriff," I said easily. "I'm not a Papago, but they are a good people and the name's an honor. I got called that because I rode through their country a couple of times."

"You say you saw the two men who shot Ludlow? Did you get a good look at them?"

"I saw them, but they were too far away. One of them ran for his horse, but the other one grabbed for his gun. Naturally, with a dead man on the ground and a man about to take a shot at me I didn't waste any time looking him over."

"How many shots did you hear?"

"One."

Dolliver turned around from the coffee. "I heard three."

"That's right," I agreed. "One shot apparently killed the old man. Then one of these men shot at me and I shot back. As you saw, the old man was shot twice. The way it looks to me is he was shot elsewhere, then they trailed him back to his own ranch and shot him again."

"What gives you that idea?" Lynch demanded.

"If you noticed, sheriff, the rain had not washed out the old man's tracks. They came from the corral. Even from where I stood I could see he'd fallen down twice before he was finally killed."

It was obvious that the sheriff had seen nothing of the kind, but he studied me carefully. I was doing my own thinking. The reason the sheriff had not seen those tracks was because all his attention was centered on me. Now that was natural enough, considering that I was there with the dead man, and was a stranger. Still, he should have looked around. He should have noticed.

Dolliver, whose attitude I liked, brought coffee to the table, and cups. He was a clean-cut youngster and no fool. I had a hunch that had he not been present I might have been in a lot more trouble than I was.

It struck me as faintly curious that Sheriff Lynch was making no effort to pursue the possible killers nor even to see in which direction the tracks led. Did he already know?

The thought was unbidden, but once in my mind it would not leave. His actions worried me. It was as if he had decided who was guilty or who he intended to prove guilty and that he had no further intention of investigating.

This was strange country to me, and I knew no one here. The man I had been told to find, and who was supposed to give me a place to hide out, was now standing with his back to the fireplace and his attitude was not friendly.

Nobody needed to tell me that I was in serious trouble. Nor had I any desire to shoot my way out of a situation such as this even had it been practical. I had committed no crime, although I was wanted for one, as Hugh Taylor had warned me. I did not wish to break any laws or get in any deeper. Every sense I had warned me to move carefully.

I tasted my coffee and it warmed the chill from me. Dolliver filled his own cup and sat down. I had an idea he knew I was in trouble and intended to stay close.

"You ever been in this country before?" Lynch asked.

"Never. When I left California I crossed into Arizona near Yuma. Then I headed off down into Mexico. I worked there for a spell, then decided to drift."

"How'd you find this place? It ain't the easiest spot to find." He stared at me suspiciously, but I put on my most innocent face.

"Did you ever cross the desert right behind here? The only spot of green you can see is right in the notch back there, so I headed for it. I figured where things were that green there'd be water, and more than likely people who could set me on the trail to a town."

That was obvious enough even to him, but he was not satisfied.

"You come from California? You sound like a Texan to me."

"Hell," I said carelessly, "it's no wonder! That outfit I rode for in Mexico all talked like that. Fact is,
out in El Monte where I come from half the people who
settled the place were from Texas."

That was plausible, too, but he still was not ready
to accept it or me. He spooned sugar into his cup and
stirred it around, then drank with the spoon still in his
cup.

"What's the problem, sheriff?" I asked. "Is this a
posse?"

"We're huntin' a Texas outlaw name of Wat Bell," he
said, grudgingly. "We got word he was headed west so
we're cuttin' all trails."

"Bad weather for riding," I sympathized. "Is this
Bell a bad hombre? Will it take four of you?"

Dolliver chuckled. "I am not one of them," he said.
"I have a small ranch right over the mountain from here.
I joined these boys back in the pines to see who was
shooting who. My ranch is the Tumbling T."

COMMENTS: In the introduction to this volume I mentioned that
Dad took us on an extended trip around England and Ireland in the
late 1960s. Rural Ireland was a different place in those days; Gaelic
was still occasionally spoken, to the exclusion of English in a few
places, and electricity, telephones, and central heating were rare in
many of the towns and farms at which we stopped. While our hotel in
Dublin was pretty fancy in an Old World sort of way, it still had black-
out curtains on the windows from the time of World War II.

Somewhere in our travels, we came to the ruins of a huge old
stone house. The story I remember was that, hundreds of years ago,
it had been sort of a local execution chamber. If you wanted someone
killed off, and had enough clout, the man who owned the house would

issue an invitation . . . and visitors never returned. There was also a version in which the invitation was given to the wrong person—or perhaps it was given by the intended recipient to a friend or family member—leading to the death of the wrong man. It was a long time ago and my memory is not what I'd like it to be. Regardless, Dad loved the possibilities associated with such a setup.

I get the feeling that the Tin-Cup Ranch in this tale is that same sort of place and a similar situation is being played out. For that reason and based on the style of the writing, I would set the era of this fragment to sometime in the 1970s.

Dad and my sister, Angelique, in one of the ruined
manor houses we visited in Ireland.

KRAK DES CHEVALIERS

A Treatment for an Adventure Story

In Alexandria, to a meeting place for drifters from
all the world comes BARAMUS, a man of the Levantine
coast, of no particular nationality or origin, a go-
between, a procurer, an occasional thief and occasional
murderer. He comes looking for a group of men to do the
impossible, to enter an impregnable fortress and extract
an old man and his granddaughter and then escape with
them to the coast.

Alexandria in the 12th century appeared to be a dying
port. Yet it was still one of the most cosmopolitan cities in the world. Always more Greek than Egyptian, it had
become a staging area for mercenary soldiers awaiting a
war, merchant seamen between voyages to the East or Europe, adventurers and soldiers of fortune from all quarters of the world.

It was a period of change and excitement. The Cru-
sades, which had offered employment and quick wealth to
fighting men, were tapering off; the Mongols of Genghis

Khan were settling down in Russia or retreating to Asia;
for the Vikings the great days of raiding were coming to
an end.

Here, in this place, were men from Bristol, Dieppe
and Cadiz, from Venice, Constantinople, the Malabar coast
and Madagascar, men with no present loyalties, and with
no interests beyond gold, women and wine.

Observing the room, Baramus spots three whom circum-
stance had washed up in this backwater of the world:
KEVIN O'MORE, Irish chieftain, swordsman, fighter who
fled his own country to escape the English conquest; SIR
WALTER DE MALEBISSE (pronounced Malbis), a Crusader
knight who had given up vast estates in England to go to
the Holy Land; and ERIC THE GOLDEN, a Viking, his ship
destroyed in a storm, his crew lost at sea. YAKUT ALI, a
noted warrior from the castles of the Assassins in the
Elburz mountains of Persia, sits nearby. At his table
sits BATU KHAN, a Mongol . . . lately they were enemies,
now friends.

Suddenly there is a crash of an over-turned chair.
Nine men, swordsmen all, are approaching one who stands
alone, facing them feet apart, waiting. This one is MINA-
MOTO TAKANORI, a samurai.

O'More starts to rise. "One man alone? I'll help
him."

From the adjoining table Batu Khan puts up an arresting hand. "Wait," he advises, "and learn."

The nine rush. There is a terrible moment of flashing
swords and death, and the nine are destroyed. (This feat,
portrayed by Toshiro Mifune in THE LEGEND OF MUSASHI with
12 men, is both spectacular and believable.) O'More in-
vites Takanori for a drink, and the group are approached
by Baramus.

He makes an intriguing proposition: For 25,000 gold pieces they are asked to enter a castle no army has ever captured, and get out with the girl and her grandfather.

To aid them they also recruit CHAWAMBI, an African warrior of the Watuta, a war-like tribe, and ZALIM SINGH, a Rajput warrior from India.

Baramus takes them to a house on the sea shore where they meet PHILLIP ARCADIUS. It is he who wishes the girl and her grandfather free of the castle.

As they make their way up the trail to the house AN-TONIUS, Phillip's nephew, asks, "Will they succeed?"

"If anyone can, these men will."

"And how many will survive?"

A shrug. "One or two . . . perhaps three."

"It will be much money for those who live."

Arcadius glances at him, amused. "You are very naive, Antonius."

"You mean--?"

"After all, as you say, it is a lot of money, and only two or three will be left . . . perhaps they will be wounded. So why waste money on such as these?"

"But--?"

"Leave such matters to me, Antonius. In time, you will learn."

Baramus enters: "These are the men."

Arcadius studies them. He is cool, composed, worldly. He is a man who has come up from the gutters of Constantinople and Alexandria to wealth and power, and is eager for more of both.

"25,000 pieces of gold," he suggests, "it is a great sum. All the greater because some of you will die."

"And those who return?" O'More says. "They will be paid by you?"

"You are afraid I will not pay?" Arcadius smiles.

"Oh, no!" O'More replies cheerfully. "The sum will be placed in the hands of the Banco Giro, of Venice. They will pay."

There is no pleasure in the eyes of Arcadius. "What do you, a savage from a wild northern isle, know of the Banco Giro?"

"Enough to know their future depends on their faith. If they do not pay the word will go round the world, and they will no more be trusted. As for the savages of a wild northern isle, why, we had poets and sages when your ancestors were dabbling in the shallows for shell-fish."

"You say that to a Greek?"

"You call yourself a Greek, but would a Greek call you a Greek?"

"I do not think I like you, Irishman."

"Does it matter? Do you woo my affections or my sword?"

Arcadius brushes it aside. "No matter. Now what will you need?"

"A boat . . . not large, not new, with but one sail. Food for thirty days, spare weapons, much rope. I shall make a list."

"Do that. And for now?"

"Thirty gold pieces to drink your health . . . and ours."

"Very well. And you leave . . . when?"

O'More shrugs. "Have the boat tomorrow night by the ruins near Cape Lochlas. We will take it when we have need of it." When they are gone, Antonius says, "The Banco Giro? You did not think of that, Uncle?"

Irritated, Arcadius shrugs it aside. "No matter. I know the Banco Giro . . . and they know me."

Baramus is to guide them to their destination. He is to supply them with the plan of the castle, the great KRAK of the CHEVALIERS, perhaps the strongest castle ever built. There will be four men to sail the boat, and to guard it while the fighting men are ashore.

En route they are attacked by pirates, the pirates are defeated, and aboard their ship a girl prisoner is found. She sees Baramus, although he does not see her, and she is frightened, begging not to be seen by him. They hide her below.

That night, anchored in a cove awaiting a SECRET AGENT who will apprise them of conditions within the castle, O'More and Sir Walter see somebody from the ship encounter somebody from the shore. It is too dark to identify, and they whisper. O'More suspects betrayal.

Sure at least that it is not Chawambi, O'More gets him to track the men. Two men upon horse-back, who ride away, but not toward the Castle.

Who are they? What does the midnight meeting portend?

Yakut and Batu capture an OLD MAN with a donkey. Holding him, they disguise themselves and enter the village at the foot of the mountain where the castle is.

A SOLDIER from the castle reports them. He has recognized Yakut as an Assassin. "I saw him once. He was from Alamut, a protégé of the Old Man of the Mountain."

Suspicion is aroused--someone from within may have been carrying out information regarding their captives. Only three have been out of the castle. Under torture the Secret Agent talks. He is the creature of Baramus and Arcadius, but they believe he lies because there are so few men.

Girl and her grandfather questioned. They know nothing. They wish to pray . . . can they enter the chapel at night? Well, why not? They are given permission.

A reconnaissance reports no ships off shore, only one small trading vessel. Since no force of any consequence

seems to be nearby, the commander does little more than
to increase the guard at the gates in the outer wall.

The Grandfather trusts Arcadius; the girl, GABRIELLE,
does not. They have been informed they are to be rescued.
What the Grandfather does not realize is that the danger
is greater to them from Arcadius than from their captors.

The Krak of the Chevaliers was considered by T. E.
Lawrence of Arabia and many others to be the most formidable castle ever built. It was constructed toward the
end of the castle-building era, and summed up the best
defensive knowledge of the time. It is massive beyond belief, with towering walls and guarded approaches. The entrance from the main gate is narrow and covered with
openings above so that an enemy can be attacked while in
the passage, if they should get so far.

Kevin O'More leads the attack. They scale the hill,
and surmount the massive outer walls by a method, never
used in film, to be told in the story. A highly exciting
method, and very effective.

Once inside they send three of their men to capture
the other postern gate near the main gate by which they
will retreat.

Eric, Zalim Singh and Batu Khan have this mission.

Thus far there has been no alarm. They have moved
with speed and skill, yet they must now get to the upper
ward of the castle and to the chapel where, if plans have
gone well, Gabrielle and her grandfather will be waiting.

One by one they cross the lower ward and attain the
wall near an inner gate. Chawambi disappears in the
night. GORDON, Sir Walter's squire, moves closer. O'More
saunters up to the gate and is challenged; making believe
he is drunk he tries to push on in and there is a clash
of swords, and instantly the others are behind him. In
the close confines of the entrance the fighting is brief
but intense, and then they enter the upper ward and move
silently to the chapel.

Then Gordon turns and runs from them into the center of the ward. Puzzled, they turn to face him. Suddenly he blows a shrill whistle. "You fools!" he shouts at them. "I have tricked you all! All! Every one of you will die!"

He whistles again, and suddenly many men appear, armed and ready.

They retreat into the chapel, only to be attacked by GUARDS who await them there, and then they see across the room the old man and the girl and Chawambi is there. He has dropped in through a window in time to prevent the guards from taking them away. There is a bloody fight in which each do heroic deeds, and then the chapel door is forced shut and barred.

Chawambi leads them through the window to the wall and along the wall to the main gate where their friends are fighting fiercely to hold the gate. They have horses. Gabrielle and her grandfather are swiftly mounted. Batu Khan dies fighting. "Go!" Zalim shouts. "I will hold the gate!"

"And I!" Eric joins him.

On horseback they flee down the stone-paved ramp which lies in a sharp V shape. At the point they turn and start toward the main gate, fired at with arrows from loopholes, or sudden attacks from concealed posterns. Directly before them a portcullis drops and they are cut off. O'More quickly reverses and charges back up the covered ramp, but Sir Walter is a couple of jumps ahead of him. At the gate toward which they are headed two armed guards leap out to stop them. Sir Walter's sword cuts them both down, but he takes a bad blow in the process. Charging the gate, they fight their way through and ride for the shore where the boat is to be waiting. Within moments a group of horsemen are in pursuit.

En route to the coast, Yakut is shot from his horse by an arrow. O'More rides back to pick him up, but he is dying and waves him away. He tries one more shot with his bow, then dies as O'More rides away.

There is a tremendous fight on the lonely beach with
the boat lying off shore in which O'More, Sir Walter and
Takanori fight off the encircling enemy with swinging
swords, while Chawambi uses arrows to pick off enemy ar-
chers.

Meanwhile Gabrielle and her grandfather are smuggled
aboard the boat by Baramus and his men.

Instantly, the sail goes up and the boat pulls away,
leaving them on the beach, faced by their enemies.

The four prepare to defend themselves to the death,
but now their enemies, seeing the girl and her grandfather escaping, ride away. They have no wish to go against
such fighters when there is nothing more to be gained.

Dejected, abandoned, the four mount their horses and
start back along the shore. Then, O'More remembers the
mysterious meeting in the cove, and a remark he had over-
heard at the last. Now that remark returns to memory:
". . . and afterward? Here?" And the reply, "Here."

Instantly, the four bring their horses to a gallop.
If there is to be a meeting at the cove . . . if there is
even a chance . . . they might make it first and be there
waiting.

Antonius is at the cove with two men. The two men
with him are his own fighting men, and he tells them,
"The old man and Baramus . . . kill them. We need them no
longer. If Gordon is with them, kill him also."

The sail appears, a smoke signal goes up, and the
boat comes in. Baramus comes ashore with the old man and
the girl.

Antonius walks toward him, hand out-stretched. As he
clasps the man's hand, the two slaves move in and kill
Baramus.

The four riders arrive, O'More catches a hand of the
girl as her grandfather is killed by Antonius, then as

Sir Walter is fighting with one of the huge slaves, Antonius plunges a knife into his back, and is killed himself
by Takanori.

Sir Walter is buried up the shore and the three remaining men, O'More, Takanori and Chawambi, take the
boat.

"To Alexandria?" asks Takanori.

"Venice," O'More says.

In Venice, Gabrielle goes with O'More, Takanori, and
Chawambi to the Banco Giro.

The banker is there, and with him, Phillip Arcadius.

The money is paid. Arcadius shrugs. "It was a gamble.
One wins, one loses . . . I lost."

"Antonius, also."

"Ah, yes. Do you know he planned to kill me, too? But
I suspected as much, and planned to kill him." He shrugs.
"And with the old man gone, the secret of the treasure is
lost. Now nobody will find it. It is lost forever."

Outside in the street the four stand together, and
Gabrielle says, "With this we can get a larger boat."

"Larger?"

"For the treasure, darling. I know where it is!"

The End

COMMENTS: I suspect this was written in the mid-1960s, because I
have a vague memory of some discussion about it between Dad and
British film producer Euan Lloyd. It certainly has the sort of "high
concept" pitchability necessary in Hollywood: "The Magnificent 7 vs.
the World's Greatest Castle." And, of course, there are a variety of
great casting and action opportunities. I can remember sitting in my
father's lap and him leafing through a book containing many color

photographs and architectural details of the castle. I'm guessing that was just a few days before he took a break from whatever he was working on and pounded this treatment out, a process that took only a few hours. It's a fun beginning, but to get it to the point where it would have been truly producible there are still a lot of loose ends to be wrapped up and a lot of fleshing out to be done.

What role was the girl, taken on after the pirate raid, supposed to have played? Why did the squire, Gordon, suddenly betray our heroes to the men in the castle? Who are the mysterious (though possibly known to history) residents of the Krak des Chevaliers who are holding the old man and Gabrielle prisoner? And, seriously, why intentionally kill the old guy who knows where the treasure is? I have to assume that was just a mistake. These and more questions would have needed to be answered before Louis tried to sell this to Euan Lloyd or anyone else.

The group of misfits and mercenaries would also have needed some time and adventures (like the pirate raid) in which to bond. Their gallant, in some cases suicidal, defense of one another during the attack on the castle would be meaningless without their road to friendship being fraught with conflict and tests of one sort or another.

Euan and my father showing off their new hats in the early 1980s.

The Krak des Chevaliers is a real crusader castle in Syria, though prior to the nineteenth century it was actually called Krak de l'Ospital after the order of the Knights Hospitallers, who were its longtime residents and who, over a period of many years, dramatically improved the original Kurdish fortifications on the site.

The unnamed secret weapon our band uses in the attack, the special way over the outer walls that Louis alludes to but is keeping to himself, is almost certainly the use of a large lizard, like a monitor lizard. He had used this same gag (filmmaker slang for a stunt) in the short story "The Hills of Homicide" to allow a murderer to scale a cliff:

```
        . . . the smaller monitor lizards are from
India, running four to five feet in length . . . It
is those lizards that the thieves use to gain access
to locked houses.
        A rope is tied around the lizard's body, and he
climbs the wall, steered by jerks on the rope from
below. When he gets over a parapet, in a crevice, or
over a sill, the thief jerks hard on the rope and the
lizard braces himself to prevent being pulled over,
and they are very strong in the legs. Then the thief
goes up the wall, hand over hand, walking right up
with his feet on the wall.
```

It is my guess that our Rajput knight, Zalim Singh, might have brought this trick to the group's attention as they planned their attack. One can only imagine the fun you could have with our heroes trying to locate, capture, or steal such a lizard!

There are a couple of details mentioned in connection to this story that I find particularly interesting. Sir Walter De Malebisse might have been intended to be a fictional relative of my mother's. Hugh de Malebisse, an actual relative, came to England with William the Conqueror and several generations later there really was a Walter and he did go on a pilgrimage to the Holy Land.

In some of the notes associated with this draft Louis uses the following description of the spot where the men first meet in Alexandria:

In an alleyway near the Gate of the Moon, within a minute or so from the Canopic Street, was a leather-worker's stall. There were saddles made, bridles, whips, and all manner of leather goods, and at the back of the stall and on the left as you faced it, was a rack of already made bridles hanging from a point near the ceiling. They hung close together and in great numbers, effectually concealing a door to a passage that led to the back of the building.

The leather-worker seemed always to be there, an ancient man with a face that might have been made from his own goods, yet wrinkled and seamed with age, wisdom, and evil. Attending him were his two sons, huge, irritable men, and his daughter.

To those who knew the old man or who seemed to be of the right sort, a son would step aside and let the visitor pass by . . . if no one watched or seemed interested . . . going through the curtain of bridles and into the hidden passage.

And within might be found all nationalities from the shores of Norman England to those of China, from Madagascar to India and Sumatra.

For this was the resort of men of the sea and of the wars, here they might free themselves of their burdens of wealth . . . if any . . . or find employment.

Footsteps echoed along the passage, and a great oaken door studded with iron opened, and the newcomer passed through to an odor of roasting meat, incense, and sweaty humans. Another door, the odors stronger, and then a room filled with tables, benches and the sound of music drowned by the murmur of voices.

This idea of the leather worker's stall and the screen of bridles being a cover for a haven for mercenaries appears in other places in Dad's notes about his own life and in reference to other stories he might write about North Africa. Sometimes the location is one city, sometimes another, but the description of the entrance remains basically the same. I'm guessing that it reflects something he read or was told, since, as far as I can tell, the only time Louis had access to North Africa was during the short time a ship he was serving on transited the Suez Canal. He may have had some time ashore in Egypt, but not very much.

There are two oft-used L'Amour themes present in this treatment. The first is the idea of a payoff that would be divided among all those that survived. Thus the fewer who survived, the greater the reward. That concept is echoed in other places in this book and in Louis's previously published works.

The second is that of finding a treasure. Treasure shows up many times in Dad's work, and I have always found that fact sort of interesting. Louis was a very hard worker and had no problem paying his dues. He was not a gambler, and certainly one of the subjects I discuss in this book deals with how cautiously he approached his career. It's my guess that the sort of windfall symbolized by a treasure is the highly material (and male) version of "and they lived happily ever after." It may be a holdover from the poverty of his younger days and his dream of being able to afford some leisure time in which to perfect his craft.

Additionally, treasure is not only a staple of the adventure fiction of earlier generations, an era when access to great riches was denied to average men and women through vagaries of class and education; it may also reflect a time when Dad was searching for an audience of paying customers. To him, fame and the remuneration that could come with it may have seemed like the "bestowed by God" or "good luck" aspects of finding a treasure. And for a writer, a treasure, a fortune of valuable items once owned by man but now lost, implies a story . . . and a good story is a real treasure!

IBN BATUTA

A Proposal for a Nonfiction Book

LT

COMMENTS: In early 1960, Louis tried to promote a series of nonfiction books based on the lives of the great scholar travelers of the Middle Ages and Renaissance. Included were to be Hsuan-tsang, who lived from around 602 to 664; Ludovico di Varthema, 1470 to 1517; Jean-Baptiste Tavernier, 1604 to 1689; Nicolao Manucci, 1638 to 1717—and Abu Abd al-Lah Muhammad ibn Abd al-Lah l-Lawati t-Tangi ibn Batutah . . . or, for those of an informal bent: Ibn Batuta, 1304 to 1368.

Batuta claimed one of the most extensive travel itineraries in history, a series of journeys and adventures that boggles the mind. His travels are considerably better chronicled today than in 1960, although some historians doubt Batuta actually traveled to all the places he described. Regardless, the Moorish adventurer's tale definitely struck a chord with Louis, who found in Ibn Batuta both a kindred spirit and an inspiration.

THE WORLD OF IBN BATUTA

A Proposal for a Nonfiction Book

A proposed nonfiction book based on the journeys of
the great Moorish traveler of the 14th century. His world
is the world of the Arabian Nights, of mystery, adventure, romance, caravans, the diamonds of Golconda; the
Vale of Kashmir, of betel and hashish, of myrrh and
frankincense, of harems and beautiful slave girls, of
strange empires, singing sands, of the Golden Horde, the
Mongol khans, of Samarkand, Tashkent, Delhi, Bukhara,
Baghdad and Damascus; of scimitar and Greek fire, of pirate galleys and the sciences of the East.

Born of Berber parentage at Tangier on February 25,
1304, into a family with a tradition of judicial service
as qadis, he received the usual education of his class
before setting out, at the age of twenty-one, on his pilgrimage to Mecca. It was his intention not only to fulfill the duty of his faith by making this pilgrimage, but
to prepare himself for future judicial offices by broad-
ening his education through contact and study with the
great scholars of the East. It is likely, from his care
in listing the scholars and saints he encountered on this
first trip and the diplomas conferred on him at Damascus,
that this may have been his primary object in making the
journey.

Gifted with a mind eager for learning, a quick eye
for detail, and a consuming interest in everything he
saw, by the time Batuta reached Egypt he was already obsessed with travel. He reached Mecca by the way of Syria
on this first pilgrimage, and then explored the classic
lands of Islamic culture. He proceeded by a complicated

route through Iraq and southwest Persia to Baghdad,
thence to Tabriz, and northern Mesopotamia before returning via Baghdad to Mecca.

Although young, he was already a person of consequence, and living in an age and area where scholars were
greatly honored and respected, he attracted great attention wherever he went. He was interested in the personalities and histories of the countries and sultans along
the way, yet at the same time contrived to benefit from
their generosity.

Nearly everywhere he stopped he was given purses
filled with gold, Arab horses, slaves or silk robes. And
everywhere he was lavishly entertained by the amir, bey,
sultan, shah or whoever happened to be ruler. All wanted
to talk with him, many wished to acquire his services. An
astute young man of inquiring mind, Batuta studied as he
traveled and talked with the best minds everywhere. He
was a good judge of personality, and had amusing and
sometimes caustic remarks to make about the various people whom he encountered.

He then devoted several years (more than two, and
probably almost three) at Mecca preparing his great plan
of travel. During this period he went down both shores of
the Red Sea, visited Yemen, experienced monsoon rain for
the first time, and sailed from Aden to the trading ports
of Africa, then back along the southern shores of Arabia
to Oman and the Persian Gulf. During these travels he
heard many tales of far places that aroused his desire
for further adventure.

It must be remembered in this connection that while
many European authorities claimed the monsoon winds that
carried ships from the coast of Africa (region of Zanzibar) to India were discovered by Hippalus in approximately 45 A.D., ships sailed by Arabs had been making
this voyage for a very long period of time. In the period
from say 30 B.C. on through to about 90 A.D. up to 120

ships a season were sailing from Myus Hormus on the Red
Sea coast of Egypt to India.

Actually, one of the rarely mentioned but contribut-
ing causes of the decline of the Roman Empire was an adverse trade balance with India.

Another pilgrimage to Mecca was made in 1332 or about
there, and he planned a trip to India and to the court of
Muhammad bin Tughluq, who was noted for his generosity to
scholars, but destiny intervened and he traveled through
Egypt again, and through Syria to the land of the Turks.
He became the basic authority for the history of the region during this period at the beginning of the Ottoman
venture.

He then crossed from Sinope to the Crimea and visited
the territory of the Khan of the Golden Horde, then the
ancient capital of Bulgaria, and Constantinople in the
retinue of the Khan's third wife, a Greek princess who
was returning to visit her family.

There is more than a possibility, which I intend to
develop, that the relations between this Greek princess
and the young Islamic scholar were something more than
platonic.

After travel in Russia, Batuta returned in the winter
to Sarai, the capital of the Golden Horde, and then
started for India overland through Khiva, Bukhara, Samarkand and Balkh, then by a difficult route through Afghan-
istan and Khurasan, to reach the Indus on September 12,
1333 with an imposing array of attendants.

Batuta, it might be said, was very adept at securing
gifts from the various kings he encountered. Most of
these were freely given, but where this was not so, Batuta had his own methods, many of them devious, for getting what he needed to continue his travels. Like
Varthema, who came later, he seemed interested only in
traveling and learning, and there was little interest in
wealth for its own sake.

Batuta spent some time in India which made a deep impression, but there was a court intrigue in which he barely escaped with his life, although he was later restored to favor and entrusted by Sultan Mohammed with a mission to China. Before this he held the job of Malikite grand qadi in Delhi for some time. It was during this period that he became the victim of the intrigues mentioned above. Batuta, it seems, was a stern judge, and his ideas of morals were rather more severe than those in some of the areas where he served. He was envoy to China in 1342 . . . a trip he was long in carrying out due to a series of adventures and delays.

He made an adventurous trip through central India and down the Malabar coast. He spent 18 months in the Maldive Islands (off the coast of India) as qadi, but left for Ceylon. He went along the coasts of Coromandel and Malabar, again to the Maldives, and then resumed his trip to China.

While waiting for the sailing season he took trips to Bengal and Assam, then went by ship to Sumatra, traveling from there to China by junk, and on to Peking. He returned to Malabar by way of Sumatra in 1347, through the Persian Gulf to Baghdad, then Syria (while the Black Death was ravaging that area) and again to Mecca via Egypt.

He sailed from Alexandria to Tunis, and in a Catalan ship via Sardinia to Tenes in Algeria, overland to Fez. Later he crossed the strait to visit Andalusia where the kingdom of Granada still flourished. Returning to Morocco he crossed the Sahara to the empire of the Mandingos, and is one of the few authorities on the great African empires which existed in the region of the Niger during the Middle Ages.

Returning to Fez, at the behest of the Sultan, he dictated his memoirs. He probably ended his days as a qadi. His travels covered the period from 1325 to 1354.

As exciting as is the material in Batuta's original
work, the one translation that is in any respect adequate
has been written by a scholar for scholars and is replete
with footnotes, many unimportant and unnecessary village
names, which are fine for the historian but of no importance to the casual reader. Much in the way of context
has been left out that could be included.

What I propose is to write an entertaining, exciting,
and substantial book based on the travels of Ibn Batuta.
It will be a thorough study, yet written for the layman
who wishes to be entertained while he is learning. In his
own account Batuta is inclined to pass over a shipwreck
in a couple of paragraphs and a court intrigue in
scarcely more, and he devotes little time to his affairs
with women. The outlines are there, so without digressing
or throwing the book out of proportion, I expect to enlarge upon these stories to add to the color and entertainment value. As a man of that world Batuta saw little
reason to discuss what conditions elsewhere were like or
how his times fit into the greater historical picture;
that too will be placed in context.

My knowledge of the area and the period are quite
complete. I have traveled in person over some of the same
routes, have studied the histories, religious beliefs and
sciences of the countries he visited, and know something
of the personalities with whom he came in contact.

The travels of Ibn Batuta are, I believe, one of the
greatest experiences a reader can have, for it opens a
world largely closed to Western readers. From frequent
lectures I have discovered there exists an enormous market for such a book, and a vast curiosity about the subject matter. Above all, it opens a relatively new field
of interest to the general reader. Alexander, Charlemagne
and Tamerlane have been done. The story of Marco Polo, a

mere commuter by comparison to Batuta, is known. Above all, this is an intelligent viewpoint from behind the scenes . . . this is a Muslim commenting on the Muslim world, a participant telling the story of what he has done and seen. Too many of our scholars are purely European scholars, unaware that there is any scholarship other than their own, or any viewpoint different from the one they hold.

What I hope to write is an exciting, colorful and highly informative book for laymen, one in which a scholar will find few faults.

GOALS:

1. To cover the travels of Ibn Batuta as described in his books.
2. To provide added background on those places he visited, conditions at the time, circumstances of travel beyond what he himself tells, and further background on people he mentions.
3. To locate towns and places according to their modern names. All this without footnotes.
4. To provide further background on customs, education, medical practices, some of the things he missed.
5. To place all these things in relation to what was happening in Europe at the time so the reader is fully aware of the period of which he is reading.

COMMENTS: This proposal has been pieced together from several different documents. The original was sent off to Henry Holt and

Company, one of the oldest hardcover publishers in the United States. Initially, Louis pitched them the idea of doing one nonfiction and one fiction title a year . . . a proposal that they balked at immediately, claiming, "That increment may be too frequent for us, or any other publisher, to handle profitably."

They were, however, willing to look at his Ibn Batuta book proposal. Unfortunately, their response, while probably appropriate considering Louis had, so far, only written fiction, was somewhat less than what he was looking for . . .

```
We have read the outline for IBN BATUTA with
great care and interest . . . The material you
sent is indeed an informative description of Ibn
Batuta's life and does serve to support your
points about the exotic adventures and historical
importance of the subject . . . [I]t does not
really show how you will handle that material in
the book . . . Nevertheless, we are nervous about
how we could sell this book without a sample of
the book treatment itself.
```

I suspect Dad was looking for the credibility a substantial work of nonfiction would give him, but the real issue was whether he could afford to take the time to write such a work. Serious research would be required, not the sort he put into a Western but work that was specifically sourced and carefully documented in the text. That would have created additional expense and a clerical challenge the likes of which he had never undertaken. Perhaps it was all for the best that he did not find support for this project . . . all for the best because my father also had another idea brewing: a work of fiction, the story of another young man, another wanderer in the medieval and Islamic world . . .

By December of 1960 Louis had finished *The Walking Drum*. Whether the life of Ibn Batuta inspired the adventures of my father's fictional hero, Mathurin Kerbouchard, or was simply a research source is unclear. However, there are many resemblances, including planned but unwritten sequels that followed a path similar to Batuta's to both India and China.

Over the next six years Dad sent *The Walking Drum* to Bantam, Doubleday, St. Martin's Press and, no doubt, Holt and a few others. He rewrote it based on notes he had received. He retitled it *May There Be a Road*, hoping that would help. Nothing worked. No one was the least bit ready to allow a writer of paperback Westerns to try his hand at a swashbuckling historical adventure novel, any more than they were ready to let him publish the history of a fourteenth-century Moroccan traveler.

By 1984, however, the world was a different place.

SHANTY

Two Beginnings to a Western Novel

CHAPTER I

So I gave my heart to a bend in the road, and off I went, a'yondering.

There was nothing behind me but trouble, and nothing before me but dreams, but there was sunlight on the hills that morning, and stories I'd heard of the Western lands to color the thoughts in my head.

There was a yearning in me, too, a kind of uneasy yearning back to a ghost-memory land, for I'd been born in the West and lived there a time.

Of that I remembered little, just vague drifting things in my mind of a night time, memories of long grass blowing in the wind, of icy peaks against the sky, and the hoarse bark of rifle guns.

Yet the wide sky gave me a call, and the prairie left me something to dream on, so I saddled my old roan and pointed her nose into the West.

Sometimes there had been worrying voices in the night time, voices I knew belonged to my father and mother, but the things they said were not clear, nor had I any memory of the conditions that might have caused such anger.

Two days later I fetched up to a creek bank where a man was cutting cedar posts. My belly lining was chafing my spine from hunger, so I hired out for a dollar a day and found, to cut posts.

It was hard work, and John Burdick was a driving boss, one who worked less after I came up, but spent his time yammering at me. Being a fair hand with an axe and a cross-cut saw, I did my work, and well. But when a week had passed and I'd smoothed some wrinkles out of my belly, I told him he could pay me off.

He was a big shouldered man with a lot of mustache and a hard, free way about him. He'd also a liking for the bottle and some notion of himself as a fist fighter. "You got nothing coming," he said, "you et enough for three men."

"It was a dollar a day and found," I said, knowing as I said it this was no time for arguing, nor would I get any place.

"If you work two weeks longer I'll give you ten dollars," he said.

"Seven dollars," I said, "and you pay me now."

He grinned at me. "Kid," he said, "I got a lot of wood cut for nothing. Now you beat it, before I give you a hiding."

So I walked up to him and hit him.

"Mister," I said, "I earned seven honest dollars. You going to pay me?"

He got up off the ground and made as if to wipe the blood from his mouth, and then he came at me. So I fetched him a clout alongside the ribs, and when he swung a wide right at me I went in and belted him with another right in the belly. He went down to his knees and stayed

there, and I said to him, "Mister, I got seven dollars
coming."

He gave it to me.

So I caught up that roan and crossed the river, going
on into the woods. Come night fall, I stopped by a cabin
and hollered at the house.

The man who came to the door had him a shotgun.

"I was riding by," I said, "and figured I might work
out a bait of grub."

He looked me over, and then he nodded. "All right,
get down and come in, but if you're one of that Ryerson
outfit the best you'll get is a dose of lead."

"Only Ryerson I ever knew was a steamboat captain on
the Ohio," I told him.

When I put up the roan in his barn and went inside I
found he had him a neat little cabin, right well made,
and a pleasant faced woman with two youngsters. He had a
plowed field outside the barn yard and a few chickens. A
body could tell by the way the house was made that this
man was a workman, a first-rate carpenter or millwright.

"Name of Sturgis," he said, "Henry Sturgis. We settled here five, six months ago. Sorry to meet you like
that, but there are toughs around. They stole two cows
from me last night. You forget about working--I do all
the work to be done around here. The wife and I are just
pleased for the company."

She put on a cloth and fixed the table up some, and
time to time she glanced at me, pleased like. Women folks
set store by company, and this was a lonely place, with
woods all around and dark except where they'd cleared
land.

"Thank you, ma'am," I said, "you cook a might fine
meal. I'll often remember this in the Western lands."

"We came from Pennsylvania," she said, "and started
west. Where are your folks?"

Me, I looked up at her. "Ma'am, I've no folks, any-

where. They were killed when I was a boy, maybe six,
seven years old. Truth to tell, ma'am, I must have been
younger. I don't rightly know my own name, nor how old I
am, nor where my folks came from."

She was some cut up at that, and we set around the
table until real late . . . why, it was after nine
o'clock before we went to bed. They gave me a place to
sleep in the hay-mow, with blankets and all.

Setting out there in the hay, a'looking out the door,
I got to thinking how many homes I'd been in, and none of
them my own. Seemed like everybody but me had a place to
go to, come night time.

They were fine folks. Mrs. Sturgis, she told me come
day-light I could have breakfast with them and they would
fix me a packet of grub to take along, which was kindly.

Setting there thinking, like that, I heard a noise
outside. It was a whisper of a noise only, but next thing
I knew there was a man standing in the doorway.

"New horse in here," I heard him whisper. "Where'd he
git the horse?"

Me, I just set there. Struck me a mite funny, that
man going to take my roan. That roan being one of the
most miserable animals a man could find in a year of
looking. Born with a sore tooth, I guess, but that roan
didn't like anybody at all. Except maybe me. Animals take
me friendly, and I sort of make up to them . . . nothing
ever belonged to me before, except that roan.

Meantime I felt around. I didn't move, because that
floor would creak and those men were armed. That hay
would rustle, too. Moreover, I was afraid if a disputa-
tion started up Mr. Sturgis would come high-tailing it
out to help me, and maybe he would get hurt.

Since I was old enough to hold up my hands I been
fighting my own battles, and I don't know how to do much
of anything else that matters. Except how to do a lot of
hard work.

There were three, four of them, and I set there
a'waiting for that man to go to the roan's stall. He
stepped forward and that roan kicked out and knocked that
man sprawling across the barn.

"Why, that--!"

Another man stepped in and I saw him draw back his
rifle to swing on the mare with the rifle butt, and I
took off from that loft edge and piled him up alongside
the kicked man. He hit the deck in a heap, and I drew
back my fist and slugged him, then I wrenched that rifle
from him and shot at the man in the doorway.

Here is another, more personal, version:

CHAPTER I

Somewhere my love lies sleeping behind the lights of
a far-off town.

So I gave my heart to a bend in the road, and off I
went, a'yondering.

Each rise in the road was a challenge, each bend in
the road a lure, each light a beckoning finger that drew
me onward.

How many times had I looked upon house lights with
longing? How many times had I stopped upon the road to
look into the window of a home, watching a father reading
a newspaper by lamp-light, his wife sewing, his children
doing their school-work? To all of this I was a stranger,
for I had known no such home, nothing but a haunting memory that flickered, a tiny flame, in the back-shadows of
my mind.

My home had been a campfire, and there is nothing
like a campfire for dreaming. A lonely man can find in a
campfire those things for which he is forever longing,

and no crystal ball will ever read the heart of a man with half the campfire's truth.

There was nothing behind me but trouble, and nothing before me but dreams, but there was sunlight on the hills that morning, and the stories I'd heard of the Western lands to color the thoughts of my head. And I had memories, too, for it was from the West I'd come. There was a yearning in me, a yearning to go back to those ghost-memory lands before the time I'd lived with the Sioux.

Of that I remembered little, just drifting will o' wisps of thought that slipped from the background of the mind during darkness or when busy with something else, memories of long grass blowing in the wind, of icy peaks against the sky and the hoarse bark of rifle guns.

These, and something more . . . the sound of a woman's voice singing, of a man's quiet tones, of strong arms that carried me and soft arms that loved me. There were other times, worrying voices in the night, voices I knew belonged to my mother and father. I remember fears of troubles I was all too young to grasp.

Until now mine had been a sorry life by all standards but my own. Growing up any way at all, working since first I could remember, learning to trust few of those whom I met, for a boy without family can expect little enough in this world.

Always there had been within me a feeling of destiny waiting in the West. I suppose all young men feel destiny awaiting them somewhere, but this went beyond that, and always there seemed something awaiting me just over the horizon, something connected with those intangible memories.

Each time I looked upon a town strange to me, I looked upon it with hope.

The wide sky gave me a call, and the prairie gave me something to dream on, so I shouldered my pack and pointed my nose to the westward.

My age was an uncertain thing, and of my rightful
name I knew nothing, but it was likely that I was scarce
eighteen when I started to the west again.

Yet, how old is a man? Is he to be measured by years
or by accomplishment, by energy or despair, by strength
or hopelessness? When does a man cease to be young and
begin to be old?

For surely, all men do not age at the same rate. Of
one hundred men of the same years, some will be forty,
some eighteen, some already seventy. With some the age is
physical, with most, it is of the mind; some men are born
old, and some are forever young.

He who lives an even, uneventful life, who knows few
women, marries young, works long at the same tasks, troubled by little, eating the same food . . . is he seventy
then, or is he ten in the years of experience?

He who knows strange, far places, customs varied with
each port, the tastes of exotic foods, the lips of lush,
foreign women, the mysteries of the jungle, of dark, narrow streets, the beat of surf on an icy shore, the sounds
of a ship's bells tolling the half hours, the bow-wash
about the hull . . . is he who has known hunger, despair,
hatred, fury, the agony of thirst and hatred and the glo-
ries of love, is he of the same age as that other, although their years are alike?

No man can cut himself adrift from the life he has
lived, or the things he has felt, the food he has eaten,
the people he has known. For these are stored in the memory, each to become a part of the man, each to have its
place in the color of his future actions, each a part of
what he has become and is becoming.

Of the memories that come to me in the night all are
wiped out by that last, terrible night of fire, gun smoke
and hoarse yells, ending in darkness, quiet and a boy
alone.

There had been before that a long time of wagon-

riding, and I can hear today the rocking, rumbling roll
of wagon wheels, loaded heavily. For the longest time before that there had been nothing but prairie and sky.

The gentle hands of my mother I remember, and the
quiet voice of my father . . . but I recall a time when
his tones had a deadly sound, too. And sometimes I seem
to hear both their voices speaking in a different tongue,
a strange, musical sound that I loved to hear.

The morning after the massacre I do remember.

Sunlight sparkled upon the water when I awakened, the
water of a small creek that chuckled amiably among the
rocks.

For a long time I lay still, smelling the smoke from
across the creek and knowing what it was, yet afraid to
cross the stream, to see what fire and nightmare had
left.

Three Indians found me.

They were big men, as tall as my father had been, and
strong. They spoke to me but I had none of their words
and so one of them gave me a strip of jerked beef on
which to chew, and that I understood well enough. He took
me up on his horse and patted my shoulder.

And then for several years I was an Indian.

How old was I when they found me? Was I five or six
or seven?

More likely five, although it might have been even
younger. Months passed in which I learned what Indian
boys learned, and with them. Months when I hunted and
fished and played at war with Indian children.

They were Sioux, and I was with them for four years,
sometimes in Montana, sometimes Canada, more often in
Wyoming, but it was in Canada they took me at last to a
Hudson Bay post. The white man there asked my name but I
had nothing to tell him, for all had been wiped clear by
that night of terror and death.

The Sioux remained long in the vicinity of the post

and I was much with them. Often I went into the woods
with Man-Who-Walks-With Birds, a medicine man who had
taken a liking to me. More than any other he taught me
how to live with the woods, the plains, and the mountains.

The factor at the Hudson Bay post was a friendly,
bearded man who occasionally sat down to talk to me, and
once when I said a word which my father had often used,
he was curious about it.

Did I know any more such words? I remembered a
few . . . I believe he hoped to find a name among them,
but there was none.

There were books in the library at the post, for many
of the trappers were great readers and they traded books
as they did all things. In one of them he showed me the
first map I had ever seen, and he showed me on the map
where the post was, and where the Sioux told him the
wagon train had been massacred.

Often I would take that book from its shelf and look
at it, and the map seemed strange to me because there
were no woods and streams, nor did it show wagons or
fear. But I did not forget the map.

One day they took me away. They carried me off to the
east and left me at a home for other children without
families.

Until then I had been among friendly people, but when
they first allowed me to walk in the yard with other
children a boy walked up to me and struck me. He struck
me hard in the mouth and laughed at me.

Suddenly out of the mystery that was my past I heard
my father's voice, speaking to someone in that tone which
had frightened me. "Come around here again, and I'll kill
you."

The boy hit me again, and laughed again, and within
me burst something white-hot and I struck out at him.

Four years in the woods I had run and played with In-

dian boys, wrestling with them, fighting with them. Now I
sprang at this boy and hurled him hard to the ground and
when he got up I battered him down again with my fists,
so filled with anger that I was frightened of myself.

The headmaster of the school came at me, but I ducked
away from him and backed to the wall, frightened at this
strange place where I found myself.

The yard was square and stone-walled and floored with
coarse gravel, and other children stood around, staring
at me, and the boy who had struck me got up slowly from
the ground, his mouth bleeding.

The headmaster reached for me, and then the boy I
struck opened the gate to go to the pump to wash away the
blood and I ducked under the headmaster's arm and ran
past the pump and into the woods. The headmaster and some
others came after me but they were not men who knew the
woods. Hiding quickly, I let them search all around and
waited until darkness came to move off.

For more than a week I walked, living from the woods
as I had been taught. When I walked it was on the roads,
but when I slept it was in the forest. I knew how to make
fire and three times I caught fish, and the other times I
lived from roots or the inner bark of trees.

One day I came out upon a sandy shore where the wind
was cold in the morning and where the sea was. The sea
rustled upon the sand and my feet made crunching noises
as I walked along the shore toward a dory where a man was
mending nets. Beside him there was a fire, and food cooking.

For several minutes I watched him, smelling the cooking food and feeling my stomach growl with hunger. At
first I think he did not see me and when he did he said
nothing for some time, but at last he said, without looking up, "How are you, boy? Hungry?"

His accent was familiar, but I knew not why. He took
the pipe from his mouth and looked at me. He had shrewd,

friendly eyes and an easy way about him. He shifted the
net upon his knee. "The net is old," he said, "and my
fingers are clumsy. How are you, boy, at mending nets?"

"I never mended one," I said. "I never even saw one
before . . . not like that."

"It is time for eating. Will you join me?"

Some faint memory stirred with me. "Thank you, sir,"
I said, and he looked up at me, surprised and pleased.

"Well, now. There's a thing. A boy who speaks like a
gentleman. It is an accomplishment, boy, and don't you
ever lose it. There is nothing," he added, "like proper
speech and manners for impressing people, and they are a
gracious thing."

He was a slender man, but wiry and strong, with gray-
ing hair and tiny laugh wrinkles at the corners of his
eyes. He had hot coffee with many slices of bacon and
some baked bread, and it tasted very good.

"You look to have traveled some," he said. "Have you
run away from somewhere?"

At this time I had not learned caution in dealing
with people, so I told him I had been a week in the woods.

He looked at me with some doubt, but when I responded
to his questions by explaining how I had lived his doubt
turned to respect. "Think of that, now. I doubt if I
could do as well. Perhaps at sea. Where did you learn the
like of that?"

"I was four years among the Sioux."

So after a bit of bacon and the warming of hot coffee
in my stomach I told him of my few years and the home to
which I'd been sent and the fight I had.

"You hit him then? Good lad. You'll find his type all
too often in this world, and it's little else they understand but blows.

"Well, I should send you back, but I am something of
a rebel myself, and if you'd like I shall make a fisherman of you. For the time being."

He gestured at the sand dunes about us. "This is a
place I often camp. My home . . . if it can be called
that, is off shore on Monhegan Island." He glanced at me.
"I'm Welsh, you know. David Penderyn's my name."

The red crept up my neck. I could feel the hot, sham-
ing flush of it climbing up my face. "I've no name," I
said, "I've no name to call myself."

"Ah?" He added fuel to the fire. "A name can be an
important thing for a man, and you'd best pick one out.
For a convenience . . . until you find your own."

The Sioux had given me a name . . . Haokah . . . it
was no rightful name. At the home to which I'd been sent
they had told me they would find a name for me, but
they'd not had time. They didn't even have a name for the
records there now, unless they invented one after I left.
More likely they were pleased to be free of me . . . who
wants a boy without a name?

Why could I not remember? Why I had lost that, too, I
did not know. Yet lost it I had. Since then I'd said over
all the names of which I could think, and so had the Hudson Bay factor, trying to help me, but none of them had a
familiar sound.

"There's no need to hurry," Penderyn added quietly.
"We'll camp here tonight, and tomorrow we will go to the
island. I live alone there . . . in a little shanty I
found myself."

"Call me that, then," I said, "since you found me,
too. Or I found you."

"Call you what?"

"Shanty. It's as good a name as any."

We fished the next day, and made it back to the island after dark. The shanty in which he lived had three
rooms. There was a kitchen, a bed-room, and a large living room filled with drawings, books, and all manner of
odds and ends in which he was interested. He had a collection of arrowheads, another of shells, and some odd

bits from old wrecks found along the shores of Maine and
the off-shore islands.

"Cabot came here in 1497," he commented, indicating
some odds and ends of old iron, most of which I could not
identify. "He was exploring the coast looking for a way
to the East, but I think there had been others here before him. I've found old campfires along the coast that
certainly were not made by Indians. Basque, Breton or
Norman fishermen, probably, and there are some ruins over
across the island."

He pointed out a cot along the wall. "You will sleep
there," he said. That was the beginning of it.

We fished off the Grand Banks, and sometimes we
traded for furs along the Brunswick coast, and I learned
how to handle a boat under oars or sail, to mend nets and
to fish.

Sometimes we would stay at the cabin for days while
he puttered around with his drawing . . . mostly drawings
of old wreckage, of ships or boats or trees . . . sometimes of waves.

"A rebel I was, and a rebel I have remained," he
said,"although they trained me for a barrister in England. It was not the life I wanted, and the girl they
wished me to marry was not the one I wanted, so I walked
away from it all, married a girl I loved and we came here
to fish and paint. Marie died, and the boy too." He
glanced at me. "He could have been your age, and I hope
he'd have been the man you are."

He walked across the room, listening to the wind.
"Storm blowing up," he commented, "and until you've seen
a storm off these islands . . . a real storm . . . you
will have seen nothing."

My hands grew strong with the hauling of nets, and my
shoulders with the cutting of wood for the house, but he

had started me learning from the books he had at hand, and from the tales he told me at odd moments throughout the day, or in the evening hours.

"You should go to school," he told me, "but the best school is in these books and others you will come upon. Let them lead you one to another, for all any school can give you is the barest outline of an education, then you must fill in the spaces yourself.

"Nor will acquiring information make you wise. Wisdom comes when you begin to draw conclusions from what you have learned or observed."

He was Welsh, as I have said, and in him there was a strong mystic vein. He was half a poet, I think, and half a seer, but a quietly practical man always with a gift for fishing and feeling for sea and wind beyond that of common men.

"Don't believe too much, boy. When you believe too much you must also disbelieve too much."

He told me that one day, the thought coming from nowhere. Nowhere, that is, but the recesses of his own mind.

He knew poetry, and loved it, and it was he who first brought The Iliad and The Odyssey to my mind, and read them aloud in the long hours of the evening. Yet he was not a well man.

Each time now that we went for the fishing, it seemed that drawing the nets took longer, the pull for shore was slower, and more and more I began to take the weight of it upon my shoulders.

When I first came to him upon that windy shore of Maine, I was ten . . . perhaps eleven years old. Four years went by, and they were good years for me, and for him, I think, for he had been lonelier than he realized.

Toward the end there was a kind of haste in him, a realization, I think, that he had not long to live. Dur-

ing those last months he tried to teach me everything he
knew, and once far out at sea he stopped, his face gray
from hauling the heavy net, and he said, "Knowledge was
meant to be passed on, boy. Do you always remember that.
Sometimes I feel . . . there was a German who wrote lines
that went something like this . . . 'I am like a bee that
hath gathered too much honey, I need hands reaching out
for it.'"

That was the last time we went far out from shore.
When we reached the cove at last, I was hauling the oars
alone, but strong enough to do it, for I was fourteen by
then.

It was that night he sat up suddenly and spoke across
the room to me. "Boy, if anything happens to me, go to
Henry Trefethren. He will see that I am buried beside my
wife. He has been told about you, and will sell what is
left and give it to you.

"Also, there is a black box in the trunk. Open it
with the key that's around my neck and mail the letter
that's written and sealed. Keep the rest of the contents
of the box for yourself, but keep them close to you."

Two weeks later when I returned from the fishing, he
was dead. The letter was mailed that night, addressed to
some place in England or Wales with a long, complicated
address. Otherwise there was little in the box except two
hundred dollars in gold pieces and three letters addressed to me.

In the first of the letters there was a will, leaving
everything in my name . . . or the name we had decided on.

In the second letter addressed to me, he said this:

The years you have spent with me have been the
happiest since losing my family, and I have felt
as if you were my own son. During this time I
have listened to the inflections in your voice,

noticed a few words you have used from time to
time, and your own behavior as well as the rare
odds and ends you remember of your own parents.

I believe I can safely say your family were
of Welsh, Cornish, Irish or Breton extraction;
that they were people of good background and of
some education. I believe they were better off
than most families going west in the 1850's.

There may have been a reason for their going
west other than the desire for land or gold. I do
not believe your wagon train was massacred by Indians. I believe your father, or perhaps your
mother, had an enemy they feared and that it was
this enemy who followed and attacked the wagon
train.

Knowing you are curious about your family, I
offer these comments for what they are worth.

The enclosed letters to you are to be delivered to Mr. Jefferson Hodge, in Boston. Mr.
Hodge is my attorney, and on your eighteenth and
twenty-fifth birthdays these letters will be
returned to you.

                              My best wishes.

When I had delivered the letters to Mr. Hodge, I went
down into the street and stood there alone.

I was fourteen years old and after buying clothing
and my passage to Boston I had but sixty-three dollars
remaining, and no place to go until I chose such a place.

The three years to come were to be three of the hard-
est and most brutal of my life.

COMMENTS: The first of these Boy-With-No-Name drafts, though relatively straightforward, doesn't get very far, nor is it anything but a typical Louis L'Amour beginning. I believe it was written several years prior to the second attempt.

But the second fragment is much more interesting. The first several pages wander around a bit. I get the feeling that Dad might have been waxing a bit rhapsodic about his own life, exploring some exaggerated or fantasy version of it as a possible background for this particular character. However, this might have indicated that, at the time this was written, Louis was thinking about putting together some sort of autobiographical or semi-autobiographical project. That could explain why he chose to lift the first few lines of this story to use as the lyrical introduction to his very personal short story collection, *Yondering*.

Around 1960 Louis mentions coming up with an idea for a novel using that title. He states in his journal:

```
Decided to do a novel called Yondering. A western
in hard-back, and will try to write it in May.
```

I doubt that either of the two attempts you have just read dates that early, but I do believe it was this story he was considering. The reference to it being "in hard-back" also suggests Dad was going to try to up his game a bit, to make it a more significant, potentially personal, piece.

In the *The Bastard of Brignogan* section that starts this collection, I note that in the 1970s we went on a long trip through eastern Canada. Dad's family lived on both sides of the border and he wanted to explore the territory of his ancestors in order to use it in future stories.

I suspect we took our eastern Canadian trip between the writing of these two versions and that something about connecting with his mysterious Canadian roots inspired Dad to revisit this story. This personal connection might also have brought him back to that wonderful first sentence when he started gathering the material for the short story collection he eventually titled *Yondering*.

Both *Yondering* and Louis's "memoir," *Education of a Wandering Man*, are fascinating projects, because they were examples of Louis's compromising with himself over writing an autobiography. He wanted to do it. Other people—his fans, his publisher, and his family— also wanted him to do it. But there was something (perhaps a number of somethings) keeping him from it. He often claimed he would write an autobiography only as fiction, thus not making it a true autobiography at all. Whatever the tension was that both pressed him forward and held him back, it helped create two wonderful books that we might not otherwise have.

KRAG MORAN

The Beginning of a Boxing Story

When the bell sounded Krag Moran went out fast. Gomez was coming right in because that was the way Gomez fought, the only way he knew how to fight. He was a short, thick-muscled bruiser with a square jaw and a flat face. And he could punch . . .

Moran saw the left start and went inside with a belting right to the heart that landed solidly. Even as the punch connected Moran was rolling to miss the right aimed for his head, and he was hooking his left to the ribs. Then he completed the combination with a right hook to the ear that shook Gomez and slid away.

Gomez looked at him, looked into his eyes, startled. Moran ignored the expression, feinted to bring Gomez on in, then stiffened the left into a blow that smashed his lips into his teeth. Moran's right crossed and connected hard to the cheekbone and Gomez staggered, momentarily off-balance.

Moran did not follow it up. Gomez was at his most

dangerous in wild slugging matches and Krag Moran was not
a gambling man. He moved around, looking Gomez over.

The Mexican had been hurt, and another fighter would
have been cautious. Gomez was not because it was not his
way. There was a growing welt on his cheekbone where the
right had landed.

Moran jabbed lightly, three times to the face. Two of
the jabs were to the eye above the welt. Gomez circled
and tried to work Moran into a corner, so Moran went
along with the game. Gomez rushed and Moran side-stepped
so swiftly that Gomez unloosed a punch at an empty corner, then furious at the laughter of the crowd, he
whirled. His turn was sudden, violent, and complete. He
met a right hand that struck like a bat hitting a line
drive. He turned over at the count of eight, but that was
all.

Gillerman had his money on the desk. "You can hit,"
he said, "you can really punch. Want a fight next month?"

Krag Moran shook his head. "I won't be in Panama next
month," he said, and he walked outside.

A thick-set man was standing on the street smoking a
long cigar. "Let's eat," he said, lifting his eyes to
Moran.

"What do you want?" Moran's voice was rough.

"To make a fast buck. How about you?"

"Where do we eat?"

"Feliciano's suit you?"

"If you pay for it."

"Sure," the man said, unsmiling, "I pay for it."

When they had ordered the man lit his cigar again. He
was shaved too clean and smelling too strongly of lotion.
He had thick, moist lips and wet, slightly protruding
eyes. He was a man, Krag was sure, who was strictly on

the make for a buck, who could not be trusted with anything out of eye range.

Krag Moran was twenty-eight but looked younger. He
was an inch over six feet and weighed one-eighty. His hair
was rusty-brown, his eyes slate-gray, his cheekbones high
and his jaw strong. He had no marks of the ring. He wore
a rumpled linen sport coat, a blue shirt and gray slacks.

"I'm Zavatarri. You got fifty bucks for tonight. I
can get you a grand for the same job."

Zavatarri took a clipping from his pocket and put it
beside Moran's plate. It was a magazine picture of a
fighter. It was Johnny Coleman, the light-heavyweight
champion of the world. "Who does he look like?" Zavatarri
asked. Then he pointed at Moran with his middle finger.
"He looks like you. You could be his brother."

"So what does that get me?"

"Dough . . . big dough and fast dough. There's a town
called Tangabar. A month ago it was a dozen mud huts and
a boat landing. They found a mountain of iron there, then
oil. Today there's fifteen thousand tough men in that
town, all loaded with money they have nowhere to spend."

When the waiter put their food down Moran started on
the steak. Let the man talk--this much was his.

"They've got a fighter there. He looks good, he hits
good, he talks a good fight and they like him . . . and
he couldn't go five rounds with you."

"So?"

"So we drop into town by plane. You're Johnny Coleman
on vacation but not backward about picking up a fast
buck. They make an offer, we fight this guy, we collect,
we lam."

"You're nuts. They sign this fight, Coleman reads it
in the papers, then we're in trouble."

Zavatarri shook his head. "Look. How many times you
seen in the paper where a champ signs but doesn't fight?

How many times does some jerk promoter say he's signed
the champ when he never even saw him. Publicity, that's
all. That's what they'll think this is."

Moran cut into his steak. It was a thick steak, a
juicy steak. It was the first steak he had seen in three
months. It was his first good meal in two weeks.

"You look good in there," Zavatarri said through a
mouthful. "You can move around. You box like Coleman. You
can hit, all right. You ain't as good as Coleman, but who
is?" He waved his fork. "Far as that goes in a place like
Tangabar I can hold up any news release until we're out
of town." He rubbed his fingers. "Tell them you're tryin'
to make a buck without your manager, who takes you for
everything."

Tangabar was two double rows of sheet metal on frame
buildings. Only the hotel had two stories. The town had
fourteen gambling houses, twenty saloons, five restaurants and a half dozen greasy spoon joints. It had fifty
shacks with women sitting in the doorways.

It was a town where they had a fighter named Monk
Burman. He weighed two hundred pounds even and his name
was not Burman, but Krag Moran did not know that . . . or
care. It was a town where a lot of guys had a lot of
money that said their fighter could take Johnny Coleman.

Krag Moran moved into a thin-walled hotel room and
from his suitcase he took three pairs of dirty socks
which he washed in the basin. He took out an extra pair
of slacks, his boxing gear and a dirty shirt. The dirty
shirt was wrapped around a .380 Colt automatic with three
extra clips, all loaded.

He put the clips in his pocket, the automatic behind
his waist-band under his shirt and went down into the
street. It was a tough town full of tough men. Men who
weren't going to like it if they got gypped.

Women followed him with their eyes as he walked along
the street and men took a second look at his shoulders.
He bought a clean shirt for twice what it was worth.

Zavatarri was sitting on his bed when he got back to
the room. Moran's suitcase was facing opposite from the
way he had left it.

"We're in, kid. Took just that long. Night after tomorrow. Publicity's no trick here. All they do is mention
it in a couple of saloons. Anyway, there's nothing else
for them to do but drink, gamble and go after women. They
can do that any time."

"What do I get?"

"You get a grand, like I said."

Krag Moran rolled up his sleeves and ran water into
the basin. His forearms were brown and powerful, his
hands thick and square across the knuckles. He looked at
Zavatarri in the mirror. "Get yourself another boy.
There'll be four, five thousand men there. Maybe twice
that many. You're dealing for Coleman now. You asked for
fifty percent, at least."

Zavatarri didn't like it. He didn't like it even a
little. His eyes got mean and he took his cigar from his
mouth. "You cheap bum! You got fifty bucks for Gomez. You
didn't have a quarter when you got in there with him.
Why, you lousy--!"

Moran took him by the collar and lifted him. He held
him like that until his face started to turn purple and
his eyes bulged. Zavatarri struggled uselessly. "Don't
call me a bum." Moran's voice was flat, conversational.
"I don't like it." He dropped Zavatarri on the bed.
"Sure," he said, "I didn't have any money. But you didn't
have a fighter that looked like Johnny Coleman, either."

He lathered his face and put a blade in his safety
razor. He looked at Zavatarri's mottled face in the mirror. "We split fifty-fifty."

Zavatarri started to complain but Moran was watching

him in the mirror. After a minute he shrugged and said,
"All right, all right."

Zavatarri sucked on his cigar. "You think you can
lick this guy? We could make a buck bettin'."

"I can lick him."

"This guy's big. He's rugged."

"If he was any good he wouldn't be here."

"You're good."

Moran chuckled without humor. "Not good. Just good
enough. I've had 'em on with the good ones, though." He
looked at Zavatarri. "Anyway, I'm not a fighter. I'm just
a guy who can fight who needs a buck."

When he was cleaning his razor he said, "You bet the
way you like. I'm bettin' my end on me."

When Zavatarri was gone Krag took off his shirt and
bathed his body. He took the .380 and cleared the shell
from the chamber. Then he put the gun in his suitcase.

There was a saloon and gambling place called the
Queen's Bar. Krag walked to the bar and ordered rum and
looked around. He had a good memory for faces but he knew
none of these.

There was a girl dealing blackjack. She had a still,
expressionless face and large, beautiful gray eyes. She
dealt very fast, never flickering an eyelid, and she said
nothing at all to anyone. She looked up and saw Krag
Moran watching her.

He sat without drinking, just keeping the rum in
front of him. She did not look curious. She did not look
anything. She just turned back to her game. She played
fast, straight, and while he was watching, she made money
for the house.

The bartender came up to him. "You Johnny Coleman?
Heard you were in town."

"Who's the babe dealing twenty-one?"

"Mag Kelly. She's all right."

After awhile he drank his rum, got off the stool and went to the door. He glanced back and saw Mag Kelly watching him. He lifted a hand, then went out. She had not smiled, had not answered his wave.

He went up to the hotel and stretched out on the bed with a two-bit Western. He read until he was sleepy, then undressed and got into bed. At three a.m. he awakened and the town was still alive. He heard Zavatarri stirring around, heard a low woman's laugh. He went back to sleep.

At daybreak he rolled out and dressed, putting on a sweater. He was always in shape . . . he walked fast, avoiding the mud flat and taking the road down the coast. He trotted a hundred yards, walked fifty, sprinted fifty. When he had covered a couple of miles and felt good, he shadow-boxed a little, then stripped off his clothes and went into the sea.

It was a warm, milky sea. He swam for only a few minutes and then came in. He stretched out on a rock until his body was dry, then he dressed. While he was dressing he saw a house standing alone down the coast among some rocks. He was slipping on his shoes when he heard a step and turned. It was Mag Kelly.

Her hair was down to her shoulders this morning and she looked younger and softer. "You shouldn't swim in there," she warned, "there's sharks."

"I didn't see any."

"A boy was killed, just last week." She turned to go. "I didn't know who you were. I just wanted to warn whoever it was."

"What's the rush?"

She stopped and turned. "I'm getting breakfast." She started to go on, then stopped. "Have you eaten?"

He got up and hung his sweater around his shoulders, looping the arms in front. "Thanks," he said, "I don't mind if I do."

There was an old man sitting on the step with a shotgun. He looked up at Krag Moran and then at Mag Kelly.
"This one all right?"

"This morning."

They went inside and Krag watched her. "What did that
mean?" he asked abruptly.

"That's Hongkong. He takes me to work. He brings me
home. I don't like to be bothered."

"Always with the shotgun?"

"In town it's a pistol."

Krag Moran had seen old men like that before. He had
looked into the old man's eyes. He had a feeling the old
man would kill him without a qualm.

Over breakfast they talked of books, of the town, of
the sea. Then she said, "You're in trouble. Burman is
good."

"So?"

"So you're not Johnny Coleman. So maybe even Johnny
Coleman couldn't beat Burman. And his name isn't Burman.
And some place, some time, he was very, very good."

"What makes you think I'm not Coleman?"

"You're not. I've seen him close enough to know
you're not him; maybe a little in build. But you've got
better shoulders."

"You haven't mentioned it?"

"Of course not. That's your cup of tea. But I'm not
coming to the fight. I don't want to see what happens to
you."

She was younger than he had believed, and her father
had owned a plantation but had lost it when she was in
her twenties. He had died when she was twenty-five.
"Since then Hongkong's been with me. I take care of him,
and he takes care of me."

"He looks like he could."

"He can."

She walked to the door with him and pointed out the

path. He thought she lingered a little, and he knew he did not want to go. Finally, he did. When he looked back, she looked after him and waved.

Zavatarri came to his room. He looked worried and sat down on the bed. "Where you been?" His voice was impatient.

Moran stretched out on the bed and looked up at the ceiling. It was made of one by six boards with small spaces between. There was a peaked roof over that. Moran yawned, "I took a walk," he said, "a work-out."

Zavatarri was obviously relieved. He lit a cigar and smoked, talking at random. He kept coming back to the fight. "This guy is good," he said. "You sure you can take him?"

"You can always hedge your bets," Moran said quietly, "but remember: lay off my dough."

Later he went down to a restaurant for lunch and saw a half dozen rough-looking men sitting around. One of them said something, and the others laughed. One was a big man with a thick stomach and a beefy red face. "I could myself," he said. "He don't look so tough."

"Even his manager doesn't think so." The speaker was a little man with a crooked face. "He's bettin' on Burman."

When Moran finished eating he started out and the red-faced man said, "Better take a good look, he'll not be the same again."

Moran was behind him and he reached over and clapped a hand over the man's face and jerked back. The chair and man went over backward and Moran stood waiting, his stand indolent but ready. The red-faced man started to lunge up, then thought the better of it.

Moran looked around. "Any time," he said, and walked out.

He had a bad feeling about the town. The stinking mud
flat, the thrown together buildings, the riff-raff . . .
none of these was the matter. The place just did not feel
right. He went back to the hotel and got his gun. He
checked and it was all right. He lay down on the bed and
looked up at the cracks. A lizard came through one of
them and angled down the wall. He threw a paper wad at it
and it scuttled indignantly away.

It was very hot . . . there was no breeze. He wanted
to swim but the sharks gave him something to think about.
He got up from the bed finally, and slipped into his coat
and walked outside. He could hear the sound of hammers
from the open space beyond the town. They were throwing
up a ring there. There was a natural bowl where specta-
tors could sit around on the ground to watch.

He walked that way but stopped some distance off. He
saw Zavatarri talking to Pete Salmi, who was promoting
the fight. He went back to town and very thoughtfully
looked around. Monk Burman had followers all right, and
most of the betting was on him. He sat down on the steps
of a saloon and waited, watching the road down the coast.
In a little while he saw them coming, Mag Kelly and the
old man, Hongkong. She glanced at him but said nothing
until he spoke, getting to his feet. "I want a man in my
corner," he said, "an honest man."

She nodded, "All right . . ." She walked on inside.

He was sitting on his bed in the hotel when there was
a knock at the door. The man who came in was thin and
tall with lack-lustre eyes and a cadaverous face. He wore
a shirt outside his slacks and he looked at Moran.

Then he closed the door and said, "You ain't Coleman."

"Coleman draws more money than I would."

"To fight this guy you'll wish you were Coleman."

"Who is he?"

The man shrugged. "Looks familiar, but I don't know
him." He held out a thin hand. "I'm Tilho. Worked behind
a few fighters."

"Seen him go?"

"Uh-huh. He's got it all. So much he shouldn't be
here. There's got to be something back of him that ain't
good. But that won't help you."

"How do they like it here?"

"Rough. Above the belt anything goes."

"All right with me." Moran sat up. "I'll give you
fifty bucks. If I win, a hundred bucks and ten percent of
my bets."

"You must figure you're bidding."

"Maybe," Krag said. "And they could go stronger than
I can. But I figure you're on the level."

Tilho got up. "You better." He started to the door,
then stopped. "You better think about leavin', too. If
you win," he said, "there'll be some who won't like it.
You better also think about collectin'."

"Yeah," Moran agreed. "Thanks."

He had been thinking about both of those things. He
had been thinking about them a lot. He did not like the
feel of this town, and he had been in a lot of tough
towns. He knew the tough streets in the tough towns. He
knew Malay Street in Singapore, Blood Alley in Shanghai,
Grant Road in Bombay and District Six in Cape Town. But
he didn't like the feel of this place.

Zavatarri and Salmi were betting on Burman. They were
betting heavy, and part of what Zavatarri was betting was
from his part of the purse. "It better only be his part,"
Moran said, and went into the saloon where Mag was dealing.

After awhile she closed the game and came over for a
drink. They sat there without talking until he said, "You
like that place of yours?"

"Not much."

"How about this?" He glanced around.

"Not at all."

"All right." He turned on his stool. "Mag," he said, "I like you."

"I like you, too," she said softly.

There were not four or five thousand at the ringside, there were twice that many. Everybody was there who could walk. This was probably the only different bit of entertainment they would see all year.

Krag Moran went down to the ring and alongside the ropes. He took off his coat and folded it carefully. He made sure which way the pocket opened. He took off his shirt and folded it, then his slacks. He wore his old blue trunks under the slacks. He folded the slacks. The Colt .380 was in his coat pocket.

He got into the ring. He moved around lightly, getting the feel of the canvas. When the crowd roared he knew why, and when he felt the jar of the ring he knew his opponent was climbing in. The referee called them for instructions and Krag looked out from under his brows.

Kid Morowitz . . .

A tough Polack who came up from the wrong side of the tracks, from the small clubs to a title contender in two years. For three years he whipped everybody in the light-heavy class until he outgrew it. He had whipped the old champion twice in over the weight matches, and he had fought to a draw with Johnny Coleman.

He was sneering, powerful . . . thirty pounds heavier than Moran and he grinned when they came face to face. "You? Coleman?" He chuckled. "This here's gonna be good."

Kid Morowitz, now Monk Burman. He was wanted on a murder charge . . . a waterfront killing. He had vanished after that, just dropped from sight. But here he was.

Tilho took the towel from Moran's shoulders. "That's
Morowitz," Moran said, "the Kid himself."

"Yeah," Tilho said, "you take your time out there."

Tilho had not seemed surprised . . . Moran saw Mag
Kelly in a ringside seat, old Hongkong beside her. Mag
looked up and smiled. It was a sad smile.

The bell rang . . .

Krag Moran went out, taking his time. Burman tried a
left and was short. Krag feinted but Burman ignored it.
Moran feinted again and was surprised when Burman came
all the way in. Burman's jab jarred on his forehead and a
solid right clipped his chin. Moran felt the wicked jar
of the blow clear to his heels. He worked around Burman,
boxing carefully. The big mug could hit.

Burman came in, jabbed twice to the head, crossed a
right that missed and took a smashing left to the ribs.
Moran went inside, hooking short and hard to the body,
then clinched. Burman was a bear in a clinch but Moran
liked it rough. He always had. He pushed the bigger man,
treading on his instep and trying to twist him. Burman
broke away and stopped Moran's rush with a left to the
head. The left came again and Moran went under it with a
right to the heart, left to the ribs and a right to the
ear. He broke away, and as Burman started in, stopped him
in his tracks with a jarring jab that split Burman's lip
and drew first blood. The bell rang and he walked back to
his corner.

"All right," Tilho said, "you're moving."

"You know this guy."

Tilho looked down at Moran, touching the sweat from
his face with a towel. "Yeah, I know him."

Moran walked right on in when the bell sounded. He
slipped a left jab and crossed a right over the left.
They went in close and suddenly he was winging them in
with both hands. The attack surprised Burman. Toe-to-toe
they slammed it out for ten fast seconds and then Moran

broke ground suddenly and when Burman came in, Moran
nailed him with a right uppercut that set him on his
toes.

Burman was shaken. His eyes grew ugly and he rushed
Moran into the ropes where Moran side-stepped fast trying
the same stunt he had pulled on Gomez. Burman turned
swiftly, dropping at the knees as he turned. Moran's blow
missed and he took a wicked punch into the belly. He
backed up, gasping, and Burman moved in, hitting him on
the chin with both hands. Moran fell and hit the canvas,
rolling over.

Moran took a count of six, then came up. Burman moved
in, tried a left which Moran pulled away from, then Burman shot his right and Moran slipped it, smashing his own
right to the head. Burman backed away, surprised.

"How d'you like it, Kid?" Moran said.

He felt Burman stiffen and he shoved him away and in
the instant of surprise, stabbed a hard left to the
puffed lips. Burman tried to clinch again, and Moran
said, "You dirty killer! I'm takin' you back!" And he
fell away to his left as he spoke, one hand on Burman's
shoulder, and then he whipped a jolting right to Burman's
chin.

Burman caught it turning and it shook him to his
heels. Moran hit him with one fist and then the other and
Burman went down. Moran backed off, waited, and when Burman got

COMMENTS: Stylistically, I suspect that this slightly Hemingway-
esque story is from the immediate postwar period, though there is no
mention of WWII itself. However, it also has some crossover with a
tale from Louis's life prior to WWII, a story about him getting into a

boxing match with a very large, very tough guy in a Borneo oil camp. There is little evidence that proves the Borneo tale is true, but this story fragment has a few similarities to the various versions I have heard of it.

Dad was briefly in Panama in the 1920s, just long enough to soak up some of the atmosphere. I love the moment where the character "stretched out on the bed with a two-bit Western." I have always wondered if Dad had any inkling that he would be the guy writing those 25-cent Westerns within a few short years.

Louis emerging from a workout at a
mining camp locker room.

STAN DUVAL

The Beginning of a Crime Story

The big man walked to the empty stool beside him. He probably weighed twenty pounds more than two hundred, and his face was splotchy red.

Stan cupped his hand around the Bourbon and soda. He could feel the big man staring at him in the mirror. He was in no mood for trouble but he could sense something building up in the man.

The big man ordered a drink and the bartender put it on the bar in front of him, standing with his hands on the edge of the bar, waiting for the man to pay. The red faced man took a thick wad of bills from his pocket, tossed one of them on the bar without looking at it and stuffed the rest back in his pants.

There was a girl down the bar who was on the make. She was sitting with another woman who looked like the girl would twenty years from now. Probably her mother. He smiled to himself. The girl looked like a chippie off the old block.

He avoided her eyes. In avoiding her eyes, he caught

the sardonic expression of the big man beside him. There
was something in those eyes that made anger rise within
him. He started to speak, then took a drink of liquor and
tried to forget about it. He was a stranger in town and
about to start looking for work. Getting arrested in a
bar would be a poor way to start.

"You're wasting time," the big man said suddenly. He
had spoken without lifting his head. Neither did he turn.
"If I were you, I'd light out."

"What do you mean?"

The big man was turning his glass in his fingers, and
suddenly, Stan was afraid. This man was not trying to
start trouble, that was his imagination. There was something else going on.

Lifting his glass to his lips the big man spoke
softly. "Well, she's lying back there dead. There's sure
to be somebody dropping by at some point. Then the cops
will be looking for you."

"Are you nuts?" Stan stared at the big man in the
mirror. He had a wide neck. His hands were thick fingered
and heavy. He was a bruiser. In a brawl he would be hard
to handle.

"Me? You're the one that's nuts. If I'd killed my
wife I wouldn't be sitting here!"

Killed his wife?

Stan felt a chill of apprehension go over him, and
his hands shut down hard on the bar. He glimpsed his face
in the mirror and he looked pale.

Then it hit him. The man was insane. Stark mad. Stan
forced a smile and shrugged. "I wouldn't either," he
said, "but then I haven't killed anybody."

"You don't have to kid me," the big man said, "I
ain't a bull. But the cops won't figure it that way. If I
were you, I'd blow out of here, but _fast_!"

Stan was puzzled and angry. Who was this guy? Who did
he think he was talking to? "Listen, chum," Stan said, "I

don't know what your angle is, or who you're trying to kid, but I don't have a wife, never had a wife, and I wouldn't have killed her if I did!"

The man hunched his big shoulders and leaned his elbows on the bar. He was one of the most powerful men Stan had ever seen. "Isn't your name Duval?" the big man asked. "Henry Stanley Duval? Weren't you in Klamath Falls for awhile?"

Stan felt the tightness go out of him. He felt at that moment much as he did before a close shot at a tiger. The cold sense of awareness, the instant of waiting before the big head shoved through the bushes, the knowledge that one shot would be all he might get. His muscles and his mind relaxed and he felt wariness creeping over him with a faint, remote chill.

He spoke, and his voice was quiet, very calm. "Yes, my name is Duval. I have been in Klamath Falls. I am a man who has been many places. But I am not married, I never have been, and I know no one in this town."

"Nobody but her, and she's dead. You better blow, bud. I ain't a squealer. Nobody else knows so far."

"But _you_ know," Stan suggested. "How do you know? Maybe you killed this woman you say is my wife?"

"Me?" The big man chuckled. "I liked Madge. She was a good kid, only maybe she had too many friends. But don't get any ideas. I got an alibi. I got a honey of an alibi. How's yours?"

Alibi? He didn't have the shadow of an alibi. An hour before he had come into town with a man in a Buick sedan. The man's name was Gardiner. He had dropped Stan off at the bar and told him he would meet him there in a hour or so and they would have dinner together.

Madge?

The name struck fire in his brain. Madge? Klamath Falls? He took a swallow of liquor, then said without

turning his head, "This supposed wife of mine. What was
she like?"

"Hell, you should know. A honey of a blonde. Tall,
willowy babe, with a little scar on her ear lobe.

"Don't get me wrong," the big man was saying, "I
don't blame you. You guys come back from overseas and
find your wives playing around. Hell, I wouldn't blame
you."

Stan wasn't listening. Madge. That would be Madge
McClean, but his _wife_? Why, he had known her for no more
than a week. They had dinner, he recalled. She was a
dancer and singer, and pretty good . . . well, pretty
good for Portland.

She had been going up Morrison Street tucking some
things in her bag. As she passed him she dropped her coin
purse. He had to follow her two blocks and through two
traffic signals before he could catch her to return it.

They had talked a little, had a drink together, and
then dinner.

It was one of those cases of two lonely people, mutu-
ally attracted. He had some business in Klamath Falls,
and by that time they were liking each other quite a bit.
She knew who he was, had read all three of his travel
books, and he liked her. They had decided to make it a
twosome.

They had registered at a hotel there . . . it hit him
right in the wind . . . as man and wife.

Stan Duval took another drink and stared at the big
man's reflection. "I don't get it," he said, and his
voice was suddenly hoarse. "What's your angle?"

The big man shoved back off the stool. "Hey," he
said, "I'm just a friendly guy. Always doin' things for
people! My name's Fin Campo, if you want to know. I just
hate to see a good guy in a bad spot. And brother you're
in one!"

Campo turned and went out. Stan sat there, staring at
his drink. It didn't make sense, none of it did. He
hadn't seen Madge McClean in four years . . . almost
five. Before he went into the Army. Nor had he heard from
her in all that time.

The whole thing was insane. He was married to no one,
and had never been married. How had Campo found him in
that bar? Who was Fin Campo? And what, he wondered suddenly, had become of Gardiner?

If there was anything to this he was going to need
Gardiner. Gardiner could prove when he got to Los Angeles, where he had been until he walked into the bar.

Stan got up suddenly. The telephone directory gave
Madge McClean's address as 2203 Parkington Row and the
map in back showed it to be close by, a stiff twenty minute walk . . . shorter if he could get a ride.

"Listen," he said to the bartender, "if a small man
with a broken nose comes in here asking for Duval, tell
him I'll be back in about an hour."

He walked out into the street, his mind suddenly made
up. No matter what happened, he must know. He saw a cab
and flagged it down. "Twenty Two O Three Parkington Row,"
he said, and sat back in the seat, staring ahead of him.

It didn't make sense no matter how you looked at it.
He had returned from overseas two months before. He had
gone through the war, and then because of his experience
they had asked him to stay on. Having made some good
friends, he volunteered to remain one more year.

When he got back he was tired of everything. He
wanted some time to adjust himself, to relax, think, and
make plans for the future. Before the war he had been an
explorer, hunter, and professional wanderer who wrote
books of his travels and lectured.

A friend in New York had a car he wanted to sell so
Stan bought it and started west. He was in no hurry. He
had stopped many times, wrote a little, camped out here

and there. In San Diego he sold the car, and while trying
to make up his mind on the next move, dropped into a bar.

That was where he met Gardiner. They were sitting
side by side, and started talking. When Stan mentioned
his name, Gardiner was immediately interested. They had
talked and Gardiner had told him he knew just the man he
should see in Los Angeles, somebody who wanted some jungle films made. The plan was to head north by the end of
the week; it had seemed like an opportunity to restart
his life.

The cab rolled up in front of the door and he got
out. All the lights were on in the house and a police car
stood at the curb.

"Looks like the joint's been raided!" the cabbie
said.

He paid the man off and started up the walk. Four men
were standing in the front room, looking at the body of a
girl.

Stan stared down at her. Her golden and beautiful
hair lay around her head like a halo, a halo stained at
the top with blood. There was a widening pool of it on
the carpet and floor.

They looked up when he entered. There was a tall,
very lean man with sandy hair and a sad face. "Who are
you?" he asked.

"My name is Stanley Duval."

"Duval?" The sandy haired man smiled. "You're her
husband, then?"

"No," he said. "I'm not."

"I'm Lieutenant Haynes," the officer said. "Let's get
this straight. You say you aren't her husband? She's
listed as Mrs. Stanley Duval?"

"There's a mistake somewhere. Her name is not Duval,
and I am not married to anyone and never have been."

A plain clothes man with a beefy face and small mustache smiled cynically. "I suppose next thing you'll be saying you didn't know her!"

"Oh, no," Stan said. "I knew her all right. I met her about five years ago in Oregon, but her name was McClean, not Duval. We saw a good deal of each other for about a week, and I haven't seen her since."

Haynes shook out a smoke, then handed the pack around. He studied the girl thoughtfully. "You say you haven't seen her in all that time? Then how do you account for this?"

In his hands he held a letter, which he showed to Stan. It was addressed to Stan Duval, General Delivery, San Diego. It was a letter he had picked up at the post office the day before. He controlled the urge to check the pocket in which he had placed the letter . . . that would be the action of a guilty man.

Fear came to him then, a cold fear that crept up his legs and left him standing in an icy chill. "I don't account for it," he said, "I can't account for it. You found that . . . here?"

Haynes was looking at him through the cigarette smoke. "Yeah. Right over there by the divan."

"You say," the other plain clothes man said, "you weren't married to her. Here's a rental receipt made out to Mrs. Stanley Duval. She's been paying rent under that name for two months."

"How did you know this address if you haven't seen her in five years?" Haynes was speaking in a conversational tone, quiet, almost lazy. "How'd you happen to come here tonight?"

"Why, there was a man in a bar gave it to me. A fellow named Campo. He said a woman with my name was murdered here."

"My God! I've heard some yarns in my time. How'd this guy know you?"

"I don't know." Stan's mouth was dry and he felt empty in the pit of his stomach. "He just came in and sat down beside me and started talking, said this girl was murdered and that I'd better get out of town."

"In spite of this letter you say you haven't seen this girl in five years?"

"That's right. I just got in town tonight. Came up from San Diego."

"How'd you come? Plane or train?"

"Neither. I rode up with an acquaintance. A fellow I met in San Diego."

"Oh, where's this guy now?"

"I don't know. He was coming back to meet me in the bar where I met Campo. But after I talked with Campo I thought I'd run out here and try to find out what this was all about. He may be there now. His name was Gardiner."

"In other words," Haynes said, "you've no alibi for the time of the murder?"

"No," Duval said, "I've no alibi. I'd no idea I was going to need one. This girl," he added, "was just an acquaintance. She was okay, a pretty nice kid, but except for one week I never knew anything about her."

"That," Haynes said, "is the thinnest yarn I ever heard. You understand," he glanced up at Duval, "I'm not saying it isn't true, but without doubt it is the worst yarn I ever heard anybody tell. You say you haven't seen her in five years, but there's a letter of yours on the floor. A letter that from the date must have been dropped here tonight or yesterday.

"You say you got her address from a guy in a bar who told you she was murdered. Hell, man, we hadn't been here over three minutes when you got here. How could anybody know? We found the body."

"Maybe this guy Campo killed her."

Haynes rubbed his chin. "Duval, you don't know what you're saying. I haven't a doubt you met Campo in a bar.

He spends a lot of time in bars. But him telling you anything like this . . . it's just plain goofy."

"You know him?"

"He's a special investigator for the District Attorney. Not much goes on in town that he doesn't know. I
might add that he's got enough political pull to make it
felt anywhere."

Haynes looked around at the other plain clothes man.
"Potter, see what's wrong with the medical examiner. He
should be here by now!"

"The car's just pulling up, Lieutenant. He'll be
right in."

Two men walked through the open door. One of them had
a black bag. He knelt over the body, and Haynes leaned
over to watch. The policemen were craning their necks and
Potter had stepped into the next room.

It was a moment, a fleeting instant that might never
come again. Stan Duval turned and walked quietly from the
room.

His heart was jumping and his mouth was dry. When he
got to the door he stepped out on the porch, then off
onto the lawn, and walking across it, leaped the hedge
into the next yard. He was going through the gate into
the alley when he heard a yell from the house.

He started running. He was frightened now, frightened
as he never had been. Running on his toes, he made the
end of the alley, his heart pounding. A siren started
somewhere behind him, and he walked across the street,
forcing himself to walk, then sprinted another block.

Stan came out on the street. Ahead of him and on the
corner was a drug store, and beyond it, as he turned the
corner, was a neighborhood theatre. It was a large theatre, and several people were buying tickets. Coolly,
forcing himself to be calm, he stepped into line.

The siren was whining behind him, and he could hear
it turning a corner, then stop. They would be flashing

their spotlight down the alleys. He got his ticket and walked into the theatre.

He had no more than a few minutes at best, and no plan of action. They might not think of the theatre; it would seem a trap. Maybe it was. He went into the men's room and glanced at himself in the mirror. His face looked white. Turning, he walked out. The usherette had stepped inside the curtains to watch the picture; the lobby was empty. Directly opposite him was a huge Chinese vase, over six feet high. There was one on either side of the lobby.

Stan started for one, and then he saw the girl. She was watching him, but when their eyes met, she looked away. Her figure was trim, neat and her eyes beautiful. She walked toward the curtains.

There was an overstuffed chair near the vase. Putting one foot on the back, he caught the top and pulling himself up, dropped lightly inside. Then, his heart pounding, he sat down.

His heart was throbbing painfully and he was perspiring profusely. Sitting still, scarcely daring to breathe, he waited. It was late. Within an hour and a half the theatre would close. He would be safe. He would have a long night before him to plan.

Then he heard the voice. It was so soft he scarcely heard it, but it was unmistakable. "Why did you get in there?"

A woman. It must have been the girl who had been watching him. "I'm powdering my nose," she whispered then. "Even if anyone sees me they won't guess about you. Why did you get in there?"

It sounded silly, but he whispered back, "I'm hiding." He hesitated. Oh, well. She knew he was here. "From the police," he said.

"That siren was for you? I saw you buying a ticket. What did you do?"

"They think I killed my wife. I'm not even married. I got away."

There was silence, and he could almost hear the girl thinking. Who was she? Why hadn't she reported him at once?

"Better stay here all night," she said.

He heard her moving away, and he could hear voices from the outer foyer, from the snack bar. Footsteps approached again, and he could hear her humming. Then her voice. "Catch."

Stan glanced up. Two candy bars came over the top. He caught them deftly, then heard her moving away.

He put the candy in his pocket, suddenly aware that he was hungry. Next time he ran away from the police, he told himself, he would wait until after dinner.

Time dragged slowly. The bottom of the vase was just large enough for him to sit with his knees against his chest. There was no room to stretch his legs, and he dare not stand up for fear someone would hear him.

The girl puzzled him. Why her interest?

His flight had been instinctive. Considering the plight he was in it had seemed the only obvious course. Haynes could not be blamed. His story was absurd. It was absurd, and it was the truth, all of it.

What _was_ it all about? Thinking back over it, he began to realize that his involvement had not been due to accident nor to a coincidence.

A lot of things began to click into place. The letter was the key to it all. He had received that letter in San Diego. He had put it in his pocket to be answered the next day. Then he met Gardiner, and decided to take a chance on the jungle film deal. In any event, he had planned on going to L.A.

The last he had seen of the letter was when he put it in his pocket. Had his coat been off since? No. Therefore, if the letter left him, and it had, it had to be taken from his pocket while the coat was on him. That necessitated opportunity. Who had the opportunity?

Gardiner. Stan remembered then that he had fallen asleep several times on the trip north from San Diego. But that meant that Gardiner was involved.

Well, why not? Campo had come into the bar while Duval waited for Gardiner. Could Gardiner have sent Campo there? How else could Campo have known?

But what was behind it? Why?

Why had Madge been killed? Why was she using his name? Who had killed her?

He remembered how struck Gardiner had been when he heard his name. Stan had merely believed he was another man who had read his books; now it seemed to mean something else. Somehow, or some way Gardiner had known something about him, or about Madge. Perhaps Gardiner was the murderer. Possibly he had been planning the crime even then, when suddenly a scapegoat was offered in the person of Stanley Duval!

A coincidence, but it still didn't make sense. He was satisfied with his solution of his own involvement. Gardiner could have lifted the letter from his pocket, got in touch with Campo, who was somehow involved, and arranged the whole setup.

The show was ending and he could hear people leaving. Somebody tossed a gum wrapper into the vase. Bit by bit people drifted out of the show, and he could hear their comments on the picture.

"I thought he was simply wonderful! Don't you like his voice, though? It just does something to you!"

Then another voice, close beside the vase. "Listen, Ruth, it's early yet. Let's go up to my place for awhile?"

"George, I've told you that I'll never--besides, Andy's home."

They drifted out, and silence settled. Then he heard

a rattle of brooms. "Let's get it over with," somebody said, "I want to get home. My kid's sick."

"Yeah? What's the trouble?"

"I don't know, the Doc says . . ." The voice dwindled.

They moved away and Stan let himself relax. He waited, his legs asleep. Finally, he heard them leave. By the luminous dial of his wrist watch he waited a half hour longer. Then he got to his feet, straightening his cramped legs. He chafed them, rubbing the circulation back into action. Then he reached up and catching the top of the vase, pulled himself up.

Waiting an instant for correct balance, he dropped to the chair, and then the floor.

All was dark and still. Through the doors he could see the street. A police car stood by the corner. The drug store was still open. No, it was closing. The reflected light snapped out, and then he heard voices. Two policemen got into their car, but they just sat there and did not go away.

Stan sat down in the chair and took out a bar of candy. He couldn't remember ever being so hungry before.

Under the wrapper was a white card with a name—Judith Baird Kegley Apts. On the back was the note.

If before 8 a.m. or after 5:30 p.m. come.

He ate the candy thoughtfully. Why the devil was she helping him? Or willing to help? Who was she?

Undoubtedly the police would be patrolling the area. The prowl car in front of the theatre was an example. They had lost him near here, and they would be watching closely. In any event, he would find a better place to hide. The vase was too dangerous.

Going down the side aisle he walked through the vast

and empty theatre. All was pitch dark here, the light
from outside killed by the thick, velvet curtains.

Striking matches, he found his way backstage. There
was a small backstage office, probably used now by the
janitor. In the office, he prowled, striking many
matches, but putting the stubs in his pocket. In one
drawer he found a flashlight.

If he left the theatre now, and he was sure he could
leave through one of the exits used for fire or emergen-
cies, he would be on the streets in a section of town
where anybody might be questioned . . . after all there
had been a murder nearby.

His best chance was to wait until morning, and to
mingle with people on their way to work. Money was no
handicap. He had nearly three hundred dollars in his
pockets. That should be sufficient for any immediate purposes.

Stan got up and, using the flashlight sparingly, he
made a careful reconnaissance of the theatre. The door of
the manager's office was unlocked, and he stepped inside
and looked around. Seeing a knob in a panel, he turned it
and found another door. It was a small closet with a wash
basin and mirror, and . . . an electric razor!

When he had the plan of the theatre clearly in mind
he chose a loge seat and sat down, leaning back, and went
to sleep. He was not worried about sleeping too late. He
had always been able to awaken when he wished.

Yet it was after six when he opened his eyes again.
He got to his feet and for five minutes by the watch,
listened for any sound. Assured that no one had yet entered the theatre, he went to the manager's office,
shaved, washed and combed his hair.

Replacing the flashlight he went to a ground floor
exit and pushed down on the handle. It opened easily, and
holding it open a crack, he studied the situation. The

exit opened on an alley. Opposite the theatre was a market. A truck was backed up, unloading boxes and crates.
It was a new truck, still bright and without dust.

When the driver had a load in his arms and turned
toward the market, Stan Duval opened the door and stepped
out. He walked over to the truck and was standing there,
admiring it, when the driver came out of the market.

Stan grinned at him. "That's a slick looking rig
you've got there!"

"Yeah," the driver was in his twenties, "she sure is.
Better'n the one I been driving."

"You in the service?"

"Sure was. Infantry. How about you?"

"Tank Destroyers. It was just about as bad."

"Yeah." The fellow wiped the sweat from his brow.
"What you doing now?" he asked, looking curiously at
Stan's tailored suit.

"Thinking about buying me a couple of trucks. That's
why I was looking."

The driver glanced at the remaining cases. "Stick
around until I get those last cases off and I'll drive
you where you're going. You can see for yourself how she
is."

"I'd like that! Okay, I'll wait."

The driver came out and they got in. Stan commented
on the cushions. "Pretty nice, all right," the boy said.
"Softer than those G.I. trucks!"

He swung the truck around and slowed at the alley entrance, then seeing the way clear, pulled out. A prowl
car was standing at the corner, facing them. Stan looked
straight ahead, making conversation.

"Which way you headed?"

"Going down to Spring," he said, "Seventh and Spring
or anywhere close to it."

When he got there, the kid dropped him off. "Thanks!"
he called, then he walked over to a newsboy and bought

two papers. He started up the street. "I hope," he told himself softly, "they don't have a picture!"

Stopping in a small café he sat at the counter and opened the papers. They had a picture, all right. He should have known they would. After all, before the war he had been a sort of minor celebrity.

It was not a good picture. It was undoubtedly the worst ever made of him. A newspaper photographer had snapped the photo when he was returning from Guatemala and recovering from a hard bout of malaria.

He ordered coffee and a sandwich, and then looked at the headline. It was a jolt.

EXPLORER FLEES MURDER SCENE

Henry Stanley Duval, noted explorer and author of three books on his adventures, is the object of a statewide search today. Duval is wanted for questioning in regard to the murder of a woman alleged to be his wife.

COMMENTS: Here we have a fragment of a crime story written for the postwar pulp magazines. It's a classic concept, a regular in noir fiction: a man caught between two unforgiving forces—a criminal conspiracy and the relentless and impersonal process of law enforcement. He must escape the law and confront the criminals to clear his name.

Below are some of Louis's notes. These were created prior to the story fragment above in an attempt to work out the plot. Typical of a healthy writing process, Louis's manuscript did not stick exactly to the plan. In my opinion, the critical juncture in any story comes when what you are writing begins to diverge from what you intended. Those differences can, of course, stop a story in its tracks (as, perhaps, it did with this one), but it can also be where the magic happens. It's where the elements of the story take on a life of their own and lead the author through the process.

Later in his career, Louis learned to forgo the planning to a great extent and dwell more and more in that magic creative zone. Though *Louis L'Amour's Lost Treasures Volumes 1* and *2* document the times he did not immediately succeed, the Lost Treasures materials that we have added as "Bonus Feature" postscripts to many of Louis's completed and long-reprinted novels are testament to the fact that he was able to pull off that combination of skill and minor miracle more often than just about anyone.

CAST OF CHARACTERS:

Stan Duval--ex soldier and explorer.
Judy Baird--secretary to Pres. of Culloden Airlines.
Madge McClean--casual girlfriend of Duval.
Cord Becker--multimillionaire inventor and manufac-
    turer.
Gardiner--racketeer and crook.
Fin Campo--spec. inv. for D.A. and in pay of Becker.
Donna Gregg--show girl friend of Madge.
Sam Gaynor--inventor, murdered before story begins.

Stan Duval returns from overseas. He is tired, and wants to relax. Also, he just wants to get around the country a little.

He goes west to San Diego and . . . one night comes into a club and [meets] Gardiner [who] tells him about heading to L.A. He himself is going to Reno . . . would Duval like to ride to L.A. with him? Duval would. The journey up is leisurely. Twice Gardiner turns off the road to look at pieces of property.

They arrive in L.A. at night and Gardiner lets him off near a bar. He is there when a big man who

calls himself Fin Campo tells him he had better leave
town as the police will be wanting him for murdering
his wife.

He has no wife. The man mentioned her name, Madge
Darnal [also referred to as Madge McClean], and he
places her as a girl he once knew and liked, and once
spent a night with in a hotel, registered as man and
wife.

He has not seen the girl in five years. He goes
to the address Campo gives him, and finds the police
making an investigation. He denies being married to
Madge, denies killing her, denies ever having been in
the house before.

The detective shows him a letter, addressed to
him, with a date only two days earlier. They had
found it on the floor.

Also, a neighbor woman declares she has seen him
coming and going, declares she heard a conversation
in which his wife said "Oh no, Stan, wouldn't . . . !"
And "But, Stan!"

Madge has been killed by a blow on the head with
a water pitcher. She has been dead for about an hour.
No fingerprints are on the pitcher except those of
Madge.

Several men had been seen coming and going to the
apartment.

--Stan finds himself faced with these facts!
• He has no alibi.
• The letter and the testimony of the woman next
  door place him at the scene of the crime at the
  right time.
• The letter proves to the police he is a liar.
• The motive: jealousy.
• The girl had been passing herself off as Mrs.
  Stan Duval.

- Records prove they were registered that way at a hotel in 1941.
- He says he was given the address by Campo.
- Campo when found denies it.
- No Gardiner can be found in Reno or elsewhere.
- Record of a marriage is found in Stentora, Arizona.

While the police are occupied, he walks out. He escapes after quite a chase, registers in a small hotel, and tries to figure something out.

- Why should Madge be killed?
- Why involve him?
- How about the marriage?

It becomes obvious that he is the victim of an elaborate and carefully worked out plot.

- Yet why was Madge using his name?
- How did the letter get to her floor?

Obviously, Gardiner must be involved. How else could the letter have gotten there? A letter that was in his pocket when he left San Diego. How could Campo have known where to find him? Yet why? What was behind it all?

Madge, he discovers, was one of three nieces of Bernard Thornton, millionaire impostor. There is also a nephew. He also learns that Madge had been blind for three years.

Elsie, one of the nieces, had been killed in an auto wreck a year previously.

Another niece is married to Roderick Howard, owner of a large Funeral Home.

The key to the problem lies in a conversation
Madge Darnal had with Stan on the weekend in Klamath
Falls.

It was a chance remark, a remark that returns to
him and enables him to find the solution to the crime.

Stan discovers that Madge had drastically changed
her way of living in the past two years, living in
seclusion and moving often.

He decides she was afraid of something. Yet, of
what? The origin of the fear seems to begin with his
meeting with her. Could it have been something he
said? Something she learned while with him?

He wonders: why does one kill? What are the mo-
tives for murder? He decides: for wealth, for love,
for protection.

He believes he can eliminate love as there is no
evidence of it.

Therefore the killer must have killed for wealth
or for protection.

Madge had no wealth. She was an heiress to no
fortune.

Therefore, the killer must have killed for protection.

Protection from what?

Madge was making no effort to harm anyone. She
herself seemed in fear.

Hence, the killer must have been afraid of something she knew.

What did Madge know?

The answer would lie in Madge Darnal's past life.

He had met her in Portland. She had seemed willing and anxious to leave Portland. Therefore the answer might lie in Portland.

What had she been doing there?

He remembered her saying something about being a
bridesmaid at a wedding.

Had the killer committed a previous crime? One
that would warrant murder to prevent its being known?

That would seem to imply two possibilities. Either the previous crime had also been murder or the
killer now held such a position that his previous
crime being known would cause disgrace and ruin him.

That held that either the crime had been murder,
or the position held was a good one.

The solution lies in the past life of Madge Darnal. He has little time and few resources. Perhaps
the solution lay in his own subconscious.

He and Madge had talked. What had they talked
about? In intimate moments women talk of many things
close to them. They had been together for days. He
remembered her eagerness to leave Portland. He recalled one occasion when she showed fright while they
were in Klamath Falls. What was that occasion?

. . . He must dig out every memory, write all he
could think of on paper and try to reconstruct those
past hours. Where had they gone? What had they done?

He remembered then her reluctance to leave him.
How she had clung to him at the last moment. Love, or
fear?

She knew something, became aware about the time
he met her that her knowledge was dangerous, and
stayed with him for protection.

Then he remembers a girl she knew. A girl who had
once worked in a show with her. The girl's home was
in Whittier. He finds she is working in a night club.

She tells him that Madge often spoke of him with
affection. That he apparently was the one man in her
life. That she had loved him. He discovers Madge had
moved frequently, had used other names, finally his
name.

Had Madge ever expressed fear of anyone or anything?

No, but she had seemed frightened. She hated to
stay alone. She often moved. She patronized various
stores in different parts of town. She watched
closely for any mention of Stan's name, wanting to
find him again.

Had they [the women] been together in San Francisco? Yes. Why had they left? A sudden notion of
Madge's. They had been at the Top o' the Mark, came
down in the elevator, and she bought a paper. Something in the paper seemed to disturb her.

What day? She didn't know. What paper? She didn't
recall. On an inside page? Yes. The month? August.
The week, perhaps the first week of August.

He delves into the papers, searching for a clue.
He finds one. He returns to Madge's friend to ask
more questions. She is dead. She has been murdered.

What next?

He will be murdered.

He has no clue.

Something in the papers? What?

What could suddenly make her wish to leave town?
All had been well. Only one of two things, probably:
that the police had started investigating something
in which she was implicated, or someone had come to
town of whom she was frightened.

If it was mentioned in the papers, it meant the
man was of some importance.

He has a feeling the police are closing in on him
now. All right. He must find and lead them to the
real criminal. He must force him to act, force him to
fear, force him to disclose himself. The . . . murder
was evidence that he was becoming desperate . . .

Suddenly, Stan realizes something. The killer
would no longer want him captured!

The killer would want him free! He would be
afraid of what Stan might have learned. Therefore

there was a chance that he might aid Stan to escape and therefore disclose himself!

Yet, that meant Stan must put himself in the killer's hands!

When on their trip they had stopped all night with a friend in his home near Ashland [Oregon]. When they entered, Madge had two bags, and when she left, but one!

He must contact his friend. Find out if that bag still existed. He starts north. Discovers he is being followed. Tries to lose his pursuer, and fails. He recalls a small hamburger place, and stops there to eat. A car pulls up and two men come in. One is Fin Campo, the other Gardiner. One sits on each side of him.

When he finishes eating, they try to take him out with them. He refuses to go. Succeeds in throwing Gardiner, then slugs it out with Campo. He rushes out, a third man fires at him but he escapes.

He gets to his friend, finds the bag, and learns that Madge had mailed a package [to the friend] only a week before! The package is addressed on the inside, to him. It is a diary . . .

In the diary he finds a report of Madge dating a man. A man named Cord Becker.

Cord Becker! The inventor, the manufacturer! He reads on.

They had played cards one night with a man named Sam Gaynor. He and Becker had talked for a long time, and later she had met Gaynor on the street, and he had seemed worried, had asked her many questions about Becker, his honesty, how long she had known him.

Then there had been a boating accident and Gaynor had drowned.

Shortly thereafter, Becker patented some new process and began building a fortune based on that process.

She had unwittingly mentioned to him that she had
a long talk with Gaynor, his [Becker's] manner had
seemed very strange . . . he had pried into her conversation, finding out enough to become suspicious.
Then putting two and two together, he had decided she
knew more than she told. Then she had become frightened, and left.

Stan, through a private detective friend, digs
into Becker's and Gaynor's past. He discovers that
Gaynor had been working on these processes for a long
time, that he had come to Portland to secure capital.
There was no record of previous experimentation on
Becker's part.

Stan goes to the former district attorney in
Portland. He talks to him of Becker and arouses his
interest.

He explains he is wanted, does not tell his name,
begins the discussion of the case.

You can tell from the scattered nature of these notes that Louis
was putting every idea forward that might help him work out the
mystery and therefore the plot. At some point Dad began a less bewil-
dering outline:

Duval is deliberately involved in a plot to cover
the murder of Madge McClean, a girl who had once used
his name. In struggling to clear himself, he escapes
from the police, enlists the aid of Judy Baird, and
begins investigating Madge's background. He discovers
she knew of an invention by one Sam Gaynor. That
Gaynor had been murdered and Becker patented the discovery.

      Donna Gregg is also murdered to prevent her talk-
ing. Duval recovers bag and diary, but is slugged and
the bag taken away. He retains the diary.
      Gardiner, in San Diego, encounters Duval and
calls Campo who directs him to bring Duval to L.A.
The crime has been decided upon, and with Duval in
L.A. the time has come. Not only can they rid themselves of Madge, but have a made to order suspect!
      Duval meets Judy in the theatre.

Unfortunately, my father never went further with this second set of notes, which might have given us a simpler overview of his concept for the story. You can see, however, that it was becoming more stream-lined and easier to tell . . . all part of the process of working through the details.

Within this story fragment there are a number of slight refer-ences to places and events in Louis's earlier life. Dad had lived in Portland, Oregon, for a couple of years and in Klamath Falls before that. While there he visited Ashland on a number of occasions.

Dad served in the Tank Destroyers stateside until the combina-tion of his age (too old, at thirty-four, to begin combat duty) and his unit's deployment forced a reassignment to the Transportation Corps. While in the Transportation Corps and managing cargoes for the Army in the Bay Area, Dad was billeted at the Mark Hopkins Hotel . . . where there is a penthouse restaurant and cocktail lounge by the name of Top of the Mark.

During his getaway, Stan talks to a young truck driver who is a war vet, and they commiserate about how hard-riding G.I. trucks were. Louis had ended up as a lieutenant in a Quartermaster Truck Company delivering tank and aviation fuel all over France, Holland, and Germany. Most of the time he was lucky enough to have a jeep and driver, but he knew all too well the fatigue driving a heavy-duty truck could cause.

LOWIE

The Beginning of a Western Story

The tunnel belched and their candles went out and in the darkness there was a smell of dust.

A heavy, cushiony sigh went through the mountain and with it a sound like a fat man sinking into a deep leather chair, only vastly greater.

Sand trickled . . . somewhere pebbles rattled briefly, and then the sounds dwindled and died. Nobody stirred, their minds suspended in blackness, transfixed by the awfulness of what had happened, beyond the need of words, knowing the mountain had trapped them.

In the same instant of realization and shock came the knowledge that it was probable they would never, could never escape. They were beyond help except what they could give themselves. Nobody, anywhere, knew where they were. Very likely nobody cared. They were sealed here, to die of suffocation, unless they could make their own escape, find their own way out. Inexperienced as one or two of them were, they knew the fall had been great, that it had been no minor cave-in, easily dug through and shored up.

"Anybody hurt?" Lowie asked. In the stillness that followed the collapse of the drift the sound of his voice was flatly casual, conversational.

There was no reply until Dud said quietly, "And nobody even knows we're here."

"Scared?" Skinner's voice held a faint uncertain sneer.

"If he's scared I wouldn't know," Lowie said, "but I am."

They had been wary of this, knowing their danger. Never before had all four entered the drift at one time. Working two to the shift had the advantage of keeping Dud and Skinner apart, but it also meant there were always two men outside to start rescue operations in case anything happened. Yet this morning they had all entered to discuss a change of direction to trying to cut into the vein of the old Spanish working, a tunnel that entered the mountain from the south. As if the mountain had waited for just this moment, the hanging wall had caved and they were sealed in, trapped.

"You all right, Charlie?" Lowie asked.

"Uh-huh. Has anybody got any water?"

"I filled the olla," Lowie said, "and my canteen is with me."

The nearest white man was sixty miles away and knew nothing of their presence here. They were in Apache country, the location of their claim a carefully guarded secret. If they escaped it must be by their own efforts.

Skinner shifted his feet. "Maybe we're wrong. Maybe it only caved a few feet. Maybe only eight or ten. It wouldn't take us long to cut through that."

"Sounded like the whole mountain came down," Charlie said, "but the drift is holding here, so it's not that bad."

"That was bad ground," Dud said. "There was twenty feet of tunnel we had to shore up with plank an' timber,

remember? That was all loose ground, above there. But
when we used that timbering I thought we had it whipped."

"Nobody ever whips a mountain," Charlie said. "Those
Spanish couldn't whip it. We found some outside, an' you
can bet some were trapped inside."

It was Lowie who brought them here. He heard a rumor
of the old Spanish mine from a friendly Indian. He had
traced the rumors, searched out the old Spanish trail on
several careful forays into Apache country, and he had
found proof of the mine's existence.

Lowie was twenty-two but had lived his life in the
West, while Dud and Skinner were in their late twenties
and Charlie was forty or more. They had pooled their efforts and come on in, taking a risk, for Cochise was on
the warpath and all this country was covered from time to
time with Indians. Yet the canyon was lonely and their
camp carefully concealed. Only twice had they seen Indians, and none close by.

"No use to sit here and die," Dud said, "I'm starting
to work."

"Go ahead." Charlie struck a light to the candle
which had gone out when the air belched. "I'll spell you."

"It's going to be tough with that loose ground caving
all the time," Lowie said, "but might as well get
started. I'm going up to the face."

"What's up there?" Skinner wanted to know.

"Maybe nothing. But I've a hunch we're not far from
the spot the Spanish were working, the one with the open
drift. If we could cut to it, we might have an easy way
out."

Dud moved to the muckpile, shovel in hand. He looked
at it, then stooped, the candle throwing a colossal
shadow of him on the rock wall.

Dud was a big man, wide of face and of shoulder. Impatient of restraint, he had a flaring temper and a quick
fist. Skinner, whom he had chosen for enemy, was slim,

saturnine and bitter. The two had begun snarling at each
other on the first day of travel. Skinner had the reputation of having killed two men, and Dud was known to be
quarrelsome. Not the men to be chosen for such a trip,
but there was little possibility of choice. Men who would
venture into Apache country were few, and quarrelsome as
the two might be, they were equally fearless, and had
proved hard workers.

The ore had been rich. The few samples they collected
carefully from the old Spanish working had proved that,
yet that drift was a death-trap to be avoided. Hence they
started their own attempt to penetrate to the vein, and
had almost reached it when trapped. Yet they had already
gathered some gold. The creek had shown some placer gold,
and they had each taken a turn at the pan, with some
luck. If they had to abandon the larger prospect, they
would at least have a stake.

Dud bent his back and began to move dirt. Taking his
time not to foul the air with dust, he worked steadily.
Yet each time he moved his shovel, the sand-like soil
slid down to fill the space. Lowie scowled at the sand
and then turned away and with his own candle walked to
the face of the drift.

He was a tall young man with broad shoulders and a
lean body. At six feet two inches he weighed only one
hundred and sixty, but hours and days and months of using
a single-jack and drill had packed beef into his shoulders. He tapped the wall and it gave off with a flat,
hard, unrewarding sound. He tried the side walls and the
hanging wall with the same result.

Thinking, it seemed to him that the old Spanish tunnel had come this way, and their own drift had trended a
bit south. Hence, the two might be separated by only a
few feet. Yet it was all guess-work, and they might work
their hearts out only to find it useless--and the short
time they had left was regulated by the supply of air.

He thought again of that sliding sand. It was peculiar, here in the heart of a mountain, to find loose
sand. By rights the pressure should have packed it to
sandstone by now. Unless there was no pressure, and that
meant an open space above. Yet, supposing such an open
space existed, how much sand was there? It might be more
than enough to fill their drift before they could break
through. Yet it was a chance.

Would they ever see sunlight again? Or drink cold
water? Hear the birds singing? Lowie got restlessly to
his feet and walked back to the others. Skinner was working now, and he was working steadily, carefully. His
shirt was off and sweat and dust coated his body. There
was fine dust in the air. Lowie extinguished his candle
and watched, studying the hanging wall of the drift.

Slowly and steadily they worked. An hour passed, then
two. A third followed. Still the fine muck sifted down,
and they had made progress, but not enough. One candle
burned. Lowie himself worked. Dud lay on the floor, face
down, breathing carefully. Skinner leaned back against
the wall. Sweat trickled down his body. The heat was stifling.

Charlie got up slowly. "I'll take it, boy."

Lowie leaned on his shovel. "She's rough, Charlie."

The older man's face was drawn. "We gained six feet,"
he said. "But it ain't enough."

"How much longer we got?"

Charlie shrugged. "Not long. Air's mighty bad. Dud's
about all in."

"Look at this stuff," Lowie said, "it isn't sand and
it ain't just rock. It's finer than dust."

Charlie took a pinch of it in his fingers. He felt of
it, he sniffed it. "Smells a mite musty like. Funny sort
o' stuff to find in here."

Lowie grabbed Charlie's wrist. "Charlie! It's guano!"

"Guano? What's that?"

"Bat manure! And bats live in caves! There's a cave above us somewhere!"

Charlie looked up. The edge of the hanging wall was visible. At first what they had dug out was broken rock and muck with a few ends of the splintered hand-hewn planks used for shoring, but this dust had been sifting down through that hole, filling up all the crevices.

"How long you reckon they lived in that cave? An' how many of them?"

"Maybe millions of them," Lowie said, "maybe for thousands of years."

The impact of his words registered slowly. The guano could be many feet thick, there might be more than enough to fill all this space and more before they could break through into the cave above. Yet it offered a possible solution. If they could not get out through their own tunnel, they might make it into the cave above, and if there was a way out for the bats, they might enlarge a way out for themselves . . . or find one ready made.

Dud got slowly to his feet. He swayed drunkenly. "Ready for me?" he whispered hoarsely.

Lowie shook his head. "Stay close to the floor. Only move back. Take Skinner with you."

Dud stumbled away, and Charlie leaned against the wall, staring at Lowie. The candle flame seemed to have grown smaller; breathing was an effort now. The air was hot and stale. It was stifling in the narrow drift. "What you goin' to do?" Charlie asked.

Lowie shrugged. "Got to figger," he said. He mopped his face with his hands. "We must sort've be on the edge of that cave," he said. "Don't appear that guano would weigh heavy enough to make that break. I reckon it was forward o' the cave. If we had any plank we could shore up that hole an' maybe dig out."

"We got no plank," Charlie said, "we've got nothing."

Lowie's head was throbbing. He sat down, heaviness in his muscles. He stared at the sifting dust, thick over and between the rocks. It was enough to break a man's heart.

Skinner got to his feet. His eyes were sunken and he moved like a man walking in his sleep. But he got hold of a shovel and moved up to the pile.

Looking at Skinner, Lowie knew how he must look. Like he felt. There wasn't much time now. He felt sleepy, and his head ached. He got up. Skinner was working steadily, like an automaton, and surprisingly, he was forging ahead. He cleared as much in a few minutes as they had in more than an hour. Charlie found some slabs that had fallen, and built a wall to hold back the sliding muck.

Skinner continued to work, and then suddenly he slid forward on his face. They dragged him back and splashed water on his face. "Leave him lay," Lowie said, "air's better down there."

He picked up the shovel and went to work, yet he had moved not more than three shovels full when Charlie yelled.

Instinctively, he half sprang, half fell backward. With a gasping rush, the sifting, bone-dry guano shot down, carrying a few chunks of rock. It hit the space cleared and filled it, then piled up. A few final grains sifted down; the trickle stopped.

They stared dully. All their work for nothing. They were trapped. They would never get out. They would die here. Dud was far away at the face but they could hear him gasping slowly, straining for breath. Lowie lifted his eyes and suddenly, he stopped, his gaze riveted on a black hole.

COMMENTS: Louis started this story twice, so he had something in mind; it wasn't just an experiment to see what would turn up. People regularly write to me, asking questions about Louis's real-life experiences in the West. I'm sure most would like to hear that he spent some time as a cowboy, and I hate to disappoint them, but that just wasn't the case. Louis had plenty of typically Western jobs, but they were more of the farming and mining sort than punching cows. He spent a lot of time underground and thus you get stories like this one, "Dead End Drift" in the collection *Yondering*, "Under the Hanging Wall" in *Beyond the Great Snow Mountains*, and novels like *The Comstock Lode*, *The High Graders*, and several others.

Louis and his father, L. C. Lamoore, on the steps of
the Katherine Mine bunkhouse, Arizona.

SOUTH OF PANAMA

A Treatment for an Adventure Story

LARKIN FURY had been on lookout during most of the night, but he found that daylight brought no beauty to the shores of Sotavento Bay. Behind the rocky shoreline the rugged hills lifted in a bleak and tawny mass unrelieved by any growth of tree or bush.

Through the morning mist the Caribe moved ghost-like upon the dark water, feeling its way up the channel toward the dock. Details at last began to arrange themselves. Two rocky islands, white with guano and seabirds, appeared briefly to starboard, then vanished into the mist.

At the head of the cove buildings took shape, and a long dock pointed an inquiring finger toward the incoming yacht. Along the dock was a narrow tramway ending in an ore chute. Close beside it stood the gaunt and rusting skeleton of a giant crane. Shoreward, its gray bulk dwarfed by the magnitude of the mountain behind it, was the smelter. No smoke issued from the tall chimneys.

Closer to the dock and lining a street facing the water and a second street at right angles to it were a scattering of weather-beaten, nondescript buildings. A low-roofed store, a long warehouse, and a cantina, among others. Behind them along the mountainside, a scattering of huts and houses, most of them mere shacks.

It was nothing or less than nothing, an outpost of civilization at the foot of the cordillera, a place seemingly forgotten, and located upon one of the most bleak and lonely coasts in the world. From the deserts of Chile came nitrates, from the mountains copper and sulfur, and the rest of the coast offered nothing but heat, mighty winds, and the sudden chill blasts from off the Humboldt Current, a river in the sea carrying cold water north from the Antarctic. Along this coast men live only to work. There is nothing to attract them but the mining. The climate is severe, the landscape bleak and unpromising.

The town they approached was over a half mile up the channel from the lonely sea, and seemed cut off from all that was real, familiar or normal. Even the barren sea with its threats of a coming storm were preferable to this loneliness.

Larkin Fury had thought of nothing for days but to get home and get ashore. The situation aboard the Caribe had gone from bad to worse, an ill-assorted group of people subjected to all the strain of the close confines of a yacht on a long voyage, and now that strain had reached the breaking point.

At a movement beside him Fury turns to find that WENDY FORREST has come up from below. There is no one else on deck although they are visible from the wheelhouse where there is a sailor at the wheel.

Wendy is a slender, graceful girl in a linen dress. She is poised, lovely and exciting, all of which Fury

knows only too well. She is also reported to be the fiancée of BLAIR MURDOCK, who owns the Caribe . . . and who
is Fury's employer.

Larkin Fury had returned from the Korean war, was
discharged, and shortly after was offered a job by Murdock as a bodyguard. At first this seemed unnecessary,
but Fury soon discovered Murdock was a man who made enemies, and his need for a bodyguard was very real. Fury is
a tall, rugged-looking young man of nearly thirty with
considerable experience getting around in the rough
places of the world.

Now he turns to Wendy. "You shouldn't have come
here."

"I couldn't sleep." She looks around. "What is this
place? A ghost town?"

"On the chart it is Sotavento Bay. Last night the
starb'rd engine broke down and we're going to put in for
repairs. There should be some help, and a machine shop."

To proceed up the coast in the face of the impending
storm would have been foolhardy at best, yet Larkin Fury
would have preferred it. He wanted nothing so much as to
be ashore in the States.

The voyage had begun on a golf course. Murdock, Fury,
DAVE BRACELIN, and KEN FARRELL had been playing. No one
of them was well known to the others. They were simply a
group of men who had made up a foursome after reaching
the clubhouse. Murdock had drafted Fury to make the
fourth man; he had been working for Murdock only a few
days, scarcely enough to know his employer.

As the game developed Murdock commented on the trip
down the coast he was planning and the difficulty in
finding a navigator for his yacht. Bracelin replied that
he held a master's ticket and had commanded a Navy supply
ship during the war. Farrell, a mining engineer by pro-
fession, had been a navigator aboard bombers during World
War II. Murdock already knew Fury had once been something

of an amateur sailor. All were free at the time. Bracelin
was looking around for some investments and Ken Farrell,
a lean, pleasant man, was between assignments.

Both Bracelin and Farrell were married so it was decided to bring their WIVES along, and Murdock would invite his "fiancée" and another girl.

The Caribe was a beautifully appointed diesel-powered
craft of eighty feet over-all, and carried a cook, steward, waiter and four seamen, two of whom worked on deck
and two below. Their work was supplemented by the guests
themselves, who took turns standing wheel-watches. The
plan had been to cruise south along the coast of Chile
and Peru, fishing the Humboldt Current.

Blair Murdock was a short, heavy-set man who proved
to be extremely arrogant. Given to a master-of-all-he-
surveys attitude, he was determined to have all his ac-
quaintances in some way beholden to him. He has helped
Wendy out of difficulties and Larkin Fury is employed by
him. The others are indebted as his guests. This attitude, not obvious until the voyage was well along, made
conditions aboard increasingly difficult.

Animosity eventually developed. Bracelin, an able man
when sober, rarely was. His wife was neurotic, lonely,
and envious of Wendy's youth and beauty. The Farrells
were tactful and considerate. They developed a liking for
Fury and for Wendy. GAIL MATTESON, the other girl, was an
athletic, attractive brunette with a quick tongue, often
edged with acid, but a capable, interesting person. Youth
and their natural attractions drew Wendy and Larkin
closer together as the voyage continued.

Until the return trip had begun all had been fairly
amicable. Ashore in Valparaiso, Larkin Fury had met Wendy
and they lunched together, returning to the yacht, laugh-
ing and talking. Murdock had seen them come aboard and
had become angry. This Ken Farrell observed, and he
warned Fury.

"Watch yourself, Lark. He's an ugly customer."

Realizing for the first time that Murdock was jealous, Fury began to avoid Wendy. He was not afraid of Murdock, but the small space aboard the Caribe was no place for trouble. It was better, and certainly more polite, to avoid friction.

More and more the task of handling the Caribe had fallen upon the shoulders of Farrell and Fury. Murdock made no pretense of doing anything beyond taking the wheel occasionally, and Bracelin was drunk or nearly so most of the time.

The trouble that had been impending finally broke the surface as the yacht was proceeding up the channel at Sotavento Bay. Wendy explained her situation to Fury. She was not, she insisted, engaged to Murdock. He had proposed and she had agreed to give an answer when the voyage was completed. He had been friendly and helpful when she had fallen ill, and she owed him money. He had suggested that be forgotten and that she come along on the trip to recuperate. When they returned would be time enough to discuss repayment . . . or marriage.

Murdock had dated her several times. She had found him good company and genial. It had taken the close confines of life aboard the Caribe to convince her that living with him would be impossible. She has avoided bringing the matter to an issue, wanting no hard feelings while aboard the yacht. Like Fury she is eager for the trip to be ended. What had started as a glorious and exciting vacation was ending in a deadening feeling of futility and animosity.

Murdock arrives on deck while they talk and this leads to angry words. Agnes Bracelin adds a catty remark of her own to an already tense situation.

Further trouble is stopped by Ken Farrell with the comment that there's trouble enough without fighting among themselves. They can see no evidence of life

ashore, although two very dirty fishing boats are moored
at the end of the dock. Not even a stray dog is visible.

"Deserted," Bracelin comments, looking ashore.

"No," Farrell says, "look."

A MAN in dirty whites and a battered straw hat has
appeared from between two buildings. He does not move
forward, but merely stands watching them. Another appears
beside him, and then still another, until there are at
least a DOZEN. They show no evidence that they wish to be
friendly. In response to shouts, they make no reply, but
merely stand, staring.

Blair Murdock goes to the dock and starts toward
them, muttering irritably. His short, thick-set figure
shows both arrogance and anger as he strides forward.
"Hey, you!" His voice is harsh. "Who's in charge here?"
There is no response, no movement, no indication that he
has been heard.

"We'd better go with him," Farrell suggests, "he's
apt to get us all in trouble."

Their footsteps echo hollowly on the ancient wooden
dock. There is nothing in the faces of the men to reas-
sure them. Most of them seem sullen and menacing. Only
one or two have a more positive attitude, but these are
afraid to speak or step forward.

It is obvious to both Farrell and to Fury that something is drastically wrong, that they have unwittingly
stepped into a situation loaded with danger. Furthermore,
nothing in Murdock's attitude is likely to alleviate the
situation.

The men on the shore look toward the graceful white
lines of the yacht. On the deck are four women, young,
attractive women. There is greed in the eyes of some of
the men, greed and hunger.

Glancing beyond the group, Fury can see nothing but
solitude and emptiness. Obviously, the mines have been
abandoned and the town is all but deserted. But why have

these few stayed on here? And what is wrong? Fury speaks
to them in Spanish and one man finally replies. A tall
man of gaunt face and thin body.

The mines have, as they had surmised, recently closed
down. The rich vein of copper that had been worked there
has been lost . . . first the smelter closed down, then
after some futile attempts to find the lost vein, the
mine closed down. The machine shop is closed and the ma-
chinists and mechanics are gone. No one is in charge here
now.

To his question as to why they have remained, the man
hesitates, then replies this has always been his home,
the grave of his father is here, and that of his mother.
His wife is here, and his son. Where else will he go?
What will he do?

As to the others, some are like him. Some, he admits,
have remained behind for other reasons. Some, he adds,
are "the men of Arango."

Arango, it seems, is a local bandido, a rider of the
hills, and a most dangerous man. With the closing of the
mine this place has occasionally become his hideout.

At this there are some angry remarks from some of the
rougher men in the group. Fury does not like the way
these men look toward the yacht, and he is impressed anew
with their helplessness. What, he wonders, is to prevent
an attack upon the boat, a looting?

Farrell is professionally interested. He wishes to
examine the mine. He is, he tells the tall man, whose
name is PIETRO, a mining engineer. If the vein did not
play out, but was broken off, he might be able to locate
the lost vein. He is an expert in this sort of thing and
has been employed by many of the largest mining corpora-
tions to uncover lost ore bodies.

Fury suggests they might find tools in the machine
shop, but his comment provokes immediate reaction. Sev-

eral of the men come forward threateningly. They are not
to go near the machine shop. It would be dangerous in the
extreme to persist at present. Fury can see this.

Murdock interrupts and declares they must have tools
and spare parts. This is not exactly a wise comment, and
from the exchanges between some in the group, Fury can
see that there are those who would like to keep them from
leaving.

They return to the Caribe to debate the problem. The
few good men of the crowd disappear and only the gentuzas
(riff raff) remain. They crowd to the edge of the dock
and look at the yacht and at the women. Gail Matteson, a
tall, shapely brunette, is wearing shorts and a halter.
Wendy is dressed in the same way. Bracelin comes on deck
carrying a bottle and a glass. This excites further muttering among the group on the shore.

Only when rain begins do they leave. Looking out a
few minutes later, Larkin Fury sees the dock deserted,
likewise the town. During the first hours of darkness,
Pietro slips aboard and tells them they must go, that
word will be taken to Arango. The men know the yacht is
helpless and they will seize it. Murdock scoffs and refuses to be impressed. Bracelin is drinking and seems unaware of any trouble. The crew are working about the
yacht, but obviously do not like the situation.

To try to escape in the face of the storm is extremely dangerous, and Murdock refuses to allow them to
drop down into the channel. As he says, the men ashore
have boats and could attack anyway, if they wished. He is
not afraid, and implies Fury and Farrell are building up
fears from nothing.

Larkin Fury determines to have a look at the machine
shop. If they can get the necessary articles to make the
repairs, and the tools they need, it is possible they
might complete the work in a few hours. In the darkness

and the rain he lowers a dinghy and gets into it. At the
last minute, over his objections, he is accompanied by
Wendy.

A driving rain is raking the harbor waters. They go
up the shore to the smelter, a great, gloomy building,
creaking and groaning in the wind.

They open a window and make their way through the ma-
chinery to the mechanic's shop. Occasionally they believe
they hear unnatural noises, only to pause and find nothing. They go into the machine shop and searching about,
find tools, and some lengths of pipe. Suddenly, Wendy
catches Larkin's arm and points. He looks up, and there
hanging from a rafter is the body of a man!

This, then, has been the reason for the fear and
threatening atmosphere in the village. This is the reason
why they were not wanted near the smelter. Realizing that
if they are caught here they might be killed, they start
to move out, and get back into the main building. Suddenly, they hear muttered conversation, and in a lightning flash, glimpse three men. Then one lights a
cigarette, and in the flare of the match they see a dark,
mustached face under a wide hat. He is a fat, sloppy,
dirty man . . . but one look is all they need to know
that he is also a dangerous man.

Carefully, they ease their way out of the smelter and
return to their boat. They make their way back to the
yacht and climb aboard.

Bracelin, who has been on lookout, is drunk and has
passed out. Fury finds several of the gentuzas are
aboard. One is raiding the bar, another is stuffing himself with the night-lunch put out for the watch. At the
point of a pistol Fury drives them from the yacht, but
they get away with several bottles and the knowledge that
the yacht is ripe for the plucking, stored with quanti-
ties of food and wine.

Murdock had slept through it all. Gail Matteson has
succeeded in escaping to her cabin, and although a man
tried the door, he did not attempt to break it down.

Despite the seriousness of the situation Murdock will
not be impressed. Part of it is obviously that he is con-
temptuous of the Chilenos, part of it that he wishes to
show Wendy how unafraid he is. He scoffs at their story
of the murdered man . . . they saw a sack or a shadow.
Nothing to it.

Day breaks with great storm clouds at sea and white
caps on the water. The crew falls to work to attempt repairs. This is all kept secret for the knowledge that the
yacht is being repaired might precipitate trouble.

Ruth Farrell comes to Fury. Her husband has gone
ashore with Pietro before daybreak to have a look at the
mine. He believes something may be done, and Pietro has
told him that only fear of the policia would prevent
trouble. If the mine was to be reopened and the policia
were coming back, the worst of them would take to the
hills with Arango and there would be no danger.

Pietro has told Farrell and his wife of the dead man.
He was the smelter boss, hated by some of the men who
favor Arango. They had tortured him, believing he was
taking away a large amount of gold. It had turned out to
be very little, but some of them believe there is more
hidden around the smelter. They say that along with the
copper the mine produced some gold, and this man had kept
it hidden for himself.

Fury slips ashore and talks with Pietro's son. The
boy tells him there are good men in the village, and a
half dozen women, but that the gentuzas outnumber the
good men, and are dangerous. Yet they will begin nothing
by themselves. They fear Arango.

Fury tells the boy that he believes Arango is already
in the village, and described the man he has seen in the
smelter. The boy agrees he must be back and looking for
the gold. Some of the good men, the boy tells him, are
being swayed by the gentuzas. They are horrified that the
smelter boss was tortured and killed but they are hungry,
for food is short, and they are being told there is much
food on the yacht.

The mine, the boy tells him, was a rich mine. It was
the life of the village, of the people. Here they wished
to stay, and they had remained, hoping without cause that
the mine would live again. Farrell, the boy says, has
told his father there is hope. That he had seen a formation like this, that an earthquake might have faulted the
ground . . . and there are many quakes here.

Fury returns to the Caribe and is fortunate to get
back aboard for now a dozen tough-looking men have gathered on the edge of the dock near the gangway. Sounds of
the work going on below have been heard.

Fury warns them away and they laugh. They are doing
nothing, but who is to stop them no matter what they do?
And if the yacht disappears, who will know it was not lost
at sea? Suddenly the crowd opens and Arango comes through.

He wears sandals and has a bulging waistline, and a
straggly black mustache. He starts to come aboard and
Fury orders him back. He smiles what is meant to be an
ingratiating smile and tries to convince Fury that he
wishes to help. He indicates several men whom, he says,
are mechanics. They will make repairs. When this fails
his manner shifts alarmingly. He becomes furious. He ges-
tures. He threatens. There is a moment of tenseness when
it might come to shooting, but Arango is covered at close
range by Fury's pistol and he backs off . . . then
shrugs, laughs, and implies he was only having "fun,"
that he means no trouble. He starts away, then suddenly

he turns and spits on the deck, anger and vindictiveness
alive in his expression.

The crew are working desperately on the engine and
believe it will soon be ready to go. It is late in the
day but Farrell is still ashore. Larkin Fury decides to
go after him, for when the time comes to move, they must
move fast. When Fury prepares to leave, his pistol is
missing. Murdock offers his own. Wendy wishes to go
along, but Larkin will not have it and Murdock offers objections also. Larkin goes ashore.

Later, Wendy overhears Murdock telling one of Arango's men that Fury is ashore, and the men leave at once.
Wishing to go ashore, and warn Fury, Wendy is forcibly
restrained by Murdock. Hurrying below, she attempts to
awaken Bracelin and tell him. That fails, and leaving
Gail to work on him, Wendy goes below to where the crew
are working on the engine. They refuse to believe that
Murdock has deliberately sent the men after Fury. And
anyway, unless the diesel is repaired they may all get
caught.

The steward will not go ashore. He is afraid. The
waiter is warned by Murdock that if he leaves without orders from him, he had better not return.

Ashore, Larkin Fury moves among the abandoned buildings. He is aware that Arango would like to catch him
ashore where he could be murdered with impunity. Arango
is no fool, and whatever he does he wishes to have as few
witnesses as possible. It is one thing to know a man is a
thief and a murderer, it is quite another to prove it.

Soon Fury realizes he is being stalked, yet he evades
his pursuers in the darkness while working his way
through the village toward the mine. Somehow they have
learned he is ashore. He can tell that much. Leaving the

buildings he works his way over the rocky mountainside
toward the mine.

Gentuzas are waiting there, too, waiting for Farrell,
who is inside the mine. Fury starts a small rockslide to
divert attention, then runs for the mine, but is seen
just as he enters. They rush him, he tries to fire, the
gun clicks . . . he realizes that Murdock has sent him
ashore with an empty gun.

Fury escapes into the mine and sees lights bobbing
toward him. It is Pietro and Farrell. They have drilled a
round of holes and spit the fuses. At his warning, they
duck into a cross-cut. Their lights are hastily put out,
there are running footsteps and lights that bob by the
cross-cut, then a shout as the runners smell the burning
fuses. Footsteps rush in the other direction. There is a
roar and then silence.

Farrell returns to see what has happened at the face
of the drift. Farrell is sure that work in the mine was
ended on the verge of rediscovering the old vein. Fury is
shown by Pietro another way out of the mine, an old working used now only as an air shaft.

Back in the abandoned streets, Fury runs across a
sentry. He disarms the man and keeps the gun. At the edge
of the dock he finds the yacht gone . . . then through
the drifting fog he sees her out upon the water. Murdock
has at last moved away from the dock.

In the distance Fury sees men climbing aboard through
the rail from a fishing boat. He hears a shout of laughter from the boat, and a woman's scream. He rushes down
to where he had moored the dinghy in which he came ashore
to avoid the crowd at the gangway. He pushes off and fog
closes around him. He listens. Yells and cheers from the
boat draw him on. He comes alongside and crawls aboard.

There is loud laughter from the after deck--they have
already found the liquor cabinet. They have formed a
rough circle and in the midst is Murdock. His shirt is

torn to ribbons, he is battered and bleeding. Each time
he attempts to escape the circle of his tormentors, he is
hurled back or struck.

Slipping aboard, Fury finds Bracelin in the chart
room. He has been beaten unconscious. Gail Matteson and
Ruth Farrell are there also, working desperately over
him. His wife has shut herself in her cabin and the crew
are locked below. Bracelin is coming out of it; shaken,
he tells Fury, "I'll be all right. Just give me a few
minutes." Fury leaves Bracelin, telling him to release
the crew and arm them . . . any way at all.

Bracelin starts for the crew. Fury hears Wendy scream
and he goes down the ladder. Suddenly he is face to face
with Arango, who has Wendy by the wrist. Murdock lies
against the rail in a bloody heap. Arango stares at the
gun in Fury's hand, then at Fury.

Arango smiles, he insists they are friends, his boys
are just having "fun"--they want no trouble. He starts
edging closer, talking softly. Fury orders him to stop,
to release Wendy. Arango's smile fades into a snarl.

Bracelin appears behind Fury with the released crew.
They all have clubs and heavy spanners, and are ready and
anxious for action. But they are outnumbered three to one
and several of Arango's men have pistols and rifles.

Fury orders Arango to release Wendy and get off the
boat. Arango suggests that if they let him keep Wendy, he
will go. After all, they have a boat, they have money,
they can get many women. After all, he leers at Wendy,
she is "thin" and "not too much." They will not miss her.
Fury lifts his pistol and Arango jerks the girl in front
of him.

Arango backs toward the rail, keeping the girl close.

Suddenly, they are hailed from the water. It is Pietro and Farrell in the other fishing boat. The blasting
in the mine has exposed the vein . . . the mine will be
working again!

This penetrates the consciousness of the few good men who have been swayed by desire for food and liquor. They draw back. A few of the gentuzas, the more cautious or cowardly ones, also hesitate. The police will come back, Pietro shouts--and they all know their police are not to be trifled with.

One by one they slink toward the fishing boat. Seeing himself deserted by all but a handful, Arango is suddenly vicious. He swings Wendy to arm's length and hurls a knife. The action is sudden, but Fury has never taken his eyes from Arango. As the bandit hurls the knife, he fires. The knife misses by a hair, but Fury does not.

Arango goes down and the remaining gentuzas rush. There is a few minutes of pitched battle, and then from below comes a full-throated throbbing. One of the men has remained below to put the last bit of work on the broken down diesel.

As suddenly, the fight is over. The battered gentuzas clamber over the rail after the better men, and one leg over the rail, his shoulder and hand dripping blood, Arango looks back at Wendy.

"Oh, well," he shrugs, "she probably wouldn't know how to roast a goat, anyway!"

COMMENTS: It is likely but not certain that this was the first draft of a motion picture treatment. It definitely has the feel of an early '50s, low-budget adventure film similar to Louis's *East of Sumatra*.

Though I've removed a good deal of excessive and redundant description and rejiggered the odd paragraph structure in this manuscript to make it more readable, those issues tell me that Louis stopped and started this piece fairly often. I get the feeling he was frustrated with it or having second thoughts about bothering with it at all. As usual he was uncomfortable with the present tense requirement for treatments. Often it was only in his final polish that he got this problem squared away.

In the hard days between the decline of the fiction magazines and his breakthrough into paperback originals, Louis was often tempted to sell ideas directly to the film industry. In the end it was probably no easier than mailing away a manuscript to a publisher or agent and hoping for the best, but at least he could meet the people who were doing the buying one-on-one, and it was an additional market. Unfortunately, it is very common for people around Hollywood to tell writers that they know—that they are absolutely sure—that some star or some studio wants to make a particular sort of picture. If only a treatment could be produced or a pitch developed on the double, the idea could immediately be sold and everyone involved would be on their way to greater fame and fortune.

I've been there myself and ninety-nine percent of the time it's a delusion, a figment of the Tinseltown dreamer's imagination and the writer's desperate hope. Writers in Hollywood end up with stacks of

these unused and often half-baked ideas; they burn them to stay warm on winter nights. Although Louis sold a fair number of treatments over the years, I fear he also fell victim to "producer's dream syndrome" more than a few times.

It is amusing to read the description of the stereotypical bandito Arango, because I know just who Louis had in mind: the man who had almost single-handedly immortalized that unfortunate caricature in Hollywood culture, Alfonso Bedoya. Louis and Al were good friends, and I have a feeling that Dad may have pulled him out of many a fight in many a bar. I suspect Dad was trying to make the type so unmistakable that, if it was ever produced, Al would be first in line for the part.

Bedoya was a veteran character actor who made hundreds of films in Mexico and is best remembered for his delivery of the classic line "We don't need no badges! I don't have to show you any stinkin' badges!" in *The Treasure of the Sierra Madre*. From what I understand, Al was a *serious* badass. Louis didn't allow a lot of people like that into his life lightly, so I've got to assume they were quite good friends.

Louis was fascinated by the Chilean coast. This story seems to be set in the north, but the southern stretches appear in a number of other stories. He had extensive charts, "Sailing Directions" guidebooks, and various traveler's accounts of the southern areas from several different time periods. "Sailing Directions," or pilot books, contain specific information for ships approaching various ports, including descriptions of the coastline and threats to navigation like reefs, sand bars, or sunken vessels. I suspect that the early description of the location of this story, and thus a good deal of the plot, was directly inspired by an old entry in one book of sailing directions or another.

THE ROCK MAN

Notes for a Television Series

DAN BYRON is a mining engineer & geologist, a cultured, sophisticated man of the world.

BORN to wealth, his family lost all they had in a bank failure, and Byron worked his way through school with a series of jobs, and through college as a karate instructor and Shift-Boss in a hard-rock mine.

HIS FATHER had been a diplomat, a stern but capable man; his mother an actress on the stage, an accomplished, intelligent woman. Many doors are opened to Byron because of his parents and who they were.

HE STUDIED the martial arts in Japan and Korea as a boy when his father was connected to the U.S. Embassy. His first teacher was his father's chauffeur, the sole survivor of a school of karate from western China, almost unknown in Japan or Okinawa.

BYRON studied at Cal Tech and moved from there to

further practical experience in his field in Australia, South Africa, Mexico, Guatemala, Brazil, Iran and the western United States.

HE is now a consulting geologist and mining engineer with a background supplemented by extensive reading and travel. He works with the latest technology, makes surveys by plane with a magnetometer and other such equipment, or on the ground. He will also have occasion to make minute examinations of aerial photos . . . on which many things aside from minerals may appear. He will occasionally be consulted by the FBI or the CIA where his knowledge is needed.

HIS WIFE of many years was lost when her plane crashed during a hi-jacking. So far as he is aware she is dead, but not legally dead.

HIS DAUGHTER, now in college, often went into the desert and mountains with him; she is skilled at getting around on her own and takes no nonsense from anybody. She has a good sense of humor, is critical of and often amused by her father's occasional girl friends, and when she disapproves, often makes mild fun of them for her father's benefit. They are in the best sense of the word, comrades. She is the one person he can talk to, for since the death of his wife he is a lonely man, immersed in his work.

INCLINED to be easy-going, Byron is a man who knows his own skills, knows he is tough and is under no pressure to demonstrate it. He will often yield a minor point to avoid trouble, but once moved to action he is a veritable engine of destruction. His physical encounters are apt to be brief, sudden, climactic.

HE SERVED in the Korean War, saw a good bit of action, and knows how to handle himself in any kind of trouble.

HE likes women, not only sexually but as people,

mixes easily in any kind of company, and being a single man to whose name there is a hint of tragedy, and
a lonely man as well, he is especially attractive to
women, many of whom believe they can make him forget
his wife.

THE MYSTERY of his wife's disappearance will be
held over for future stories: In a foreign city he
sees a man in a crowd that he recognizes as having
been on the plane. He tries to follow, loses the man
in a labyrinth of streets.

END, perhaps, with man or other man denying other
survivors. First, however, it is essential to see
Byron in action as the geologist, on the ground, in
the American West or British Columbia working as he
will.

Nothing to do with above, but what of a man who
steals a steamboat loaded with gold on a Western
river? Disguises the boat and heads upstream at the
season's end? He gets a dancehall girl to put on a
fantastic show, tips off the crew and passengers so
they all rush ashore on a dark, rainy night. He casts
off, with two or three men to help, and takes the
boat upstream knowing the stream will soon freeze
over. He has received word a chinook is blowing and
moves out quickly in the night. When they return the
boat is gone . . . vanished. Everyone assumes the
boat has gone adrift and floated downstream. Perhaps
the boat is frozen in? [The crew is] All bored. He
feels the Chinook start, or--?

After that digression Louis goes back to his notes on *The Rock
Man:*

A geologist-mining engineer of international reputation who in the course of his work becomes in-

volved in plots, crimes, investigations of all sorts.
He is on a first name basis with premiers and national figures of many kinds and because of his
knowledge is frequently called in for aid or consul-
tation.

In these days when minerals, rare earths, etc.
are in great demand so are the services of those who
can find them.

Open with a sequence in which attempts are made
to kill him, he has no idea why. An attempt to run
him down with a car; a shot taken at him with a si-
lencer; then a man approaches him for information; he
wants the information before it can be given to the
party who is paying for it. He is threatened.

Office in Century City; a ranch in Colorado; his
meetings can take place in resort hotels, country
clubs, luxury homes or remote cabins. He has a secretary and a right-hand man.

Interesting locales--bizarre characters--
suspense--international importance--

Use the dead man from the Suez Canal bit from
Lucas; analysis of dust or sand; in certain areas
only such dust can be found; they find a body in the
desert but the man was drowned . . . in salt water.
His body flown out and left in the desert. He tracks
to the plane that brought the body. Hence man was
killed on or near salt water. Draw heavily on police
books.

The first story must show him in action, working
as a geologist. Perhaps the secret missile base in

the Colorado Mts.? He discovers clue to oil or min-
eral from ancient missiles.

COMMENTS: In the mid-1970s Louis put together these notes for a possible TV series. A well-known, but aging, actor of the time had come to Dad to see if he could create a show for him to star in . . . Dad came up with this idea and pitched it to the actor and his agent, but ultimately no deal was made. Louis wrote the following description of one of the meetings in his journal, saying that the star was enthusiastic:

> . . . his agent less so. Agent believes networks
> will not even know what a geologist is . . . I dis-
> agree. I have more respect for the people out there
> than the agent does. As for the Networks, that may be
> another question. In any event all that needed to be
> said was said in a few minutes and the rest was re-
> hashing of the same topic to no point. [The star]
> called afterwards and wanted to keep up my interest.
> I really don't care as I've too many books to
> write . . . I haven't time for much else.

Century City is a complex of office towers that went up on what had once been part of the 20th Century Fox back lot. Local legend has it that the spectacular amount of money lavished on the Elizabeth Taylor–Richard Burton version of *Cleopatra* (which exceeded the film's original $2 million budget by over $40 million) caused the studio to sell off its back lot for an amount that was not much more than the film's final cost. Regardless, from the late 1960s into the 2000s it was the prime corporate real estate in Los Angeles.

I assume the comment about "ancient missiles" is some sort of a mistake, though I'm not really sure what Louis was trying to say.

I love the digression about the steamboat story right in the middle of the material on "The Rock Man." Although the structure of the *Louis L'Amour's Lost Treasures* volumes doesn't give us many opportunities to appreciate it, when Louis was working, one idea frequently fed directly into another. For better or for worse, many of the ideas we see here are the results of, or the victims of, multitasking.

BORDEN CHANTRY II

The First Ten Chapters of a Western Novel

CHAPTER 1

No man knew where the wind began nor how its shadows
moved through the sun-silvered grass.

Borden Chantry sometimes thought such things but told
no one, not even his wife. She was a good woman, one of
the very best, but without poetry and she would have been
made uneasy if he expressed such thoughts.

He took the roan diagonally up the slope of the long
hill and from the crest could look four directions into
infinity.

Only the grass where the wind played shadow-games,
only occasional out-croppings of bare black rock, the
broken bones of old lava flows breaking through the
earthly flesh. He sat still in the saddle, listening to
the wind, feeling it, sensing something upon it. A distant cloud of antelope floated across the plains.

This was not a place for a man but for the wild
horses who ran, manes and tails streaming or the occasional buffalo, very rare now, remembering their distant
thunder upon the earth.

These moments he loved, alone upon the plains that
ran on for endless days of riding to the east, south and
north. Only to the west, over beyond the horizon, did the
plains come to an end against the vast eastern wall of
the Rockies, the Sangre de Cristos here, but a part of
the Rockies none the less.

A little more than two years ago he had been a
rancher, with wide acres of land and over three thousand
head of white face and long horn cattle. The land was
still his but the cattle were gone, some caught in an unexpected five-day blizzard, others sold at a loss to pay
his debts. To make a living he had become town marshal.

This, where he now sat in his saddle under the wind,
this was where he belonged. Here he was at home. Here he
knew what to do. In the town where he lived he was uneasy, restless for the hills, uncomfortable even among
those who respected him and had asked for his services.

He frowned, watching a distant buzzard against the
sky. Something was wrong in his town, something he should
know about but did not. He was a sensitive man, and he
felt an uneasiness that should not be there. He shook his
head, irritated with himself. He was becoming a fool,
imagining things that were not there.

He glanced again at the buzzard. Buzzards. There was
more than one. A dead critter, no doubt.

The sooner he could save enough to re-stock his
ranch, the better. He had saved money, then bought cattle
with it just before the freeze-up. He reined his horse
sharply around, turning away from the thought that never
in his life-time could he save enough money to start
over.

In the days when he began ranching it had been eas-

ier. Many cattle ran unbranded on the range and he had
found strays in the valley of the Purgatoire that had
been there for years.

It was different now. All cattle were branded, all
the land claimed by someone, and even though he still
owned land, starting over would be difficult. He had gone
to Hyatt Johnson, the banker in town, but Hyatt hedged.
Nobody wanted to loan money on land, there was too much
of it.

He was riding toward the buzzards, still some distance away. His eyes cast for the tracks of horses. Nothing fresh. He would have been surprised had he seen any
for this was empty country. Nobody came here except to
hunt for strays at round-up time when they brought everything in. And last night's rain would have wiped out
signs of recent movement.

He saw tracks of unshod horses. That would be the
wild bunch who roamed his own range. There were a dozen
to sixteen in the bunch led by a gray stallion with black
tail and mane. They knew each other, he and that stallion.

Five years ago he had come upon him suddenly in the
Mesa de Mayo country. The stallion had stopped, facing
him, nostrils flared, ready to fight or run.

"Go on!" he said tolerantly. "Get out of here before
I put a rope on you!"

With an angry snort the stallion had turned and
herded his mares back up the canyon.

Now he drew up and let his horse suck water from a
shallow pool caught in a hollow of a rock they were passing.

He glanced again at the buzzards. He was closer now,
and there were four or five of them. Something was dead
down there, or something about to die. Whatever it was
must be down in Sheep Canyon, in its lower reaches where
it started to flatten out.

When he topped the next rise he could see it, something resembling a heap of discarded clothing, but he knew it was a man.

. . . Or had been. Death had been here and the man was gone; only the shell remained.

Nothing had been at it yet. The buzzard is a wary bird, and from long experience they know some creatures die very hard, indeed, and some will fight until the last breath.

Borden Chantry sat in his saddle and studied the situation. The worst thing he could do would be to charge down there and mess up any tracks that had been left.

The body lay sprawled on bare sand among patches of grass and clumps of brush. He had been a short, stout man wearing a store-bought suit and a town man's shoes, incongruous in this wild and lonely place. A carpet-bag lay open beside the body. Somebody had gone through it and through the dead man's pockets.

There was no horse, nor were there tracks of one. Borden Chantry had been walking his roan closer and now he drew up again to study the body and the position in which it lay.

A glance told him most of what he needed to know. The body had been lying there all night because there had been a brief shower, a hard-driven pelting shower that indented the well packed sand. It had left the clothing damp and muddy where it touched the ground.

Shot through the head. He could see the bullet-hole clearly enough. Borden Chantry dismounted and squatted beside the body. The pockets had been gone through, yet had they taken everything?

How did the man come to be here, of all places? It was only a short distance from Borden's now empty ranch-house, a short distance, he reflected, by Western standards, but several miles, actually.

This was an area where no one came, not even he him-

self and nobody lived closer. A year might pass with no
more than one or two riders even passing within several
miles of this area. So how did this man, a stranger, come
to be here?

Where was he coming from? And where was he going?

Back there was an area known locally as the Black
Hills, and all that was wild country except for the stage
station.

Had the man left the stage? If so, why? Was somebody
pursuing him?

Beside the body was a stick, lying loose on the sand.
That stick did not belong where it lay, and it was too
short for the man to have used it as a cane or a staff to
assist his walking. A stick lying among sage-brush or
cacti acquires a fine silting of dust and the sand beneath it acquires an indentation where the stick has been
lying. None of this was present, and yet one end of the
stick had sand in among the slivers of the broken end.

Half-concealed by the body was a hole in the sand
into which the end of the stick might have fitted.

"Well, I'll be damned!" he said aloud. "I'll be
double-damned!"

He looked again at the position of the body and the
way the stick was lying.

"Somebody," he said aloud, "brought the body here,
propped it up in a sitting position with that stick and
then shot into the head."

Now, why in the devil--! He sighted from the body's
position toward the bank of the arroyo, some sixty yards
away. Leaving his horse ground-hitched, he walked toward
the bank, climbed it, and looked around. It needed several minutes before he found anything, and it wasn't
much. Somebody had knelt on the ground, leaving a very
slight knee-print and a somewhat deeper toe-print.

It was here a man had kneeled to take his shot into
the body that lay below. Why anybody would go to such

trouble he could not guess, but that was for tomorrow,
today he was concerned only with this.

He looked around for something to use in measuring,
but no stick was available and the yucca leaves were not
long enough. Taking off his belt he measured the distance
from the knee-print to the toe-print, then marked the
edge of his belt and put it back in place.

This was none of his business as he was only the town
marshal whose jurisdiction ended with the town limits. He
would have to inform the sheriff or the Deputy United
States Marshal.

Returning to the body he studied it again. Whatever
he could learn might help his fellow officer, and in any
event any crime in the area might sooner or later come to
rest in town, his town.

Squatting on his heels beside the dead man, Borden
looked him over with care. Not a very clean man, certainly. The under-side of his coat sleeve was polished as
from rubbing on a desk or bench. The cuffs of his pants
were somewhat frayed. The shirt was dirty at the collar
and cuffs, unchanged for several days. The hands showed
no familiar calluses but the nails were dirty and there
was something dark, ink perhaps, on the fingers.

The pockets had been searched but he found a couple
of small coins, unlikely in a Western man's pockets as
nothing was used smaller than a two-bit piece. Either
this man was from the East or he had recently been East.

Several times he had stopped his examination to look
around, and was becoming increasingly uneasy. The killer
was probably miles away but he could not be sure. Borden's roan was waiting patiently, not twenty yards away,
yet suddenly he began wishing he had his rifle in his
hands. He doubted if the killer was anywhere around but
he had the uneasy feeling of a man who is watched.

Gathering brush he piled it over the body to keep the
buzzards away. It would worry them for awhile and before

they became confident he would have a wagon here to pick
it up.

Mounting, he rode away at a rapid canter, his eyes
alert for any movement or anything like a clue. He rode
on to his own abandoned ranch-house, coming down from the
north into the small valley with its big old cottonwoods
and the shabby little cabin standing in their shade.

The corrals were empty; the open-faced barn that had
offered shelter to his saddle-stock during good weather
and the stronger, tightly built barn for winter storms
remained as he had left them.

He walked his horse down the slope and looked at the
cabin. He did not want to go in. Too many memories there.
He had built that cabin with his own hands, and he had
brought his bride here with some small pride, yet he remembered how she had looked when he carried her over the
threshold and put her down.

"This? This is it?"

He would never forget her tone. Of course, she could
not be expected to know how he felt about it, or how
other such places were. She was an Eastern girl and evidently had expected more. Yet she had been a good wife,
and was a fine person. He wished he could have had more,
and but for that turn of bad weather he would have been a
rich man by now, able to afford what he wanted, what she
wanted.

He did not know what she had envisioned when he spoke
of his ranch. Evidently it had not been this. He loved
the place: the cabin, its cold spring, the rustling cottonwood leaves, the small vegetable garden he had planned
so carefully. He sensed her disappointment yet he believed she had come to love the place.

Borden glanced around a little, walking his horse
from place to place, then he took the trail for town. He
would have to get a telegram off to the U.S. Marshal.

His thoughts returned to the body. He did not know

but he was sure the man had already been dead when shot
in the head. For one thing there was no blood. The air
was crisp and cool, really cold at night, so there would
be little change in the body.

Brought from some distance away, deliberately shot,
then left. In such a place it might have lain there two
or three years unfound, so why the bullet? Insurance, he
suspected. Somebody wanted an obvious cause of death in
the event the body was found.

Why not just leave the dead body? If found, the
killer must have decided, there must be an obvious cause
of death so investigation would go no further.

That implied there was something more to be found; it
also implied the killer had something to be worried
about, something he did not want investigated. It also
implied that whoever disposed of the body knew the country, knew this was an empty area, that Borden Chantry no
longer worked his ranch, that even a round-up in the area
was unlikely. That implied somebody with local knowledge.

When he left his ranch behind he let the roan choose
his own pace and settled down in the saddle to do some
thinking.

Where had the dead man come from? What was he doing
in this country, obviously a city man? Where had he been
killed? And why? And by whom?

Somebody with local knowledge, and that meant somebody who knew him, somebody who might wonder where he had
been riding today. Somebody with something to hide who
was willing to kill to keep it hidden.

This was ranching country with a railroad that ran
right across the state. His town was only a whistle-stop.
It was cattle country, and sheep country as well. What
could the dead man have wanted here, of all places?

And he had not been around town or Borden would have
seen him. Borden swore softly, with amused exasperation.
When he went to wire the U.S. Marshal, Harold, the tele-

grapher, would take the message. And what Harold Cuff
knew, the whole town would soon know.

Nevertheless, he rode his horse up to the window
overlooking the tracks. "Wire to the Deputy U.S. Marshal,
Harold. To Thurston Jones . . ."

"No need to waste your money, Bord. Thursty's in
town. He's up at the cafe, lookin' for you."

"Thanks." He turned his horse.

Sometimes it helped to know Harold Cuff.

CHAPTER 2

Borden Chantry rode up to the cafe and swung down,
tying his horse at the hitching-rail. Automatically his
eyes took in the street. Big Injun was sitting in his
chair outside the jail. Borden gestured to him, and the
Indian got up and walked slowly down the boardwalk to
him.

"You'll need the buckboard, Injun," he said, then explained where the body lay. "Cover it with a tarp and get
it over to the old barn where Doc can have a look." He
paused. "And Injun? Take a look around. You might see
something I missed." He explained about the stick and the
kneel marks he had found.

When Big Injun had gone he went inside. Thursty was
seated at Borden's usual table. He stood up and extended
a hand. "Good to see you, Bord. Wish you were still sheriff around here."

Chantry sat down. He wished he was, too. The additional money had helped for the two years he had been in
office, but he was no politician, knew nothing about cam-
paigning, and he had lost by a few votes to Nathan Johnson, Hyatt's brother.

"Breaks of the game," Chantry replied. "He knew how

to run for office, and I stood on my record. It wasn't enough."

Ed brought coffee to the table. "You wanna eat?" he asked.

"Bess will have supper waiting, so I'll just have the coffee and maybe a doughnut."

"I have to take a run out to Frisco," Thursty began. "Be gone a couple of weeks. I'm to testify in a court case out yonder, and I need somebody to stand by for me. I talked to the marshal and he suggested you." The other man's smile was hidden by his cup. "I was about to ask for you, anyway."

"What's going on?"

Thursty sipped his coffee and looked out the window at the gathering darkness. "Nothing that needs to worry you," he spoke carefully, "except for Turren Downer."

Borden Chantry accepted the coffee and doughnuts Ed brought to the table, then glanced out the window.

"What about Turren Downer? Isn't he in prison?"

"Was. He isn't now. He's out and around."

"Do you think he'll come back here?"

"He's already here. Somebody saw him over at Trinidad a few days ago. He got some time off for good behavior and there's a story he saved a guard's life when some rocks caved on him, but Turren's a tough man and where Turren is, there's always trouble."

Borden Chantry knew all about Downer. He'd been a top hand on several outfits, then started running with a bad crowd. Borden had heard that was partly because he had a thing for Zaretta Clyde.

Zaretta Clyde? Borden frowned, disturbed by the thought of her, living so close yet out of his jurisdiction. She had made no trouble but from time to time there were rumbles of suspicion and gossip.

Zaretta lived well on a small ranch, running a few cattle and quite a few horses. The trouble was that she

lived too well for the outfit she had. Of course, she
might have money.

He did not even know what she looked like although
she had been spoken of as a handsome woman.

"I'll stand in for you, Thursty, but don't be gone
too long. I may give up the job and take the family back
east."

"You? You're a Western man. This is your country."

"I know it, but Bess came from the East and she's
wanting to go back. She figures I'll do well there."

Thurston Jones shook his head. He glanced at Borden.
"You're Western, Bord, as Western as any man could be.
You'd die back there."

"Tell that to Bess. She wants Tom to get a proper education and go on to college. She may be right, though.
The country is changing."

Chantry changed the subject. In as few words as possible he explained about the body he had found, that he
had sent Big Injun to bring it in, and the puzzling aspects of the discovery. "Doesn't make sense," he summed
it up, "a man like that in such a place. It's a cinch
whoever dumped the body did not expect it to be found
right off. The bullet was a precaution."

"Precaution against what?" Thurston wondered. "Why
did they want an obvious cause of death?"

Borden Chantry was silent, thinking. After a moment
he said what had been in his mind from the beginning.
"I'm going to have Doc do an autopsy. There's something
funny about this. I think they did all they could to keep
anybody from guessing who he was or where he was killed.

"First, they hoped the body would not be found until
it was torn up by animals or wasted away, but they did
not trust to that. Just in case they wanted an obvious
cause of death that could be readily accepted.

"This one is for you. I'm a rancher, not a detective."

"You did pretty well on the Lang Adams thing."

"Just common sense, that was all, and cow country savvy. This is different."

He finished his coffee. "Bess will be worried. I'm going home."

"Bord? I'll be gone for two weeks. Look into this and give me a report, then if you want me to take over I'll do it."

"Well . . ." He hesitated, but had to admit the hesitation was not honest. He did want to investigate. Puzzles bothered him, and leaving the body close to his own ranch, that almost made it his problem. "All right, but hurry back. Meanwhile I'll see what I can scare up."

Tom and Bess were at the table when he came in. Bess got up and went to the stove. "How are things at school?" he asked his son.

"All right, I guess, but Ol' Lady Graham is sure piling on the home-work."

"Old Lady? She's no old lady, Tom. She's young and almighty pretty."

"You noticed that, did you?" Bess said.

"I sure did, Bess." He smiled at her. "But I saw you first."

He paused. "I came by the ranch. Those wildflowers came up where you scattered the seed, a whole mess of them."

"Pa? Can I ride out there with you someday? I miss the place."

"One of these days. We've a little trouble out there right now." He explained about the body.

Bess brought his food to the table and sat down opposite him. "I wish you had another job. I live for the day when we'll be away from here."

"There's crimes back east, too, Bess."

"But you won't have anything to do with it." Or with
anything else, probably, he told himself. What would he
do for a living? What could he do? He had spent a lot of
horse-back time just thinking, in the saddle. Or over a
cup of coffee at the restaurant. He would have to come up
with some kind of a plan, something he could do. They
wouldn't have much money because he wouldn't sell the
land for what Hyatt would give him for it, and he was
sure that was just what Hyatt was waiting for. Sooner or
later he expected Borden to get into a jam and come to
him for money.

The night was cool and he added some sticks to the
fire. Bess was knitting and Tom was at the table with a
book open and writing on a tablet. He had never had much
schooling himself and whenever Tom wasn't around and his
books were, Borden liked to dip into them and read a little. Someday, if there was time . . .

"Thursty's going out to California," he volunteered.
"Got to testify in a case. I'll be taking over for him
for two weeks."

"You'll be investigating that murder?" Bess asked.

"Sort of. Nathan Johnson will be on it, too."

He did not like Nathan Johnson nor did Nathan like
him. It went beyond the election, and was, Borden realized, a matter of personality. Nathan had been county
clerk before he ran for sheriff, and had visions of running for the state legislature. He would not be Borden's
choice for any office. Yet, the man had a way of making
himself liked and he could get the votes. Better than I
could, Borden reflected. Give the man his due. He knows
his business. And his business was politics, it was not
solving or preventing crimes.

Soon everybody in town would know about the body.
Some must have overheard him talking to Thursty Jones,

others would see the dead man when Injun brought him in. The talk might stir up a clue. After all, there was no other town within miles.

It also might warn the killer that his crime had been discovered sooner than expected.

Borden Chantry considered that and warned himself to walk carefully. So far the killer had been quite sure of himself. No doubt he still was, but there was always a point when fear came, and the instinct of a frightened killer was to kill again.

He did not fear for himself, but suppose, just suppose the killer tried to retaliate against his family? He glanced quickly at Bess and then at Tom. Maybe Bess was right. Maybe he should get out of this business.

Yet the discovery of the body and the talk about it might help. His experience, limited though it was, inclined him to believe that if a criminal is pushed he makes mistakes. And all criminals, he believed, were optimists. They had to believe they could get away with it, they had to believe everything would go right for them. The trouble was somebody was always noticing, and the criminal could never be sure he had not been seen or that he had not, inadvertently, left some clue.

Borden Chantry knew little about the detection of crimes, but of one thing he was sure. The greatest ally the law had was the mind of the criminal itself. In a larger city it might not work so well, but he knew what it could do, for better or worse, in a small town.

What he must find out was who the dead man had been, and how he came to be where he was.

The first thing was to find out how he got to this part of the country. He had to have come on the steam cars or from the south by stage. Obviously, he was no horseman.

Of course, he might have been driven in by somebody, by buckboard or wagon. The killer, perhaps?

Tomorrow he would begin inquiries. If he had arrived
with somebody or been met by somebody someone would have
seen it. People liked to talk. They liked to know, to be
able to tell others what they had seen. It gave them a
sense of importance. Of course, they might be afraid.
Those who knew might be frightened by the killing.

He would talk to Cuff. The dispatcher rarely missed
noticing who got on or off the train. After all, he sat
behind his telegraph key looking out the window at the
tracks where the trains stopped.

Then he would talk to the livery stable to see if
anybody had hired a rig. A difficulty was that he had no
time limits. He did not know when the man arrived, yet
wearing those clothes he had not been here long.

Priscilla, at the post office, might know something.

In fact, she always did. She was uncommonly nosy, but
on the other hand, she was not inclined to gossip and
rarely spoke of what she knew.

If the killer was in town or even in the country
close by he would soon know what Borden was doing. He
would be able to observe every step of Chantry's progress, and would know when Chantry was getting close and
take the necessary steps to prevent discovery. In the
morning he must see Nathan Johnson. By that time the body
should have been brought in. He would have to get Doc
Terwilliger on the job, too.

"I had a letter from Ethel," Bess said. "She says the
Dornbecker farm will be for sale. Old Charlie died and
the boys are working in Boston now. I remember it well,
when I was a child. They had such a lot of maple trees
and we used to go over for the sugaring."

"How big a place?"

"Eighty acres. There's a small orchard, mixed fruit
trees, just for their own use, and a big barn. The kind
you always wanted out at the ranch.

"Ethel said they would sell it on time, to the right person."

Borden shifted in his chair. He had enough of being in debt, of fighting the weather for crops. At least he knew what he was doing out here, and back there he would have it all to learn. Still, it sounded like a good place.

"Did she give you any idea what they were asking?"

"She said she'd find out."

Ethel was Bess's sister, a nice woman. He knew how they missed each other.

He got up and reached for his hat. "I've got to make my rounds," he said. "Don't wait up for me, Bess."

"Borden? Be careful. Please?"

Outside he moved away from the door and stood listening to the night. Caution was as natural to him as breathing.

The piano was going in Time Reardon's Corral Saloon, and he heard somebody ride down the street, heading out of town.

He supposed it must be hard on Bess. When a man was keeping the peace his wife never knew when he walked out of the door whether he would come back, or not. Yet things had been quiet in town, and the jail was empty. Nothing for Big Injun to do but keep the place swept out.

Kim Baca, his former deputy, now had a small horse-breeding ranch just out of town. Well, that was one thing he had done, if nothing else. He had turned Kim from a horse-thief headed for a hanging into a good deputy and a man on whom he could depend.

He did not go out through the gate in the low picket fence. Instead he walked under the cottonwood tree and stepped over the fence, keeping himself in the dark until he reached the street alongside the cafe.

Three horses were tied at the Corral's hitching-rail and a buckboard with a sorrel team. He knew the horses.

They were M-Bar-W stock, cowboys returning from a small
drive over to Trinidad. The buckboard was one he had not
seen before, but it was old.

He crossed the street to the saloon.

CHAPTER 3

Time Reardon was tending his own bar. He nodded
briefly to Chantry. There was mutual respect between
them, not friendship, but each understood the other very
well indeed.

The three M-Bar-W cowboys were at the bar, and a
stranger sat at the nearby table. He was a square shouldered man in a gray suit coat and matching vest. His ears
were tight against his head and his eyes busy. In front
of him was a stein of beer. He wore a handle-bar mustache
and his face showed signs of the sun.

"How are you, Bord?" Reardon asked. "Everything
quiet?"

"Yes, and I hope it stays that way."

Time mopped the bar, then he said, "Hear you found
some work for Nathan."

"For me, too."

Reardon looked up. "You? Here in town?"

"Thurston Jones has gone to Frisco. He asked me to
handle whatever came up so Nathan and I will be working
together."

"Does Nathan know about this?" Was Reardon disturbed,
or was it his imagination?

"Not yet. I thought I might find him in here."

"He hasn't been in." Reardon leaned his forearms on
the bar. "This body you found? Local man?"

"Stranger. City man."

The M-Bar-W cowhands were listening. All three were

known to Chantry as they had ridden on round-ups together
when he was still a cattleman. "In Sheep Canyon?" The
cowhand's name was Hayes. "How the Hell did he get away
out there?"

"Not by himself, he didn't," Hinge, another of the
cowboys said.

"Murder?" Reardon asked.

"He'd been shot in the head. My guess would be a
rifle, fired from fifty, sixty yards off. That's just a
guess."

These men, if interested, could be a help. They rode
the range south of where the body had been found, and
they were friends. Borden Chantry was one of their own
kind. When you ride an empty land you notice things another might ignore. You see the tracks of a strange horse
or glimpse a rider in the distance, you are curious. It
was a country where not too many were moving around and
those who were knew each other, and understood what the
other was doing and why he was where he was. Anything or
anyone who did not fit into that pattern was reason for
curiosity.

Nathan Johnson came in. He was a few inches shorter
than Borden Chantry, and had grown a little fat sitting
behind a desk.

"How are you, Borden? Hear you found some work for
me?"

"For me, too, Nathan. Thursty asked me to stand in
for him. He's gone out to Frisco to testify in a case."

"Glad to have you aboard." Despite the fact that they
had run against each other for office there was no obvious animosity. But so far there had been no need for co-
operation, and their paths had gone off in opposite
directions. "I'll be glad to have any information you can
give me. I'd like to get this closed up fast."

Borden Chantry lifted one boot and rested it on the

brass rail. "That may be tough," he said quietly. "This isn't any ordinary killing."

Two men had come into the saloon and seated themselves at a table near the door. From the corner of his eyes he saw that one was a stranger, the other a man whom he knew slightly as a small rancher in the southern part of the country.

Nathan turned to face him. "Now what does that mean?" He was suddenly interested, and Borden could understand why. A big case now might mean much in the future, if as many believed, Nathan aspired to higher office.

"It is not a simple murder," he said quietly. "The man himself, the obvious attempt to prevent his body being found until nature had destroyed it, and other aspects. It makes a man wonder, Nathan, just who would go to all that trouble, and why. If it was simply a robbery his body would have been left where it was robbed."

He stepped away from the bar. "I'm having Doc take a look at the body. After that we should know more."

He walked to the door, glancing at the newcomers as he went out. Their eyes were averted and they did not glance his way, which seemed unusual. One's eyes almost automatically observe movement when close by, but neither looked up, either so engrossed in conversation they were not aware of his passing or deliberately avoiding his eyes.

Two horses had been added to those at the rail. Both wore the Double O brand. He knew the brand belonged to the man inside. What was his name? Mitchell? Hitchell? Something of the sort.

Borden Chantry walked along the street to the bank, then crossed the street to the front of the Express Office, where he checked the door. He waited there in the darkness under the over-hang, his eyes studying the street, alert for movement. He was expecting no trouble, but he was thinking as well.

Who was the man with Hitchell? And that other man? With the somewhat sun-burned face? He was not from around here and was also not used to exposure to the sun, or at least not lately.

The marshal of a small town had to know who strangers were and what their business might be. Usually he understood at once, but these were not stock buyers, nor were they prospectors. This was not mining country yet there were always a few optimists.

His thoughts returned to Bess and the East. He might try farming but he had done nothing like that since he was a boy when he had helped his father, before they came west. He knew next to nothing about raising crops, or even what crops might grow back where Bess wanted to live. He would have to look into that.

Was he actually thinking of it? Seriously? He took off his hat and ran his fingers through his hair, watching the street. He had to think of it. Bess was serious, it was clearly what she wanted. He hitched his gun into an easier position and checked to see if the thong was off the hammer. He only kept it in place when he was riding, and here in town, where he might need it quickly, he kept his gun free.

A light was on in the office when he stepped in. Kim Baca was playing solitaire on the desk, using their battered cards.

"All quiet?" Kim asked.

"Hitchell's in town. Know anything about him?"

"Small outfit, runs about three hundred head, I think. Neat little place, neat house, backed up against some low hills. He doesn't come this way very much. Usually rides into La Junta or Trinidad."

"You seem to have him pegged?"

Baca shrugged. "A man can't make a living with three hundred head, not with prices the way they are. It's

mostly young stuff, of course, and likely he's building
up a herd."

"Does he own a buckboard?"

Baca shrugged. "Not that I know of, but it could be.
He's got a nice barn, well-built, strong. In fact, he's
got the best barn I've seen around this country."

Except for the saloons and the cafe it was a nine
o'clock town. By that time everybody was in their own
home, concerned with their families and preparing for bed
or tomorrow. He saw the three riders from the M-Bar-W
come out and mount up and he walked out on the street
where he could be seen.

As they rode abreast of him he said, "Hayes?"

They pulled up and he walked over to them. "You boys
get around out there. If you see any strange tracks, I'd
like to know."

"Anything in pa'tic'lar?"

"Maybe a buckboard or a wagon, but just anything at
all."

"All right, Bord." Hayes lifted a hand. "See you
around."

He strolled on down to Alvarez's cafe and stepped in.
There were a half dozen Mexicans in the place and a couple of Anglo punchers whom he knew. He nodded, went to
his usual booth.

Alvarez came over with two cups of coffee and sat
down opposite him. The population of the town was almost
a third Spanish-speaking and Alvarez was something of a
leader in the community. He had two sons and a daughter
attending school and his sister was a teacher.

"Al? Is everything all right with your people? No
problems?"

"Nothing, Bord. All is quiet." The Mexican sipped his
coffee, then put the cup down carefully. "But it is not
among our people for you to look." He paused. "You are my

friend." He drank his coffee, then looked over his cup
into Borden Chantry's eyes. "Be careful. Be very, very
careful."

Borden Chantry knew better than to ask questions.
When Alvarez knew something, if he knew something, he
would tell him. They talked idly of range conditions, of
horses, and their families. Borden finished his coffee
and got up to leave. Alvarez rose also and said quietly,
"We have a new sheriff now. It is better that he handle
those things not of the town."

"Gracias, amigo." Borden Chantry lifted a hand. "I
think I shall go home now."

When he looked back, Alvarez was still in the doorway, watching him go. Puzzled, Borden stopped in the
shadows and looked around again. There was nothing, yet
the Mexican had been trying to warn him, suggesting he
confine himself to the town, and he could do just that.
Thursty would not expect him to solve any crimes, just to
keep the lid on until he returned.

Yet he had an uneasy feeling that he was missing
something important. Crime in a community is like a
cancer--it grows, eating away at the underside of a town
until there is total corruption. It is all too easy to
tolerate an evil if it avoids the public eye, and something was wrong here.

He had small experience with crime. He was no detective, and had come into law enforcement by the back door,
so to speak. True, he had been asked to take the job, and
without it his family might have gone hungry. Well, maybe
that was stretching it a bit, but he had needed a job,
and desperately.

Until he had taken the job as town marshal he had
known the towns-people only casually. He bought supplies
at the general store, picked up mail at the post office,
ate occasionally in the cafe. Sometimes he dropped in at
one of the saloons for a drink, although he wasn't much

inclined that way. He and his wife attended church here
in town and, eventually, Tom had gone to school here.

Since he had become marshal the town had taken on a
new look. These were people he had to protect. He had
solved the murder of Joe Sackett and he had, with Tyrel
Sackett's help, frustrated the attempted bank robbery by
the outlaws Monson and Clatt. If he was going to go back
east he had to leave the town clean, so whatever was happening, he had to know.

Bess was sitting by the fire when he came in. She was
reading <u>Quentin Durward</u>, by Sir Walter Scott. "You should
read this, Borden, you'd like it."

He filled his cup and sat down at the table. "Bess,
what do you know about Zaretta Clyde? I mean, what are
people saying?"

"What can they say? Nobody knows anything about her.
She's been here more than a year and hasn't been in town
three times, although they do say she has visitors."

"Visitors?"

"Men, mostly, some of them city men. They don't come
to town, either. They get off the train at a place near
her ranch and are met there. She meets them sometimes
with a buckboard, and sometimes it is that foreman of
hers, Clint Meyers."

He chuckled, shaking his head. "You ladies don't miss
much."

Bess shrugged. "It's mostly Priscilla. There at the
post office she hears about everything that's said, and
Clint Meyers gets his mail there. He writes to some woman
in Denver. She used to be at Cheyenne Wells, according to
Pris, but moved to Denver a few months ago. Pris knows
it's the same woman. She recognized the hand-writing."

"And Zaretta?"

"Mr. Meyers picks up her mail, most of it business,

judging by the printing on the envelopes. Pris thinks she has investments."

Borden Chantry sat long over his coffee, thinking. All to no purpose, for he came up with nothing. Zaretta Clyde was the only new person in the area of whom he could think, and those men in Reardon's place, but there were always travelers coming through. He would have to check with Elsie Carter at the hotel.

Morning dawned bright and clear. He sat by the window of his home and watched the train pull in. No passengers left the train and only a couple of packing cases were unloaded. "Bess? I'll be around town all day." He paused. "If you talk to Pris--"

"Why don't you talk to her? You know she thinks the sun rises and sets in you. Really, she does."

"Doesn't act it. She's scolding me most of the time for letting things happen over which I've no control."

"That's Pris. But she still thinks you're the best and she would tell you things she would never tell us."

His house stood on a narrow lane that ran along behind the stores and shops on Main Street, directly behind the cafe.

On the other side of the house and some hundred yards off was the railroad, and from his kitchen window he could watch passengers dismount from the train.

Kim Baca was at the desk when he entered the office.

"All quiet," he said. "Doc says he wants to talk. He'll be at the cafe." Baca paused. "Said you an' your corpse kept him up half the night."

"You talked to Big Injun since he got back?"

Baca jerked a thumb toward the jail cells behind him.

"He's back there, sleepin'. He was up most of the night, drivin' down an' back."

Doc Terwilliger was alone in the cafe but for Ed, and Doc was dozing over a cold cup of coffee. Borden dropped into a chair opposite him. The doctor was a small man in a worn gray suit, a white collar and red tie.

He opened his eyes when Borden sat down. "Took you long enough," he grumbled, "for a man who wants everything done right now."

"Have you seen the body?"

"Seen it? Inside and out! White man, about forty-five years old, advanced case of tuberculosis and a bad heart along with it. And you were right. He was shot after he was already dead, been dead for several hours, I'd guess."

Ed brought two cups and a pot of coffee, carrying the cold cup away.

"How did he die?"

Doc poured some coffee into his saucer and blew gently to cool it. He looked over the saucer into Borden's eyes. "You ain't going to believe this, Bord. You ain't going to believe it at all."

"Well?"

"He was drowned. He was held face-down in some shallow water by somebody with a mighty strong grip."

CHAPTER 4

The coffee tasted good. He took another sip and put his cup down carefully.

Drowned.

A dead man found on the plains of eastern Colorado, miles from water, and death by drowning.

"Got any idea what kind of water he drowned in?"

Doc Terwilliger chuckled. "Now I just knew you'd ask that question! An' not many would think of it. Matter of fact, that was almighty obvious. He was drowned in alkali water. Lungs, nostrils and throat had that white stuff. He swallowed a good bit of it in gasping for breath."

"Shallow water, then. Face pushed down into it and held there." Borden Chantry turned toward Terwilliger. "Have you told anybody about this, Doc?"

"Only you. Nobody else was around but that little McCoy boy. You know, the youngster who lives alone."

"Billy won't talk. He's mighty cagey. Just the same, I'll have a word with him."

Doc nodded. "I like that boy, Bord. And I think he's got a good feeling for medicine. He should get a chance to go to school."

"Narrows it down, Doc. This narrows it down." He glanced at Terwilliger. "Why would someone move a body in the first place? Simply because it was too close to home, or to something they didn't want seen. No doubt they hoped it would be torn up by animals or would simply fall apart before anybody saw it. Nine times out of ten that would be exactly what would happen."

"Only you happened along?"

"The buzzards found him first. And you know any Western man knows buzzards mean something dead. Whoever left the body wasn't thinking of that."

Borden Chantry looked at him. "You'd think of it, wouldn't you? Billy McCoy would think of it, too, and Time Reardon or Ed here, they'd think of it."

"What are you gettin' at?" Doc asked.

"Whoever left that body wasn't thinking of buzzards, and that, too, might narrow the field."

He pushed back from the table. "What about his clothes?"

"Big Injun took them. Said you'd want to see them."

"Good!" Chantry got up. "Doc, there are a lot of curious people around. The cause of death was a bullet wound, wasn't it?"

Doc shrugged. "Of course! Anybody could see that.

Right in the middle of his forehead." He smiled. "Got to
get over to see Elsie's aunt. She's ailin'."

Borden chuckled. "Is she ailin', or does she just
want the good doctor to hold her hand?"

"You got enough to worry about without bothering
about sick women. That's my department. Besides that,
she's right handsome when you get down to it."

The sun was bright when he walked into the street. He
paused there, looking around. Ed had followed him from
the cafe and was sweeping off the walk. Far up the street
Judge Alex McKinney was talking to Priscilla in front of
the bank.

There was nothing much to the town when you came
right down to it, but he'd miss the place. He would miss
the people, too.

Billy was loitering nearby, tossing small rocks at a
circle marked in the dust. He was pretty good. Nearly
every rock was landing in the center.

"Billy? I wouldn't talk about being in the stable
with Doc when he did that autopsy."

"No, sir. I won't." He tossed another rock. "Mr.
Chantry, I'd be careful if I were you. Somebody's been
staked out near your house."

"What's that?"

"Yes, sir. Last two nights. Maybe it's not anybody
watchin' you, maybe he's watchin' the railroad, but he's
been behind that stack of ties yonder alongside the
tracks."

The stack of railroad ties were alongside the tracks
and just opposite the house. A boy like Billy was a canny
youngster. His father had been a good friend and Borden
Chantry had brought justice to his murderer.

"Thanks, Billy. You're a top hand in any man's outfit. You be careful, now."

He paused. "There's something wrong around town,
Billy, something very wrong, like when your father was
killed."

"I think they're scared, sir. Why else would they be
watching you? Maybe it's like before."

"How do you mean?"

"Like Lang Adams, sir. He killed all those people because he was scared, and there was no reason for it. I
think these folks are scared."

"Good thinking, Billy, but you stay out of it, you
hear? I've got enough to do without looking out for you,
too."

"Yes, sir. But if I see anything--?"

"I'll listen. You know that, I'll always listen, just
like your dad would have. You have any problems, you come
to me, or if I'm not around, to Bess."

He walked back to the office, hung his hat on the
rack and sat down. The dead man had drowned, and in alkali water, shallow water.

He had been drowned and then taken miles away, probably by night, and his body dumped in a remote place. He
had then been shot.

What did this imply? Just as he had decided, somebody
did not want the body found where he had been killed.
Somebody did not want the cause of death known. The pattern of thinking was not Western, although he could not
rely upon that.

A body would attract buzzards, which any Western man
would know. However, the buzzards might not be noticed as
the area was rarely visited, so even that deduction was
questionable.

The dead man was not from around here. The soles of
his shoes did not indicate rough walking. The polished
seat of his pants and coat sleeves to the elbow seemed to
indicate some work at either desk or table.

Several things he needed to know. Who was the dead

man? How did he get to this part of the country? What was
he doing here? Why was it necessary to kill him? And
above all, who had done the killing?

People had warned him to be careful, and Billy had
said somebody seemed to be watching him. Billy was only
twelve, but Billy missed little that went on around town
and a small boy was often ignored. It also meant that he
must not be seen talking to Billy or the boy might be en-
dangered.

Where to begin? The answer was simple. He had the
man's clothes. He had gone through them once, but he must
do so again, with more attention.

Borden Chantry went to the desk drawer where he kept
Wanted sheets sent by other jurisdictions. Idly, he
leafed through them, not hoping to discover a familiar
face but to be nudged into thinking of something that
would help. Many of the posters were of men or women not
likely to be found in the West--pickpockets usually kept
to large centers of population where they could work the
crowds, and sneak thieves, too. In a Western town like
this everything a body did was open to somebody's eyes.

A safe-cracker now, he might try the bank or Reardon's Corral Saloon where he occasionally kept valuables
for people who were briefly stopping in town. The express
office was another possibility, but a slim one. A man
trying to rob the express office would be aware it was in
plain sight of Hyatt Johnson's house as well as the bank.

All in all, this town was not a good place for a
criminal to operate. When Monson and Clatt tried to take
the bank they had a good-sized gang but a plan that had
not included him. Nor had they expected Tyrel Sackett to
be in town.

Outlaws were fools to tackle these Western towns,
anyway, because every man had a gun and knew how to use
it. Not only that, they would use it.

He needed to think, and he did that better in the

saddle, but first he would have a look at the dead man's
clothing.

Rising to go back to the cell where the clothes had
been left he caught a glimpse of himself in the mirror.

He glimpsed a man with a lean brown face, a handle-
bar mustache, carefully combed dark hair and quiet eyes.
He paused for a moment, regarding himself speculatively.
What would people think of that face back in those Eastern states? There were outdoorsmen there, of course, so
in the country, at least, he would not appear strange.

He shrugged, looking away. He had never thought much
of how he looked at any time. Mirrors were not found on
the range and until he married Bess he had never owned
anything beyond a piece of broken glass he used to shave
with. If he went east he would be wearing a collar and
tie most of the time, he supposed.

Again that question: What could he do? What work
could he find that was within his range of abilities?

The suit taken from the dead man lay on the empty
bunk in the nearest cell. He stared at the nondescript
jacket and the shirt with the soiled collar. It was not
much for a man to leave behind.

Of course, he had come too late. The killers had been
through the pockets before he saw the man, removing everything that might offer a clue, and also whatever money the
man had on him. Maybe there was nothing here. Maybe they
had cleaned him out so thoroughly there would be no clue.

Borden Chantry pulled over a chair and sat down facing the suit.

After he had examined the clothes he would have Big
Injun beat the dust from them and collect it. He did not
know if that would help or not, but he presumed there
might be some indication of where he had worked or lived.

The suit was several years old. The inside of the

right coat pocket, particularly around the top edge, had
a dark stain which might be ink. There had been ink on
the man's hands, washed off carelessly but still ingrained in the wrinkles and under the finger-nails.

The same was true of the right pants pocket. So the
man had worked with ink or used it somehow enough to
stain his hands and clothes.

A printer? Perhaps. Borden Chantry did not know much
about the activities of city men beyond the usual sort of
thing. Yet this man, an untidy one, had undoubtedly
worked with ink.

There was no label on the clothing. The buttons were
of bone, and of a common sort. He had picked up the coat
when he heard a light step in the office, and then a
woman stood in the door of the cell.

Unreasonably, the first thing he thought of was his
gun. The thong was over the hammer.

Then he chuckled. Such a thought! For this was no
outlaw, it was a woman, and a damned good looking one
into the bargain.

"Howdy, ma'am." He put the coat down and got to his
feet. "I wasn't expecting visitors."

"And I thought it was about time a new resident became acquainted with the town marshal. I am Zaretta
Clyde, how do you do?"

"Of course, Miss Clyde. If you would go back into the
office--?"

He folded the coat and put it down on the bunk. When
he followed her out he turned the key in the door.

"You lock your empty cells?" She was smiling at him.
"Or is there a ghost in there?"

"A ghost? Come to think of it, there's two ghosts.
One is of the murdered man who wore that suit, the other
is his murderer."

She smiled again but her eyes were cool, measuring,
studying him. "You mean the murderer is dead?"

"Not yet. But his shadow is somewhere close to that suit and when I'm through with it, I'll find him."

Her smile was gone. "You are confident, Mr. Marshal." She sat down in a chair.

He shrugged. "I'm really not much of a marshal, Miss Clyde." He waved a hand to indicate the town. "But the folks out there know me and are comfortable with me."

He glanced at her again. "I have been meaning to run out to see you, but you've beat me to the punch. Same idea, getting acquainted with folks new to the area."

On the desk lay the sheaf of the Wanted circulars. She glanced at them. "How interesting! Do you get those all the time? I mean is there one out for every crimi- nal?"

"No, ma'am, just for those wanted for some reason. The marshal who was here before me kept 'em all, so we've got quite a library." He glanced up at her, smiling. "When I'm settin' around doing nothing I kind of leaf through them. Keeps me up on what's happening."

"But aren't most of them out of date?"

"A criminal is never out of date until he's dead. Mighty few ever go straight, so the law is always on the look-out. Of course, in a town of this size we never see the fancy big city crooks. Crime here is mostly local, unless it's something like that Monson an' Clatt outfit."

"I hadn't heard about that."

"Happened before you came. Organized gang tried to rob our bank, but they didn't quite make it."

"What happened?"

"Two of them went to prison, got twenty years apiece. We buried the other five yonder on Boot Hill."

Zaretta Clyde shivered. "I'd heard the West was vio- lent, but--"

"No more than back east. It's just more out in the open, like. I represent the law here, but every man an' woman in town takes pride in the place and none of them

want folks makin' trouble. That Monson an' Clatt outfit
now? Most of the shootin' was done by citizens."

He paused. "You've got a nice place out there, Miss
Clyde. Are you plannin' to run cattle?"

"Horses, I think, but that's not the reason I'm
here." She smiled at him, and it was a lovely smile.
"Doctor's orders. He said I must live where the weather
is dry."

"Sorry to hear that, ma'am, but you've got it here.
Last few years we've had a spell of dry weather." He
shrugged. "It's partly what did me in. Drought first and
the grazin' was bad for my stock. Winter came on with
them in bad shape and it wiped me out. Wiped out some
others, too, but most were in better shape financially
than I was."

She got up from her chair. "It has been nice talking
to you, Marshal." She paused. "How is the restaurant
here?"

"Can't be beat. Ed was an ol' cow-camp cook, an' most
folks think that's all he was, but as a matter of fact,
Ed was raised to be a chef in one of them fancy hotels.
He got his trainin', worked some an' was doin' well, then
he had the same trouble you've got, I guess. He had to
come west for his health. He fell in love with the country an' stayed.

"He cooks reg'lar for those who like it that way, but
ever' now and again he does somethin' fancy. My Bess,
she's my wife, she takes to his fancy cookin' so ever'
once in awhile he fixes somethin' special for her."

He was standing. Big Injun was outside the door,
looking in. "You go along down there and tell Ed I said
he was to fix you something special. You have any favor-
ites, you tell him. Nothing he likes better than to throw
together something for the women-folks. Most of us are
steak an' potato men, or steak and beans."

When she had gone, Big Injun came in. He was well

over six feet and despite his age the two braids that
hung over his shoulders showed only a few strands of
gray.

"Hitchell. He buckboard back of store. Buy many
t'ings inside."

Borden Chantry thought for a minute and then he said,
"Maybe if you wiped out his buckboard he'd give you two-
bits," he suggested casually, "wiped it out with a sack,
an' bring the sack to me. If he gives you trouble, tell
him Ed pays you." A muscle twitched in Big Injun's cheek;
it was what passed for a smile. The man had no interest
in impressing anyone, but he was no fool.

Borden dropped into his chair. What did Alvarez know
that he did not? The Mexican was his friend, and he had
warned him. Time, too, had seemed a little nervous.
Saloon-keepers often knew things or heard things others
did not, although sometimes they were only whispers of
things. Unless he was wise and kept his ear to the
ground, too often the last to know was the town marshal.

Why would somebody watch his home? Was somebody
scared because of something they thought he knew, or
might know? Was that why Zaretta had visited him today?
The trouble was, he didn't know anything. He didn't know
if there was danger, or where it might come from.

CHAPTER 5

Borden Chantry returned to the cell where he had left
the dead man's clothes. Seated again, he examined each
article of clothing with care. On the vest now, he turned
it over in his hands. That third button looked different.
Obviously the original button had been lost and replaced
with another. It was likely that the dead man had done
the sewing himself. He had taken several turns of the

thread, using more than was necessary. He had known little about sewing.

The button itself was not even bone, but some sort of
metal of an almost identical color with the other buttons. Something was printed on the back. He rubbed the
dirt from the button, some of it alkali, and cleaned it
off. Gundy Min.

Gundy Min? What the Hell did that mean? Was it the
name of a company? He doubted that. Or an organization?
The button must have been one immediately available, and
perhaps from another suit or buttons saved for an emer-
gency.

In one of the hip pockets of the pants he found some
broken leaves; evidently dried leaves had gotten into the
pocket when the body was dragged along the ground, for
there was some earth along with the leaves. Carefully, he
put them in an envelope with some of the sand and earth
and marked it as evidence.

Replacing the suit, neatly folded on the bunk, he
left the cell, locking it behind him.

Gundy Min? The name meant no sense.

That is, it made no sense to him. Obviously, it would
have made sense to the button manufacturer or to whomever
the original garment had belonged. Idly, on a tablet, he
scratched out diagrams and drew pictures, always thinking, wondering. He wrote Gundy Sunday, Gundy Mundy . . .

He tore off the sheet and stuffed it into his pocket.
Irritably, he got up and went out on the street. Kim Baca
was just coming in and Borden said, "I'm going for coffee," and started down the street. At the post office he
stopped abruptly, then went in.

Nobody was around. The mail distribution had been
hours ago. Behind the wall of post office boxes he could
hear Priscilla's pen scratching.

"Well," he said aloud, "somebody is working, anyway."

Priscilla pushed back her chair and came over to the

window. "I am not working, Borden. I am writing to my sister."

"Ever hear the name Gundy?" he asked.

"No, I can't say I have." She brushed the question aside. "You had a visitor this morning. That Clyde woman."

"Nice-looking woman," he commented. "Just wanted to get acquainted with the town marshal."

"You wait until I tell Bess about that!" Priscilla teased.

"She seems all right. Get mail here?"

"That's her business, Marshal. Business mail, all of it--brokerage firms, seems like." She paused. "Must be an orphan or something."

"Why do you say that?"

"No personal mail. Women-folks like to keep in touch. Most of us write to a sister, mother, aunt or maybe an old friend. She never gets any mail like that."

Or, he thought, she gets it somewhere else, some other post office or maybe--

He shook his head. That would be unlikely, he thought, but possible. "She invite you for tea?"

He was startled. "Me? I'm not a tea drinker. Bess is, but not me."

"She's invited Hyatt. Elsie Carter told me she over-heard it. Right in the door of the hotel. Invited Hyatt and he went, too."

"Well, why not? She's an attractive woman and a woman's company might do Hyatt some good."

He turned toward the door but she stopped him. "Marshal? You be careful, I've got a bad feeling about things."

He nodded. "So do I, Pris. Worst of it is, I can't think of any reason why I should feel that way."

"I can," Pris replied. "I've seen it happen, Marshal, but not always the same way. Maybe somebody in town knows

something, or gets a hint of trouble in his family or
close by. So he gets watchful and doesn't talk as much.
Somebody else notices it, maybe without even thinking of
it, and begins to feel the same way. First thing you know
a lot of people are on edge. There was a time there before you solved that Sackett killing when folks were
right suspicious of each other, and nobody wanted to talk
about anything." She paused again. "It's like that now,
Marshal. You be careful."

Borden Chantry walked back to the street and stood at
the corner of the post office building. Between that
building and the cafe there was a space maybe forty feet
wide and he could see his own home, his corral and barn.
Nothing was stirring there. Through the leaves of the big
cottonwood he glimpsed the pile of ties Billy had spoken
about. He scowled, then shook his head.

He went into the cafe and Ed brought his coffee. He
curled his fingers around the big cup, the heat seeping
into them. The smell was comforting.

Suddenly the door opened and Turren Downer came in.
He was a broad, powerful man with big hands and shoulders, thick, curly bronze-like hair and a square jaw. He
glanced over at Chantry, then at the badge on his vest.

"Marshal, is it? I heard you were marshal but
couldn't believe it." He walked over and drew back a
chair, sitting astride of it and leaning his arms on the
back. "Heard you killed Boone Silva. Down the country
where I was folks were almighty surprised. They'd have
bet Silva would take you without turnin' a hair." He
grinned. "I could have told them different. I mind the
time we were roundin' up strays over near Lone Butte an'
you killed that rattler. He never got finished with his
rattle before you shot his head off. I told myself then
I'd never get into a shoot-out with you."

Borden Chantry shifted a little in his chair. He did
not like talk of such things. Especially talk about him-

self. He was a modest man and it all made him uncomfortable.

"Who you ridin' for, Turren?"

"On the loose. Saved up a mite and I'm sort of
lookin' around." He wiped a hand across his face. "Time I
shaped up. I'd like to get me a place of my own and go to
raisin' stock. You don't need a deputy, do you? I might
do all right in your line of work."

"You might, at that." Chantry smiled at him. "You'd
have to lay off the hooch. Folks don't take much to having a lawman who hits the bottle."

Downer nodded. "You'd not believe it, but I haven't
had a drink in two months. Fact. Amazes me, but it's so."

Downer got up and swung his chair back into place. As
he turned away, Borden Chantry said, "Turren? For old
times' sake? Be careful."

Turren turned sharply around and seemed about to
speak, then turned back to the door. As he reached it he
looked back again. "I'll do that, Bord, an' you do the
same."

Borden Chantry shook his head. The Turren Downers of
the world he could handle; the trouble was with things
like this murder he did not know where to begin.

Drowned in shallow, alkali water, and there were a
couple of dozen places in twenty miles where that might
happen. After rains, anyway.

So what did he have? A body to be buried in an un-
marked grave, an old suit of clothes and a lot of suspicion. Zaretta Clyde had just added to that suspicion. She
had occupied that ranch property for several months now,
so why take this time to come in and get acquainted with
the town marshal? Why not before? Months ago? Was she
trying to find out what he knew?

Borden tasted his coffee and put his cup down. Let's
suppose, he suggested to himself. Having no evidence,
let's speculate a little. Suppose somebody has a nice

little criminal operation going. What it was didn't matter for the moment. Suddenly, for one reason or another,
one of their number gets killed? Or maybe he was not one
of them but just somebody who knew too much? Suddenly the
lid was off and the operation was in danger.

But what kind of operation? Operated by whom?

The line of thought intrigued him. It was the only
solution that occurred to him to account for the body
being found where it was, an obvious attempt to dispose
of a body without risk of discovery.

Had it been murder by a traveler or even someone
local, a murder for robbery, jealousy or what not it was
unlikely the body would have been moved but left beside a
stage trail or the railroad. A body found under such circumstances would certainly require investigation but
would not have aroused the attention this one had. Somebody had tried to be too smart.

Rain had washed away any tracks near the body. He repeated that to himself then stopped. Near the body? What
about further away?

I'm not cut out for this job, he told himself. Any
fool would have considered that possibility and looked
further away from the body. Horse or human tracks could
well have been erased by the rain, but what of buckboard
tracks? Places where the narrow wheels had cut through
drifts of sand or over embankments.

A dead body was not the easiest thing to load on a
horse, and that was given the fact that you had a horse
who would stand for it all. A Western man might tie a
body securely enough so it would not fall off, and some
others might too, but it would not be easy.

From the first he had assumed a buckboard was used.
Why, he asked himself, had he accepted that idea? Because
it was the easiest way to move a body across country? Or
because there had been no abrasions on the skin where a
rope might have been tied? On a couple of occasions he had

tied unconscious men into their saddles. He was a big man,
considered unusually strong, and it had not been easy, and
difficult if the horse side-steps. A body, dead or unconscious, is awkward to handle, being both limp and heavy.

Was that the only reason why he had so quickly accepted the idea of the buckboard? Suppose, just suppose
he had unconsciously seen something that because of more
immediate concerns did not register consciously?

Just so he might have passed over tracks or indications because he was not looking for them and because he
was watching the buzzards or at last, the body. With his
attention focused he might have over-looked much.

So what to do? To ride back, to swing in a large and
then a larger circle about where the body was found, and
to particularly observe those places in which a buckboard
might most easily be driven. He doubted if the man he
sought would have been thinking of hiding a trail. His
attention would have been on getting the body to a place
where it might be dumped and getting away without being
seen.

Tomorrow. He would ride out tomorrow and look. He put
his cup down and got up but as he did so the thought
flashed through his mind.

He would be riding alone, away from observers, and if
anyone did want him dead, their opportunity would be perfect.

A man alone on horseback in empty country makes a
nice target.

CHAPTER 6

The roan he was riding was range-bred from mustang
stock crossed with a Morgan stud, and it was a stayer, a
horse who took to wild country and rough going. He

started off to the west but when well away from the town
and seeing no one on his back trail he swung toward the
south. He took his time, stopping occasionally to give
the roan a breather and to check behind him. Only when he
was sure he was not followed did he turn toward his ranch
and the place where the body had been found.

He was under no illusions. Whoever had killed would
kill again if he believed himself at risk. The loneliness
and the quiet gave him a chance to think, and slowly, for
he was a slow-thinking man, he turned over all aspects of
the problem in his mind.

Why had the man been killed? Over a woman? That
seemed doubtful, although possible. Over money? Possible.
Or had he known too much? Unlikely, although it was possible the man was engaged in something illegal. He was
not a horse or cow thief, the first two possibilities in
this country. He might be a yeggman preparing to rob the
bank or the express office. As it happened that was one
aspect of crime about which Borden Chantry knew something.

Long ago, maybe ten or twelve years back he had
worked on an outfit with a yeggman who had gone straight.
Well, he had gone straight for awhile. Chantry now knew
that the man had told him all he did in hopes of recruit-
ing Chantry into helping him, explaining in detail how
yeggs operated and how easy it was to not only live off
the country but to pull off a big one.

Could it be that? It was something to keep in mind,
at least. Again and again he checked his back trail but
saw no evidence that he was followed.

Or were they simply waiting for him?

He circled warily, taking his time, studying every
aspect of the terrain. He was west of the place where he
had found the body when he saw it. A narrow cut in a
small drift of sand, such as might be made by the wheel
of a buckboard.

For several minutes he sat his saddle studying the angle of the cut and looking for some sign of the other wheel. He saw nothing so slowly he began to back track. It was over a hundred yards before he found another track but this time it was double and there, under a bush, was an edge of track that might have been made by a horse's hoof.

Four hours later he had tracked the buckboard almost a mile. Rain and wind had obliterated most of what might have been a good trail, and he found nothing with which to identify either the buckboard or the horses. The one clue with which he was left was the direction from which the buckboard had come.

The buckboard had come in from the east. Of course, it might have circled around but he doubted it. Whoever the driver was he would have wanted to be rid of that body as soon as possible. No doubt it had been covered by a tarp or some such thing, but the driver would not have wanted to be seen, and to have met anybody would have demanded some sort of an explanation.

How long would it have taken? At best, over this terrain the buckboard could have averaged three miles an hour, and he would be traveling by night.

Borden Chantry considered that again. Probably by night. He might have chanced the daylight hours, trusting there was no one about, but the risk would be great. Unless, of course, he was a man not of the country. A stranger might have believed this empty looking country was really empty and not realized that occasional cowboys might cross it at any time.

There was a point here that disturbed him. All the evidence inclined him toward believing whoever left the body was a stranger to the area, except for the place in which the body was left. Or had it been simply chance? Simply an accident as to his choice?

"Bord," he said aloud, "you just ain't cut out for this job."

The sky was impossibly clear, and in the far-off distance he thought he could see the Spanish Peaks. The wind stirred the bunch grass and a tumbleweed left its resting place and rolled over, then again. He took off his hat and let the wind cool his brow, stir in his hair. "I'll miss this country," he spoke aloud again, and the roan twitched an ear.

He rode east, seeing no further sign, considering the nearest road over which the buckboard must have traveled. Thinking of that, he remembered Mable.

She was an Indian woman who lived on a lonely ranch with her two daughters. As a younger man he had worked with her husband, punching cows. A few years later Jacob had been killed when a horse fell on him. Several times while the girls were small he had taken sacks of groceries by the ranch, never stopping long, just dropping them off with a tip of his hat.

Mable, who lived on a low knoll, kept a few sheep, a couple of milk cows and some other stock as well as a few cow ponies. If anything was happening within miles, the chances were that Mable knew of it. Whether she would talk or not was another question. An Indian might simply not be concerned with certain things, and they were not as loose-tongued as a white man.

He rode across the mesa toward Mable's ranch, in plain sight for well over a mile, and he took his time. When he reached the ranch there were three ponies in the corral but no one about. He stepped down from the saddle and led his horse to the creek for water. It was not considered polite to ride right up to the door, and he was giving them time. Finally, he tied his horse at the corral and removing his hat, walked over to the door.

Meralda came to the door. She was about fourteen, he figured, and bright-eyed and pretty.

"Howdy, ma'am," he said, smiling, "I'm a stranger hereabouts and was wondering if you had coffee on?"

"You're not a stranger! You're Mr. Chantry. Will you come in?"

He ducked his head and stepped in. Mable was sitting near the stove, mending a dress with a torn sleeve. Felicia, the older girl who was seventeen now, went to the stove for the coffee pot. She was a quiet, serious girl, not as attractive as Meralda, but he remembered she had done well in school.

"Passin' by," he explained. "Wondered how you getting on?"

"It is a good year for the sheep," Mable said.

He accepted a cup of coffee and relaxed. They talked idly, with long periods of silence. He knew they knew he wanted something and were waiting.

"Not many people out this way," he suggested. "Have many visitors?"

"No."

"I've been looking around," he said. "Somebody in a buckboard, three or four nights ago."

"We want no trouble," Mable said.

He could not honestly say they would have none, and simply sipped his coffee and waited.

"At night there is no travel," Felicia commented. She gestured, "It is a road that comes here, and goes on to Old Mike's."

And Old Mike had been dead for these past ten years, he reminded himself.

"The buckboard would go out and back," he suggested. "Twice along the road."

The coffee was good, the way he liked it, the way Jacob had liked it.

"Sometimes the dogs bark," Mable commented.

"Dogs are like that."

"They barked when Hitchell come by. He was with a big old man. They drank coffee, and the big old man wanted to pay. He say 'I 'spect you can use this.' He put ten dollars down.

"I tell him keep his money."

"Mr. Hitchell tried to stop him," Meralda said.

A stranger, looking around, might think they were poor, but such was not the case. Indians lived the way they wished to live, and to many the old ways were the best ways. Chantry was not sure they were mistaken, but even if there had been a bad time after Jacob died, Mable now owned over a thousand sheep. Hitchell would know that, a stranger would not.

Felicia refilled his cup. "Hitchell come this way often?"

Mable shook her head. "Never before."

"The big old man," Meralda said, "kept looking toward the road. Maybe he expected somebody."

Or maybe he wished to see how far away it was, and if they could hear somebody passing. Why would Hitchell come unless something bothered him? His cattle rarely drifted this way, for there was water and grass closer to the southeast.

He finished his coffee. "Thank you." He took up his hat. "I'll be riding on." He paused in the door. "I miss Jacob."

Mable looked up. "Me, too."

He went out to his horse and gathered the reins, taking his time. Felicia came to the door, then walked over to him. "Four nights ago, the dogs bark. It is somebody on the road. Again, before daylight, they bark again." She paused. "Now they are with the sheep. Tomas is with them, too." Again she paused. "They are not foolish dogs."

He swung into the saddle. "Thank you, Felicia, and thank you for the coffee."

He turned his horse away and headed for the road.

When he reached it he hesitated briefly, then turned back
the way he had come.

Hitchell again? And a big old man? Now who would that
be? Somebody who did not know Mable. Somebody not from
around here.

It was long after dark before he stripped the saddle
from the roan and spilled some oats into the bucket. He
stepped outside the shed, still standing in the shadow
and looked toward the pile of ties. He was some thirty
yards from the house and the yard was in shadow except
for one place of about thirty feet which lay bathed in
pale light. If they were scared, as Billy McCoy believed,
were they scared enough to risk a shot at night in town?
Had it come to that?

He doubted it. He reached the light spot and crossed
with quick steps. He must remember. It would not pay to
take chances.

Tom was already in bed, but Bess was up, reading.
"How's Quentin Durward coming along?" he asked, as she
put the book down.

"You'd like it," she repeated. "You're riding late."

"Stopped by Mable's," he explained.

"How are the girls?"

"Gettin' prettier by the minute. At least, Meralda
is. She's doing well in school, I hear."

He sat down, suddenly tired. Bess put food before him
and he realized he had not eaten since rising. "Anything
happen in town?"

"Priscilla was by, looking for you."

"She came here?" Priscilla did not often leave Main
Street.

He took his watch from his vest pocket. It was almost
ten, too late to see her now. It was an early to bed,
early to rise town and most of the houses were already
dark.

Moreover the last thing he wished was to call attention to Priscilla. As postmistress he could see her at
any time but if she called at his home or he at hers at
this hour there would be comment which might alert the
very people he wished to find.

Bess left for bed and he finished his small meal,
took the dishes to the sink and spilled water over them.
Turning, he cupped his hand over the globe and blew out
the light. Sitting down at the table he pulled off first
one boot and then the other, with a slight jingle from
his spurs.

He leaned back in his chair. It felt good just to
sit, to relax. Now if he could just--

Something moved in the darkness outside. He sat very
still, every sense suddenly alert. It was a man, rising
from behind that pile of ties, a man who seemed to be
staring toward the house. Then slowly, he moved off.

For an instant Borden Chantry thought of following,
but by the time he got his boots on the man would be
gone.

There were other ways--there had to be other ways.

CHAPTER 7

He awakened at the first gray light. Borden Chantry
had worked cattle too long to not awaken before sun-up,
yet on this morning he did not immediately rise. Instead,
he lay quiet, staring up at the ceiling.

Suppose Billy was right and they were running scared?
He had done nothing to frighten anybody except to find
the body.

It had not been intended that the body be found, but
might there not be a reason why it must not be found now?

Suppose, just suppose, the reason for taking the body so far was that it not be discovered at once? Suppose other plans or actions depended on not stirring up any dust?

He could think of no other reason why they should be alarmed. Possibly something was happening or about to happen that demanded no suspicion be aroused?

Suppose, and he was stretching the point, only a few weeks or days were needed to complete whatever it was?

The dead man was an Eastern man, so probably any crime he would be associated with would be known in his part of the country? The dead man had not been a cattleman or a sheepman, and had no indications of being interested in mines. So what remained?

Land? That did not make sense, either. Land was a drug on the market as he had reason to know.

Borden Chantry sat up as carefully as possible and swung his feet to the floor, reaching for his socks. He dressed quietly, not to awaken Bess, and tip-toed from the bedroom in his sock feet. By the time he had slipped on his boots sunlight was coming through the curtains of the kitchen windows.

He made coffee and sliced some bacon into a frying-pan, thinking all the while.

Hitchell? What did he know about Hitchell? He cut several slices of bread, toasted it lightly and carried it to the table with the bacon.

Hitchell had ridden on the last round-up before he, Borden Chantry, had gone bust. He had been repping for his own ranch and several others down that way, and he had been a fair to middling cowhand. Slowly, he dredged his memory, making little notes on a tablet as he did so. That must have been four years ago and it was the first time he'd seen Hitchell, a well set-up man on the slim side, who looked like he'd been sick.

Now why had he thought that? He looked pale, like he might have been in a hospital. It was easily seen because in that bunch they all had been burned brown by the sun, or red like Pat Costigan, who just burned as many of the red Irish do, and never got tan.

He had repped for Rocky Wade's Four-Forty-Four outfit, too. Rocky ran a lot of cattle down in New Mexico, just below the line.

He looked down the railroad tracks toward the station. Harold Cuff was sweeping off the platform. Chantry considered him. Cuff talked a lot, but he knew a lot, too. Suppose despite all his talking there were things he never discussed? Perhaps because he did not consider them news? Or just from some reserve? He talked largely of things everyone would soon know, but what else was there?

Cuff was the dispatcher, and he would know when trains were coming, where they stopped, where they were side tracked. It might be worth talking to Cuff, or listening to him, a little push here and there, maybe.

He had no idea how a real officer investigated, yet a few things must be done. He must try to discover the identity of the dead man and just how he had arrived in the area. He had to have known someone here, yet Chantry was positive that the dead man had not left the train in town. There were sidings where trains occasionally stopped, however, and one was near Zaretta Clyde's. Her visitors rarely left the train in town. Had the dead man been one of them?

He shook his head. The man was too untidy. It was unlikely such a man would be accepted socially by the Clyde woman, who was if nothing else, fastidious. From all he could see and learn, she herself was always neat and nicely gotten up and her place was a ranch with everything in place. Still, there could be a connection. What was Nathan Johnson doing, if anything? Attuned to the political winds as he was it was unlikely he would miss the chance to crack this case, especially if it looked like it could gain him attention. The more Borden Chantry

thought about it the more certain he was that he had
stumbled into something important.

He put on his hat and left the house, strolling down
to the depot. As he walked by he noticed the pile of ties
again. There were tracks around, some scuffing of the
ground. Harold was working his key rapidly and Chantry
merely nodded, walking on by. Several packing-cases lay
on a baggage truck, all marked for the general store. To
take time to look around would also let people in town
know he was curious, for little passed that was unobserved.

He was turning back when he saw the suit-case. It was
battered and old, standing in a corner of the baggage
room. He walked over to it, a well used suit-case, bulging with what it contained and tied around the middle
with a heavy strap.

Harold Cuff came out of his office. Today he was
wearing his green visor and bright red sleeve garters.

"Found it, did you? I was fixin' to call you, Marshal. That there bag showed up on the night train about
five, six days ago and as it seemed to come from around
here, the boys put it off to be claimed."

"What do you mean 'it seemed to come from around
here'?"

"Bob Neighbors, he's conductor on the night run, he
said they found the bag settin' just inside the door on
the one passenger car, except there was no passenger."

He studied the suit-case thoughtfully, then he said,
"Harold, where'd your train stop that night?"

"Usual. They came out of Trinidad on time, made it in
to here on time. No problems."

"No stops?"

"Well, there was one stop, that siding near Iron
Springs, name skips me at the moment. There was a signal
there to pick up somebody but nobody showed."

"Could that suit-case have been put on then? By somebody who might have planned to get aboard?"

Cuff shrugged. "It's possible, but Neighbors didn't
mention that he saw anybody, and he looked around."

"Harold, I'm going to take that suit-case as evidence. If anybody shows up to claim it, send them to me."

"Glad to be rid of it. Sure, take it along. You just
sign a release here, for taking unclaimed baggage."

Suit-case in hand he walked back home. So far as he
could see he was unobserved, but knowing his town he
doubted it.

Borden Chantry sat down in his kitchen and looked at
the suit-case, but he was not thinking of it, but of the
problem itself. Possibly, the man had gotten his suit-
case aboard and gone back to the ground for his carpet-
bag, which had been found beside the body. At that moment
something prevented him, or perhaps the train took off
with him left on the ground?

What if the man was involved in something and wanted
out, either scared or felt he was being cheated, perhaps.
If this suit-case was his, and the circumstances seemed
to fit, he had evidently planned on catching the train
out of town where he would not be seen, and had gotten
far enough to get his suit-case aboard, and something or
somebody had then prevented him from following.

He knew the siding, and had loaded cattle there once,
several years ago. That had been his first shipment of
beef from the ranch. Just one car-load, but his first income.

Suddenly, he was worried. Suppose someone had seen
him bring the suit-case home? Might they not try to recover it? And that would put his family at risk.

Going to the shed he got a couple of grain sacks and
brought them into the house. Bess was away, shopping for
groceries he suspected, so he unstrapped the suit-case.

It was not locked, and contained some clothing, some papers, and a small roll of tools of some kind. Without
taking time to examine any of it, he transferred the
stuff to the grain sacks and carried the lot back to the
shed where he left them in his small tack-room under the
saddle given him long ago by the former marshal. Bundling
up some old clothes he packed them into the bag, replaced
the strap and carried it to his office, walking past the
restaurant and the post office to the office. He wanted
to be seen carrying the suit-case.

Ed was sweeping off the boardwalk. He glanced at the
suit-case. "Leavin' town, Marshal?"

"Unclaimed baggage. We'll hold it until somebody
claims it."

Elsie Carter, who kept the hotel, was emerging from
the post office. "I hope you don't have to hold it as
long as I've held some. One man stayed three days in the
hotel and skipped without paying. All he left in his bag
were some old newspapers and a couple of bricks. He
hadn't figured on paying at all."

"Somebody will show up. If they can identify it and
will sign for it, they can have it."

He walked to the office, feeling pleased. The town
now knew he had taken a suit-case to the marshal's office, and that it was not in his home. He doubted if
there would be inquiries. In fact, he doubted if the murderer or murderers knew there was another suit-case.

Kim Baca was in the office. He glanced at the suit-
case and Chantry explained, then Baca commented, "Something's stirring, so watch your step. Rowan MacAdam is in
town."

Borden Chantry sat down in his swivel chair. "Rowan
MacAdam, here?"

Rowan MacAdam was a gunman who had fought in a couple
of cattle wars down New Mexico way. He had done some

shooting there and had been in a couple of gun battles up
in Montana.

Why was he here? This was cattle country but it was
the slack season. Anybody in his right mind would know
that cattlemen were not hiring at this time. But then,
MacAdam had been hiring his gun lately.

"Leave him alone, Kim. He may just be passing
through, and we've trouble enough. That is, as long as he
minds his own affairs."

"Suppose he's here to get you? He wouldn't be the
first."

"Leave him alone." Borden stared out the window. Bess
was probably right. Maybe he should get out of this country, as he certainly did not want to be shooting it out
with would-be killers all the time. He wanted the quiet
life: his ranch, his cattle, Bess and Tom. That was all
he wanted, all he needed. No, he told himself, you need
money to start ranching again.

He got up and walked to the door, looking out upon
the street. For the time being this was his town and he
wanted no harm to come to it. As he stood looking ab-
sently down the dusty street his thoughts worried over
the problem of the dead man.

He would return to Harold Cuff and after him, to the
train crews. Someone must have seen the man at some time.

"Kim? I'm walking down to Ed's. I need some coffee.
I've got a couple of ideas and they need nourishment."

Nathan Johnson was in the cafe, drinking coffee with
Judge McKinney. Both looked up, nodding as he entered.

"Join us?" Nathan suggested.

"Another time, Nathan. I've got some studying to do."

"Anything on the dead man?" Johnson asked.

Chantry shrugged. "He was in your territory, Nathan.
I'll do whatever's necessary for Thursty, but I've enough
to do right here in town."

He dropped into a chair and Ed brought over a steam-
ing cup of black coffee. He was hardly in his seat before
the door opened and two men came in. The first one, he
knew at once, was Rowan MacAdam. He was a couple of
inches shorter than Chantry's six feet two, but probably
just as heavy. He spotted Chantry at once and walked
over.

"Marshal? I'm Rowan MacAdam."

"Sorry, I didn't get the name? What was it?" Chantry
looked up blandly.

"MacAdam! Rowan MacAdam." He spoke the name as if he
expected it to be greeted by a roll of drums.

"Nice to meet you, Mr. MacAdam. We've a nice town
here. Not very busy right now, but things will pick up.
If you're thinking of going into business we could use a
harness shop. Saddles, bridles, that sort of thing. We
always welcome new folks. In fact right down the street
we've a fine new church, and our school is a good one. Do
you have children, Mr. MacAdan?"

"MacAdam," he said, "Rowan MacAdam." Then he added,
"No, I've no children."

"It's too bad, children can be a comfort. Fine thing,
watching some nice youngsters growing up. Too bad, a man
your age--I had a black stallion one time. Never could
sire a colt. Tried again and again. Finally had to sell
him, but he did make a good draft horse. Spent the rest
of his life pulling a dray, I imagine he was happy."

He shook his head. "Don't feel bad about it, Mr.
MacAdan. You're a young man yet." Chantry could hardly
force back laughter, but if he laughed now someone might
die.

MacAdam was growing angry. "What the Hell are you
talkin' about? I said I was Rowan MacAdam!"

"Of course. No need to be upset. Everybody has their
problems." Chantry gestured to a chair. "Set down, won't
you? You'll feel better in a few minutes."

"I feel all right! There's nothing wrong with me!"

"There! See? You're feeling better already. Altitude sometimes has that effect on people. Will you have a cup of coffee? Ed here makes the best, believe me."

"No, I won't sit down! What are you, some kind of a fool?"

Chantry nodded, seriously. "Yes, that could be it. Each of us is a fool in his own way. I in mine, and you in yours." The time for this foolishness was nearly over. "If you're going to stay in town, Mr. MacAdan, I suggest you hang up that gun. It's a good way to get into trouble around here. The people of our town," he gestured, "no longer accept that sort of thing.

"In fact." Borden Chantry's gun was in his hand. "Maybe I'd better hold those gun belts while you're in town. We wouldn't want anybody hurt here. It gives the town a bad reputation. You just unbuckle very carefully now, very carefully, and when you're ready to leave town, just drop by the marshal's office and I'll give them back."

Rowan MacAdam froze, then he fumbled at his buckle with nervous fingers, and handed the belt to Chantry. Blindly, he turned toward the door. There he stopped. "Damn you," he said, "how the Hell--?"

"I offered you a cup of coffee, Mr. MacAdan."

"To Hell with you!" MacAdam said, and stumbled into the street.

For a moment there was silence in the cafe, then Nathan Johnson said, "Bord, do you know who that was?"

Chantry glanced around. "I know who he thought he was."

CHAPTER 8

He sat down and Ed brought him a fresh cup.

Nathan Johnson crossed the room and straddled a chair. "This murder, Borden. I could use your help with it."

"It won't be easy," Chantry agreed. "I don't envy you."

"You're not working on it?"

"Just keeping an eye on things for Thursty. He'll be back soon. You need to talk to Doc, and I'll write out a description of what I saw when I found the body."

Nathan talked awhile then wandered back to his own table and Borden Chantry stared out at the sunlit street. The first clue he had was that somebody did not want the body found at any time soon. He could not escape the conclusion that time was a key element here. Something else was nagging him, too, and he could not figure what it was. It was irritating. What had he missed? It was something, he was sure, that happened today.

So what had happened? The only thing out of the usual was the unclaimed suit-case and he had not examined it.

Yet he had emptied it of a bunch of nondescript clothing, some tools, what else he did not know. There might be a clue there. Slowly, he tried to examine every minute of the morning, among the odds and ends of rumpled clothing--

He scowled. There had been a spot of blue, blue ribbon. Now what the devil was a man like this one doing with blue ribbon?

He walked back to the house and got out the two sacks. The spot of blue was as he had recalled a strip of blue ribbon, wrinkled at a couple of points where it had been tied.

"Bess? Why would a man as untidy as this one have such a ribbon?"

"He probably received a present from his lady friend. That's been tied to something, some small box. Maybe he was sentimental. Maybe he just neglected to throw it away."

Wrapped around something, a small package of some kind? Who knew about packages? Priscilla knew. Borden put the ribbon in his pocket and walked back to the restaurant. The post office was not open yet so Pris would be unavailable. He would have another cup of coffee and do some thinking.

Except for the dead man there had been no crime, nor even rumors of one. There was just that veiled feeling of uneasiness about a town small enough to be sensitive to such things. He was still sitting there thinking when two men came in; one was the stranger he had seen in the saloon, a man with a bit of a sun-burn. As the man crossed the room to sit down, he almost stopped, staring at Chantry, then hastily turned away. As soon as he was seated he whispered something to his companion.

Borden was puzzled. Both men had seen him before and pointedly ignored him, yet now something arrested their attention. Self-consciously he shifted his coat, drawing it closer about him and his fingers encountered the blue ribbon. It had not been completely stuffed into his pocket.

So? Was that it? Why? What could it mean to them? Yet even as he considered that a small bell of warning sounded in his skull. They recognized his clue, if it was a clue, and it had caused them to worry, perhaps to fear. That might mean a cause to kill. He must be very careful.

One of the men got up and left the restaurant, mounted a horse outside and rode away up the street.

He finished his coffee. Pris should be open for busi-

ness by now. He got up and went out on the street. One of
the two horses was gone but the remaining one carried
Hitchell's brand. Borden walked up to the post office.
The crowd that came to pick up mail had gone, and Pris
was alone.

"Pris? I can use some help."

"I could use some, too. You'd think it would be easy
in a small post office like this but there's always something more to do. What can I do for you, Bord?"

"Bess tells me this was probably tied around some
small package and so I--"

"Terlandra."

"What?"

"Terlandra. That new girl Mary Ann had. Only lasted a
couple of months although she was one of the prettiest
girls this season."

"What about her?"

"She used to get those little boxes, about three
inches square, always tied in pink or blue ribbon, but
tied up tight under the ribbon. Looked like some admirer
was sending her jewelry or something."

"Notice where they came from?"

"Denver. Some place on Larimer Street."

Bord walked to the window and looked down the dusty
street. Now he had a lead, at least. He must talk to Mary
Ann but not now. He did not like to be seen going to her
house in the day time, and of course now there was the
added reason that they would be watching.

The worst of it was he did not know what he was looking for. What was going on? If, as he suspected, time was
all important, how much time did he have? Now they knew
he was alert, that he knew something was in the wind, and
they would be inclined to believe he knew more than he
did.

Borden Chantry walked back to the cafe. It was time

for some serious thinking and he must alert Kim Baca and Big Injun. And Bess, most of all Bess.

The sun-burned man? He heard him called by name, but what name? He searched his memory and after a bit it came to him. Somebody, somewhere had referred to the man as Ringwald, but that helped him none at all except to put a name to the man.

He finished his coffee and walked back up the street to the office. Kim was at the desk, his feet propped up reading a magazine.

"Kim? We've never talked much about Hitchell. Know anything?"

"He's done time, if that's what you mean. Did a couple of years for stealing a saddle. Personally, I never believed he did it, but he was convicted."

So that's why he was pale. And Ringwald? Might they have met in prison? Was that why they had come here in the beginning?

But that brought him no closer to the crime, if crime there was. The killing might have been some simple drunken disagreement and nothing more.

Yet it was more, and he knew it.

It was after nine before he crossed to Mary Ann's back door. He was the only man allowed to enter there so the girls knew who he was. Mary Ann came down and poured tea. "I know coffee is your drink, Bord, but tea is all I have."

"I drink it now and again, with Bess."

She glanced at him. "I miss that, I really do. I miss talking with women other than the girls. You'd not think I'd admit that, but it's true. I'd not say it to anybody but you."

"I know. Life takes us down strange paths, sometimes. I never figured on being the law."

"What is it, Bord? How can I help you?"

"You had a girl named Terlandra?"

"Yes, but not for long. She didn't fit in--she was a snowbird. You know, on cocaine. I can't put up with that, and never have."

"But she was here for awhile?"

"She was liked, and she was prettier than most. She could talk to anybody and would. I was inclined to over-look her using the stuff until I found she was peddling it, too."

"What was her source?"

"Denver, I think?"

He took the blue ribbon from his pocket. "Ever see anything like this?"

"Often. Terlandra used to get little packets from Denver, always tied with pink or blue ribbon, like gifts. She had only one steady customer of whom I know, a fellow named Wiemer, Harry Wiemer."

Borden described the dead man. "Is that him?"

"Sounds right. He was an untidy little man and I didn't want him around. You know how it is, once they're into coke they lose interest in women, and you can't trust them anymore. They'll lie, steal, anything just to get the stuff." Mary Ann paused, sipping tea. "That's probably what happened to her."

"What happened?"

"Terlandra was murdered. Not over a month after she left here. Less than a month, in fact. She was back in Denver. Probably by one of those she'd been selling drugs to."

Murdered? By someone she had been selling drugs to or because she knew too much? Harry Wiemer? Where had he heard that name? The dead man had been killed and Ter-landra also, but why?

"I need to know all I can about her. I'll trust you to say nothing about that, Mary Ann."

"I don't know anything else, Bord, except that the

last time he came here they had a fight. She was furious
with him about something and he with her. I heard them
arguing, something about money."

They talked for a few minutes and then with the light
out he eased himself out the back door, moved quickly to
one side and waited, listening. Had they followed him
here? Two dead, so they were not playing games. Not for a
minute did he believe the two killings were unrelated,
but how? Why?

Bess was already in bed and asleep when he eased himself into the dark house. The coffee was still on and he
poured a cup and sat down by the window. Harold Cuff was
working late. Bord liked it because the light from the
dispatcher's office was bright and friendly. It also gave
him some light almost as far as the pile of ties.

Arguing about money? He understood that dealing in
drugs, even with few laws to restrict them, was a cash on
the barrel-head business, so what could be wrong?

Had Wiemer tried to short her? There must have been
something wrong about the pay-off, something wrong about
the money.

He put his cup down suddenly. Wrong about the money?

CHAPTER 9

Three men sat in the living room of Zaretta Clyde.
The big old man sat on a sofa facing the door, Ringwald
and Hitchell half-faced him, both nervous. The big man
was truly big; he was also not that old. At fifty years
he carried the look of a man of thirty, and the body of
one. He was also mean, difficult, and uncommonly shrewd.

What his name had been in his early years had been
forgotten, left behind when he led an escape through the
abandoned sewers of the old prison. He was now known as

Lev Larson. Nobody liked him but many needed him, for
whatever involved his interest went down well. He had a
reputation for success. In the world of crime there is no
better name to have.

Rumor was that he had millions stashed away, just
where or under what name nobody knew. It was also understood that if you crossed him you were in trouble, the
worst kind of trouble.

As he looked out at the yard the gate opened and Turren Downer rode in. Lev sat up, irritated. "Who the Hell
is that?"

Hitchell said, "Cowpuncher, a tough man. I think he's
sweet on Zaretta."

"Tell her to get rid of him."

Ringwald shook his head. "No can do, Lev. Zaretta
does as she pleases and you know that. You cross her and
this whole shootin' match is gone."

"We don't need any nosy cowpunchers floating around."

"Better leave him alone, Lev. He doesn't know from
nothing and Zaretta's happy."

Lev shifted his big body irritably. He did not like
to be crossed and the presence of the big cowboy looked
like trouble. "I'll handle it," he said.

Ringwald looked over at Hitchell and said, "There's
the other thing. That blue ribbon now. Looks like that
town clown is onto something."

"Don't sell him short. Borden Chantry is no fool.
I've worked with him, seen him operate," Hitchell said.

Lev Larson snorted. "Smart? Some hick-town copper?
He's no problem. Before he figures which end is up we'll
be long gone from here."

He glanced around at Hitchell. "If he worries you
boys, take him out."

Hitchell shifted his feet, stared at the toes of his
boots and said quietly, "Leave him alone, Lev. He's a bad

man to trifle with. Nobody dreamed Lang Adams was involved in that Sackett murder, yet he figured it out and
nailed him.

"The best thing we can do is what you've always said,
keep our heads down, pull this off and you guys can get
out of here."

There was silence in the room and then Larson said,
"That Zaretta woman's gettin' too big for her britches.
Needs to be taken down a notch."

"Don't try it, Lev." Ringwald's voice was sharp. "She
has the connections. If she tells the Chinese it's no go
they'll fade out like they'd never been and we've shot
our wad."

Lev Larson sat up irritably. It was true, too damned
true. Everything depended on Zaretta, and none of her
clients wanted anything to happen to her. Her finger was
in too many pies.

He sat very still, looking out the door. The big cowboy was tying up his horse at Zaretta's rail, but he was
not thinking of that.

No more than ten days now, if all went well, and he
would be holding more than a million dollars. It was the
biggest job he had ever pulled off and he could not have
done it without Zaretta Clyde. He had gone to her with
the idea and she had helped set it up.

She had known about Hitchell and his lonely ranch.
She had known where to lay hands on Wiemer, who was the
best there was, and she had known where and how to arrange for the buyers. Yet it had turned messy and he did
not like that. First Wiemer and then that woman. Even
that went off smoothly, at least until Ringwald spotted
that blue ribbon. The hick cop seemed to have established
a connection. But had he, really?

Zaretta was getting her hooks into that new county
sheriff, Nathan Johnson, but Chantry was not sharing

ideas with him, and Johnson did not believe Chantry knew anything. Still, the blue ribbon? Was it simply a coincidence? Lev Larson did not believe in such things. Everything had a meaning, a connection.

The sun was setting over the mountains to the westward--he had not seen the mountains but had been told they were there. Denver was out there somewhere, but Lev Larson was an Eastern man, and occasionally a mid-western man. Until now he had never been west of Kansas City.

Lev Larson did not like dealing with Zaretta Clyde. He had nothing but contempt for women and believed her much over-rated. He was a brutal, self-contained man who knew what he wanted and how to get it. He had developed this deal himself and then suddenly he found he needed somebody with connections, and Zaretta had them. She knew people he needed or where to find them; she was respected in certain major seats of power that even Lev Larson hesitated to challenge.

Ten days. He could sit tight for ten days. Even if the hick cop was onto something there was small chance he could put it together in time. The deal would be consummated and they would scatter to the winds.

Lev Larson had no love for anyone. He wanted to get his money and get out and he was covering all his bases. Where there was money there were people hungry for it, and he knew somebody was probably plotting to steal his end. Well, he was ready. He trusted no one.

That big cowboy out there? Was it that he was in the way, or simply because he was big and looked like a fighter?

Lev stirred irritably. He did not like waiting. If the Chinese were coming, why didn't they come? Why so precise about the date? One particular old man had to view the merchandise, that was it. Everything hung on his word.

Lev had been warned. "Don't try anything funny. The
Hop Sing Tong has hatchet men everywhere and they'll nail
you, but good. They give their word, and it will be good,
but they don't stand for any fancy foot-work."

Lev did not plan on any. He liked a clean deal himself. That was one of the things he liked about this from
the first. It was clean. In and out, a big take, and everybody gets lost.

Never a patient man he was doubly impatient now, and
staring at the big cowboy's horse made him more so, yet
he had to confess the deal had gone together like clock-
work, fully as much because of Zaretta as he himself.

They made a team. He had to admit that, reluctant as
he was to do so. This was the big one and hopefully the
last one. A pitcher could go too often to the well, his
own mother had taught him that, and except for the first
time his skirts were clean. He had escaped, changed his
name and grown bigger, no longer resembling the man who
had been imprisoned. One of the men had died in that
sewer and they believed it had been him, so his escape
was clean and clear.

Lev Larson watched as the big cowboy came out and
stepped into the saddle. He could handle that. He would
get Turren Downer to pick a fight with him, then he would
be in the clear with Zaretta, and after that he would decide about that two-bit country marshal.

He had to admit the accommodations were good and the
food was excellent. Everything Zaretta Clyde did was out
of the top drawer.

He watched the cowboy ride down the hill. He would be
a charger and a swinger, made to order for Lev. Larson
smiled. At least he could take his mind off the waiting,
and he would teach Zaretta a thing or two.

If her man started the fight, what could she say?

Lev Larson watched the sun set without thinking of

it. His mind was on Turren Downer and what he would do to
him. The man was known as a fighter, so was vulnerable--
that he got into a fight would surprise no one. Lev had
whipped a number of the top professionals but had found
easier ways of making a living than bare-knuckle fighting.
Yet he liked fighting and he was so much better than anyone he had met that he had no problems. Moreover, different than most fighters he liked punishing his opponents.
Many times when he could have scored early knockouts he
had deliberately refrained to keep his opponents trying so
he could administer a more thorough beating.

Ten days might not be too long after all. If he
couldn't trap the cowboy into a fight he might get that
nosy small town copper; either would be fun.

He went back into his room and began leafing through
magazines that lay on the table. There was a stack of old
Police Gazettes with fight stories and illustrations on
the well known sheet of pink paper. Occasionally he came
upon old references to himself under one of the several
names he used when fighting.

Often he had been imported into some small town or
city by gamblers wishing to make a killing. He would work
up a match with some local champion. He usually wore
shabby, loose-fitting clothes that displayed none of his
Herculean frame.

He discovered he could make more money working as
such a "ringer" than with regular boxing matches. Only
once had a gambler tried to short him. After word got
around as to what happened to the gambler it never happened again.

Sitting alone he thought about all aspects of their
deal. It still looked good, despite the necessity for the
killings. Hitchell worried him a little. The man was not
really a criminal although he had done time, and Lev did
not trust an honest man.

And those Indian women? Had they heard anything? Had
they talked to that country marshal? Did they know anything to tell him?

Borden Chantry. That was his name. If he wanted a
fight he should pick one with him, put him out of action
for the next ten days, but how did he do that without
getting arrested?

He went to his luggage and opened a specially built
leather case which contained two fifty pound dumb-bells.
Getting them out he went to work and worked for a solid
hour, then sponged himself off and went to bed. It was a
three-times-a-week ritual, and he never missed.

He walked and climbed at every opportunity, wanting
to be always ready. It had become a long established
habit which he never ignored.

Ringwald stood by the window looking down at the
lights of the town. It wasn't much of a place, yet people
seemed contented and it was a supply point for a good
stretch of country in every direction.

He glanced around at Hitchell. "Lived here long?"

"Most of my life."

"Do they know you did time?"

"I doubt it. That was in another state. Baca might.
He's that deputy marshal Chantry has. Used to be a horse
thief and has connections everywhere, both sides of the
law. Folks like him."

"How'd you get into this?"

"Zaretta knew about me and she sent a couple of men
to talk to me. The way they talked I had to listen. To be
honest, I wanted no part of it.

"I'll admit it looked good for me. They built that
barn to work in, they bought me enough cows so I'd look
legitimate, and laid in more supplies than I'd ever seen

before. I figured, What the Hell? They'll finish what
they're doing and I'll be left sitting pretty."

"Zaretta will remember. She makes her living knowing
about people like you."

Hitchell stared gloomily down the street. He liked
this town and the country around. He had friends here. He
had never wanted to be rich, just comfortable.

Ringwald looked down the dark street, only a few
lights showing. He would like to be down there now, just
having a drink, and no worries.

It was a strange thing. The biggest deal any of them
had ever cut into and yet all of them were edgy, and he
for one was like Hitchell--he was running scared.

CHAPTER 10

Borden Chantry was feeling better about the situation. Things were beginning to fall into place. What was
coming off he did not know but he suspected, and he now
knew why Wiemer had been killed and probably why Terlandra had been murdered.

The trouble was he did not know who all the players
were in the game. Ringwald and Hitchell were involved but
beyond that he knew nothing. Perhaps Zaretta Clyde was,
but he had no evidence, only that she knew them and some
of them were staying at her place. But others had stayed
there also, before this. There was that big older man,
too, Larson was his name, but his connection was doubtful. So far he had seen no more than a nodding acquaintance which would be natural with men staying at the same
hotel or boarding place, if Zaretta's place could be
called that.

Ringwald and Hitchell were small figures on the board
if he was guessing right. Any move to grab them would not

only tip his hand but would give him nothing. He must
know what was coming off and who was holding the reins.

Who were the top men in the game and what were they
waiting for? If they were waiting. He had guessed that
time was the key element, but why? Was somebody coming to
make a pay-off? If his own timing was off he might miss
on everything and the killers might escape him and suddenly all would be gone.

He doubted that Turren Downer was involved. Turren
was Western. He was big, strong and tough, a mean fighter
and a good one, and if he got into trouble it would be
from brawling, a gun battle or something of that nature.
He was not a criminal as such. Of course, he had now done
time and there was no guessing what connections he had
made in prison. That would have to be considered.

When he walked in the door Bess was putting supper on
the table and Tom was deep in a book, as usual. He looked
up quickly. "How'd it go, Pa? Are you any closer to those
men?"

"A little. I believe I know what's happening, and
some of those involved, but I can't talk about it now."

Tom was full of questions but he knew his father well
enough to know that he had said all he was about to say.

"If we go back east will you be an officer?"

Borden shook his head. "How could I be? I won't know
the country or the people as I do here. I'm not a good
officer, Tom, I just know this country and use a little
common sense."

"Everybody says you're the best."

"That's nice of them, but enough of them didn't think
so to re-elect me as sheriff."

"Are we going east, Pa?"

"When I figure out what's happening here we'll decide. I don't know how I'd make a living, son. All I know
are horses and cattle."

Tom was silent. His mother's desire to go east and to

have him in school there had blinded her to reality. Tom
loved his father and knew that here, in the West, he was
an important man. Back east that would simply not be
true. Yet he himself wanted to go east, and to attend
Eastern schools.

He had sneaked back on the street the day the outlaws
Monson and Clatt's gang had tried to rob the bank, and he
had overheard Time Reardon, no friend of his father's,
say, "He's one of the very best. Whatever you do, don't
low rate Borden Chantry. With a gun in his hand he's as
good or better than anybody I've ever seen."

Tom was fiercely proud of his father yet he had a pen
pal in the East who scoffed at the idea there might be
such men. Gun-fighters and cattlemen were the stuff of
romance. A lot of people believed that and Tom knew
enough to know that having survived gun battles and having once built a ranch would do his father no good back
there.

Sometimes he was jealous of his friend, Billy McCoy.
He felt Billy was closer to his father than he was, yet
he could understand why: Billy was part of this place, a
boy at home in the harsh Western landscape just as his
father was. He himself had been raised to think like his
mother and, despite the influence of his father, he had
taken on much of it, partly through the desire for a
broader, deeper education.

Billy McCoy had his own ideas about those pink and
blue ribbons. He had seen them in the rubbish thrown out
at Mary Ann's where the girls sometimes fixed meals for
him. He had seen them and decided where they came from
before Borden Chantry had. People talked a lot in front
of a youngster, taking it for granted he did not understand. Or that he was not paying attention. No matter how

busy or absent-minded Billy happened to be he was always
paying attention.

Sitting in the kitchen by the window, but just far
back enough not to be a target, even though it was early,
Borden Chantry went over the few items he had in his
mind.

Harry Wiemer had incurred somebody's anger, enough so
they wished him dead, and he was dead, his body left so
hopefully it would not be immediately discovered.

How had he incurred the displeasure of those who
killed him? And why had it been necessary to kill Terlandra as well?

Something had gone wrong, if Chantry was surmising
correctly and there had also been a difficulty between
Terlandra and Wiemer.

What had happened?

There had been a dispute about money. Had he not
paid? Or had he not paid enough?

He certainly had paid or she would not have delivered. And for the same reason he had probably paid
enough.

Harry Wiemer was a man who dealt with ink. An en-
graver? There had been a dispute about money. Suppose it
was counterfeit? Suppose he had unwittingly or on purpose
because he was short paid Terlandra with a phony bill and
she had passed it on to her people? She would be in trouble and he would be in trouble with Terlandra.

And perhaps with his people?

Somebody had built a mighty fine barn for Hitchell.
Suppose that barn had been used to make queer money? Suppose it had been made and was awaiting shipment?

To whom? Where?

Suppose that was the time element?

It was a lot of supposing with very little concrete
evidence. He had seen no counterfeit money nor had he
heard of any. Suppose that was the idea? Counterfeit
money made in the West but for shipment elsewhere? Far
from its point of origin?

And suppose in his need for cocaine Wiemer had spent,
accidentally or on purpose, some of the counterfeit
bills? Bills that weren't his to spend. Even more likely,
what if he told Terlandra about the operation? What if
they were using some of the counterfeit on the sly to
solve some problem that she might be having?

COMMENTS: Louis started planning this sequel to *Borden Chantry*
in 1987, around the same time he began laying the groundwork for
his memoir, *Education of a Wandering Man*. Although he had been
plagued with heart issues and pneumonia throughout the year, it was
only around January of 1988 that doctors discovered that both were
caused by the lung cancer that eventually ended his life.

The chapters you have just read were written during a time
when he was on oxygen and often dealing with the aftereffects of che-
motherapy. I fear that even though I have done some judicious editing,
you can still tell he was not as focused as usual.

Whenever Louis L'Amour characters sit around drinking coffee
and asking themselves questions about what is going on, that is actually Louis trying to figure out what he wants to do with his story. In
fact, you can pretty much bet that he either had just returned from
doing the same thing himself or was about to go get himself a cup.

By the end of Chapter 8, he was still struggling to raise the
stakes, get all the pieces in place, and keep the plot moving. However,
it is interesting to see that shifting the point of view to include the bad
guys sort of gave the story a second wind.

Writers of mysteries often face a problem where their detectives, especially if they work in law enforcement, have to be reactive rather than proactive—that is, unless enough momentum has been built up and a good chain of evidence created. Since Lev Larson, Zaretta, Ringwald, and Hitchell are the ones actually driving the story forward, shifting to scenes that included them added an energy that even Borden seems to feel is lacking. It also allowed Louis to live inside those characters for a while and figure out what they had done and what they would do in detail.

The other element that shows up while we are dealing with the criminals is the possible involvement of a Chinese Tong. Tongs are sworn brotherhoods or secret societies that often have political goals (in the last sixty years many have been pro-Taiwan, pro-Kuomintang, or anti-Communist groups), but that have also been tied to organized crime. Chinese criminals would have been an excellent way to dispose of counterfeit money, because they could spend it overseas, using it in places and in ways that would take U.S. authorities a long time to even notice. At the time of our story it would have been nearly impossible to trace.

The Tongs have a bit of a connection to Louis's personal history. It is possible that Dad was exposed to Tong organization or activity, or at least to stories of the Chinese societies, while in the Far East. However, his closest connection to the criminal aspect of the Tongs was in Arizona. Louis was an eyewitness to the escape of five "Bing Kong" Tong assassins after they killed a member of the rival "Hop Sing" Tong, the owner of a restaurant in Kingman. Having just returned from Asia, Dad had enjoyed a number of conversations with Tom King, the murdered man.

Also of interest is Dad's mention of "yeggmen," a type of criminal that I imagine he got to know while hoboing around the country. Yeggs were itinerant crooks who were reputed to "peel" their way into vaults with a single jack and chisel, or an axe. They might also boil the nitroglycerine out of dynamite so that they could drip the unstable liquid through a hole in a safe door using a string to guide the droplets into place. Then, wrapping the safe in mattresses, they would hit the door with a sledgehammer to fire just enough of the explosive to break the door free.

One last detail taken from Dad's history is his depiction of the stifling social atmosphere of small towns. He had lived in, and been an outsider in, many places where people's every action became the subject of gossip. Even I have been in places (as late as the 1970s!) where a local police officer might hesitate to follow up a lead because he feared what being seen talking to a criminal, vagrant, or prostitute might do to his reputation.

There are two generations of notes for this story. The ones that apply directly to the chapters above begin like this:

```
Who? Was he?
Why? Was he killed?
How did he get there?
Who is involved?
What clues?


Ink ingrained in skin of hands
Unlikely if using pen.
Ink on inside of pocket-edges.


Who works with ink?
A printer -


Chantry visits newspaper, watches printing--doesn't
  fit.
```

There was also an earlier concept that led to a very different version of the counterfeit money plot. It all started with the following note:

```
Queer as collateral? Never to be used?
Perhaps teller used some of it in emergency?
```

"Queer" in this case is old-time criminal argot for counterfeit money. Louis seems to have been considering a version of the classic bearer-bond con, where millions of dollars in fake bearer bonds are shown to the mark and validated by an "expert" of some sort. Then the con man takes out a loan that is just a small percentage of the value of the bonds, using the bonds as collateral, pretending it's all so he won't have to go through the "trouble" of cashing in the extremely valuable bonds. The con man then disappears with the loaned amount, leaving the mark with a safety deposit box full of worthless paper.

Later Louis expanded those two lines into a pretty complete treatment of the "counterfeit collateral" version of this story.

Borden Chantry Sequel

Hyatt Johnson appears preoccupied and worried. CHANTRY is sensitive to the feelings of his town, is disturbed by some premonition of trouble he cannot understand.

Some time before Chantry has met a newcomer in whom all are interested, a fascinating, interesting man with a couple of men who are his hostlers and guides. The newcomer is planning to invest largely. He will get r.r. [railroad] through the town, and may build a new and better hotel. He looks over the town, buys several lots for which he pays in promissory notes against a large sum of money he has held for him in the local bank. Hyatt has glimpsed this money, but it is being held, not on deposit, but simply held by the bank. Hyatt and his teller have each signed a receipt for it but the money is not to be deposited for several weeks.

Chantry is disturbed by the newcomer. Although he supposedly knows nothing of the country he has

several times taken the right turn on the streets
and seems to have a familiarity with the town.
Chantry's wife says he is too suspicious, Hyatt
smiles tolerantly, the saloon-keeper is noncommittal
but, it develops, has invested no money in the newcomer's schemes. It is well known that the money is
at the bank. The newcomer has borrowed several sums
against it, for immediate cash needs; it finally develops that he has borrowed quite a lot of money
from various citizens, or has obtained the money on
false pretenses. An old man is found dead apparently
killed by a fallen timber, Borden proves such was
not the case. Yet he was a harmless, friendly old
man who has no enemies and no possessions. Borden is
sure it is murder. But why? Actually it is because
he recognized a scar on the newcomer's finger and
knows him.

The newcomer has been entertaining some of the
big ranchers in town, and also their cowhands. One
young cowhand is found struck on the head, apparently
left for dead, but he is not dead. Borden takes him
to a woman on a nearby ranch who attempts to nurse
him back to life. He has been struck hard and is in a
coma.

Keeping this man's existence a secret, Borden
hopes to keep him alive and hopes he can identify his
assailant. Borden spends time on her ranch, and his
wife becomes suspicious. Borden believes the young
man can tell who attacked him, and why. He is sure
something is wrong and wishes to know, to uncover the
mystery.

Boy from the ranch where the man is kept is buying items at the drug store to care for the young
man, and newcomer is present; the old druggist asks
if somebody has been hurt out that way? Boy says no,
just usual stuff they keep on hand, but newcomer's

interest is aroused. The body of the cowpuncher has
not been found, and this has worried him. [He was
left for dead] not too far from the woman's ranch.

Newcomer must find out if puncher is alive.

Meanwhile a rider returns from delivering some
horses and is going back out to his ranch. He refuses
a drink and in the altercation that follows, is
killed in a gun battle. On the surface it is a fair
shooting, all agree the puncher was armed, that he
had an even break, but the henchman of the newcomer
who killed him is obviously a deadly man with a gun.

Slowly Borden begins to tie things together. He
believes there is some connection between the killings, although there is no outward tie. He is accused
of trying to find a pattern as he did before [in the
novel Borden Chantry]. One is a simple shooting, another an accident.

Borden goes about his job with the aid of Kim
while the town prepares for a big fandango and cele-
bration. There are to be some contests, cash prizes
awarded, saddles, etc. and all the cowpunchers want
to compete. An attempt is made to murder puncher in
coma but he comes out of it, explains that he had
gone up a draw where there were always cattle and
there were none. He was studying tracks when slugged
by a strange puncher who said "he was looking for
strays." Kim comes in to report there are no cattle,
the range has been swept clean. Borden and Big Injun
trace lost cattle to a distant valley where the cattle are held . . . several thousand head. Perhaps
with Indians to help they move cattle to reservation
or--?

Return to find big fandango going on, everybody
enjoying themselves.

Hyatt obviously concerned; several others seem
less than happy and it appears two or three citizens

have compared notes and found all are holding notes
from newcomer. Some have sought assurance from Hyatt,
yes the money is still there. Then he becomes disturbed and Borden puts two and two together and goes
to him with a suggestion he check the money. It is
counterfeit.

One of the girls on the "line" has given Borden a
clue without realizing it, when she mentions one of
the newcomer's followers reminds her of a man she
knew who is now dead. Borden has routinely checked
the name, discovers the man is now in prison for
counterfeiting. He supposedly had been working hard
at making money before arrest but it was never found.

Or . . . the murdered man had a packet he would
not let out of his sight. Man was very jumpy at
night. Thought he was followed.

Murdered man spoke of his old outfit in Civil
War. Borden writes to Washington for info on outfit.
He finds it had engaged in counter-guerilla action,
including break-up of gang of counterfeiters. Equipment never found.

So, the newcomer murdered man with plates, made
large amount of queer. Sells some, but due to fatal
flaw in plates it cannot be passed . . . some other
way of using it must be found.

Newcomer hates town, because of something that
happened to his father. So he and his followers loot
the town of money and the range of cattle wanting to
effectually destroy it.

An earlier cash payment to a creditor has been
held up so it would not be discovered that the money
was counterfeit.

Borden kills gunman in a shoot-out and proves to
newcomer his father was not framed but caught in the
act.

Additional, though somewhat cryptic, notes on the plot read:

```
    Con man using counterfeit money--Has left bad
[bag?] containing $100 bills & [a few] gold eagles
. . . This is left at the bank as surety to impress.
Bag locked.-First he uses real money, deposits,
withdraws deposits--leaves bag. He has successfully
passed himself off [as] an investor--in land, cattle,
mines.-Man has left large amt. in bills in bank to
be deposited later.- . . . banker will over-extend
counting on big deposit.-Draws on other money left at
store for supplies, cattle. He buys much on credit
due to money left.-He plans to loot town, milk it dry
of cash.-- . . . everybody seem[s] to profit.
```

It is interesting to follow the evolution of this plot from these notes, which explore a con game that relies on the townspeople's naive belief in the money a man supposedly has in the bank, to the concept of selling imperfect counterfeit bills to a Chinese gang that may circulate them overseas. Clearly the latter version is more sophisticated and more in line with Louis's desire to free the Western genre from its traditional conventions and connect it to the rest of the nineteenth-century world. The Chinese experience in the West was something that Dad always wanted to deal with but never really got around to. As with many subjects, it was really just a matter of having too little time.

In other notes Louis left behind, he mentioned that he was interested in using the fact that there are "two sides of the street, or an end of town [that separates classes or ethnicities or both]." He wanted to "have a poor woman speak longingly about the quality and style of the prostitutes' clothes." The "scarcity of Indians on the plains" was something else he wanted to comment on, as opposed to the "great village referred to in Spanish accounts." This may be a note regarding the spread of disease that occurred after contact with Europeans and the other pressures on the Native American population. "Cover some of plains Indians activities before white man" is also a note in this section. Obviously, Louis had some social and cultural commentary in mind.

Reading through this fragment and the original novel, *Borden Chantry*, I sensed something familiar about the contrast in the relationship Borden has with his son, Tom, who is more protected, bookish, and under his mother's wing, and Billy McCoy, who is a rough-and-tumble street kid and operates more in Borden's world. It is quite similar to the relationship that Louis's father, Dr. L. C. LaMoore, had with Jack, a boy that the family adopted. Jack Otto was a scrappy kid from an Eastern orphanage, and Louis occasionally seemed to feel that his father might have liked Jack better than him. The adoptive father and adopted son had a lot in common in their earthy approach to life, while Louis was more intellectual and introverted, a kid more interested in getting lost in a book than getting out into the world. It is ironic that Louis went on to have adventures beyond anything Jack probably could have imagined.

Buried deep in this manuscript there is also a brief moment out of my own past. When Tom Chantry asks, "Pa? Can I ride out there with you someday? I miss the place," it is likely my father was remembering something I had asked about a number of times. In the early 1970s we moved from West Hollywood to a much nicer neighborhood near UCLA. But our old house didn't sell for nearly two years. I was very attached to that place, and the fact that it was somehow still there, that no one else had taken it over and made it theirs, made it harder to give up.

The move occurred just at the time that I made the transition from grammar school to junior high school. I realize today that the few trips I made with my mother back to the old place to clean up this or that or to show the house (I really can't remember what exactly) were like a haunting return to my childhood, a dusty, empty shell of what it once had been.

It's amusing to realize, now that I am an adult, that many years later Tom Chantry would return to the ruins of his old home and be forced to take refuge in a place where he had played as a child. "The

Hole," in *North to the Rails*, seems to be a combination of the tunnels through the deep growth of hillside ivy that the neighborhood kids and I used to travel unseen (or so we thought) between the houses on our West Hollywood street, and the small grotto containing a spring that existed on some land we owned in the Tehachapi Mountains of Kern County. Looking back, I wonder how many times my sister and I were, at least partly, the models for characters in my father's books.

Lastly, but perhaps most important, it is worth noting that my father chose to return to this particular story after finishing *Education of a Wandering Man*. He must have been fairly sure that one or the other would be his last book. After succeeding in his long struggle to publish material in other genres, he had clearly decided to try to complete one last, fairly traditional, Western. He knew that this was something his fans would enjoy and, as much as he had planned to write other, more personal, works, I don't think he wanted to give in to any maudlin, self-absorbed acknowledgment that his time was ending. He wanted the last thing he did to reflect his life at its best. He wanted it to be about moving forward, getting the next thing done, and entertaining the people who had supported him for the previous four decades. While I'm sure he wanted to finish this book, I'm actually glad he didn't. There was nowhere he was happier than in the middle of an unfolding story.

About eighteen months before Louis started this draft, and about ten months before he discovered he had cancer, he wrote the following in his journal:

> Don't know how much productive time I have left so must ration my work with more care. Sometimes I work like I had all the time in the world. I have 17 books I must do--34 I'd like to do and more coming all the time. But I will be 79 next March. Feel great most of the time and like I could go on forever . . .

And then:

I am on the verge of becoming a good writer, all
I need is time.

ACKNOWLEDGMENTS

I would very much like to thank my mother, Paul O'Dell (who worked on the earliest incarnation of this book and came up with the title for this entire program), Jeanne Brown, Angelique Pitney, Charles Van Eman, Sonndra May, Daphne Ashbrook, Jamie Wain, Jayne Rosen, Jessica Wolfson, Mara Purl, Cathy Sandrich Gelfond, Trish Mahoney, Jordan Ladd, and Paula Beyers for all their help and the sorting and transcribing of the original manuscripts.

On the publishing end of things kudos go to the great Stu Applebaum, Gina Wachtel, Ratna Kamath, Nina Shield, Elana Seplow-Jolley, David Moench, Colleen Nuccio, Joe Scalora, Cynthia Lasky and her crack team, Scott Shannon, Matt Schwartz, Paolo Pepe, Scott Biel, Heidi Lilly, Ted Allen, Larry Marks, Bill Takes, Libby McGuire, and Gina Centrello.

Too rarely thanked in the acknowledgments sections of books are the people who create audiobooks, in this case Penguin Random House Audio. To remedy that, I wish to offer my sincere gratitude to Amy Metsch, Orli Moscowitz, Katherine Punia, Heather Dalton, Sue Daulton, Alexis Patterson, Nicole Morano, Laura Wilson, Kaitlyn Robinson, and their fearless and wonderful leaders Amanda D'Acierno and Nina Von Moltke.

In addition, I would like to thank Universal Studios for allowing us to reprint *The Jade Eaters* and Michael Allen for giving me his take on music history, hippies, and cowboys, and to recommend to anyone who is interested Kenneth C. Davis's book *Two-Bit Culture: The Paperbacking of America* as a grand source on the history of the mid-twentieth-century book business.

ABOUT THE AUTHORS

Our foremost storyteller of the American West, LOUIS L'AMOUR has also thrilled readers with his work in the adventure, crime, and science fiction genres. He wrote ninety-one novels, a book of poetry, and over two hundred short stories. There are more than three hundred million copies of his books in print around the world.

BEAU L'AMOUR is an author, art director, and editor. He has also worked in the film, television, magazine, and recording industries. Since 1988 he has been the manager of the estate of his father, Louis L'Amour.

louislamour.com
louislamourslosttreasures.com
louislamourgreatadventure.com